KT-425-524

Will Wiles was born in India in 1978. He lives in London and writes about architecture and design for a variety of magazines. He is the author of two other novels, *Care of Wooden Floors* and *The Way Inn*, also published by 4th Estate. *The Way Inn* was shortlisted for The Encore Award and *Care of Wooden Floors* won a Betty Trask Award.

Praise for *Plume*:

'A superbly observed "how we live now" satire on life and media in contemporary London' *The Times*

'The reader is sucked along unstoppably, but glorying too with uncomfortable recognition. Fabulous in every sense' *Spectator*

'*Plume*'s cast of semi-sinister clowns aren't the most sympathetic, but it's the suffocating, Ballardian sense of place and mental and physical deterioration that Wiles, a design and architecture writer when not a novelist, does so horribly well. *Plume* is about a man trapped in a prison of his own making who endlessly gets nowhere at all' *Financial Times*

'Wiles takes us deep into a subtly altered London at the mercy of the malign forces of gentrification, and seemingly in the hands of a mysterious tech maven whose new app can track every user at all times…an eerie and sometimes pretty sharp satire on the more sinister commodifications of modern life' *Daily Mail*

'Relentless in its energy, wit and imagination' *Mail on Sunday*

Also by Will Wiles

Care of Wooden Floors
The Way Inn

PLUME

Will Wiles

4th ESTATE • London

4th Estate
An imprint of HarperCollins*Publishers*
1 London Bridge Street
London SE1 9GF
www.4thEstate.co.uk

First published in Great Britain in 2019 by 4th Estate
This 4th Estate paperback edition published in 2020

1

A catalogue record for this book is available from the British Library

ISBN 978-0-00-819444-4

Typeset by Palimpsest Book Production Limited, Falkirk, Stirlingshire

Printed and bound in Great Britain by CPI Group (UK) Ltd, Croydon

MIX
Paper from
responsible sources
FSC   FSC™ C007454

This book is produced from independently certified FSC™ paper
to ensure responsible forest management.

For more information visit: www.harpercollins.co.uk/green

For my parents, with love.

'People begin to see that something more goes into the composition of a fine murder than two blockheads to kill and be killed — a knife — a purse — and a dark lane. Design, gentlemen, grouping, light and shade, poetry, sentiment, are now deemed indispensable to attempts of this nature.'

'On Murder Considered as One of the Fine Arts'
Thomas De Quincey

ONE

We want beginnings. We want strong, obvious beginnings. Start late, finish early, that's the advice from people who write magazine features. Ditch the scene-setting, background-illustrating and throat-clearing and get stuck in. It's not a novel.

Lately, however, I've been fixated on beginnings, and their impossibility. I trace back and back through my life, trying to find the day, the hour I started to fail. Whenever I alight upon a plausible incident, where it might make sense to begin, I find causes and reasons and conditions and patterns that can be traced back further. And then I discover that I have gone back too far, that I have reached a point well before the event horizon of my failure, where the mass of it in my future overcomes any possibility of escape in the present. No fatal slip, or fatal sip.

Start late, finish early. Start with a bang. Later, a couple of my colleagues would claim that they heard the explosion. The rest would insist that it was too far away to be heard and that the others were mistaken.

I did not hear it. I felt it. The shockwave, widening and waning as it raced through east London, passed through my chair, through my notebook, through my phone, and through the people seated around the aquarium conference table. As it passed through me – through the acid wash of my gut, through raw, quivering membranes, through the poisoned fireworks of my brain – the wave registered as a shudder. It tripped a full-body quake, a cascade of involuntary movements beginning at the base of my spine and progressing out to my fingertips. These episodes had been getting worse lately, but I knew this was more than the usual shakes: as I felt the wave, I *saw* it. My eyes were focused on the glass of sparkling water in front of me. I had been trying to lose myself in its steady, pure, radio-telescope crackling. When the shock of the blast reached us, it had just enough strength to knock every bubble from the sides of the glass, and they all rose together in a rush. No one else reacted. No one else saw.

No ripple could be seen in the rectangular black pond of my phone, which was lying on the conference table in front of me. Within it, though, beneath its surface, ripples . . . But the Monday meeting had rules, strict rules, and my phone was silenced. Really, it should have been turned off, but I knew that it was on behind that finger-smeared glass, awaiting my activating caress.

'Explosion' was not my first thought. I guessed that a car had hit the building, or one nearby. These Victorian industrial relics all leaned up against each other, and interconnected and over-lapped in unexpected ways. Strike one and the whole block might quiver. But it could have been nothing. Without the evidence of the glass in front of me, I might have believed that I had imagined the shock, or that it had taken place within me, a convulsion among my jangling nerves, and I had projected it onto the world.

Even the bubbles were no more than a wisp of proof that an Event had taken place; they were gone now, and no further indications had shown themselves. None of my colleagues had stirred – they were either discussing what to put in the magazine, or looking attentive. As was I. There were no shouts or sirens from the street, not that we'd hear them behind double glazing six storeys up.

But on the phone, though, through that window . . . Whatever had happened might now be filling that silent shingle with bright reaction. With a touch, I would be able to see if anyone else had heard, or felt, an impact or quake in east London; I would be able to ask that question of the crowd, and see who else was asking it. And I might be able to watch as an event in the world became an Event in the floodlit window-world – the window we use to look in, not out. It was magical seeing real news break online, from the first hesitant, confused notices to the deluge of report and response. An earthquake, a bomb, a celebrity death. And if you scrolled down, reached back, you could find the very first appearance of that Event in your feed or timeline, the threshold – the point where, for you, the Event began, the point at which the world changed a little. Or a lot. In front of me, in real time, the Event would be identified, located, named and photographed. And the real Event would generate shadow events, doppelhappens, mistaken impressions, malicious rumours, overreactions, conspiracy theories. More than merely watching, I would be participating, relaying what I had seen or heard or felt, recirculating the views of others if I thought they deserved it, trimming away error and boosting truth. Journalism, really, in its distributed twenty-first-century form.

(I sickened as I thought of the Upgrade, the digitisation effort taking place on the floor below, all those features I had written being plucked from their dusty, safe, obscure sarcophagus in the magazine's archives, scanned, and run through text-recognition software. Soon they would be online. It couldn't be stopped.)

Being denied the chance to check if an Event was indeed happening felt physical to me, withdrawal layered over withdrawal. The action would be so quick: a squeeze on the power button, dismiss the welcome screen, select the appropriate network from the platter of inviting icons on my home page. I no longer even saw those icons: the white bird of Twitter against its baby-blue background, the navy lower-case t of Tumblr, the mid-blue upper-case T of Tamesis, enclosed in a riverine bend. For something happening in London, Tamesis might be best, the smallest and the newest of those three. It had started as a way of finding bars and restaurants, and prospered on the eerie strength of its recommendations. But it was evolving into much more than that, rolling out new functions and abilities, constantly sucking in data from other networks, informing itself about the city and its users. If there had been a bomb, or a gas explosion, or even a significant car accident, Tamesis would know about it before most people, pulling in keywords and speculation from Twitter and Facebook and elsewhere, cross-checking and corroborating, and making informed guesses – preternaturally informed. Maybe that, really, was twenty-first-century journalism: done by an algorithm in a black box.

With the passing minutes the importance of the vibration diminished, but my desire to escape this room and dive into the messages, amusements and distractions of the phone only strengthened. It was right there in front of me, but inaccessible – Eddie would be greatly displeased. He was relaxed about a lot of things that might bother other bosses, but the no phones rule in the Monday meeting was sacrosanct, and I saw his point.

Allow one, just for a second, and everyone would be on them the whole time. But the thought had taken root. Not only was I cut off from the sparkling constellation of others, I was cut off from myself, the online me, the one who didn't tremor and sicken at 11 a.m. on a Monday morning, the one who charmed and kept regular hours and lived a fascinating life, not this shambles who sweltered in the aquarium. The old image of life after death was the ghost, which inhabited without occupying, and observed without possessing or influencing. But here I was, in this meeting, alive and a ghost. Death, I imagined, would be more akin to being stuck on the outside of an unpowered screen – the world still blazing away there, wherever there was, but imprisoned behind vitrified smoke.

If I could be reunited with that shining soul behind the glass, though, the happy success, not the ailing failure, I could check in with the others – Kay, for instance, sitting across from me but looking at Eddie, as mute and inaccessible as my phone. I could send her a message, see what she had been saying on Twitter, Tamesis, Facebook, Instagram . . . I doubted there would be anything to see. I greatly preferred the other version of me who would be doing the looking, though, the assurance and charisma of his interactions with others. He had no hands that might shake or knees that might buckle. His visage appeared only behind moody filters, hiding the sweat and pallor. He was always on his way somewhere interesting, not fleeing rooms full of people. What would become of that Jack Bick when this one was finished? I wondered. His was the greater tragedy. He had not brought failure upon himself. How I wanted to be in his company, but how bittersweet I now found those times together. It was like seeing an attractive house from a train window and thinking, Yes, what a fine place to live – and realising that the railway line ran right past its windows, the passing trains full of strangers gawping in. This was the relationship between my online and my offline. The phone is the dark reflecting pool for the monument of the self.

'Jack?'

Kay was looking at me now, and so was Freya, and so were the Rays, and Ilse, and Mohit and the others. They were all looking at me. Eddie was looking at me – he had spoken.

'You with us, buddy?' Eddie said, and some of the others laughed. I forced a smile.

'Feature profile,' Eddie continued. Everyone looking.

How must I look to them? I wonder: the thin layer of greasy sweat pushed up by the warmth of the aquarium, the unlaundered shirt over an unlaundered T-shirt, unshowered and unshaved on a Monday morning. Was there odour? The air around me could not be trusted; I feared the tell-tale vapours that might be creeping into it. My index finger was resting on the rim of my glass, where I had been watching for tremors and thinking about the bubbles.

'Something just happened . . .'

Thirty or so eyes on me. No one spoke.

'Did anyone feel that?'

No one spoke.

'Feature, profile,' Eddie said. 'What do you got for us, Jack?' He enunciated this carefully, savouring the carefully remixed syntax.

The really bad part was that I actually had an answer to this, I was in fact prepared, but I had completely tuned out while Freya was talking, lost in ascending bubbles and the vibrating gulf between the icy crystalline world of the water and me, its observer, a low-voltage battery made by coiling an acid-coated length of bowel around a spine filled with tinfoil and bad cartilage. I searched for the correct page in my notebook, sweat prickling.

'Oliver Pierce,' I said.

One of the Rays pulled their head back, an almost-nod of recognition. Ilse appeared to tighten. Kay smiled, though only specialist devices aboard the Hubble Space Telescope could have detected it. The others did not react.

'The mugging guy,' Eddie said.

'Yes, the mugging guy.'

'He's been interviewed a lot.'

'No,' I said. 'He *was* interviewed a lot, when the mugging book came out. But he hasn't said anything to anyone in years. Not a word. Deleted his Twitter, doesn't answer emails . . .'

'Does he have a book coming out?'

'No,' I said, too quickly, a mistake. Then, scrambling to recover: 'Well, he must have been working on *something* – when I—'

'Maybe he's got nothing to say,' Eddie said. 'No book, no hook. How do we make it urgent?'

'He must have been working on *something* . . .'

'I haven't even seen any pieces by him lately,' Freya said. She was as bright-lit as the rest of us, but it was as if she had stepped from the shadows. I had tuned out of the meeting during a lengthy argument about feature lifestyle, her domain. We used to have a food correspondent, but after she left, food was added to Freya's brief. Freya hated food. Her one idea had been a feature about the next big thing in grains – trying to sniff out the next quinoa, the spelt-in-waiting – which Eddie, Polly and Ilse had united in hating. Boring, impossible to illustrate. It had been a bruising business for Freya, and part of her recovery was to try to make someone else's ideas and preparation look worse than hers had been. That someone would be me. Every month the flatplan served me up after Freya, a convenient victim if the meeting had gone badly for her. Unless I booked an interview high-profile enough to lead the feature section (not for a while now), feature profile followed feature lifestyle like chicken bones in the gutter followed Friday night.

'Nothing on *Vice*,' Freya continued, 'nothing in *Tank*. What if he's blocked or something?'

Pain, a steady drizzle behind my eyes. The quake visited my right hand, which was resting on the table in front of me, on top of my pen. I stopped it by picking up the pen and making a fist around it. The aquarium air was acrid in my sinuses, impure. What time was it? The Need wanted to know. I had to push on.

'Isn't that interesting in itself?' I asked, emphasising with the pen-holding hand, keeping it moving until the quake subsided. 'A writer has a smash hit like that mugging book. Big surprise. Awards. Colour supplements. Then, he goes Pynchon. Recluse. Emails bounce. Changes mobile number. Why? Isn't that worth a follow-up?'

'But he's not a recluse,' Eddie said. 'He's talking to you. Why's that?'

I wished I knew. 'He must have something to say.'

'There were loads of interviews when that book came out,' Freya said. There was brightness in her tone, no obvious malice, but I knew her game. She was trying to smear my pitch. And as she spoke, it was as if I could detect the gaseous content of each word, the carbon dioxide in each treacherous exhalation, subtracting from the breathable air in the room, adding to the fog around me. 'And besides . . . A novelist . . . Not much visual appeal.' She pursed her lips into a red spot of disapproval.

No one else spoke. Eddie pushed back in his chair. 'When are you meeting him?'

'Tomorrow,' I said. 'Morning. Tomorrow morning.'

'Let's have a back-up,' Eddie said. 'I want you to meet Alexander De Chauncey.'

An action took me without my willing it, an autonomous protest from my body. My head fell back and my eyes rolled; my lower jaw sagged; and I made a noise: 'Euuhhhh . . .'

Another boss might have regarded this as insolence – it was insolence, after all, a momentary lapse into teenage rebellion, not calculated but real – and hit back hard, but this was Eddie, our friend. He smiled at it. 'Look, I know you don't rate the guy . . .'

'He's a prick.'

'Have you met him? You wouldn't say that if you met him. Ivan introduced us. He's actually a great guy. Fun, creative, down-to-earth. An ideas guy.'

'He's a fucking estate agent.'

Eddie was away, fizzing with enthusiasm for his own proposal. 'That's the angle. An estate agent, but a new breed. Young, hip, creative. Progressive. One of us, you know? Not one of them. He's got some really amazing ideas. You'll love him.'

Every particle of my body screamed with cosmic certainty that I would hate him. 'Maybe next month?'

The change in Eddie's manner was so slight that perhaps only half the people in the room picked up on it, if they were paying attention: a hardening, a cooling. 'What, you're too busy this month?' A chuckle from the ones who had detected the change in Eddie-weather. 'Look, it's win-win, Jack. If your mugging guy pays off we can go large on him and maybe hold De Chauncey for next month. It won't hurt you to have one in the bag, to get ahead of yourself. If mugging guy is so-so, we do both. If Mr Mugging is a dud, we do De Chauncey. Yeah?'

There was no real question at the end of Eddie's statement

– more a choice between consenting by saying something or consenting by staying quiet. I chose to stay quiet. Eddie turned to his flatplan and struck out six spreads, over which he scrawled PROFILE PIERCE? / ALEX. The spread after this block he put an X through.

The flatplan was the map of the magazine – a blank A3 grid of paired boxes indicating double-page spreads, used to plot out the sequence of stories, features and adverts, letting editors decide the distribution and balance of contents: too word-heavy or too picture-heavy? Are there deserts to be populated or slums to be aerated? Editors, not generally a whimsical breed, often attribute mystical properties to the 'art' of flatplanning. They talk – their eyes drifting to the middle distance – of matching 'light' and 'dark', of rhythm and counterpoint, and the magazine's 'centre of gravity', its terrain, its movement. But basically, the flatplan is a simple graphical tool and can be mercilessly blunt in what it shows.

Those Xed-out spreads that came between features were advertising. And each of those ads would be for a high-status brand – BMW, Breitling, Paul Smith – appropriate to the magazine's luxury-lifestyle brief. One spread, very occasionally two, between each feature. No one commented on that, as if it had always been that way. But when I had started at the magazine there had been three or four ad spreads between features. Sometimes ad spreads would interrupt features. Advertisers would insert their own magazines and sponsored supplements into ours. The ads would experiment and try freakish new forms. They would have sachets of moisturiser glued to them, or fold-out strips reeking of perfume, or the page would be an authentic sample of textured designer wallpaper or a hologram or it would come with 3D specs. It had been quite normal for the magazine's writers and editors to complain about the ads, about features getting swamped by them, about the magazine becoming cumbersome. We were afloat on a sea of gold, and whining it was too thick to paddle, that the shine of it hurt our eyes.

There were still grumbles about the adverts, but now they dwelled on quality, not quantity. Was this Australian lager, or that Korean automobile, really the kind of advertiser we wanted? Couldn't the ad team do better? But Eddie was able to turn away these gripes with a sympathetic yet helpless shrug – a shrug that said, 'I know, but what can you do?' – and no one pushed past that.

Every year there were fewer of us to complain.

Ilse was unhappy with the inclusions, the loose advertising leaflets tucked into the magazine. One was a sealed envelope printed with a black and white photograph of a child's face, dirty and miserable. Underneath the face was the message IF YOU THROW THIS AWAY, MIRA MAY DIE.

'This kid, I don't know – this kid is threatening me? They are holding a gun to this kid and threatening it? It's a threat?'

'It's a charity appeal,' Kay said. 'They are just trying to create some urgency.'

'It is ugly,' Ilse said. 'Not the photograph, a good photograph I suppose, lettering fine, but what they are saying with this is ugly, it is a threat. When I open my magazine, my beautiful magazine' – she acted this out, closing last month's edition on the envelope, then opening it again – 'and, oh my goodness, this kid, I don't even know. It is not the correct mood.'

Eddie pushed a hand into his thick black curls. Ilse had been with the magazine longer than anyone except him, and along with him was the only surviving remnant of the Errol era. Dutch, brittle, she had a temper that was the basis of several office legends: that she was unsackable, that she had once hit a sub-editor with a computer mouse, that her giant desk was not a reflection of her status as art director but rather an exclusion zone established to keep the peace. When I was new, before the office became the roomy, under-populated space it was now, I had to sit near Ilse for two days while the wall behind my desk was repainted. Two days of terrified silence. On the second day, I ate lunch at my desk and for some reason – a self-destructive, reckless impulse, a death wish – that lunch included a packet of Hula Hoops. As I crunched my way through the fourth or fifth Hula Hoop, I became aware of eyes focused through steel-framed glass, of pale skin taut over sharp cheekbones. She said nothing, just looked. The remainder of the pack I softened in my mouth before chewing. It took about an hour and twenty minutes to finish them all.

This was back at the beginning of my time, and it was commonly held that she had mellowed. Recent budget cuts she had borne with (public) silence, if not good grace. Nevertheless, art directors are dangerous as a breed. They spend too much time playing with scalpels. Here we are in the age of Adobe Indesign and Photoshop, and still they won't be separated from those vicious little blades that come wrapped in wax paper like sticks of gum, and those surgical green rubber cutting boards. Why, if not for murder? Or at least recreational torture.

Before Eddie could answer, Freya spoke. 'Last month it was the National Trust. That seems off, to me. I mean, stately homes?' She threw up her hands and grimaced.

Eddie smiled. 'Good high-quality product. Not starving kiddies.'

'But it's just so Boden. Where do we draw the line? Those fucking catalogues of William Morris shawls and ceramic owls and reproduction Victorian thimbles?'

'If their money's green,' Eddie said with a teasing little shrug, clearly relieved to be arguing with Freya and not Ilse, who could thus be answered by proxy. 'Look, these pay, and quite frankly beggars can't be choosers. You want to sit in on one of my meetings with the ad team. You don't want.'

One of Eddie's tics – along with the suffering-in-silence hands-in-the-hair – was starting sentences with the word 'look'. You could see why he liked it: there was that note of Blairish candour, of plain dealing. It insisted on your attention and assent. But it was also a tell. It cropped up when he felt a discussion was not going his way. When he felt, for whatever reason, that he was not being sufficiently convincing. This was a double-look.

'Look, they're not going to do anyone any harm, they're not going to kill anyone. You might not like them, I don't care for them, but we need them.'

A silence fell.

'Is that everything?'

Polly, the deputy editor, whispered, 'Friday . . .'

'Aha, Friday, yes,' he said as he caught her eye. 'A reminder of what we agreed last week: I'm not here next week, so the next Monday meeting will be on Friday, and it's an important one. Has everyone kept the morning free?'

There were nods and mumbles of agreement. The change in schedule had been mentioned at the last Monday meeting, and its importance had been emphasised. Since then, it had been much discussed, out of Eddie and Polly's hearing, in quiet, nervous huddles. Eddie or no Eddie, the Monday meeting was sacred. When Eddie was away, Polly took his place, and the meeting went on. A Monday meeting on Friday was a patent absurdity, and an ill omen. But how to express the suspicions of the group?

After a tense silence, Kay spoke, and was direct. 'Are there going to be redundancies?' Seeing Eddie wince, she added, 'I don't like to ask, no one does, but we're all thinking about it and, frankly, the atmosphere is beginning to get a little stifling.'

Stifling was about right. Could Kay see it too? The room was filling with smoke, slowly, silently. It was going to choke us all, me first, unless we got out. No one else appeared to notice it – was it not affecting them, or was it killing them invisibly, undetectably, like carbon monoxide? No, I reasoned, probably not them, they would be just fine. The smoke was for me alone, it would fill my lungs and drag me down, and I would end right here in front of everyone before Eddie rapped the table with his knuckles and said, 'That's it.' How would they react if I expired in the middle of the Monday meeting? Would they be sad, would there be a tasteful black-border tribute in the next issue, using that photo they took last month for the new website? Or the other photo, the one from four years ago when I was entered for an award, the one with the puppy fat and the smile, not the gaunt, hollow-eyed creature I had become. I feared the new picture, crisp shadows in 8-bit greyscale.

Or would the expressions of grief be limited to: 'Sadly Jack has let us down again, so we have ten pages to fill . . .'

My death might save Eddie a redundancy. Kay was right. She had asked the question we all feared to, the question we asked each other when Eddie wasn't present, preferring to swap ignorant speculation for an actual answer.

'Look,' Eddie said, grabbing a fistful of his hair as he spoke, 'I'm not going to sugar-coat it. It's tough. Tougher than it's ever been. But I promise you I will do everything it takes to avoid . . . having to do anything like that.'

He looked around the table, carefully making eye contact with each of us in turn. Freya, at his left hand, was reached last, and she did not raise her eyes from her pad, where an extensive pattern of angry spirals had appeared.

'So for the time being the inserts stay,' Eddie continued. 'We'll just have to live with them. Even those fucking pewter eggcups, if it comes to that, God help us.'

A couple of people managed to chuckle. Eddie rapped his knuckles against the table. 'OK. Friday then. That's all.' And the meeting broke up, like a cloud dispersing.

In spite of my desperation, I did not immediately rise from my seat, fearful of wobbling in front of the others. Polly had been sitting at Eddie's right hand, on my side of the table, and my view of her had been blocked during the meeting by Ilse and Mohit. As the others left the aquarium, she was revealed. And she was staring right at me, chair swivelled in my direction, no trace of a smile. Her clipboard, a stainless-steel thing that was in effect a corporate logo for Brand Polly, lay on her lap. At first I thought she was going to speak to me, so I turned my own chair her way and looked attentive, trying to straighten up and compose myself. But she said nothing, and just stared at me, as if I were an inanimate object that presented a problem; a knackered sofa that needed to be taken to the dump, for instance. She was still staring as she stood, and only looked away when she reached the door and left the meeting room.

My head swam. I had to get out.

It was a relief to be out of the aquarium, out of the meeting, but I was not free yet. The earliest, the absolute earliest, I could justifiably leave for lunch was after noon, and it had only turned eleven thirty. The Monday meetings used to start at nine thirty sharp and had been known to run until one or even two. Now they started at ten and rarely ran past twelve. Fewer pages to fill, smaller, simpler flatplans, less international travel to coordinate in the diary, fewer voices around the table. Today we hadn't even started until ten fifteen – my fault, I had been late.

I wanted to talk to Eddie, to try to excuse myself from the office until Friday. That was the one advantage of being expected to do two interviews: I could justifiably work from home all this week and perhaps half of next week, in theory using the time to meet the subjects, type up the transcripts and then write the pieces. And other things.

But Eddie was talking with Polly in his 'office'. This was not truly a separate room, more a stockade in the corner of our open-plan expanse, made more private by metal archive cabinets on one side and chest-high acoustic panels on the other. The publisher – who had a very nice office – had fixed ideas about editors working in the midst of their staff. And so it had been, back in the Errol days: he had a big desk opposite Ilse, right in the middle of the floor, surrounded by his team. By the time I started on the magazine, Eddie had migrated to the corner. The archive cabinets and acoustic panels had appeared during a reorganisation a couple of years ago, a reorganisation made possible by our declining numbers. We would tease Eddie about his fortress, and he would tease back, saying he needed a bit of space to himself, to give him a break from all of us. Then those deep, gentle brown eyes would turn serious, perhaps even a little sorrowful, and he would say that sometimes people, us, came to him with delicate matters, sensitive personal or professional issues, and he wanted us to feel secure in doing that, to have some privacy. Really it was for our benefit, not his. And didn't we prefer having a bit of distance from our boss? Not having him looking over our shoulder the whole time?

He really was an amazingly thoughtful guy. But he was talking with Polly, and it looked tense. Polly was holding her steel clipboard in Clipboard Pose #4: Body Armour, clutching it to her chest in crossed arms. As Eddie spoke, she gave a series of little nods to punctuate what he was saying, a human metronome on a slow beat. She was behind the De Chauncey stitch-up, I was certain of it. Two interviews – the injustice of it was planetary, galactic.

As if to confirm my private suspicions, she abruptly turned to leave Eddie's office, and as she did so she looked straight at me. Our eyes connected, and something burned in hers, something that could be read as ruthlessness, or even cruelty.

Eddie looked up wearily as I entered his enclosure, announcing myself with a knock on the acoustic panel, a knock robbed of almost all its sound, reduced to a submarine bump. I had gone over as soon as Polly left, wanting to catch him before he picked up the phone or was detained by someone else.

'Jack . . .' he began, and his expression said, *Never a quiet moment*.

'Eddie,' I said. 'These two interviews . . .'

He rolled his eyes. 'No. Stop. We discussed this in the meeting. You're doing both.'

'It's fine, that's fine,' I said, holding up my hands in surrender. There was a little armchair by Eddie's desk for visitors to sit in but I chose to stand, as Polly had done. Business-like. On task. 'I just want to make sure it's OK to take the time I'll need to do them properly. I'm seeing Pierce tomorrow, Wednesday for transcribing, then Thursday and Friday for writing. So if we arrange De Chauncey for Monday next week . . .'

'No,' Eddie said. He frowned, eyebrows coupling. 'No. No. I'm not having you out of the office for two weeks, not when I'm out as well. You don't need that much time. You're meeting Pierce tomorrow morning, right?'

I nodded.

'You can do De Chauncey in the afternoon, while you're out. Transcribe both on Wednesday. On Thursday I can take a look at both transcripts, and we'll know where we stand.'

I shifted from one foot to the other, uncomfortable. Standing suddenly felt like a lot of effort.

'Come on,' Eddie said. 'Don't give me this. I know you can do it, you used to do it all the time. Come Thursday, I want you back in the office, and we'll make decisions about which feature to prioritise. I want clear progress before I go on leave, something I can have confidence in. Ready to show on Friday. Important day, Friday. Then you'll have a clear run at writing, OK? Without me breathing down your neck.'

My ankles were doing a lot of extra work to keep me upright, I realised. I was being undermined – the pleasant sensation of the sand being sucked from under the soles of your feet by a receding wave on the beach, reborn as a nightmare. Undermined, yes, that was it – Polly digging away at my basis, unseen.

'Sure,' I said. I wished I had sat down when I came in – it might have looked less formal and professional, but there was nothing formal and professional about falling over.

'Look, I don't enjoy micromanaging you this way, but I also don't enjoy it when you let us down, and when I have the others complaining that they have to pick up your slack.'

Polly – that had to mean Polly. Or Freya?

'I don't want a reprise of last month, or the month before,' Eddie continued. 'You were in the meeting this morning – it's a tough time. The toughest. We can't carry anyone. No passengers, get it? Need you up front, stoking coal.'

'Sure,' I said, squeezing out a smile. Had I been in the meeting? What had been said? It was a swirl already, nothing but half-gestures and loose words.

'Great.' Eddie smiled back, a comforting sight, which gave me hope I might make it out of his office and back to my chair without total collapse. 'Pierce is a good catch. How did you get him?'

'Uh, I'm a fan,' I said. 'Quin – F.A.Q. – put me in touch with him.'

'The Tamesis guy? F.A.Q.?'

'Yeah.'

'I thought he wasn't best pleased with us?'

I shrugged. 'I smoothed him over.'

'Anyway, Pierce could be great,' Eddie said. Even in my depleted state, I noticed this was a bit more equivocal than 'great catch'. 'Get the goods from him, something new and exclusive, and you'll have a great piece. Listen for a strong opening. Once you've got that the rest'll write itself on the Tube home.'

'Sure thing,' I said, and my affirming smile took a little less effort.

'Big week, then,' Eddie said. He nudged his computer mouse, waking the screen, to indicate that the meeting was over. 'Real chance to do something great. Make us all proud.'

'Sure. Great. Thanks, Eddie.'

It was 12.04. That would do. I slipped out of the office. Having had my dreams for the rest of the week dashed, I had no desire to be interrupted over lunch, so I 'accidentally' left my phone on my desk. The bubbles, the vibration, had completely left me.

It was about ten to two when I returned. We were allowed an hour for lunch and I liked to do some generous rounding in my interpretation of that rule. Eddie was pretty relaxed and didn't count the minutes. I figured that if it was twelve-something when I left and one-something when I returned, that's an hour. The people who left at one wouldn't be back yet, the people who left at twelve thirty would have only just returned. It was normally quite easy to slide back into the office without anyone paying attention to how long I had been gone.

Normally. Today, however, there was a small crowd of my colleagues gathered between my desk and the window: woman Ray, Polly, Mohit, Kay, Kim from promotions, and even a couple of golf wankers and craft weirdos from downstairs, whose names, of course, I did not know. My desk, with its dank heaps of notebooks and magazines, was not their focus, thank heavens. They were looking out of the window.

'Walthamstow?'

'Don't be silly, Walthamstow's over there. It's the estuary somewhere.'

'Royal Docks?'

'City Airport? Oh God . . .' A murmur of horror passed through the group; a couple of people covered their mouths.

We were on the sixth storey of an eight-storey building, and the windows on my side faced east, 'offering', as Wolfe / De Chauncey would put it, 'panoramic views of east London and Docklands'. In the foreground were the roofs and tower cranes of Shoreditch; much further away, to the right, were the towers of Canary Wharf, and behind those the yellow masts of the O2 Arena; to the left, at about the same remove, you could make out a little of the Olympic Park. On a clear day you could see a distant, dark line of hills on the far right and in places the mercury glimmer of the river. But in winter a grimy white dome, twin to the Teflon tent in Greenwich, was clamped down on the city.

Today, however, a new landmark had appeared. A column of black smoke rose from the ill-defined low-rise muddle of the horizon city. Further out than the skyscrapers on the Isle of Dogs, it nevertheless bested them in height and weight. While their glass and steel edges blurred in the cold grey air, the smoke tower was crisp and shocking, appearing as the most solid struc-ture in sight, an impression only strengthened by its slow distensions and convolutions. It was blackening the dome, pumping darkness into the pallid sky.

'Not City,' a voice said behind us. The other Ray, man Ray, was hunched at his Mac. 'It's on the BBC, just a couple of lines: fuel depot in Barking. Explosion and fire. Oh, that's awful. It says here people are being evacuated.'

'Better than being in danger,' Polly said.

Ray shook his head. 'But people aren't evacuated. Places, buildings, neighbourhoods are evacuated. Evacuating people would mean scooping out their insides.'

'And that's the BBC?' the other Ray asked. 'Really, you expect better.'

Man Ray shook his head in sad agreement.

'Are we in danger?' Kim from promotions asked. 'From – I don't know – gases.'

'I doubt it,' Polly said. 'It's a good long way away. If they were evacuating here, they'd be evacuating half of London. It's just a fire, a big fire.'

'It's drifting this way,' Kim from promotions said.

'It's just smoke,' Mohit said.

'When did it happen?' I asked. I had reached my desk, which put me to the rear of the group, and I don't think that any of them noticed my approach. Their eyes were on the plume.

'When did what happen?'

'Ray said it was an explosion . . .'

'It doesn't say,' Ray said. 'This morning.'

'I think I . . .' How to explain about the bubbles? If I said I saw the explosion I would sound ridiculous. 'I think I felt it . . . The vibration . . .'

'The earth moved for you?' Kay asked, and a couple of people chuckled, Mohit and a golf wanker.

'Now you mention it,' Ray – woman Ray – said, 'I think I felt it too.'

This prompted a more general and impossible-to-transcribe group conversation about who thought they had heard or felt what, whether it was possible to feel anything at this distance, and so on. I didn't contribute much, and the group's focus, such as it was, broke away from me. But Polly was still looking at me, and I frowned back, trying to figure out what I had said or done to earn this special attention. Her eyes darted down to my desk, which I was leaning against. My right hand was resting on one of the stacks of papers that are permanently encroaching on my keyboard and work space. It was this heap that Polly had glanced at, just a pile of torn-off notes, news-papers and magazines like the others, but I saw the top sheet, the one pinned under my hand, was not in fact mine at all. It was a yellow leaf from an American legal pad, and it was clipped, with many others like it, to a steel clipboard, which must have been left there by its owner while she was distracted by the drama at the window.

'Excuse me,' Polly said, and she grabbed her clipboard out from under my hand just as I lifted it to see what was written on it. Then she flipped the pages that had been folded over the back of the board to cover the sheet I had seen. But I had seen it. Columns of numbers – dates, times. The lowest line, the only one I saw in detail, read:

MONDAY: 10.11 12.05

Then two blank columns. I knew immediately, instinctively, what was recorded there, and what it meant. It was the time I had arrived that morning, and the time I had left for lunch, with spaces left for the times I returned from lunch and left the office at the end of the day. Polly was recording my move-ments – my latenesses, my absences, the myriad small (and not so small) ways I was robbing the magazine of time. The purpose of this record was obvious: she was building a case for my dismissal.

I did my best to hide the fact that I had seen the numbers and guessed their meaning. Grey oblivion enclosed my panicking mind on all sides, squeezing in. I pulled the chair from under my desk and sat down heavily. Polly was no longer looking at me. Instead she was staring fixedly out of the window, jaw tense, clipboard clutched to chest, being scrupulous about not looking at me. The grey closed in, appearing in my peripheral vision, cutting off my oxygen. I hit the space bar to rouse my computer and that small action felt like an immense drain on my resources. Fainting was a real possibility. No air. Horrible implications were spreading outwards from what I had seen, a thickening miasma of betrayal and threat. Firing an employee was cheaper than making them redundant – perhaps that was Polly's game. Perhaps she was collecting a dossier against me to spare someone else, a friend, an ally: Freya? Kay? Mohit? But of those names, none was more clearly on the axe list than mine. If I was already doomed, and they could save themselves that redundancy payment into the bargain . . .

Unread emails. Hundreds of new tweets. Fifty new Tumblr posts. I looked at the latter, not able to face the clamour of Twitter, and it was a good choice – calming. Attractive concrete ruins. Unusual bus shelters in Romania. Book covers from the 1970s. Silent gifs of pretty popstars. *New Yorker* cartoons. Feel-good homilies and great strings of people agreeing with heartfelt, bland statements against racism and injustice.

But the smoke was there, too. A camera-phone photograph on the blog of another magazine, showing the same plume we could see but over a different roofline. A much better photograph from the feed of Bunk, F.A.Q.'s company, taken from a higher angle and showing the column's base, orange destruction under buckling industrial roofs, in a necklace of emergency-service blue lights.

More of my colleagues were returning from lunch, some unaware of what was going on in the east, others brimming with urgency, disappointed to find that we all knew about the fire already. There was a volatile, excitable atmosphere in the office. Having an unusual event like this, a news event, so very visible in front of us all was turning people into restless little broadcasters, vectors for the virus of knowing, eager to find audiences as yet uninfected with awareness of it. This floor of this building was dead, saturated, so the group broke up and the spectators went to their phones and their keyboards to email, tweet, update Tamesis, Facebook, Instagram, WhatsApp, Snapchat – transmit, transmit, tell, tell. And all with this weird glee, the perverse euphoria that accompanies any dramatic news event taking place nearby, even a terrible event. Any other day, I would be among them – I felt that rush, that fascination, but at a distance, behind a firewall of private pain – but all I could do was gaze at my screen, barely seeing, hand dead on my mouse.

'Crazy.'

Polly was at my side. I had no idea how long she had been standing there, but I knew I had done nothing in that time, not the slightest movement.

'What?'

She nodded at my screen. It was still showing the Bunk picture of the fire.

'Crazy,' she repeated. 'I wonder how they got that shot? The high angle . . . Helicopter? From the look of it, it's amazing no one was hurt.'

Her tone was pleasant – just a regular chat between co-workers, as if nothing had happened, or was about to happen. A very casual assassin.

'Long lunch?' she asked.

Aha, I thought, here we go. I patted the book I had taken with me – Pierce's *Murder Boards*, decorated with a jolly fringe of fluorescent sticky bookmarks. 'Was doing some background. Working. Notes. Ready for tomorrow.'

'Oh, good.' Polly appeared genuinely pleased by this, which only intensified my suspicion that a trap lay ahead. 'Have you looked at your emails? I've set things up with De Chauncey's people – 3 p.m. tomorrow, at their Shoreditch branch. Easy-peasy.'

'Right,' I said. Grim tidings, but it didn't feel like the gut-shot I had been expecting. Her chirpiness was concealing something, I knew. Sure enough, the trap revealed itself. She adopted Clipboard Pose #2: Moses, supporting it with the left forearm and laying her right palm on the attached papers, as if drawing from them some inviolable truth.

'I wonder if you could do something else for me?'

I didn't reply. Maybe I shuddered.

'I'm trying to do some planning. To see if we can get past living hand-to-mouth, as we have been. When you have a spare moment, do you think you could jot down some future subjects for profiles? Your top ten people you would like to interview for the magazine.'

'The thing is, what with De Chauncey . . .'

'Eddie's keen to see this as well.'

'I just spoke with Eddie.'

'I think he said to help me out with the front? This is what I want you to do. Just this.'

I coughed, throat dry, and the action churned the liquid lunch in my stomach, acid frothing, rising.

'Just give me your target list,' Polly continued, no less sanguine. 'You must have people you're pursuing? Ideas? Ambitions?'

Once I did, sure. 'Sure.'

'Just stick 'em on a page and give them to me. Say by Friday? Then we can get planning for the future.'

'Sure.'

'Great!' And she hurried away cheerfully, clipboard swinging like a scythe.

The photograph of the plume on my computer screen disappeared, replaced by the writhing rainbow tentacles of my screensaver. But I didn't need photographs to see it. I could just raise my eyes to the window and look at the real thing: a tight black column at the bottom of the frame, an ominous addition to the dusty publishing trophies lined up on the sill; filling the sky at the top of the frame, choking out the light.

The tasks I had been set were impossible. Not for the others, but impossible for me. I knew I would not be able to do them. I knew that I was going to be fired. I knew the *how*, and I knew the *when*. And I already knew the *why*.

TWO

Latenesses, absences, missed deadlines, empty pages. I knew how it looked. It looked idle. It looked like the work – the lack of work – of a man who no longer cared. No passengers, Eddie said. We can't carry anyone. He wasn't the sort of boss to crack the whip unless he had to. No, his methods were persuasion and consensus. But I could see the change in him. The moment was coming. The moment when I could no longer be excused, when the accumulating evidence toppled into a landslide that would sweep me away.

Facts, accumulating. Polly's scrupulous notes, the implacable grid of the flatplan. Gather enough facts and you have the truth. But an interviewer, a profile journalist like myself, knows different. There are, for a start, too many facts. Far too many. Punch a name with even modest achievements into a search engine and back come hundreds, thousands, of relevant results.

Search someone like Oliver Pierce or Francis Quin – someone who operated online, someone with a following, an active fan base – and there are tens of thousands if not more.

Add to that what you gather yourself. People have no idea how much they say in the course of a normal conversation. Talk to someone for an hour and the transcript can approach 5,000 words. Trim away all the worthless 'yeahs' and 'umms' and 'I thinks', cut all the bits where they're ordering a drink or asking their PR how much time they have left, and unless they are the worst kind of drone celeb you will still have far more quotable material than can be squeezed into the 2–3,000 words you have been given to write.

So you select. You edit. And here the interview stops being photography and becomes impressionist painting. Ten quotes that make the subject look generous, warm and inspiring can be found in the transcript. The same transcript can yield ten quotes that make them sound weary, bitter and self-centred. The person remains the same, what they said remains the same, but they are seen through a series of funhouse mirrors, appearing first hypertrophied, then stunted, then undulating . . .

A correction. What they said does not remain the same, not quite. The interviewer does not merely prune, then select. They edit. People talk nonsense. They speak in fragments and non-sequiturs, they repeat themselves and omit. Sometimes they skip verbs, sometimes nouns. And by 'they' I mean *we*. We are all, always, skirting total aphasia, total nonsense. But we don't mind, we don't even hear it, because our inner editors smooth it all away in the hearing. The real evolutionary breakthrough was not the ability to speak – it was the ability to understand.

Record the unedited spew that is natural human speech and write it down word for word, and the result is unprintable. The subject would be furious if you put these words – their exact words – in their mouth. Rightly so. They'd sound like a babbling fool. The work needed to correct this impression – to make people sound as they believe they sound – isn't slight. It goes far beyond cutting out the 'umms' and 'ahhs'. It can entail wholesale reorganisation and rephrasing of what was said. In other words – in other words! – the writer must extract the ore of what was meant from the slag of what was spoken. Done correctly, the subject won't believe a word has been changed.

Even after explaining these difficulties, admitting the funda-mental elasticity of the truth, the professional profile journalist will still insist that truth is the very soul of their work. Their profile, they will claim, is a fair portrayal, or an authentic depic-tion of an encounter. But I was beginning to believe that a true portrayal of another person might not be possible – not because the truth was impossible to portray, but because there might not be any truth to expose. It might be that every man and woman is a fractal Janus, infinitely involuted, showing at least two faces at every level of magnification. It might be that every human encounter is a cryptogram impervious to codebreakers.

The data Polly had collected gave the impression of idleness. If she was in a position to fill in the widening gaps in my day, that impression would only grow stronger. Perhaps she had already guessed the truth. I have considered telling the truth. I have wondered what that would sound like, what I would say, and where I would begin. But even a straightforward statement of facts is not the truth, not the whole truth.

I am not idle. I work hard. I start early, I work through lunch, I work in the evening, I work late into the night. I work until I drop. When I am kept away from work, by the Monday morning meeting or by the quiet drink I enjoyed with Mohit that same evening, work was always on my mind.

Idle, no. Polly would not see, but it is there to see, out on the streets. You are outside a pub, queueing for a cashpoint, waiting for a bus. They approach and ask for money. Maybe they have a story they tell. Look at them – the stance, the gait, the eyes. Abject, yes. But not idle. No languor, no sloth. They are busy. They are on a deadline. They are working. Addiction is work, all-consuming, urgent work. And unlike my post at the magazine, the job security is total. Addiction will never fire me. It will never let me go.

It was true that I was often late for work. But I overslept less than you might expect – I was rarely given the chance, rising promptly, at 7 a.m., when the drilling started. Next door was renovating their house. Renovate: to make new again. They were stripping that word back to its roots just as they were rebuilding their house down to its foundations. Deep into the London clay they dug, scraping out precious extra inches of floor area and headroom. They were in my head-room too. Their busy pneumatic drills were working perhaps only feet – perhaps only inches – from where my head rested on an under-washed pillowcase. They might as well have been drilling inside my skull.

I no longer got hangovers. I was never sober enough. So perhaps the universe supplied the drilling as a substitute. All the oxygen was gone from the room already. There was air, but it could not nourish or sustain. And it was thick with dust, created and stirred up by the building work. Dark grey was encroaching in the corners of the window panes, smooth surfaces crackled beneath my fingertips. My nose was blocked.

Shower first, then breakfast, I thought. But the Need disagreed. You'll have time for that later, it lied. Me first. Still wearing no more than the T-shirt and boxers I had slept in, I went to the fridge, took out a can of Stella, cracked it, and took a swig.

The grit and stain was washed from the recesses of my mouth.

Cold brilliance. Appeased for the moment, the Need receded. The choking fog around me parted and I saw the leftovers from the previous night. Grey tatters of lettuce on a sauce-smeared, greasy plate, plain newspapers balled up nearby, seven empties crowded on the little table beside the sofa – none spilled. The cushions were piled up on one side of the sofa, still indented with the impression made by my reclining form. It was dark in the living room, but it was always dark in the living room. The only natural light came through the glass roof of the kitchen extension, and that was the depleted stuff that had found its way through the winter sky and down into a canyon between the backs of Victorian terraced houses. It was further filtered by the grime that had built up on the glass roof, and the branches of the neighbours' lime tree.

'Good morning,' I said to the black skeleton of the tree. It dripped filth in response.

I started to pick up empties. One turned out to be two-thirds full, and the surprise weight almost caused it to slip from my unready fingers. Another, tucked behind the lamp on the table, had about a third left in it. How long had they been there? Were they from last night, or earlier? Three days was a gamble.

The empty empties I crushed and put in the recycling; the part-empties I left by the sink. Then I sat on the sofa. The drilling had not stopped, or even subsided, but I had a little insulation in my head now, and it was at the other end of the flat. And only on the one side, for now. I felt pretty good, relatively. The meeting with Pierce was set for eleven, a civilised time, and I wasn't expected in the office until Thursday. That was an aeon away. All that mattered was not screwing up the Pierce interview – and I was unusually well-prepared. I had actually read Pierce's books and many of his articles; that was the reason I wanted to interview him in the first place. I just had to focus and stick to it for a couple of days, and the Polly-threat might recede, give me some time and space to get my head together, to make some changes, stabilise things.

'Getting myself back on track, yes indeed,' I said to the tree. 'What do you have to say about that? Two interviews today, and they're both going to go great.'

It had nothing to say about that.

The TV and DVD player were on standby, not completely off; they had done this themselves during the night. So discreet, so obliging. I turned the TV on and switched to the news. *London Blaze*, said the red caption beside the crawl.

'. . . real concern isn't the fuel but some of the additives used in some of these related processes, which we understand were on the site.' Not a newsreader voice but the unpolished, hesitant voice of an expert, speaking over pre-dawn helicopter footage of the fire, hungry orange squirts of flame, the smoke column like a thick black neck attached to a head that was buried in the ground, swallowing, chewing, consuming. Around it, a necklace of twinkling blue lights.

'So just how concerned should we be?' The interviewer, a female voice, cut in. I liked this question. I wanted to precisely calibrate my concern.

'Well, as I say,' the interviewee, a male voice, said, 'it's not really a question of the fuel but the other chemicals that may have been present; now we don't know what these were exactly, not as yet, but we understand there were substantial quantities of material on the site, and some of these can be, well, you wouldn't want to put them on your cornflakes, ha ha, but still the question as always is one of quantifying risk.'

One of those morning interviews, then, when the interviewee's time isn't particularly important and there are unending minutes to fill. Slightly informative noise had to be created to cover the real interest, the pictures. Not the helicopter any more: footage from the ground, also shot before dawn, of fire crews directing inadequate-looking streams of water into a pulsing orange hell, the ground a reflecting pool in which coiled hoses wallowed.

My can was half empty already, its comforting weight gone, its top warm. I returned to the kitchen and topped it up from the one-third-full can I had found behind the lamp. Waste not, want not. The coldness and fizz of the remaining half of the fresh lager would take care of the flatness and warmth of the older stuff. But as a precaution, I poured it through a metal tea-strainer I kept beside the sink. In the past there had been instances when I had watched, horrified, as a glob of mould had slipped from a too-far-gone can into perfectly good beer. It was heartbreaking to have to pour it all down the sink. And there had been times when I had not washed it away, and they were even worse. But the strainer, found in a charity shop, had been a useful investment. This time nothing was intercepted, and the found beer frothed in a reassuring way. I had three cans in the fridge. That would probably do me for the morning.

'Chances of a serious reaction are one in a million, one in 10 million really,' the television voice was saying.

'Ten million people in London,' I said to the TV, 'so one poor bastard . . .'

I tried to drink from the refilled can, but misaligned the aperture with my mouth, dribbling beer down the front of my T-shirt.

'Shit.'

I ran the back of my wrist across my chin. The drilling, which had paused for breath, chose that moment to resume. I hated the pauses in the drilling more than anything, because they invited the thought that the noise might have stopped for good, which was seldom the case. The builders on the other side were now making their own contribution: a hammer-blow, perhaps metal against metal, which repeated eight or nine times, then stopped, then started again. Through the flat, from the direction of the street, came the throat-clearing sound of a diesel engine and a steady rattle of machinery.

I threw the tree an angry glance. It was planted in next door's back garden, another of their multiple insults. Through the splattered glass of the kitchen ceiling, I saw a flash of white in its black limbs.

A cockatoo, sitting in the tree, looking down at me.

No, not possible.

I changed my position to get a better view through one of the cleaner patches of grimy glass. The white shape ducked from view. I stepped back. There it was again – not a cockatoo, but a white plastic bag caught in the branches.

Pacing back to the sofa, I took my laptop from my shoulder bag and switched it on. The noise was intolerable, something had to be done. What, exactly, I did not know, and as a renter my options were limited.

To: dave@davestocktonlets.co.uk
Subject: Re: Re: NOISE
Hi Dave,

I had never met Dave, my landlord, but he was pleasant enough on email, if he replied. We had corresponded about the noise before and he made sympathetic sounds and said there was little he could do. But emailing him was my only outlet. The owners of the neighbouring houses were never around, of course – even when their homes weren't the building sites they are now, I never saw them. Even if I could reach them, why would they do anything for me, a private tenant? I was simply nothing as far as they were concerned.

The email got no further than the salutation. Through the drilling, I heard an agitated rattling of my letterbox, then a triple chime on my doorbell. That special knock, this time in the morning, meant I knew at once who it was, and I groaned. Her, one of the ones from upstairs.

I wasn't dressed but there was little point. The lager had soaked into the T-shirt and contributed to any pre-existing odours.

When I opened the front door I tried to stay mostly behind it. The icy air made me flinch. Her breath was fogging; she was dressed in running gear, a headband holding back dark blonde hair, her top a souvenir from the London School of Economics. She had been jogging on the spot, but stopped when I appeared, and took the headphones out of her ears.

'Bella.'

'Jack. Hi, you're up!' she said, surprised.

'Every morning,' I said. Bella had forced me out of bed on a couple of weekdays before the coming of the drills, and now she behaved as if I had a lie-in every day. If only I did. 'Hard to sleep with the noise.'

'I've been running,' she said.

'Cold,' I said.

'Are you in today?'

'No, sorry.'

'Really? Not at all?' Bella said. She cocked her head to one side, a gesture that said: it's OK, you can tell Bella, just admit that you will be lounging around in your flat all day and all will be well.

'Really,' I said. 'I'm interviewing people.'

'Ooh!' she said, flashing her eyes wide. How did she get her lips to be so sparkly? Just looking at them made mine feel like sandpaper. The brick-dust was so thick in the air you could practically see it.

'New job?' she asked.

This took a moment to parse. 'No. No! *I'm* interviewing people. For *my* job.'

She frowned. 'To take over from you?'

I rubbed my eyes, feeling the grit in them. 'No. I'm interviewing them for the magazine. The magazine I work for. In my job.'

'Okey-dokey,' she said, sceptical. 'Will that take all day? Only we're expecting a delivery.'

'All day,' I lied. 'Can't you get it delivered to your office?'

Her face pinched in consternation. 'Ooh, no. It's furniture.'

'Sorry. Why did you arrange for it to be delivered today if you're not going to be in?'

'Well,' she said with a little *hauteur*, 'I expected you to be in.'

I felt that she had laid out a space for another *sorry* from me, but she wasn't going to get it. ''Fraid not.'

She flicked her eyes downward and I made a small shuffle further behind the door.

Smiling brightly: 'OK. You're not dressed. I won't keep you in the cold. Hope your interview goes well!'

I smiled back and started to close the door. She popped her earbuds back into her ears and turned towards the steps back up to the pavement.

'Bella,' I said, stopping her. 'You guys own upstairs, don't you?'

'Sure,' she said, as if startled by the implication that any other living arrangement could exist.

'Have you complained to next door?' I said. 'Both next doors. About the noise. The building work.'

'No,' Bella said. 'We're out all day working, so . . .'

'But, the dust,' I said. 'The dirt.'

She shrugged. 'Thing is, it's their property, isn't it, so really they can do what they like with it.'

'I guess so.'

In truth, I didn't mind Bella as much as I might. She at least kept her low opinion of me heavily gilded with courtesy and cheer – I imagine she has no idea how she comes across. It's him I can't stand, Dan, her husband. A prime Mumford. I would happily murder Dan.

The front door sticks a little when it's closed, and on occasion it needs a real bang to shut properly. This bang dislodged something from the letter flap, and this something fell with a turn that suggested the beat of a white wing.

A postcard from my parents: pretty toy-like buildings lined up on a picturesque quay. Could be anywhere. Copenhagen, Amsterdam, Stavanger, Lübeck. Five years ago, Dad had retired, and Mum had decided to join him. So this was victory, for them. They shared a belief – a widespread and wholesome belief – in the fixed path of virtue. School, as a path to University, as a path to a Proper Job (proper – an important qualifier, that). All this was the infrastructural spine that supported Marriage, Mortgage, Family and Responsibilities. But what was at the end of this path? What lay at the sun-touched horizon? What was the reward? Retirement, that's what.

This might make them sound stuffy and orthodox – brittle mannequins of small-minded propriety cursed with a dissolute son. (My younger sister, a pharmaceutical chemist at Sheffield University, has done a little better at cleaving to the path.) Not true and not fair. They were never less than loving and supple in their accommodation of my occasional efforts to remove myself from the path. Their belief in the path manifested itself more subtly. Any unhappiness, for instance, could be diagnosed as deviation either past or planned. Miserable at school? I needed to treat it as a means to an end, the end being university. Restless and unmotivated at university? Again, its only purpose was as a step leading to the next step – head down, push on. Unable to save a mortgage deposit? Perhaps I should consider getting a more solid, more *proper* job – or moving back to Two Hours Away (by the faster train), the southern provincial city in which I was born. Love life problematic? Perhaps a Proper Job would yield more suitable candidates. None of this advice was delivered with self-righteousness or coercion, it was all meant honestly and kindly. And who could blame them for their belief in a system that had served them perfectly?

But just as the Correct Route Through Life had supplied its own built-in justifications, its completion had robbed it of purpose. My parents had spent their whole lives working duti-fully, rewarded daily with the certitude that they were doing the right thing. The arrival of the real reward – comfortable retire-ment, two decent pensions, mortgage paid off, children through university and out of the house – had deprived them of the satisfaction of dogged, stately progress.

They went a little crazy.

When I was growing up, I never saw my parents argue. They disagreed at times, or frowned at each other, but never did they engage in that basic ritual of relationships, the big argument. Not in my sight, anyway. I have no inkling of what script discus-sions or creative disputes went on behind the scenes of their performance as Mum and Dad. But on stage, they were pros.

In the first year after their retirement, they *argued*: long, flam-boyant arguments with epic scope, stirring chiaroscuro and elaborate, intertwined plots and subplots. Late in life, they found that they shared a gift for holding a really poisonous row.

They supplied their own reviews of these arguments. Ever

since I turned eighteen, Dad had routinely taken me out for 'a pint' at the local pub. A pint, precisely: two half-pints of bitter, followed by a further two ordered with hints of wicked indulgence and declamations that that had never been the plan. After his retirement, those drinks turned into discussions of the arguments. 'Your mum and I have been arguing a lot,' he would say, every time, as if he didn't say the same thing every time. He never criticised her, and I truly believe that it would never even occur to him to do so. But he would sadly acknowledge the fact of the arguments, without giving the slightest detail as to what might be causing them, and expect me to be sympathetic.

(My sister reported that she was getting the exact same from Mum, often at precisely the same moment. Mum *did* criticise Dad, but only in the vaguest, most all-encompassing terms: 'Your Father!', uttered as if his very existence was an affront we had all quietly tolerated for too long.)

Then, a transformation. After about a year of arguments, including the hellish Christmas of 2012, my parents decided they needed a holiday. For twenty-five years, French beaches had known their presence in the summer. Their knowledge of the French coast was probably rival to that of Allied high command, June 1944. But this time, in the spring of 2013, they went on a city break, to Brussels on the Eurostar.

They stayed four nights and I received three postcards. Dad ate a horse steak. Mum ate a waffle sold from a van. They were photographed in front of the Atomium, the Palais de Justice, the Tintin Museum, the restaurant where Dad ate the steak, the van from which Mum purchased the waffle, and the headquarters of the European Commission.

A mania took hold. An addiction, maybe. No city in Europe was safe. It didn't really matter where this postcard came from, and I already knew the gist of what was written on the back. It would join a small pile of very similar postcards on the kitchen counter, next to a cork board thoroughly covered with a bright collage of classical columns, Gothic spires, Moorish palaces, Dutch gables and high pitched Nordic roofs.

The era of arguments came to an end. So began the era of city breaks.

Standing in the icy doorway for so long had completely thrown me off my stride. I opened another can of Stella, forgetting that I already had one on the go.

All the cans in the fridge were empty by the time I left the house, and so were the half-empty cans I had found. I would have to pick up more, but then I would have needed to make a run in any case. Three cans or fewer was completely insufficient, dangerous. The horrible thought that there was no alcohol in the flat would be at or near the front of my mind all day.

In other regards the morning was going well. I had showered, put on (mostly) clean clothes, and set out at a reasonable time. My bag was double-checked for all the things I needed: two digital voice recorders, my old one and my new one, and spare batteries for them. After the recent disaster with F.A.Q., I was taking no chances.

Also in the bag were Pierce's books: two novels, the mugging book, and the cash-in collection of non-fiction that his publisher had put out the Christmas that the mugging book was at the top of every broadsheet 'books of the year' list. Actors, MPs, television historians, baking competition hosts, they all exerted themselves to overstate how luminous, powerful, searing, important, draining, life-affirming, etcetera, etcetera they had found *Night Traffic*. I felt quite resentful about all this, because I had been reading Pierce for years. My copy of *Night Traffic* was the softback Panhandler Press edition with the cheap cover art, not the classy Faber edition that appeared when the award shortlists and reviews started to pile up, and which is still inescapable on the Tube.

I had been reading Pierce since his first novel, *Mile End Road*, came out in 2009. This was a fairly conventional story of twenty-somethings finding love, losing it, finding it again and then losing it for a second and final time. But the few reviews it received praised its rendering of twenty-first-century London life and its (at the time) unusually realistic depiction of the mobile phone and social media habits of young Londoners. It was longlisted for a couple of prizes and did not trouble any bestseller charts.

Pierce's second novel, *Murder Boards*, had the good fortune to appear just before the 2011 riots. To capitalise, the post-riot paperback was given a sensational cover, with a movie-like strapline: THE CITY IS ABOUT TO EXPLODE. This bore little relation to its contents, 500 pages of non-linear narrative and cut-up technique told from the multiple viewpoints of its spectral cast of characters. It was concerned – obsessed, really – with missing persons and unresolved crimes, and steeped in police jargon and the imagery and phrasing of TV news. At times, it appeared to be deliberately opaque and confusing, as if the reader were an investigator confronted with contradictory accounts of events and inscrutable enmity between characters, between reader and author, between author and reality, with the objective truth of the past unknowable. To give up on *Murder Boards* was to play Pierce's game, to take on the role of the indifferent bystander, the grazing TV viewer, the desensitised inquisitor, the impatient and unsympathetic bureaucracy. The reader's natural frustration with a long and frankly exhausting experimental novel was thus subverted. Read to the end or put the book down unfinished – either way, Pierce won. Reviewers were divided.

One-third of them hailed Pierce as a genius, another third called him a charlatan. The remainder made it obvious they did not understand the book, and maybe had not even finished it, by playing it safe with cautious praise.

After the modest success of *Mile End Road*, Faber had poached Pierce from Panhandler and put out *Murder Boards* with much ballyhoo, but despite a brief life as an edgy fashion accessory and social media prop, it was a resounding commercial failure. Whatever happened, Pierce was back at Panhandler for his third book, *Night Traffic*. Maybe the big house took fright at the thought of releasing a long essay covering many of the same themes as the chunky, expensive literary novel that was stinking up its balance sheets.

But since the appearance of *Murder Boards*, Pierce had acquired a small and eager following, myself included. His post-riots essay for *3AM Magazine*, 'Beneath the Paving Stones, the Fire', had circulated on Twitter and Tumblr for more than a month, and was republished by the *New York Times*. Pierce had been writing essays about London for years, but now his writing became more adventurous, more scandalous, and funnier. He was able to arrange gonzo escapades that other journalists – again, myself included – could only dream about. A night spent with criminal fly-tippers, dumping trash on street corners and narrowly evading the police. Searching for forgotten IRA arms caches in north London back gardens. A memorably hilarious excursion with three Russian heiresses, the daughters of Knightsbridge-resident oligarchs, to find and consume authentic East End jellied eels.

In the summer of 2012 – the 'Olympic summer', we journalists are now apparently bound by law to call it, although for me personally it has darker connotations – *Night Traffic* appeared. Short, extraordinary, explosive. *Night Traffic* was an account of an incident the previous year in which Pierce had been mugged by a group of youths, no more than teenagers, in a quiet part of his native east London. Finding Pierce's mobile phone and about £20 in cash to be insufficient reward for their effort, the youths had shown the author a blade, marched him to a cash-point and forced him to withdraw £300. He spent more than half an hour in their company, crashing through an immense range of emotions from outright terror to perverse bonhomie and back to terror. Afterwards he had been too traumatised to appreciate that he should report what had happened to the police. A dark week was spent shut up in his flat, turning the events of that night over and over in his head, before he realised that he did not want to report it after all. Instead he would compose his own report, tackle the matter as a writer, as a journalist. He returned to the scene during the day and at night, and retraced his steps. He tried to find witnesses. He searched for the youths, sitting out through the small hours. He tried to get CCTV footage of the incident, without success. And he found himself coming to a transgressive acceptance of what had happened: that his ordeal had been a natural part of the ecology of the city and the economy of the night, that it was all preordained and the product of order, not disorder – and, most controversially, that violence might be a salutary urban force, 'the street seeking balance'.

Night Traffic was not quite an 'Overnight Success', as the headline of Pierce's *Guardian* interview put it. Panhandler was a small operation, based in Ipswich, and only managed to get it into a few larger bookshops. But Pierce's cult reputation got it under all the right noses, and even before its official publication there were rumours and previews promising that it was special. Then came a month-long bombardment of long, shining pieces by heavy-hitters: Will Self in the *Guardian*, Geoff Dyer in the

Telegraph, Michael Moorcock in the *Independent*, Rebecca Solnit in the *TLS*, Iain Sinclair in the *LRB*. Panhandler's first printing sold out immediately and it rushed a deal with Faber for a mass-market paperback, which hit every bookshop in the UK and Ireland just as the award shortlists started to roll in. Knopf bought US rights for six figures. By early 2013, Pierce was a rare creature: a literary celebrity. He even made a brief, ill-at-ease appearance on *The One Show*, during which, in a first for that programme, he used the word 'epiphenomenal'.

Then he disappeared, or as close to 'disappeared' as you can get while still living in London and being verifiably alive. The last post he made on Twitter was to announce the cancellation of two forthcoming events; the account shut down a couple of weeks later. Emails bounced back to their senders. The slim hardback of collected essays came out in late 2013 and Pierce did nothing to promote it – no interviews, no readings, no appearances.

Night Traffic had attracted some controversy. The police had helped sales by criticising Pierce's decision not to report the crime, and his freelance investigations. A *Daily Mail* columnist had attacked Pierce for 'celebrating' urban violence. One or two bloggers had taken against the book, claiming that it perpetuated stereotypes about the inner cities and deprived young people, although there was never much wind in the sails of this accusation; some corners of Twitter griped about 'poverty tourism'. But the reasons for Pierce's withdrawal from view remained stubbornly enigmatic. One theory was that he had taken fright at the sudden attention; another held that it was all a ploy, a stunt, an over-exposed author's effort to recharge mystique. There were rumours of grand secret projects, but nothing more than rumours. I had been astonished when F.A.Q. said Pierce had been consulting with them on the mapping software that underpinned Tamesis. Consulting how? Doing what? Tamesis's workings were obscure, purposefully so – Quin had this whole spiel about concealing some aspects of how the application worked. 'Open but dark systems', 'benevolent spookiness', 'network chiaroscuro'. You can see all that on Quin's TED Talk, or his presentation to the RSA. I forget which.

But I digress.

Writing profiles isn't hard – there are rules to remember, but anyone can learn those rules. For instance, don't slam your readers with great slabs of biography. Don't regurgitate the subject's CV all over the page. That information needs to be broken into digestible morsels and stirred into the writing. I learned that in my first job in journalism, shortly after I graduated in 2004. See?

Another rule is: don't keep the reader hanging around. Like Eddie said, listen out for that strong opening. You have to start with a bang. The beauty of this is that even a disastrous interview with an obstructive subject can be turned to your advantage. If Pierce was rude and unhelpful, if he refused to answer questions and insulted my parents, I could still write the piece to my advantage – as a gonzo exercise, to use Pierce's own tactics against him, or as self-deprecating humour. It took a bit of skill, but it was possible. I had started the calamitous Quin interview with his reaction to my late arrival. Indeed, it was a gambit I had worked hard in recent months as my preparation had grown more and more threadbare, and anyway it was so heavily used in the Sundays it has become cliché.

Yet another rule – and this applies to all feature writing, not just profiles – is that you need what's called a 'nut graf'. This is a paragraph or a line, near the start of the piece, that tells the reader what the article is about. It poses the question that the feature sets out to answer. So for Pierce, I'd like the nut graf to be along these lines: What made this acclaimed author suddenly shut himself off from the world – and why is he opening up now?

To ask that, of course, I'd need to get a good answer to that question. Because I have a nut graf of my own: Am I going to be fired this week?

At Victoria Station, there were unusually large numbers of people standing on the forecourt, not rushing about, and for a horrible second I thought the Underground entrances might be closed. This often happens in the mornings, as Victoria is always over-crowded and they have to shut the gates to stop a dangerous crush developing on the platforms. But it was well past the peak of rush hour and people were freely coming and going. Those commuters who were standing around outside were all facing in the same direction, towards Victoria Street, and they were all looking up at the sky.

I had been walking with my head down and my earphones in, thinking about Pierce, about what I was going to ask him. Little else had registered, apart from the coldness of the morning and the weakness of the light. I raised my eyes to see what the others were seeing.

The sky to the east – that is, towards the greater part of London – was poisoned. There are winter days when snow-filled clouds trap the land in unshifting twilight and the location of the sun is a mystery. But this occultation was deeper and darker than that, and lower and more sinister. Not storm-grey but the grey of truck tyres and industrial soot, intensifying to near-black at its thickest point. The plume. It had scented the air with a petrochemical tang that brought a solvent sting to the sinuses. I suppose I should be grateful to my neighbours for coating my sensory organs with a fine layer of pulverised brick and plaster, protecting me from the great fire's morning bouquet.

I picked up a *Metro* from an untidy heap by the top of the Tube stairs. 'Two Hurt in Inferno' said the front page headline; a subheading added 'Fuel Plant Blaze Rages Through Night'. On a normal morning I wouldn't read *Metro* but I wanted to see more pictures of the fire, in particular more pictures from above. I can't say what prompted this desire, but it was ardent and sudden.

'I don't like it,' a young woman standing nearby said to her colleague. 'I don't like it. I just don't like it.' They were looking at the plume, but I didn't know if they were talking about it.

A short hop on the Victoria Line, a transfer through the labyrinth of Oxford Circus, then a longer stretch on the Central Line. Rush hour had eased enough for me to get a seat and examine the paper.

As well as the cover, the fire had been given two inside spreads. The editors had clearly intuited that it would be a major topic of conversation on the morning commute and in the city's workplaces, and had done their best to cater for that curiosity. Pages four and five were straight reporting: pictures of the fire crews, details of the evacuation, hasty facts about the toxicity of the smoke, and – best of all – a top-down Google Earth view of the fuel facility with numbered spots: 'Minute by Minute: How Blaze Spread Beyond Control'.

Better yet were pages six and seven: 'Your Pictures of Barking Inferno'. What an age this was for the gawper and the rubbernecker – at last, satiety. Sam from Leyton had captured an apocalyptic black pillar dwarfing a twilit terrace of houses. Ann from Maida Vale contributed a picture from Hampstead Heath, probably taken around lunchtime: London as Mordor, an inverted black pyramid spewing darkness at its eastern edge. In the foreground of this image, other people could be seen on the Heath, also taking photos with their phones. Lee from Southend had another angle, the smoke cloud from the east, the western horizon kohled, sunset cancelled. My favourite image was by James from Crystal Palace: the view from a passenger seat of a plane approaching City Airport. The horrifying size of the plume was made clear: the leg of an elephant with a foot of fire stamping down on the estuary; London a grimy circuit board experiencing a fatal short. It's not a long journey from Oxford Circus to Liverpool Street and I made it no further into the newspaper.

At Liverpool Street I had arranged to meet the photographer, Alan, who was coming in by train from Essex. But when I got to the Kindertransport memorial by the tube entrance, Alan wasn't there. Last time we met – the Quin interview – I had had a heavy morning and had kept him waiting for half an hour. He had not been pleased. Was he taking revenge? But, no – or at least, not yet. To my surprise, I was three minutes early.

The memorial was a handy place to meet, but an uncomfortable object to spend too much time around. It's very small, almost too small, as if it is somehow embarrassed, which is a bad vibe for a memorial. Its size also makes it look a little kitsch, and I can never see the two bronze children without thinking of the charity collection boxes for the blind that used to be found in every pub. And then, having been struck by those thoughts – every time – I am embarrassed to have felt that way about a reminder of the Holocaust, and the little bronze children are full of reproach.

The equilibrium I had briefly experienced on the train was gone, and I began to choke up again. My options were limited. The pubs were just now opening, and in any case there was no time. On the station concourse there was a little food and wine shop, but where could I discreetly drink a can?

'Jack.'

I had drifted away from the memorial, into the middle of the concourse; Alan had come up behind me, packhorse-heavy with bags, tripods, reflectors and other equipment.

'Alan. Hi.'

'You look a bit lost, mate,' Alan said, full of cheer and heartiness. He was a short, muscly man somehow well-served by his receding hairline, which gave him an aura of toughness and experience. He combined this with a plain-speaking, no-airs, working-man demeanour – all 'mate' and 'pal' – that I suspected was a carefully cultivated pretence. Nevertheless, it was enough to set me – provincial bourgeois – ill-at-ease, eager to demonstrate my own (entirely affected) rough-diamond nonchalance. I had the same ridiculous problem with plumbers.

'Yeah, no worries,' I said, regretting every word as I spoke it. Was I supposed to be Australian? 'I was just thinking about getting a coffee.'

'Now you're talking,' Alan said. He checked his watch with a flourish. Chunky metal strap, hanging loose. 'Yeah, plenty time, plenty time.'

We crossed to a little coffee booth, Alan's many bags clanking against my nerves. I ordered two black coffees. Coffee might help, for a time.

'Jack, mate, this Q&A guy . . .'

This took me a moment to parse. 'You mean F.A.Q.?'

'Yeah.'

I didn't like this direction. Alan had had real trouble getting Quin's portrait. He had wanted to shoot the designer in the Tamesis nerve centre, where a giant screen streamed live data from the app. But Quin had refused, and was steadfast in his refusal, fretting about client confidentiality and industrial espionage. The alternative offered was his characterless office, which Alan hated. Eventually, using the combination of charm and un-embarrassable persistence that is a standard part of the photographer's kit, Alan got Quin up on the roof of Bunk's Shoreditch building. The London skyline made a good backdrop for the creator of Tamesis. But the very next day I got an agitated phone call from Quin – the first of many – insisting on picture approval. Compounding all this was the rush caused by our – by my – lateness. I would prefer never to hear the name Quin again, but it continued to dog me.

'Can you nudge your people?' Alan said. 'I haven't been paid.'

'Shit. Alan, I'm sorry, I'll give them hell.'

'I knew I could count on you,' Alan said.

The coffee was too hot to hold for long and I had to continually switch it between hands as the pain became unbearable. Alan did not appear to be affected. He even sipped his.

'Do you want a hand with those bags?' I asked.

'Nah,' Alan said, redistributing the load around his body with a practised sequence of heaves and shrugs. 'Used to it. Like to keep everything with me.'

'Very sensible.'

'You drinking that? We've got to get a shift on.'

'Uh, I'll take it on the train,' I said, changing hands.

The eastbound Central Line platform was quiet, but I would have been happiest turning right and walking along it to find its quietest part. Alan had different ideas and turned left, where there was only a short stretch before the platform ended. Again, he said this was habit – it was where the rear of the train would be, and there would be more room, in theory, for his bags. I doubted his reasoning. I doubted his Tube sense. And we were left standing in an awkward corner between two staff-only doors, right by the tunnel mouth. One of those doors was a concertina-like affair, which I found gravely unnerving. Warning signs. Cabinets closed with inspection tape, like a crime scene. My discomfort was ticking upwards at regular, frequent intervals. The coffee could only be tolerated for ten seconds or so in one hand before it had to be passed to the other, and was still too hot to be sipped. I tried, once, and scalded the roof of my mouth and the middle knuckles of the fingers of my right hand. While the pain of that had subsided, stickiness had spread between all my fingers, across my palm, and down to my wrist. I wanted to wash my hands in icy water, and to splash that water against my face. I wanted to be holding a cool can, fresh from the fridge. How had Alan drunk his so quickly? His innards must be Le Creuset.

'Do you got it with you?' Alan said, without intro.

'Got?' I said. '*It*?'

'The mag,' Alan said. 'The one with the F.A.B. piece in it. Want to see how it came out.'

Had he asked for one? I couldn't remember. I had considered bringing along a copy of the magazine to give to Pierce, but I hadn't written anything in the most recent issue, and I knew he had already seen the one with the Quin interview – besides, I wasn't too proud of that one. If I went through the back issues until I found a feature I was proud of, I'd be taking him a copy from three years ago, and that just seemed plain odd.

'You weren't sent one? You should have been sent one.'

'Nah.'

'Typical.'

'Muppets,' Alan said, shaking his head. Wanting to align myself with Alan, against the muppets, I tried to think of an equivalent term of cockney abuse.

'Ragamuffins,' I said. Then winced.

Alan frowned. 'You need to have a word. You guys used to be the best, a right treat to work with – good as *Monocle*, good as Condé fucking Nast. Taxis, expenses, assistants . . .'

'Times are tough.' I couldn't remember the last time Eddie had sprung for a taxi. The no taxis rule was so strict and long-established it might be in the Old Testament.

'How'd it turn out?'

'It turned out fine.' It had been, perhaps, half a step from becoming an unstoppable meltdown that rendered my career an uninhabitable fallout zone. But the photography was not at fault.

I really didn't care to have that piece – and the multiplying failures in the magazine's treatment of its freelancers – brought up again. And I had a fearful premonition as to how this morning was going to go. Alan, I suspected, was going to get on with Pierce a lot better than me. I would be left on one side, stammering, watching them form an easy, down-to-earth rapport. I had too much at stake, I was just too *impressed* by Pierce, almost star-struck. Alan would not be so hindered, and would chat freely, drop impressive names, and they'd find they had friends in common; I'd be left going oh-please-sign-my-books-Mr-Pierce and where-do-you-get-your-ideas-from. I wasn't too worried about appearing drunk – I am an expert at concealing it. If anything the problem was that I was *not drunk enough*, that I would freeze up, that my hands would shake, that I'd be visibly, palpably ill-at-ease. Not even that: visibly *ill*, lacking, empty. Perhaps Pierce would be cool, offer me a glass of wine, a bottle of something from the fridge? Those bottles were always tiny compared to a good, solid, weighty can, but it would be something. But it was futile to hope, we'd be there at 11 a.m., no one offers their guests booze at 11 a.m.

Fuck Alan and his relaxed, class-transcending bonhomie. He would ruin the whole morning.

A recorded announcement played.

'Did you hear that?' I said. 'Inspector Sands.'

'I wasn't listening,' Alan said. 'What did they say?'

'"Inspector Sands to the operations room",' I said. 'It's code. It means there's a fire alarm that needs to be checked out.'

'And this Sands guy'll do it?'

'No. There is no Sands. It's just a code. When there might be a fire somewhere but they don't know and they don't want to cause any panic.'

'I didn't hear anything.'

'That's the point, it's a very bland, boring, routine message, people tune it out, don't know what it means.'

'You know what it means,' Alan said. 'Can't be that secret.'

'Seriously, though, can you smell burning?'

I asked because I could smell burning – the acrid smell of an electrical fire, melting copper, blistering insulation. We must be surrounded by equipment handling the Underground's canalised lighting, all of it out of warranty, overdue for replacement, caked in dust. I had seen it in documentaries. The men who went into the tunnels at night. The Tube acts as a giant vacuum cleaner, sucking human detritus from the light into the darkness. I could see those documentaries again, now, in my mind's eye: a gloved hand bringing up a smoking grey fistful from the ballast around the tracks, like a robot submersible on the ocean bed. This accreted dust and hair burned very well.

'I can't smell anything,' Alan said.

He was wrong, surely. Though it did not seem to be stronger, I felt that the smell had become inescapable; perhaps because I was more focused on it, it had begun to block out all other sensations, almost as if it were welling up within me, a toxic spasm in the lungs rather than a scorched and poisoned breath from the tunnel.

I looked about to see if anyone else had smelled fire, expecting others on the platform to raise their heads, frown, sniff the air – the herd detecting danger, abandoning their quiet little worlds of phone and newspaper to confront an environment that had become unsafe. But no one raised their eyes, no one even stirred. Couldn't they sense it too? How could they all be so oblivious?

The breeze from the tunnel grew stronger, and I could see it now, see the smoke, a steadily thickening haze carried on the back of the column of air pushed out by the approaching train. And I could feel it on my skin, in my eyes, hot and stinging. I raised my hand to my face and did not lower it. I was hot to the touch. I coughed, and fell into a fit of coughing, unable to stop. Hair and skin, on fire in the darkness, one of those coal seam fires that burn for decades, inextinguishable, slow death to the communities above. I felt ready to vomit.

'You OK, mate?'

Alan was scowling at me, but not without kindness. I barely registered his expression, though; behind him, the sealed panels looked about ready to start jetting smoke, opaque and heavy yellow-stained smoke, any second it would begin.

'We've got to get out of here,' I said, barely able to speak, each word displacing more poison into my lungs.

'What? Train'll be here in a second.'

A second was too late. The air was going, it was gone, no way to get at it. Suck it in and the poison would come too, into the blood, into the brain. Then the light. It was almost too late. I needed cold air, cold water on my face, coldness in my throat.

'I'm sorry,' I said. And I ran.

THREE

Self-control came easier back in the cold street air, but I still felt that my inside was coated with grime and soot. Coughing would not shift whatever had been exhaled from the tunnel. My efforts instead brought up a belch that made me rush to the nearest bin, ready to puke. But I did not, disappointing the couple of passers-by who had turned their heads and scowled. I sat on a stone step with a view of the top of the station escalators, waiting for the alarms, the stern announcements, the fire engines.

Wishing for them, in fact. A real emergency, an event that I could *live through*. I knew the shape of it: an exodus up those escalators and a crowd forming around me. Long minutes of confusion and shared fear and excitement, people thrown together, enjoying the interruption to their routine even as they cursed it. Then the adrenalin would turn to cold and boredom and mere annoyance and we would all call our offices or appointments and tell them we were late.

Or more serious than that, and my imagination was disgustingly eager to spill the details into my reverie: a fire in the tunnel, fumes spreading fast, national news, fatalities, this stretch of line closed for days, an inquiry, a slow trickle of consequences over months and years: fund-raising, one or two of the survivors being held up as inspirational figures for saving others or overcoming horrible injuries, marathons completed, popular books written, mayoral bids considered. A plaque at this station, perhaps only feet from this cold stone step, and if I came by this way with someone, I'd go a little quiet and break my pace, and I'd say, 'I was here that day, when it happened,' in a voice that really stressed how I didn't talk about it often but it had stayed with me, picturing a great dignified weight, the memory of those x souls, my gratitude at having escaped in time, tempered with noble guilt at being a survivor, my respect for the emergency services. Perhaps poor oblivious Alan would be among the x, intimately involving me, bringing the whole sad story closer, making it far more authentic.

Or nothing. The same steady procession out of the station. No sirens, no evacuation, no space-suited firefighters, no strengthening fountain of smoke from the depths. I wanted there to be an emergency not for ghoulish reasons, but because the alternative was an internal emergency. The smoke, the suffocating need to escape – for me that was real, but it never happened to anyone else.

There was real smoke out here, though: the darkness in the east, over the roofs of Bishopsgate, behind the spires of finance, where I was supposed to be. Perhaps that was the source of my fascination with the Barking fire – that, at least, was real, really happening; other people around me could see it too, it was in the papers. For the first time in months, the city was in sync with me.

Eleven a.m. – the time Alan and I were supposed to arrive at Pierce's house. I was cold and my joints were stiff from sitting on the step. Adjacent to the station entrance was a pub.

I had been caught up in station evacuations before, as I suppose every regular Tube user has – or any regular passenger on any subway network anywhere in the world. A couple of times I had seen fire engines arrive. But I had never smelled smoke, not so much as a match's worth, let alone the thick clouds that had almost suffocated me on the platform with Alan.

When the bombs went off on 7 July 2005, I was living in a shared house in Fulham, and working my first job. My commute, District Line to South Kensington, took me nowhere near the bombs, and I had only just left the house when it all happened. The station was already closed when I arrived, and the pavement outside was filled with a restive and palpably upset crowd. No one knew what was going on, exactly, although the look on the faces of the staff made it obvious it was no signal failure. At that moment, an early report about a gas explosion was being shown to be tragically wrong. We were told to go home, and I did, to find one of my housemates already there and full of rolling news and internet rumour. We watched together. After about half an hour, when it was completely clear that services would not be resumed, I called the office, and the phone rang unanswered. I tried my boss's mobile – he was at home as well.

Thinking about it now, that was the first time I took an unscheduled day off work. After a couple of hours watching the news, mostly unspeaking but for occasional expletives and blasphemies, I went to the fridge, intending to make us both a cup of tea, and saw that there were four cans of Grolsch in there, left over from the weekend. (The very thought that beer could be lying untouched, forgotten, in the fridge from Sunday until Tuesday dates this memory for me.) I took two of these cans through to the living room and was hailed as a stalwart foe of extremism and a doctor of the human spirit. The kettle boiled, and cooled, without further attention. We finished those cans, and the other two, and went out for more. When our other housemate came back, he found us both convincingly drunk.

The mood took an uncomfortable turn not long after that when my day-long drinking partner made some broad statements about Muslims, and collective responsibility; he alluded to retaliation, without specifics; and he spoke as if confident that we all shared his urge to punish, to strike back. This seemed pathetic and futile to me, the bombers having obliterated themselves, and I disagreed strenuously, impressed with my own tolerance and ardent forgiveness – rather full of it, really. The other housemate sided with me and the day ended on an ugly note of disharmony.

I was at home during the commemoration of the tenth anniversary of the bombing. I don't recall if this was a scheduled or unscheduled absence. Next door had not yet started its renovation; I woke mid-morning and switched on the TV after opening my first can, expecting *Homes Under the Hammer*. But instead there was a live broadcast of the ceremonies at St Paul's Cathedral. I watched, disturbed at the mismatch between the ancient ritual and anachronistic dress happening *now*, and the memories of the very modern catastrophe *then*. And disturbed at the unsimple range of emotions brought up by the day, the date. Shock, anger, grief, yes, yes, yes. All those, of course. But also that strange sense of liberation when the day's pattern is broken, and the comfortable comradeship of the beers at noon, on a workday; and the unpleasant way the day had ended; because to call that 'unpleasant', could it be inferred that I found something pleasant before then? Which meant awful guilt. I hated the way my housemate had held the bombers' co-religionists to blame, the way he easily swung his anger around to face a whole community, our neighbours as well as our fellow Londoners and Britons. But I wished my own reaction was that simple and stupid. In the following days I heard the sirens in the streets, felt the tension.

For a year or two after the bombs, I occasionally had nightmares of being caught in an attack or other disaster on the Tube; trying to flee down lightless tunnels, being trapped in carriages filled with smoke, bodies everywhere. In the hellish summer of 2012, those nightmares returned to my waking mind, one of several choice scenarios served up to me as I lay shaking and sweating in bed, completely awake.

We want beginnings. Start late, finish early. Get stuck in. 'X is running late, and here I talk about how rude their PRs are', 'X was born in blah and spent their early years blah-de-blah', 'I meet X in this or that restaurant or hotel and here are three paragraphs describing that setting in not-very-amusing detail' – these are called 'long drop' intros and are frowned upon.

But what if a situation can only be understood with reference to the past? What if some behaviour just appears to be senselessly self-destructive without that reference?

And what if you look into that history, knowing the key to be there, but can't find it? It must be there, for where else could it be?

This day, then, 7 July 2005, more than ten years ago – the first day I stayed home from work and got drunk. Where the nightmares of dust and smoke and burial began. Was that the Rubicon, the tipping point? No; it was a unique and terrible day, and afterwards I went back to work as normal and it was still quite possible to leave beer in the fridge unopened and forget about it, and so it was for months or years after that. Perhaps there were underlying traits and tendencies and pathologies that could be traced back further, but at that point in my life I was only as fucked-up as the average person. Although . . .

More than ten years ago. Mine was a very long drop.

Alan was not dead, or trapped and blinded in a sweltering hell while rescue workers battled to reach him. He was alive, and above ground, and calling my phone.

I surveyed the pub: a big, bland railway Wetherspoon's. It was almost empty and nearly silent, no music, no one playing fruit machines, no football, no giveaway background noises. There was only one other customer, a guy about my age, who was using his phone to take a picture of his shoes. A radio was playing in the kitchen, but it was safe to answer the call.

'What the fuck, man?' Alan was whispering, in a quiet place himself. There was anger in his voice, but it was not ruling over other emotions: confusion, and perhaps even concern.

'Alan, hi.'

'What the fuck happened to you, man?'

'I was sure I could smell smoke. It was freaking me out.'

'That's . . . There wasn't any smoke, man.'

'I'm sorry.'

'It's Oli you want to be sorry to, you need to get here sharpish. I'm here now, said you were delayed. Where are you, are you on your way?'

'Yes.' About a third of a pint left.

'We're doing the shoot. Get here fast and I think you'll be OK.'

'OK. Thanks. Sorry.'

'Oli's a nice guy. You'll be fine if you get here in the next five, ten minutes.'

'Sure.'

'Can you do that?'

'Sure.'

I didn't like this 'Oli' business one bit. Exactly as I had feared, they were bonding. I gave thought to an additional half-pint, but on this occasion moderation triumphed.

Pierce lived just off a Victorian garden square concealed behind Mile End Road – one of those hidden pockets of the East End that could be mistaken for Chelsea or Islington or my own Pimlico. For a nauseating moment I thought he might have the whole terraced house as his own, but there were two doorbells, with Pierce's at the top. I rang, exchanged a couple of crackly words through the intercom, and heard feet on stairs.

I had seen Pierce's picture in the newspaper profiles that had appeared before his seclusion: a round face under a shaved scalp, a combination that verged on the potatoey. But no potato had those eyes, dark and furious, always directed hard at the camera. No soulful chin-stroking or writerly gazing into space – arms crossed like a bouncer, staring you down. Only the photo on the back cover of *Mile End Road* differed: dark curly hair, retreating a little, glasses, the slightly affronted look of someone caught by surprise. Before he had settled his image. In *Night Traffic*, Pierce had speculated as to what had made him a target for muggers: he was five foot eight, a couple of inches shorter than me, and a little chunky. When he opened the door, though, he seemed at least my height and more; the slight doughiness of his frame manifested as pure presence and force. The eyes didn't pin me down or fix on me like a laser or any of those clichés of command. It was as if he barely noticed me, catching my own gaze once, then breaking away, turning back into the hall.

'Jack, yeah?'

'Mr Pierce, great to meet you at last, I—'

'Alan's just left, surprised you didn't see him.'

I was relieved. 'Yes, I'm sorry I'm so late, I—'

'Close the door, yeah? Just slam it.' He was three steps up the stairs already, not looking back.

Pierce had the top two floors of the house – a flat more than twice the size of mine. At once I wondered if he owned or rented: the usual London question. Except that's not the London question, not exactly. The question is: How are you here? How do you make it work? How do you supply what the city demands? More than half my salary went on the rent of my dark little flat and I dreaded the next increase. I was not making it work. How, then, did Pierce? The secret, shameful side of the London question was the accompanying desire to hear that the answerer was *not* making it work, that they were drowning in debt or crippled by mortgage payments or the flat had untreatable toxic mould or was the site of a recent and savage string of murders. Anything that would make one's own failure sting a little less.

The flat was, at first, as you'd expect: I was led into a short corridor lined with knee-high piles of books, magazines, loose papers and copies of the *Guardian* and *Standard*. Like my own home. I knew at once what I'd find in the living room: a wall given over to bookshelves, either Ikea or built-in, wedged with books and decorated with a self-conscious sprinkling of post-cards, invitations, photographs, mementoes and so on.

Wrong. At least two upstairs rooms had been knocked through to form Pierce's living room, which ran all the way from the front of the house to the back, with big windows at each end. This yielded a long side wall that would have been perfect for metres of shelves. But this wall was instead filled with a huge map of London.

'Map' is in fact not a useful term to describe what Pierce had made. In the south, Biggin Hill and Purley were at skirting board level; the northern stretch of the M25, where it runs past Waltham Abbey, was at the ceiling cornice. The outer outline of Greater London was just about recognisable, as was the blue vein of the Thames where it widened in the east, and a few exposed green patches at Richmond, Blackheath, Epping and elsewhere. The rest of the city was obscured by a thick aggregation of matter, which lifted and shivered when Pierce threw open the door and walked into the room. It was a layer of sticky notes, index cards and clippings – several layers, from the look of it, anchored by hundreds of coloured thumb-tacks. Further notes encrusted the wall to the left and right of the map; the room also contained four metal filing cabinets and the usual living-space furniture: a three-piece suite facing a telly at one end of the room, a dining table and chairs at the other.

'Wow,' I said.

'The map?' Pierce said with a pained expression. 'I've been meaning to take it down.'

'What? Why? What is it for?'

He didn't answer, and instead waved an arm in the direction of the cracked brown leather sofa. 'Sit. Sit. Coffee? Tea?'

'Coffee would be great,' I said, taking off my coat. I had to move a couple of magazines off the sofa in order to make a place for me to sit: a *TLS* and a *Time Out*. But before I sat I remembered the need for colour. Ignore Pierce's instruction, check out the room. I approached the map.

The cacophony of information from the wall was over-whelming, and the accumulated ephemera was rarely less than five layers deep, obscuring most recognisable features. I traced the line of the river upstream until I found Pimlico. Notes on the surface included 'Monster Tavern', 'Millbank Prison – Austr.' and 'Dolphin Square sex ring'. These were all scrawled in black and red biro on small Post-its and snippets of notepaper, some no larger than postage stamps. But beneath them was a much larger note, an index card inscribed with fat black marker pen, obviously one of the first things pinned to the wall when the map was new. To read it I had to move other accretions out of the way, revealing the letters one by one. It said: MISTRESS CITY.

'Bick,' Pierce said, making me jump. An orange Post-it, its adhesive exhausted, floated to the floor; I saw one or two were already there. 'Unusual name – as in Bic ballpoints?'

'With a k,' I said, realising that Pierce must know the spelling perfectly well, having seen my name in emails. 'As in Bicker. Or Bickle.'

'Ha,' Pierce said – definitely said, spoken, not a laugh. '"You talkin' to me?"'

'That's why I'm here.'

'It's a pity it's not Bic like the pens,' Pierce said. He spoke with his back to me, busy making coffee in a small kitchen through an arch. 'That would be a good name for a writer. I'm interested in nominative determinism. The idea that your name has power, that it influences what you choose to do in life. You're, I don't know, Mr Heal, so you become a doctor.'

Should I be recording this? I wondered. I fumbled one of my digital voice recorders out of my bag, switched it on, and dropped it into the breast pocket of my shirt. 'Like our mutual friend,' I said.

Pierce stopped what he had been doing – pouring milk into a little jug – and frowned over his shoulder at me.

'F.A.Q.,' I said, surprised he needed prompting. 'Given that he's all over the internet.'

'Aha,' Pierce said. 'Well, that doesn't count. It's concocted. Francis is his middle name. Eric Francis Quin. He ditched the Eric and added the A in the nineties. The A doesn't stand for anything.'

'I didn't know that,' I said.

'Not many people do, I think,' Pierce said. 'He doesn't publicise the fact. I only know 'cause I've been to his flat. I saw some post there and asked about it. I think he's embarrassed by it now. I mean, FAQs are a bit dated. A bit web one-point-oh for Francis. A bit of sleight-of-hand with the facts on some bulletin board twenty years ago and it ends up haunting him like that.'

'Yeah, embarrassing,' I said. I was starting to feel a bit wobbly. In the past, my legs had betrayed me when others were watching and it was a misfortune I wanted to avoid with Pierce. Especially as it was all going well so far – my lateness barely remarked upon, not having to compete with Alan, Pierce proving chatty, not the surly, laconic artist-hermit I had expected. 'He should update it.'

'Ha, yes,' said Pierce. 'S.T.F.U., maybe.'

I returned to the sofa. 'Did Alan get any pictures of you with the map?' I asked, full of hope. It would make a great opening-spread image, Pierce against this conspiracy-theorist palimpsest, the city and the surgeon of its dark heart. What a way into the piece. It would write itself.

Pierce approached carrying a tray, on which there were two steaming mugs, a bowl of sugar and a milk jug. This struck me as a touch genteel, the little white milk jug in particular, which isn't bad as material goes – people acting against type. What would an 'in character' Oliver Pierce have offered me? Supermarket whisky? A line of speed? A punch to the throat?

Mention of the map made Pierce wince again. He settled into an armchair. 'Yeah, he did. But do you have to talk about the map? Like I say, I've been meaning to get rid of it.'

'Sorry. It's hard to ignore. Perhaps if you told me what it was for, and why it's not needed any more . . . Wait, hang on.' I didn't want to take any chances with this, and fished my other DVR from my bag. 'Do you mind if I record this?'

Pierce shook his head, assenting. I turned on the DVR and set it on the coffee table between us. Two DVRs, one on the table, one in my pocket – one would have to work.

'After I wrote *Night Traffic* – no, before that, even, I had been lumped in with all that psychogeography lot, Iain Sinclair and Will Self and so on, and I . . . well, I didn't like that. There are so many people doing that shit now. All the fucking lost rivers, ghost Tube stations, all that shit – I'm just so fucking sick of that. It makes me want to puke. It was getting boring ten years ago, it's just intolerable now. And the whole ideological project that goes along with it, all about tracing out the London of the Kray twins and the industrial past as a revolt against the corporate takeover of . . . I mean, I fucking hate what London is becoming, what it has become. Fucking *hate* it. This fucking shiny cloakroom for the biggest bastards in the world. But one of the reasons they come here is because of the trendiness, the grit, all that fucking mystique-sludge that's getting dredged up from the Thames 24/7. Did you read my eels piece, with the Russian girls, the oligarchs' daughters, Anastasia and that? They fucking loved all that. They had read *Mile End Road*, that's why they got in touch with me, like I was a fucking tour guide. One of them had a copy of Ackroyd's London biography, she brought it along. The East End, that's what they wanted. The Blind Beggar, sarees, National Front, Jack the Ripper, they wanted all that as much as Knightsbridge and Chelsea. So what could I do? Trying to get the city back by writing about all that stuff, that was doomed. It's just advertising, it just sucks in more cash. In the end, that's one of the things that motivated me to write *Night Traffic*, to do something that wasn't shabby-chic but terrifying, something . . .'

He trailed off, staring into space, in the direction of the window. Then he turned his attention to his coffee, putting in a slug of milk and a lump of sugar from the bowl. I wanted him to complete the quote. It was hard to believe how well the interview was going, to have this great mass of quotable, fiery material up front, but I desperately wanted him to finish the thought. My eyes flicked to the DVR on the table, making sure the red light was lit, and the timer was counting upwards.

'Something real?' I supplied. 'Something true?' If he accepted either of those, I could stitch the word into the quote and make it whole.

'Do you take yours black?' Pierce asked, offering me the milk. 'Anyway. I was trying to think of other strategies. I thought I might try to shut down the psychogeography business in London once and for all. If I could write the ultimate psychogeographical index of London, gathering up and pinning down every mystical wrinkle, backwoods fact and obscure snip of folklore – a psycho-pedia of London – I could make the field obsolete. A *Key to all Mythologies*, like Casaubon in *Middlemarch*. And that's the problem: the Casaubon Complex. It can't be done. Not that London is somehow special, although it is very big and very old. But I could take a lifetime doing it and it still wouldn't be finished. And what if I did finish it? A 5,000-page, multi-volume slab of what amounts to pub trivia; it would only fuel the fire. It would be on the Zaha Hadid coffee table in every penthouse in Docklands.'

He turned in his chair, away from me, towards the map, shoulders hunched, tense. 'I squandered months, years.'

'Is that what you've been doing since *Night Traffic*?' I asked. I couldn't help but feel disappointed. As secret projects went, it was not what I expected, not very exciting, and not even going to happen.

'No, no,' Pierce said, looking back at me, scowling. 'I stopped working on that ages ago. When Quin got involved. He came to one of my readings, for *Murder Boards*. Said he was a fan. Said he was working on a new mapping system for London, part map, part social network – this was Tamesis, but at the time they had a code name for it, Canny Valley. He wanted my input. Obviously, mapping, maps, I told him about my map. He loved it. He had this place swarming with Bunk staff, photographing, scanning, measuring, indexing, getting everything. Not just the psychopedia, some of the stuff I had gathered for *Murder Boards* too. Quin in the middle, sitting where you are now, laptop on his lap, issuing commands. Commands I didn't even understand. Then they left. And they didn't leave a trace. It was like Burning Man. But they did leave me a toy.'

Pierce leaped out of his seat, and the abrupt movement made me jump. He went over to one of the filing cabinets, opened the top drawer, and took out a tablet computer.

'An interface for updating the map,' Pierce said, returning to his armchair. He had switched on the tablet and handed it to me. 'If I added anything, they wanted to know it.'

The tablet was showing the Bunk logo, cheerful italic sans-serif capitals pushing into the future. The many-pointed star around the B was spinning as the software loaded: a sight familiar to anyone who has used Tamesis, Roamero, Trenchr, or any of Bunk's other apps. Then, a welcome screen: a picture of the wall-map with HI, OLIVER! In big, friendly letters over it. TOUCH ANYWHERE TO BEGIN. I touched the screen. A login box appeared.

WHOOPS! YOU DON'T HAVE PERMISSION TO DO THAT. PLEASE VERIFY BUNKMATE I.D.

'Yeah, it doesn't work any more,' Pierce said. 'I've been locked out. I guess F.A.Q. doesn't want me mucking around in Tamesis now that it's live and everyone uses it. We had a bit of a falling-out and I don't think he trusts me any more.'

This was news to me. When Quin had mentioned Pierce back when I interviewed him last summer, it was to name him an inspiration, collaborator and friend. 'An agent of the true city,' Quin called him. A couple of weeks ago he had suggested I interview the author, leaving no impression that the ardour had cooled.

'What did you fall out about?' I asked.

Pierce shifted in his seat uncomfortably. 'Various things. I found out he was writing navigation software for the Met.'

'For the *Met*? The *police*?'

'Yeah. They've got this drone – unmanned aerial vehicle – kind of a prototype. Except it doesn't work. It's junk. They – the Met – thought part of the problem might be the onboard software. And since mapping is Bunk's big thing, Quin's big thing – Roamero, Tamesis, all that – they asked him to take a look. All hush-hush. The trouble with Quin is curiosity. For all his radical pose, he'd agree to anything if it meant being able to poke around inside the hot brain of a police vehicle. He was embarrassed about it and he told me – partly because he wanted to excuse himself for having agreed to take a look, I think – that it was a total turkey. A dodo. Classic bureaucratic fuck-up. Barely up to the job of finding a lone pick-up in the desert, let alone spotting who's carrying the knife outside a Camden pub. "It'll never do what they want it to do," he said. And' – Pierce gestured towards the TV, which was turned off – 'it turns out he was right.'

I didn't know what this last part meant, but I was too preoccupied with the rest of what Pierce had said to pick up on it. Quin, working with the police? His image had a wide stripe of anti-establishment idealism, coloured by tech-industry optimism: giving people the tools to get around the Man, direct democracy, that sort of thing. During one of the surveillance scandals he had been on *Channel 4 News* to say that he would never give user data from Roamero or Tamesis to the police or GCHQ. They hadn't asked, but Quin had seen a public relations opportunity and seized it with both hands. He was on form – articulate, scornful, glowing with righteousness. The only time Cathy Newman managed to wrongfoot him was when she asked how he would feel if criminals exploited Tamesis. The strangest expression appeared on his smooth, innocent face, certainly not an expression one tends to see on these TV interviews: distraction, deep focus, as if he were repeating the question to a deeper part of himself. 'I can't imagine how criminals would use something like Tamesis,' he said at last.

The thought that he could go from that idealistic *naïf* to being a man designing software for a police drone was staggering. But I was here to interview Pierce.

'Let's get back to you,' I said. 'What are you working on at the moment?'

'Not very much, to be frank.'

'Nothing, really?'

Pierce sighed. 'Well, there was the grand psycho-concordance of London that ate up so much time and energy. Ever since I abandoned it I have been a bit stuck.'

'No plans? Ambitions?' I must sound like Polly, I thought, and that reminded me of her neat list of times and her, if you get a moment, mandatory tasks.

Pierce sighed again, bringing his whole upper body into the action, shoulders slumping – as if the will to go on was visibly deserting him. It was bizarre that the voluble, gossipy creature of a couple of minutes ago should yield to this exhausted, taciturn presence.

'The encyclopedia was part of a broader project – if you can call it a project, more of an ambition,' he said. 'The same project, in fact, as *Night Traffic*. An attempt to discover something about the city. I don't know where that project is going now.'

I checked the DVR, but only out of instinct, and watched the seconds climb, recording useless, dud material.

'So this larger project . . .' I began.

Pierce rolled his eyes. 'You know that stuff they used to put in shower gel? I think they've banned it. These little particles, little grains of plastic. It was always called, I don't know, "dermabrasion microbeads" and I guess most people thought it was pumice or pulverised seashells or something, but it wasn't, it was plastic, tiny specks of plastic. All this plastic going straight down the plughole, into rivers, into the ocean. Fish eating it. Seabirds eating it. It was poisoning everything. Those big swirling garbage patches in the oceans, they're not all Lucozade bottles and Ninja Turtles, most of it is this plastic dust that is almost too small to see. But it's choking up everything. Anyway, that's what I think of when I read a lot of writing about London: synthetic grit. Plastic that makes you feel a little better for a moment or two, a little invigorated, and then it poisons the world.'

This reminded me of a few passages from *Night Traffic* – Pierce had written about sitting in his flat after the attack, surrounded by novels and non-fiction about the gritty, grimy, *real* city having just encountered genuine crime, and feeling that he was surrounded by fraud, including his own work – *especially* his own work.

'You talk about that in *Night Traffic*, don't you? About craving an authentic experience in the city, something not commercial and not nostalgic, not packaged, but real . . .'

'Yeah, yeah,' Pierce said, although there wasn't much in his reply that was affirmative. Instead he appeared embarrassed, with those broad shoulders still hunched forward, staring into his coffee as if he expected the cadaver of a family member to come bobbing to its surface. 'That, that's what I wanted to do.'

I tried not saying anything – that old trick of barristers and psychotherapists – to see if he volunteered more information, but nothing came. The DVR recorded the silence of the room, the small sounds of the leather seats, a muted police siren from the direction of the main road. This was going exactly the way that Freya had predicted: he simply did not have anything new to say, and was unwilling to return to subjects he had talked about in the past. A few quotes about a years-old book and abandoned projects weren't going to be enough, and not enough time had elapsed for this to be a Whatever-Happened-To piece, all melancholy thoughts about the fleeting nature of fame and the callous muse. Those weren't the magazine's style, anyway: Eddie wanted fresh, up-and-coming, ahead of the curve, stylish. Not worn-out artists and their sadsack regrets. It'd be ten pages on De Chauncey, then, about his suits and his cars and the secrets of his success.

The coffee Pierce had made was good, but I wondered if he had left it too long on the stove. As I drank it, I was becoming more and more aware of a burned taste accumulating in my mouth.

'The reaction to *Night Traffic* was extraordinary,' I said. 'Did you feel overwhelmed? Is that why you . . .' I realised that I did not have a good way to describe exactly what it was that Pierce had done. Withdrawn from view? Become a hermit? Fucked up his career, just as he was now fucking up mine? 'Why you stopped writing?'

At last, a strong reaction: Pierce looked up sharply and the eyes got me again. 'Stopped writing? What makes you say that?'

'Everything you've been saying,' I said. 'No new books, no journalism, not even working with F.A.Q. – you sound completely blocked.'

'Blocked,' Pierce said, pronouncing the word with complete neutrality. 'That's an interesting way of looking at it. A block. You're a writer, you must know this: when you're blocked, it's never a problem with whatever you're doing at that moment, it's a problem with what you've already done. It's a problem in the past, not in the present. You have to go back in order to fix it.'

Fascinating. He could sell that to the writing magazines, maybe, but I couldn't sell it to Eddie. Was the coffee hotter than I thought? A wisp of steam flexed over my cup. I blew on it and it fled, but I didn't know if it had been steam, or smoke, coming from elsewhere, but it must have been steam. Rings formed and shunted in the black surface of the coffee. I put the cup on the coffee table with a bump and shut my eyes.

No. Not here. Not now.

'I don't understand,' I said, keeping my eyes shut. Perhaps I sounded upset, or weary, or irate, but I didn't care. 'You sounded very eager to talk to me when we got in touch, but now it sounds as if there's not much you want to say.'

I opened my eyes. The smoke was close to the floor, not yet reaching for my throat. Pierce was staring at me.

'How long has that been going on?' he asked, with a downward gesture of the eyes.

'The . . . What?' It took superhuman effort that I was able to even find those two unconnected words. 'The smoke?'

'Smoke?' Pierce said, frowning. 'That!' he repeated, pointing at my right hand.

My hand was shaking quite badly, a rapid, rocking action that started at the wrist and magnified through the fingers, causing them to quiver and quake in a very noticeable way. I stilled it with my left hand in what I hoped looked like a calm and natural action; in reality I was clamping down on it like a farm dog on a rat.

'I had an uncle who got the shakes,' Pierce said. 'He used to stay with us at Christmas. Divorced, and my cousins had their own families by then and didn't want to know. I don't have any colourful stories about him. He didn't get shitfaced and fall about or anything like that. It was painfully clear that he was on his best behaviour, for us, for his brother. By the middle of the afternoon his hands would be shaking so badly he was barely able to roll a cigarette. He died when I was a teenager – when he was only in his fifties.'

I didn't say anything. I didn't want to associate myself with Pierce's tragic uncle, and I didn't know what else I could say. What I wanted to do was to come up with a story that would pass off the shaking as something other than what it was, but my mind was blank, nothing came. I could not construct an alternative universe in which the comparison was unfair. It was fair. All I could do was stay quiet.

'I must admit, I don't often think about that uncle,' Pierce continued. 'Remembering him now, what comes to mind is . . . He was my father's older brother but you would never have guessed that from looking at them. Sure, he looked older, more beaten-up, but he completely deferred to my father, let himself be ordered about, nagged, all very meekly. Almost like a child.'

'Maybe he wanted that,' I said, and I was surprised to find myself talking at all, and interested to know what I was going to say next. 'Someone taking charge. A voice outside the head.'

Pierce stared hard at me, not with and not without kindness, as if slightly refracted by a thick layer of invisibly transparent material between us.

'Quin told me you were a drunk,' Pierce said.

I had never been called that before. The word was there, always at the periphery of my thoughts about myself, but I put great effort into excluding it.

'He said you were steaming drunk when you met him, and that you smelled of old booze,' Pierce went on. 'He wasn't impressed. You know him – a monk. Fresh pomegranate and plain yoghurt for breakfast, cycling everywhere. Determined to see in the singularity. Your thingie, your Dictaphone, was out of batteries and you tried to make notes. The interview was full of mistakes and quotes lifted from other places.'

Some sort of noise was made in response to this – a cough, an 'mm-hm' – but the organism making that noise was very far away now. If I had not been sitting down, I knew I would have fallen by now. I knew that as a fact. As it was, I wanted to close my eyes again and slump sideways onto Pierce's ancient sofa, to feel the cracked brown leather cool on my cheek, to let sleep come. The grey was closing in around my vision.

'Not the first time, right?'

I shook my head. 'I've been sloppy,' I said, the words slipping.

'Jesus,' Pierce said. 'Are you OK? You look like you're going to be sick.'

'Could I have a glass of water?'

'Sure.' He rose at once and disappeared into the kitchen. A

cupboard opened, a tap ran. 'I'm not trying to get you into trouble. You can relax.'

He was wrong about that – I could in no way relax. Just try to relax, when the gathering shadow that's been chasing you for months appears in front of you, its terrible face bared, and you know that all this time you have been running straight to it. And 'relaxing' suggested tension, tightly wound muscles, stiff sinews. That was not how I felt. I felt *undone*, as if I were unravelling, unspooling. Pierce returned with a tall glass of tap water, which he placed in front of me, but he did not sit. Instead he went back to the kitchen.

There was a single ice cube in the water, a tiny kindness that I found almost overwhelming, and which did more to convince me that Pierce meant me no harm than anything he said. In putting these truths to me, he had spoken without condemnation or judgement but in the tone of a professional, a counsellor or doctor – or a sympathetic interviewer.

'Thank you,' I said, late. I took a sip of the water. Putting the glass back on the table, I saw that the DVR was still running, its red light still lit, counter still counting. This would all make uncomfortable listening, if I ever got around to that stage.

When Pierce came back, he was holding two small cut-glass tumblers and a bottle of whisky – Maker's Mark, with the melted plastic around the neck of the bottle to look like a wax seal. Though I dearly wanted a drink, the sight of the bourbon filled me with fear. There was the usual reflexive secrecy of the addict – the fear of being seen indulging in addictive behaviour, a fear married to shame. But there was more. I tend to avoid spirits, even wine. Deep in me, I knew that it was too easy to overdo it that way. And by 'overdo it', I don't mean getting incapably drunk – that was the work of every evening. I meant killing myself.

'I don't usually drink whisky,' I said.

'What do you usually drink?'

'Stella.'

'Stella. Huh. Wouldn't have guessed. Wait.' Pierce was off again, another trip to the kitchen. A fridge door rattled open, bottles clinked, a bottle top clattered against a hard surface.

'Not Stella, but.' It was a bottle of Czech lager.

'Thank you.' Still, the reflex reflexed – *don't let him see you drink* – though it was clearly far past the point of being important, and that bottle, condensation making a stripe of light down its side, was the most welcome sight in the world. The mists receded, the world sharpened again, just from the sight of that hard green glass.

'How many people know?'

I didn't know what he meant; the question interrupted my thrill at having that cold bottle in my hand. 'About the, er, problems with the articles, or about the drinking?'

'Both. Either. I assume they are related phenomena.'

Pierce's attitude, I realised, his demeanour, was entirely journalistic. Pleasant enough, but that pleasantry was like the soft toy dangling in the dentist's office to distract child patients from what else was there. The equipment. I had been right about his professional mien, I recognised it – I was being interviewed.

'No one,' I said.

'Really?' Pierce's eyebrows rose.

'Maybe one or two people in the office have suspicions,' I said, thinking of Polly. And Kay.

'Quin likes data,' Pierce said. 'He was raised by spreadsheets, I don't know. When he is confronted with a problem, he digs out all the data he can find, digs and digs and digs, and eventually the problem just isn't there any more. When you have enough computing power, and enough eager employees and interns, you can do amazing things. When you have enough data.'

In a ball of numbness, I was hyper-aware of the cool weight of the bottle in my hand, the tiny interactions of the pads of my fingers against glass and condensation. I took a deep drink from it, realising as I did so that I had been deliberately delaying that moment – the usual ostentatious show of restraint, the one I used in pubs, drinking in company, to show that I didn't have a problem. It was entirely surplus to requirements here. All the rules had changed; they had been changed by strangers, indeed, when I had always assumed that the confrontation would come from someone close to me. I knew how that felt, from the ending with Elise: the walls folding in, the ceiling coming down, crushed, trapped, suffocated. That was how I had imagined it, when I had dared to imagine it, or found the thought inescapable: with Eddie and Polly in the aquarium, with Eddie in the publisher's office upstairs, with Kay.

But this was different. I wasn't crushed and I wasn't trapped. Which is not to say that I wasn't afraid: on the contrary, the thought of a vengeful Quin in possession of this kind of information and talking about it with others as he had plainly talked about it with Pierce – that was chilling.

'So Quin guessed?' I asked. 'About me?' What I wanted to ask was: what kind of proof does he have? Anything I can't lie my way around?

Pierce grunted, a bitter dreg of a chuckle. 'Guessed. Yeah, Quin is great at "guessing". Gifted really. Quin "guessed".'

'I don't understand what this has to do with me. Or . . . I mean, I see what it has to do with me, but I don't know what . . . why Quin said all this to you.'

'He was angry,' Pierce said. 'With you, and with me. Are you still recording this?'

'Yes.'

'Switch that off for a minute, would you?'

'Sure.' I picked the DVR off the coffee table and pressed the off button.

'Inaccuracy makes Quin angry,' Pierce said. 'Deliberate inaccuracy especially so. He says one of the biggest challenges Bunk faces is filtering out the lies from social media. Like when someone tells Tamesis that they're in the office when really they're in the pub.'

Acid bubbled up within me. Pierce's sarcastic tone earlier could be understood – Quin hadn't guessed at all.

'He doesn't care about the social reasons for that sort of thing, the niceties,' Pierce continued. 'It's just bad data, it corrupts his models. I asked him why he wanted anything to do with my map, with the kind of research I did for *Murder Boards*. He said that he was trying to run a stochastic analysis of apocrypha and myth. But he . . . I had a lot of research material for *Night Traffic* around in the flat, and he looked at all that too. Without asking.'

Pierce had been taking very small sips from his whisky before this, as if unfamiliar with its taste, or at least unfamiliar with its taste at this hour. Now, however, he took a deep draught, draining his glass.

'The thing about *Night Traffic*,' he said, with a little lick of his lips, 'is that I made it up. None of it happened. None of it is true.'

I swallowed. Pierce was glaring at me, full eye contact, judging my reaction, as if he were trying to read my thoughts about what he had said.

He wouldn't be able to. My thoughts were: He doesn't know about the second DVR. The one that was in my shirt pocket. The one that was still recording.

FOUR

'Have you ever been mugged, Jack?'

I had to take a moment to think about the answer. It was a simple question, with a simple, truthful answer. But in this room, at this time, all certainty felt suspect. The man sitting opposite me had taken an event I had experienced twice and described it nearly perfectly. That his version was a giant lie – with an orbiting debris field of lesser lies – was deeply disturbing. My own experiences felt counterfeit. It was a violation, akin to an attack. I should have been angry, but Pierce's authority and my respect for him were – curiously – unchanged. In a way, a very conditional and twisted way, I admired him: that he could invent an account so detailed, sympathetic and convincing – utterly, utterly convincing – was impressive.

'Yes, I have,' I said. 'Twice, actually.'

'Actually.' Pierce un-crossed and re-crossed his legs. 'Well, I have never been mugged.'

'You describe it so well.'

'Yes, so I'm told. What is it like? Being mugged.'

'Don't you *know*? I mean, even if it hasn't happened to you, you must have spoken with plenty of people, and your research—'

'Yes, yes.' He waved this away. 'I got emails, letters. People feeling as if they had to share what had happened to them with someone they thought would understand. Some horrible stories. I spoke at the annual conference of the National Association for the Victims of Crime. I tried to get out of it, but they were so persistent and nice. Afterwards people wanted to talk to me . . . That was towards the end, by the way, right before I decided I'd had enough, couldn't stand lying to these people any more. But what you learn from all these stories – well, no, listen, this is important. Being a writer is to realise that all experience is unique but analogous. People are good at thinking their way into other people's heads, much better than most of them realise. Anyway, tell me.'

Again, I had to think about the answer. Though they were technically very similar events – alone, vulnerable, a threat, a theft – the two experiences were very different, and it was hard to establish the common emotional ground between them.

'Confusing,' I said.

'Confusing. Very good answer,' Pierce said. He sat back in his chair and smiled. 'Can you expand?'

I shrugged. Once again Pierce had turned my interview into an interrogation of me. I was still trying to mentally accommodate his admission about *Night Traffic*. A fraud. It was a fraud. And I did not yet know my response to that. There are journalistic clichés: 'stunned', 'shocked', 'reeling', 'taken aback'. Those would work, but not well. It was more a troubling in-between state, waiting for feedback that isn't coming, and feeling nothing in the meantime. Being lost, and getting out your phone to check the map – but it doesn't load. You see the little dot marking your location, but on a field of grey. And here he was drilling information out of me. I was pitted with the sense of having shared too much from my own darkness. Pierce was impressive, for sure. The unembarrassed way he questioned, the way he handled the answers – that 'very good answer' there, a bit of positive reinforcement to help the subject, me, along, making me want to share more. A natural journalist, whereas I had spent a decade scraping by and pretending.

'The first time was very much what you'd imagine, you know,' I said. 'I was frightened . . .'

'How was it confusing?'

I drank from my beer. 'There's a moment, a time when you don't know what's happening – you're being mugged but you don't know it for sure just yet, you haven't figured it out, you don't know what this guy, this stranger, wants – you don't realise that the rules have been . . . that they don't apply any more, that different rules apply, different roles. It's confusing. You're moved very quickly from one situation, a normal situation, to an abnormal situation, and it takes some time to catch up. And the second time – the very fact it was the second time, it had happened before, made it different. I knew what was going on, but . . . it was still a very confusing experience.'

In truth, the second time had not been confusing at all. My emotions, at the time, had been very clear – more than clear, blinding, revelatory. Only in retrospect did I feel conflicted about what had happened and began to see that my reaction had been . . . perverse. 'Confusing' was a handy word to slap on that mess. Pierce was, once more, looking at me to expand, and I didn't feel inclined to.

'Let's talk about you,' I said. 'I'm supposed to be the interviewer.'

'Why?' Pierce said. 'You're not recording.'

Not as far as he knew. 'I assume you'll want to go on the record at some point.'

'To "set the record straight"?' Pierce said. 'That was the expression Quin used. More than once. I had to "set the record straight". As if everything is disordered now, crooked, and when I . . . *If* I go on the record it'll all be properly arranged and neat and tidy. "The Record"! As if there's a single, agreed text of the past somewhere, in a big ledger with metal clasps . . . Or in one of Quin's servers, now, I suppose.'

He stopped, and stared out of the window, biting his lip, frowning, those hard eyes points of radiant darkness. 'That's shit. That's a big pile of shit. You must see that. Everything would be blown to shit. There'll be a big storm of shit. Newspapers. I'll be ripped apart.'

The eyes were avoiding me now, and they swam. For the first time in our discussion, he looked vulnerable. Might he cry? Profile gold . . .

'The worst part,' Pierce continued, 'is that it won't even be that big a scandal. Not the front page of the newspaper, it won't touch the TV. Enough to destroy me, of course. A couple of days of it online, before people move on. I'll be ruined. But it won't be that important a story. Just enough to ensure I never come back.'

He was right I had not fully calculated the implications of what Pierce had said about *Night Traffic* – I had been thinking purely in personal terms, not about the wider world. I had thought, This is a huge story, but not put any real imagination into what that meant. This would bump Eddie's estate agent friend for sure. Eddie might want it on the cover. Pierce was right, national newspapers would pick it up. The magazine's name would be everywhere, we'd be at our highest profile for years, maybe since the Errol days. Money would flow: extra news-stand sales, new subscribers, extra ads sold against my piece, syndication rights. In narrow professional terms, I would be a hero. My dismissal would be off the table for a while, six months maybe, enough time for me to get my act together. And the incredible fact was that the story had just dropped from the sky. Quin volunteered Pierce, and Pierce had served up the story.

A wisp of doubt. I hadn't actually *done* anything, not yet. I could imagine the finished product: long, *New Yorker*-ish, bringing in a lot of voices, well-researched, prize-winning. But it had been months since I put words on paper, and that had been the Quin train-wreck. Could I produce 5,000 words of empathy, careful questioning, supporting quotes, legal niceties and meticulous fact-checking? Lawyers would read it, tens of thousands of people would read it, awards judges would read it. I could imagine *having written it* – stepping onto the stage to accept my award – but I couldn't imagine *actually writing* a single line.

And I would need Pierce to cooperate, on the record. I might secretly have his confession on tape, but using that alone, without a corroborating, sympathetic interview from him, would turn my piece into a ham-fisted assassination. Pierce would be denied the stage-managed interview he must want; instead he would get an exposé by a hostile and unscrupulous journalist.

With a tidal surge of nausea, I realised that I couldn't get away with that. Pierce was not powerless. He could strike back, with Quin, with the information they had accumulated on my drinking and inaccuracies and lifted quotes. Who knew how much data Quin really had? They could respond with so much muck of their own that I'd be destroyed – and, in the ensuing shitstorm, Pierce might be able to absolve himself. I began to appreciate why I, in particular, had been chosen for this job: mutually assured destruction.

Involve Pierce. Get him on board. 'If you go on the record,' I said, 'I'm prepared to craft the story with you, make sure you get your side across clearly and sympathetically. We can make your, ah, coming-out as gentle as possible.'

'Well, thanks,' said Pierce. He pinched the bridge of his nose, and shut his eyes hard, seemingly tired. 'But let's not delude ourselves. No way it'll be gentle. It'll be brutal. I'm going to get killed.'

I could not deny this, so I didn't say anything. Instead, I thought about the DVR in my shirt pocket. If I glanced downwards, I could just see the top of it. Pierce could probably see it too, if he knew to look, but that shape against my breast could be anything – phone, vape stick, pen drive. I became very conscious that my body language might betray me, might reveal that I was wearing a wire. I rolled my shoulders, pretending to rid them of stiffness, in fact trying to get the DVR to be less conspicuous, and peered into the neck of the beer bottle, inspecting its foaming dregs. To my surprise, the bottle was already almost empty, though I hardly remembered drinking from it at all.

But Pierce wasn't even looking. He was preoccupied with telling his story. 'Quin threatened to go public without me,' he said. 'He insisted that I confess and make amends. He said that it reflected badly on *him*.' He barked a laugh, eyes wide. 'On him! How fucking vain can you get? Such concern for his own reputation! He's completely naive. He thinks that if I say I'm sorry then I'll be OK. He's wrong. I made up . . . I'd say "I made up a story" but that sounds so fucking innocent, so pre-school. I invented people. I invented events. I defrauded my agent, my publisher and the public. I told lie after lie after lie and said to people every time, "this is the sworn truth". I was praised for my honesty. I'm a monster.'

I wanted, more than ever, to check the DVR in my pocket,

to confirm that it was still running, recording these words. But I did not dare. I kept my eyes on Pierce, draining the last of my beer and letting him speak, but hardly listening, thinking only of the recording.

'All those people who praised it, who praised my courage and candour,' Pierce continued. 'The people who wrote to me, the people who invited me to speak . . . All those people are going to feel like I made fools of them. And I did. Helen Mirren said that it made her cry. In a newspaper. *Dame* Helen Mirren. What are they going to do? How do I atone for something like that?'

'Is that what you want?' I asked. 'To atone?'

It was Pierce's turn to be silent. He scowled, giving the question deep, zealous thought.

'If I'm being honest,' he began – and I thought, Yes, please be honest – 'I'd rather die before the truth comes out. But I'll settle for atonement.'

'Why did you do it?' I asked. If I did decide to betray Pierce, the more information I could get out of him while he believed himself to be off the record, the better.

But he was no longer cooperating.

'I envy you, you know. You've done it. You've been there – twice. I tried to think of the most primal urban experience possible: being mugged in the street, that was it.'

'The way to avoid being mugged,' my dad said, 'is to look as if you're going to mug someone.' Memorable advice – well, I've remembered it, which is more than I can say about most of what he told me before I went to London. What made it stick was the thought it immediately prompted in me: that I could never, ever imagine my dad looking as if he were going to mug someone. This gem of street-smarts was dispensed by a diminutive, paunchy tax accountant wearing an incredibly aged blue blazer with loose brass buttons that dangled like charms on a bracelet. When my dad started losing his hair, it went at the temples first, as is quite common. But then it kept going back in two temple-width swaths, never expanding its path to take in anything from the sides or the top of the head. This left a mohican-like strip of hair in the middle of his scalp. He never did anything to adapt his hairstyle to the diminishing resources at its disposal, to try to disguise or balance the creeping baldness – a failure I saw then as a hopeless inability to face facts but in retrospect looked more like splendid unconcern. He simply did not mind.

Did he, my dad, base this advice on experience? Or was it just something he had heard and which sounded true enough to repeat without checking? So much 'wisdom' is like that, plausible but untested, repeated with confidence because it had been heard spoken with confidence. What did it even mean, in practice? A scowl on the face, a certain swagger, a certain swing, a certain strut to the walk. To appear at home in the street, as if you belong wherever it is that you are, which may be – if violence really is a possibility – what the newspapers call 'the wrong place at the wrong time'. There's data for you: if places and times can be 'wrong', then there are temporal and topological boundaries, this could all be mapped – indeed, apps like Tamesis could show you recent crime as a heat map. I knew because I hate-browsed homes for sale on those apps, seeking out the pockets where public-transport access was chilliest and crime was glowing magma red, hopeful of a miraculous, inaccessible few streets of nightly throat-slitting where a studio flat might dip towards a quarter of a mill.

You mustn't look out of place, you mustn't look like an impostor. That's when the city turns on you. But it's not quite right to say you must appear 'at home'. Because when you're drunk you often feel supremely at home on the street, altogether too comfortable, and you're at your most vulnerable.

Whatever it was you were supposed to do, I can't have been doing it. In 2005 I had just started working for *Divider*, the DVD magazine. *Divider* tried to compensate for its obvious anachronism by adopting a certain swagger in its editorial style, and I was exactly the kind of inexperienced but eager recruit it wanted, with a few energetic, pretentious university newspaper features to my name and not much else. This was little more than a decade ago, and remembering it now it occurs to me that today I would probably be expected to do an unpaid internship – an impossibility, with no resources and parents more than two hours from London (by the faster train). But in that forgotten golden age, 2005, they hired me right out of university. On a pittance, but in a real job.

Never mind that I had sauntered into the city across a collapsing bridge – I felt I belonged there, all right. Never have I felt less like an impostor. That first job was a resounding endorsement. No sense, yet, of the quiet doubts that had pursued me across that bridge, not an inkling of the trajectory that would take me to my humiliation on Pierce's sofa. In the winter of 2006, I belonged. I was *in*.

That year *Divider* had its staff Christmas party in a restaurant in Soho. A back room filled with booze. I drank far too much, but so did everyone else. I know that I flirted with at least two co-workers, without consequence. I think I told the story about my uncle's cockatoo, which isn't true, but the timing is well rehearsed through repetition. There was a lot of smoke around that table – smoking in restaurants, a lost age for sure. It was my second Christmas party at that magazine. I had shed the novice nervousness that kept me near the corner the previous year. My co-workers were my friends and I was in my place.

The restaurant ejected us after eleven, and many of the others went to a club. Unsteady on my feet, I was gripped by an instinctive desire to grab the last Tube and go to bed before I made more of a fool of myself. I still lived in the Fulham flat-share, and opted to walk to Embankment Station, from where the District Line would take me straight home.

Soho dies hard between Leicester Square and Trafalgar Square. There's a hinterland behind the National Gallery where the life goes from the streets, the lights recede and every building has its back to you. It was a cold night, and even with the pubs closing and the office parties winding down, few hurrying souls shared the pavements with me.

The choreography of what happened has stayed with me. A hand, a large hand, warm, was laid on my neck from behind – not violent, oddly intimate, almost genial, cupping itself to the curve where neck meets shoulder. I was startled, but immediately assumed that a friend from the office had been following me from the restaurant and had caught up. No stranger would do that. I stopped and turned. It was a stranger. A tall, pale man whose lined face added twenty years to his age, which I guessed was only a few years ahead of mine, mid to late twenties. His hair, straight and dark, hung lank to one side, on a spectrum between Hitler and nineties indie dropout. That's all the detail I can give. I have often tried to recall more, but even that basic outline is woozy as often as it is clear, and I wonder if any of it is invention, the imagination trying to help, supplying information not found in the memory. I'll say this: he looked both unwell and in more formidable physical shape than me. His companion was even less clear.

Our dance continued. I had stopped in the middle of the pavement, by a street corner. He circled me, coming a little too deep into my personal space, which caused me to take a step back – which was not really a step back the way I had come because I had turned when I stopped. Instead I took a step backwards onto the narrower, quieter side street, a huge step really, across a threshold, not only from one street to another but from one situation to another, a step into a new world. And the old-young man was between me and the way I had come. It was impressive, really, the way that he sheepdogged me into the place he wanted me – a skill, a real talent. Absurdly, I was still trying to figure out if I knew him.

Behind me, movement. A shadow separated from the railings that ran along the side of the pavement.

'Got a cigarette, pal?'

'I don't,' I said. 'Smoke. I don't smoke.'

'Got a quid? I'll buy my own.'

The air around me changed. My pleasant boozy buzz from the party shut off. The wider city disappeared – the millions living lives, happy and sad and indifferent, all gone, down to me, and him, and the third person, the one manoeuvring on my blind side. And the details around me: the paving slabs under my feet, wet and black, the black railings, the unlighted windows of the building behind those railings, the dirty glass skylight between railings and wall, the dark shapes of the parked cars, a dull shine on them from streetlights too far away. This whole scene, a radius of two or three metres, was my whole world, and it was empty of help.

But: I still did not know what was happening. This man did not want a cigarette, I knew that; if he did, it certainly wasn't all he wanted. Was I being begged? Was I being robbed? Was I simply free to go, to say, 'No, sorry,' and push by, suffering nothing more than an epithet spat at my retreating back? If I gave this man a quid – it was there, and more, heavy in my pocket – was that all? Would we part on good terms, with some of that spurious cheer that accompanies a successful beg? No – I was sure, on a level of animal instinct, that starting to fetch money from my pockets was a mistake.

It was confusing. There was no clarity in the situation. It didn't look promising, but it wasn't a man with a knife saying, 'Give me all your money.' There was no obvious, sensible path to either escape or self-preservation. That was the most frightening part.

'You got a quid then, mate?' Old-Young said. He stepped towards me. Aware of his colleague to my rear, I inched back, but did not take a corresponding full step. He drew closer. The streetlamp hardly grazed him.

'Sure, sure,' I mumbled, and dipped a hand into my pocket. My keys jangled with the loose change there. As it happened, I had an unusually large amount of money on me: £30 in notes and perhaps another ten in change. At the time, on my starting salary in a parsimonious industry, that was a lot. I had expected to need it for carousing, but the magazine had paid for everything at the restaurant, leaving me flush. He heard it.

'You got a lot there, yeah?' he said. 'How about you spare us a bit more?'

I froze, looking desperately towards the busier street, hoping against all likelihood that a policeman or patrol car might choose this moment to pass, or that a large group might turn the corner and give me the cover, the witnesses, to extricate myself. But I was alone.

My next move surprised me – it was, I suppose, brave, or bold, and thus I had not anticipated it.

'You said a quid.'

Old-Young lifted his gaze from mine to look at his companion – the first time he had acknowledged him, although I had never doubted they were working together. I shuddered, expecting an assault from behind – an arm round the throat, a blow to the back of the head, a knife between the ribs. How would that feel, to be stabbed? I had only really been thinking in words: 'mugged', 'robbed', 'assaulted', these were very elastic concepts, which had made fixing them to the truth of the situation all the harder – until now, anyway, and now they felt inadequate against a much larger and less abstract consideration: Am I about to be hurt, and if so, how much?

Signalled by Old-Young, Railing had appeared at my side – but still a little to my rear, covering any reversal by me. He had on a hooded jacket; not the 'hoodie' of the stereotype but a wind-cheater, something you might wear home from the gym. And, unlike a 'hoodie', unlike the boys who had (not) attacked Pierce, like his companion, he was older than I was. Black hair and an offensive little line of goatee. Other characteristics muted or blurred by fear, drink and the natural working of memory.

My hand was in my pocket, with the coins and keys. I half-re-membered something about holding keys in a fist, like a spiked knuckle-duster, and going for an assailant's face, his eyes – not an act I could see myself doing, not even in an extreme situation. Although the nature of an extreme situation is that we don't know what we'll do until we get there. Even if I could bring myself to retaliate first, would that just provoke them into worse violence? The other advice my father had given – it was all coming back now, the blazer, the dark, pitted surface of the pub table, the small velvet-seated stool I had sat on while he took to the wooden bench against the wall, the summer light low in the windows and the optics – was that, if I was mugged, I should just give them what they wanted and scram. Don't be brave, don't resist, don't be stupid. But what did they want? Where did it end? What was happening?

The two men closed in. Nothing good ever 'closes in':

pursuers, predators, storms. Without being touched I was forced back onto the railings, my little hopeless pavement-universe cut back to its minimum extent. Only the boundary of the person remained. I checked their hands. Both men had a hand free and a hand in a jacket pocket. I never saw a weapon, a knife. That's another saying, and it came back now: if they show you the blade they don't mean to use the blade. Not my dad's, that one, that came from an argument among my friends at university. Was it true? What kind of data had gone into that bit of street wisdom? Forget true: was it useful? We live our lives by these ungrounded, half-remembered bits of folklore, and when I needed help, when my mind urgently roamed its prison looking for tools, this nonsense buzzed uselessly at me: all trite and false, all of it. I knew nothing.

My hand came out of the pocket, fist clenched around as many coins as I could grasp.

'Fuck off,' Old-Young snarled when he saw this offering.

So we understood each other. I took my wallet from my back pocket. The demeanour of my robbers – I knew, now – had changed. We were into the delicate, unambiguous business of separating me from my possessions by threat of force, we all knew, and they had lost their stony composure and focus and become watchful and jumpy, eyes everywhere, lots of small movements. Railing took my wallet from me as soon as it appeared.

'Phone,' Old-Young said, beckoning impatiently. This was the least ambivalent instruction he gave me. I took my phone from my jacket pocket and Railing took it from me. This teamwork was notable: one doing the demanding, the other the taking. Did this offer some consoling moral effect, or imagined legal protection?

It didn't matter, and my thoughts were cancelled when Railing hit me. I had no time to prepare. Even consumed by fear of imminent attack, I had not expected it. (So what was the fear *for*? What good was it?) There was a fraction of a second in which I realised 'he's going to hit me' – his frame coiling back, eyes widening – then a flash of action and pain.

The punch wasn't tidy. You only learn this after you've been hit a couple of times by people who mean it, but punches are messy, slippery affairs. Think 'punch' and, for me anyway, what came to mind was *Raging Bull*: slow-motion black and white arm-back bull's-eye connection. Not a smeared moment of edges and glancing and sliding and mismatching body parts.

He hit me below the right eye, mostly on the cheekbone. It felt as if he were aiming elsewhere and missed, but that was mad, at that range surely he could hit wherever he wanted. I cried out and raised my arms to protect my face. Too late, of course, everything that happened had already happened, they were gone, off round the corner the quickest you can walk without running, all hands now in jacket pockets.

My first thought, once I had recovered my wits, was to call someone – the police, I suppose. And then I realised my phone was gone. I opened and closed my mouth, working the muscles of my face, establishing the level of damage. A wide zone of pain across the right side, a nasty headache from nowhere, but nothing broken. I was fundamentally intact. Hot, sour tears surged up and I fought with them, and the humiliation they brought and that brought them, all across the bright field of Trafalgar Square, and at last they retreated, without spilling, under the white lights of Embankment Station.

Neither of my housemates was home once I got back, which suited me as I had no wish to tell them what had happened and deal with their questions. As well as sore, my face was abnormally hot, and I knew some of that was shame.

The next morning – Saturday – I had recovered enough to explain the red patch under my eye and put a defiant, rational, angry spin on the whole business. I made some edits to the events, which helped. I felt it was my right, as victim and star witness.

One housemate was insistent that I should report the incident to the police, in the teeth of my insistence that I didn't want to, and that the police wouldn't bother doing anything, and that the men would never be caught even if they did.

It doesn't matter, Jack, they need to know for the statistics. That's important. The statistics, he kept saying. You have to report it for the statistics.

The following Monday, face showing a jaunty bruise, I was received as a hero in the *Divider* office. A crowd formed to hear what had happened (director's cut). Again I heard about the importance of police statistics. In the end I did report it, but only to get a crime number that I could use to claim insurance for my lost phone. The statistics were served.

Among the most sympathetic of my colleagues was one of the women I had unsuccessfully flirted with at the party. Her name was Elise.

Divider closed in 2009. We had both moved on by then, Elise and I, and moved in together.

'I'm not sure that's true.'

Pierce tilted his head, interested. 'What isn't?'

'What you just said,' I said. 'About mugging being "the most primal urban experience". I mean, it's a primal experience all right, but how urban is it?'

Pierce leaned forward. He was engaged. The eyes were back at full beam, the brow locked, the self-pity gone. 'It's completely urban. It is a crime almost unknown outside cities.'

'Sure, I know, but—'

'The city arose as a place of concourse and trade,' Pierce said, barging on, in full talking-to-an-audience mode. 'Mugging is a kind of trade, conducted by force, imposed on you, in a place made for trade. It's by definition in the street, or at its edges, and unlike a lot of violent crime it's mostly stranger-on-stranger, and therefore thrives where there is the highest population of relative strangers. You are brought into sudden, total contact with one of your fellow citizens, people you might be highly unlikely to encounter otherwise; it's an extraordinarily powerful and meaningful interaction, transcending some boundaries, but operating entirely within others, urban in its—'

'I know, I know,' I said. 'I've read *Night Traffic*, that's all true enough.' Except it wasn't, I had to remind myself: Pierce's thoughts on the matter were based on imagination, not experience. True enough was true enough. 'I put it badly – what I meant to say was, when it happened to me, when I was mugged, it didn't feel very "urban". The city went away. I was on my own, in nothingness, with the two men robbing me. I might have been interacting with them, but I wasn't interacting with the city.'

'You were out of your bubble, though, weren't you?' Pierce said. 'No passivity, no distance, no irony or detachment. You were involved in city life.'

I didn't say anything. I didn't disagree, I just didn't know what to think. A curious sensation had come over me. When I had read *Night Traffic*, I had admired it greatly. It had appeared both objectively true and true to my experience. Now, knowing that it was based on a mighty lie, I found myself reassessing its other apparent truths. Perhaps what had appeared to be an accurate description of my own experience only came across that way because it ennobled my experience, made it out to be more grand and important than the shabby encounters I had lived through. This deepened my appreciation of the trouble that Pierce was in. The lie had metastasised, spreading out to corrupt everything it touched. It was intimate.

I had finished my beer, and Pierce his whisky.

'What else would qualify?' Pierce asked. He was eager to get his view endorsed, almost bullying me into agreement. It reeked of insecurity.

'You mean – what's the primal urban experience?'

'Yes.'

'Buying a house?'

'No.' He rolled his eyes. '*Fuck* no.'

'OK. You're right. Modern trade? I don't know . . . working on the commodities markets?'

'No. Better suggestion than your last one, though, but it's all automated now, the preserve of very few people. Deracinated, networked, delocalised. No city necessary.'

'Walking from your home to a street market and haggling with the traders.'

'Better. Bit retro.'

'Getting the Tube.'

Pierce looked as if he had smelled something offensive, and didn't respond.

'Being caught in a disaster,' I said. I was losing patience with the game – with Pierce's games in general. 'An urban disaster. A terror attack.'

'That might be your best yet,' Pierce said. 'But, believe me, I've given it a lot of thought, and getting mugged is the quintessential urban experience.'

All at once I felt a great weariness. Pierce's games were tiring me out. I was beginning to find this talk about authenticity strangely odious. Having had the genuine experience that Pierce so craved, I didn't feel better for it. It had made a kind of sense when I had read *Night Traffic* and felt that Pierce had known what I had been through. Now I saw that someone – albeit someone very talented – was able to simply conjure up that experience, I was even further separated from it. That second attack, though. If that hadn't really happened, I might have needed to invent it. 'How about a real drink?' I said. 'We could take this to the pub.'

At this, Pierce looked happier than at any other time since I had met him.

Coats, lights, keys – the assorted chores that came with leaving Pierce's flat refocused me on the enviable fact that he had two floors to himself, and the London question.

'Do you own or rent?' I asked.

He looked embarrassed. 'Own.' No prompting was needed for the explanation, the answer to the unspoken part of the question. 'My parents did me the favour of dying while I was still fairly young.'

'Oh,' I said. 'I'm sorry. I thought the money from *Night Traffic* . . .'

'That's been paying my mortgage the past couple of years. It's a good flat and I know I'm lucky to have it, but on balance I'd rather have my mum and dad.'

We walked down the creaking stairs in silence. 'It's the London question,' I said. 'Not really "How do you afford a place to live?" – more, "How is paying to live fucking up your life?" Either you're deep in debt, or you're giving everything to a landlord, or you're doing a job you hate with no way out, or you live in a shithole. Or someone has to die.'

Pierce smiled icily and smacked the button that unlocked the front door. 'Someone has to die – and that's if you're one of the luckiest ones,' he said. 'Congratulations, someone you love has gone. You're allowed to stay. You win. That's the sacrifice London wants. And that's if you have asset-rich elders to offer up. Moloch in reverse.'

'The only ones who don't have to pay in blood are the psychopaths,' I said.

'Oh, obviously,' Pierce said. He knew at once who I meant. He had met a lot more of them than me. 'Not that it would bother them.'

'Not in the slightest.'

The time was approaching 1 p.m. The interview with De Chauncey was scheduled for 3 p.m. I had, at most, half an hour of pub time. My phone had been on silent during the interview, a basic courtesy, and I had avoided checking it, to avoid repercussions from the incident with Alan, and to postpone confronting the De Chauncey arrangements. And, as I could have predicted, there was an email from the Wolfe / De Chauncey press person confirming the time and asking for my mobile number 'in case'. Alongside half a dozen other emails, there were notifications from the various social networks – just *likes*, nothing out of the ordinary. But on Tamesis, there was an invite from Kay. That was potentially awkward. She was on my T-plus list: if convenient (and if it suited the machinations of Quin's algorithms) Tamesis would discreetly try to guide us into 'chance' meetings. A meeting I would, for the time being, prefer to avoid. I could unplus her, take her off the list, or even give her the dreaded T-minus, for people you wanted to avoid – Tamesis would then not recommend venues where it knew, or believed, she might be. But that was brutal. T-minusing was for your exes, creeps, people you weren't talking to, deadbeat pseudo-friends, creditors. The system gave you no indication you had been T-minused, just as you have no idea if someone has muted you on Twitter.

Naturally, T-minusing was one of the big selling points of Tamesis – arguably more popular than its ability to cause you to run into your friends more often. Quin affected to be embarrassed by the T-minus function as it ran against his cheerful, utopian picture of London (and, soon, the rest of the country) becoming smaller, friendlier and better connected. It wasn't even possible in the earliest releases. So why did he enable it?

'Bunk doesn't believe in denying people tools,' Quin said. 'T-minusing is feasible, it's useful, so the greater sin would be to disallow it.'

He didn't say this to me, mind, or if he did I didn't get it down – I've taken that quote from elsewhere. It's classic Quin, though: practicality held up as a moral quality in itself, overall shine of sanctimony, completely self-serving. As if it had never occurred to him that an app that helped you avoid people would be as popular as his dream of an app that helped you find people. And so it proved. Hardly a week went by without an *Evening Standard* or *Guardian* feature about the new etiquette of T-plus and T-minus. Who knew what would happen when Bunk launched Tamesis nationally later this year.

There weren't a huge number of pubs near Pierce, but several were warm-rated on Tamesis.

'Don't do that,' Pierce said, seeing the blue glow of Tamesis on my screen. 'You don't need that. That fucking . . . I'm right here. I live here. I know where to go. Look around you. Look at the city.'

I was chagrined, and quickly re-pocketed my phone. In fact I hadn't been thinking about where we might go, just about Kay, and about getting to Shoreditch to see De Chauncey. A sickly, acid emptiness in my gut, but it wasn't the urge to drink, not entirely. It was anxiety about the pub. Time was not on my side: I'd have to leave just as I started to feel comfortable. Obligations, seeing people I didn't want to see, doing things I didn't want to do. Things I wanted to escape. Escaping was, for the moment, even more important than drinking. Pierce, he was the key. I wasn't done with Pierce yet. The interview had led to . . . What? Whatever it was, it was important, and it meant, with regret, I would have to postpone De Chauncey for a day or two. Plans do change. I would be giving them advance warning, almost an hour's worth; it wasn't as if I was standing him up. Any repercussions in the office – well, that was for tomorrow. Or the day after, if I muted my phone, and by that time I might have the full incredible story from Pierce. But what could Pierce and I do together?

The sun was, presumably, somewhere overhead, but it was obscured and ineffectual. Pierce turned towards the garden square, and I followed his instruction and looked around, at the towering plane trees and the handsome stucco and yellow-brick houses. Above the white line of their parapets, darkness unnatural. I had forgotten it, and it had waited out here for me. And at once I felt it, in my sinuses, by taste, on the skin of my face, in my eyes.

'You want real, authentic?' I said, stopping. 'A primal urban event?'

Pierce stopped too, but didn't reply. He looked at me, waiting for me to continue.

'That fire in Barking. Where all that smoke is coming from. That's real. Let's go there.'

We walked to Bow Road Station and caught a District Line train bound for Barking, the seat of the fire.

Pierce lived at the eastern limit of my knowledge of London. This personal, psychic boundary coincided with a geographical boundary. My journey to Pierce was all in tunnels, apart from that unhappy moment at Liverpool Street. But the journey east was only under the sky. Pierce lived where the Underground stops being underground.

I remarked as much to him, thinking that this was the kind of observation that might get him waxing psychogeographical – a winding path through tunnelling technologies and the cost of land in the nineteenth century, perhaps, with stops for the great Victorian cemeteries and the machinations of the rail companies. Instead he grunted, as if it had never occurred to him before, and looked out of the window. Unsatisfactory, deeply unsatisfactory. I was ditching work, and ditching the pub, in order to go on an expedition with Oliver Pierce. *Oliver Pierce*. Throw in a few encounters with eccentric characters, surreal and/or threatening, and it could be considered a *caper*. If it involved drinking or drug use, criminal or semi-criminal activity of some kind, and perhaps a lucky escape from arrest or a beating, I could justifiably call it a *gonzo escapade*. This was a wish fulfilled, but only if Pierce was Pierce. He had to play along, to conform to the personality that appeared on the pages of his essays. He had to be unpredictable and dangerous and full of bad ideas. I was just along for the ride. As the writer, you are a passenger, the avatar of the reader. You can't instigate the crazy, you just happen to be there when it gets started. That's how it should work.

Or that's how it should *appear*, anyway. How did Pierce set up those Pierce-ish situations? Had he invented even more than he admitted to? If so, how? This trip hadn't even been his idea, it had been mine. He was a writer too. What if neither of us was the instigator, the protagonist? What if we were both Boswells? If we were just blokes on a train?

I looked out of the window. Material for the escapade piece I would write. A slash through unexplored outer London. The sinews of the modern city. Gas-holders and scrub. Broken, daubed walls. Industrial buildings sinking into triffidous greenery. Triffidous, that was good. Neologisms were always good for this sort of thing. Think Will Self, Iain Sinclair. London's fringe, where it breaks apart and loses its shape, before yielding to fields. But I was mistaken. This was only a temporary lapse. The city regrouped and re-exerted itself, growing denser again. With a lurch akin to vertigo, I became aware of the sheer size of the metropolis, the huge area it covered, the multitudes it contained. Builders' yards and taxi roosts were replaced by terraced lines of back gardens. Punch bags and trampolines. Blocks of flats. A train depot, its Christmas lights still up. More gas-holders. The train grew weary, getting into a melancholy cycle of slow deceleration and fitful, uneven acceleration. It terminated at Barking, and wanted us to know that well in advance, its efforts palpably waning.

We had come to Barking because that was where the fire was – the Barking Blaze, it said in the papers. Beyond that, we had not put much preparation into the excursion. I had, I think, expected to walk out of Barking Station and into a scene resembling a painting of the last hours of Pompeii. A geyser of destruction, infernal orange light, people cowering and fleeing, and so on. At the very least I expected the fire to be visibly nearby, within a few streets' walk. In fact, it was as if we had travelled no distance at all.

There was the plume in the east, but it was still removed from us, almost abstract, a threat without presence. Not even perceptibly closer, just fatter, bolder, higher resolution, its unceasing internal coilings and rearrangements more clearly defined. But not close. No one was looking towards it but us, or so I believed.

'You should have seen it yesterday,' said a voice behind us. A *Big Issue* seller, a ginger beard between red tabard and woolly hat.

'Bigger than that?'

The *Big Issue* seller frowned. 'No, not really. But newer.'

'Is it near here?' Pierce asked.

'Nah,' the seller replied. 'Down by the river.' He nodded, helpfully, towards the plume.

A silent but eloquent moment passed between me and Pierce. We both understood that the social circumstances demanded that we buy a magazine, and that it might look a little forced if both of us did. In the end, after long milliseconds of wordless deliberation, Pierce volunteered, and I immediately wished that it had been me who jumped, for appearance and out of genuine guilt. But if I tried now that guilt would be a bit too obvious. The opportunity was lost.

Down by the river. Naively, I had assumed Barking to be on the river. Out came the phones, for navigation. I remembered the map in the morning paper, the aerial photo: the industrial lands of the estuary. From the satellite's eye, not the texture of city or suburb or countryside, but more resembling a circuit board. The white buboes of oil tanks, the dull tessellation of warehouse roofs. Pierce had opened Google Maps. I tried Tamesis, which combined maps with live information and social updates. The screen raced to one side, away from the often-loaded pages of my usual haunts, into grey unloaded areas. 'Finding you . . .' it said, Bunk logo spinning merrily. Then central Barking unfolded on the screen. Menus opened like jeweller's drawers. Where's the fire? I asked it.

Ongoing event / Major fire / Barking Riverside / Police, TfL warnings in place / Ongoing air quality alert / Road closures / Related news stories (23) / User pictures (37) / What people are saying / Directions here / Share this?

I thumbed 'directions'.

While Pierce looked at timetables, I pecked out a quick email response to the press contact at Wolfe / De Chauncey. Earlier interview overrunning, unexpected circumstances, sincere apologies, possible to reschedule? And then another train east: not a Tube, a mainline train, albeit an unhurried local one. We only went one stop, but the change was startling. Beyond Barking, the city really fell apart. The railway line itself spread out as if no longer pent up by urban pressure, splitting into a wide braid of sidings and halts. Disused goods cars brilliant with graffiti fed rust to beds of weeds. Other trains passed us, rushing out of the city on separate, better, tracks. We were in the distribution steppes, the pylon orchards. Expansive wastes of tarmac patrolled by lorries and cranes, and filled with shipping containers.

Dagenham Docks Station – I liked the unregenerated name – lay under a swerve of elevated motorway, a speck of Edwardian brick caught between the concrete teeth of a later era. No one disembarked with us. Leaving the station, we were confronted by what I knew from the map to be the south-western corner of the Ford factory. This turned out to be underwhelming: no obvious forest of belching smokestacks or cathedral of automation, just unmarked, unremarkable low-rise buildings in fleshy brick. If they made any noise, it was drowned out by the motorway.

Behind us, behind the motorway and the station, the plume. To be seen across London, the plume had to climb high in the air, and so it did, an impossible tower of churning ink. But here, almost at its base, the surprise it offered was its width. It appeared to fill a whole quadrant of the sky, blacking out the south-east. A vast field must be alight to fill that footprint; more than 'alight' – that was a word for foil-tray barbecues and dinky wood stoves – this was ablaze, consumed, engulfed, erupted. Yet there must still be fuel down there to burn, to ecstatically release and send its residual filth up into that roiling pillar. My curiosity was already almost sated, we were closer than near, we were inside it. The air was foul with it. That filling-station tang I had noticed this morning had become a burning tyre under the nose, a nauseating blast against the back of the throat.

Perhaps we had already done enough: I had dodged De Chauncey for now, gone on a trip that would make for scenic colour, and now we could turn around and go to the pub. I could wash away some of this hydrocarbon stench. But no, it was too soon. We had come all this way, we had to make something of it – and Pierce was just getting warmed up. I could see his enthusiasm rising.

'Hopefully we'll get a better view from the bridge,' he said, striding off. But the bridge over the railway lines and sidings was enclosed by grey steel walls and caged in at the top, making a vandal-proof chute straight out of an abattoir. Or into one. The stairs down from the bridge were clogged with litter and weeds that had graduated into shrubbery, making me wonder if people ever came here, and who might be responsible for maintaining this miserable outpost. As soon as this thought formed, I had to revise it. Of course people came here, people *worked* here, did they not? Many people. All around were places of work: logistics centres and cement plants and, ahead, Barking power station. Even legit, old-school *factories*. Maybe the workers all drove in, rather than chance the twice-an-hour trains. Maybe they used buses instead. From where? Were there buses? So many of my fellow Londoners were, I realised, a mystery to me. Where did they live? The question: how did they make it work? All I knew was that I didn't have to duck past Triassic overgrowth on my morning journey from Pimlico to Shoreditch.

'I forget how big London is,' I said. 'You go to, say, Docklands, and you think you're near the edge. But you aren't. There's all of this. Miles more.'

Pierce smiled and squinted at his surroundings. 'If I ever want to shoot a zombie movie, I know where to come,' he said. It was the most interesting thing he had said since we set out, this humdrum observation, and it was fundamentally wrong. The footbridge and roadside had an air of desuetude and abandonment, it's true. But human activity was everywhere: a constant exchange of lorries up and down the road, the sounds of industry and the wail of the motorway. A steady metallic banging came from somewhere up ahead, and there was a general non-traffic growl of machinery and work. But no human voice, no people on foot.

To aggravate the go-away vibe of the place, a freezing drizzle began to fall. As we walked it worsened, enough for us to keep our heads down and our mouths closed.

Like the Ford factory, Barking power station was thoroughly free of awe or interest: flat, featureless blue slabs of building, and squat chimneys that issued no smoke. In any case, anything that they did produce would be quite redundant compared with the mountain of smoke rising across the way. We were close enough to see that the plume had its own shuddering orange illumination, but any actual flames were obscured by the sheds along the road.

The road from the station to the riverside was straight and wide. It and its wide pavement were not surfaced with tarmac but with scraped cement, giving them a temporary, construction-site feel. The drains, if there were any, had failed, and the gutter was a chain of giant, murky puddles. The lorries, which never ceased, sent up eruptions of filthy water, so our progress was halting. A shining stretch of cement would warn of a splash-zone, and we had to check if any vehicles were close before traversing it. I was reminded of the Nintendo platform games I played as a child: stop, wait for the swinging axe or angry ghost to pass, then jump the chasm. At the end of the road, where a wind turbine turned, was a compact constellation of flashing blue lights, twinkling and flowering in the drizzle.

'We must be close,' Pierce said, and I agreed when he said it, but again he was wrong. Perhaps it was the continual need to stop and wait for lorries to splash by, or the unfinished surface beneath our feet, or the overall hostility of the terrain, but a good deal of walking yielded little obvious progress. To our right, a collection of shiny new warehouses called Thames Gateway Park, then an online supermarket distribution centre, then the nerve centre of a popular brand of mass-produced bread. The supermarket's delivery vans had fruit and vegetables printed on their sides; the bread giant's lorries were decorated to resemble sliced loaves. The people we saw walking – three of them – shared characteristics: male, not white, hi-vis vests, an air of deep focus that suggested either tiredness or concentration on a task.

Two police cars were parked across the road ahead, one for each lane, front bumper to front bumper. Their lights strobed silently. Behind them, under the grey citadel of a cement plant, more emergency vehicles were parked: two police vans, an ambulance, two fire engines, and another fire appliance as big as an engine but not one, a mobile office or command vehicle. Yellow signs reading ROAD CLOSED stood in front of the police cars, strung with vibrating blue and white tape. Two police officers watched this frontier. They saw us coming from a distance and regarded us together as it became clear we were definitely approaching the tape rather than turning anywhere else. Words passed between them, certainly about us. As we drew closer, one of the officers walked – with deliberate, powerful slowness – to intercept us, gloved hands flexing, an expression of bored authority on his face. As soon as we were close enough to hear him, and there was no doubt we were going anywhere else, he spoke.

'Road's closed, gentlemen,' he said, pointing in our direction, through us. 'You're going to have to go back the way you came.'

'Can we just cut through?' Pierce asked, with a casual air that I immediately envied. 'We're trying to get to the river.'

The officer formed a leather-clad fist with his left hand and was massaging it with his right like a child forming a snowball.

He spoke as if he had answered the same question twenty times already.

'I don't know if you gentlemen have noticed, but' – the right hand released the left and gestured, open, towards the plume – 'there's a rather serious fire going on over there. So no one is just anything anywhere this way. The road. Is closed.'

'We don't want to get in the way,' Pierce said. 'We only want to have a look.'

'We're journalists,' I added quickly, seeing that the policeman was getting sterner and icier.

Either he didn't believe me, or he held journalists in low regard. Quite possibly both. Again, he pointed through us, back up the road. 'Media,' he said. 'Ocado car park.'

'Excuse me?' Pierce said.

The police officer indulged in a couple of slow, disdainful blinks. 'Media liaison,' he said, crafting every syllable, 'Ocado car park.' The pointing finger jabbed, once. '*That* way, gentlemen.'

'You've been so terrific,' Pierce said, taking out his phone. 'Can I get a picture together?'

The officer had not lowered his arm. '*That* way.'

A flimsy laminated sign was zip-tied to the gate of the Ocado distribution portal. Distracted by the toy-bright vans parked in neat ranks, I had missed it on our way past. It read:

METROPOLITAN POLICE

MAJOR INCIDENT

MEDIA LIAISON

With an arrow.

'Ocado,' I said, still hopeful of eliciting some psychogeographical gems from Pierce. 'The jihadists just need to knock out this facility and middle-class London starves.' Bella and Dan used Ocado. On two occasions, they had been out at the time of delivery and had called me to take in their shopping. You wouldn't believe the fuss Bella made over a melted sorbet.

'Don't knock Ocado,' Pierce said. 'When I couldn't leave the house, they were lifesavers. Their drivers were about the only people I spoke to for three weeks. I should drop in and say hello.'

I didn't say anything in reply. The roadblock had evaporated what was left of my momentum, and I was hunting for the earliest possible opportunity to call a halt and make for the pub. Not the nearest pub – I wanted somewhere I could be comfortable, where I could get myself home quickly under autopilot, not an alien boozer on the wrong side of Barking. I began to feel very far from the centre, very far from the convenience store and the fridge. But Pierce blazed on ahead.

Tucked behind the fence were two conjoined white portable huts, like the office on a construction site. Under the emblem of the Met were the words 'Rapid Response Incident Media Assistance'. A male police officer minded the door, barely acknowledging us as we climbed the unsteady steps to enter. Inside, a female police officer sat behind a desk in a smart dress uniform, her shiny buttons the brightest objects in a thoroughly bland environment of fibreboard, acoustic panels and cheap carpet. She cocked her head at us.

'Good afternoon,' Pierce said.

'Good afternoon,' the police officer said. 'Media?' she asked, doubtful.

'Yes,' I said.

'Do you have ID?'

Fortunately, I did. I pulled out my wallet and produced a business card and my NUJ card. Pierce followed my actions, hesitating a little before showing a small, teal plastic card of his own.

My NUJ credentials were accepted with a minimal nod. Pierce's card was taken from him for closer examination.

'Society of Authors?' she said.

Pierce smiled. 'I'm an author.'

'This is expired.'

'I'm an expired author.'

'Oliver Pierce,' she said, weighing the name for falsity.

'That's me,' Pierce said, cheerful. I had spent more than an hour praying for him to do something memorable or outrageous, to unleash the caper, but now he looked ready to embark on mischief I found myself praying that he behaved himself. In and out, get this over with as quickly as possible, keep moving.

'I wrote a non-fiction book about crime,' Pierce continued. Is it an offence to lie to a police officer? Even in casual conversation? Although there was nothing very casual about this conversation. The officer was sandblasting Pierce with her gaze, as if expecting the paunchy author exterior to slough away, revealing a jihadist beneath. 'About street crime. And a crime novel, for that matter. Kind of. It isn't shelved in Crime. Perhaps you've read them?'

'No,' the officer said, the words bleached of tone. That might have been lucky. The Met had not approved of *Night Traffic*. And I thought, Forget the literary scandal, was there a possibility that Pierce might find himself in criminal trouble over his fraud? Had he considered that?

'Pity,' Pierce said. The police officer returned Pierce's card, and Pierce returned it to his wallet. She said nothing, and little could be read from her face, other than homeopathic quantities of boredom and disapproval. There was no word or nod or wave to endorse or authorise our passage, nothing even slightly affirmative. We were simply no longer stopped from proceeding.

While we were having our cards read, someone had emerged from the screened-off area to meet us: a sparkling young woman in taut business attire. At a glance, I knew her – I knew her by type. I dealt with her kin every day. She worked in public relations.

'Hiii,' she said. She had a metal clipboard, like Polly's, and was holding it in pose #3, 'Small child waiting to give thank-you card to visiting dignitary'. 'I'm Lily. Hiii.'

We did hellos.

'You're writing about the event?' Lily asked.

'I am,' I said.

Lily looked troubled. 'The next full briefing's not until five, for the evenings,' she said.

'We don't need the full briefing,' Pierce said. 'Just give us an abridged version. The basic facts.'

'What kind of story are you writing?'

'Factual,' Pierce said brightly.

'I should hope so!' she said, with a laughing smile. 'What did you say your magazine was called?'

I told her.

'I know you!' Lily said. 'This isn't your usual kind of story, is it? You're more . . . modern urban lifestyle?'

'Jack's taking it in a new direction,' Pierce said. 'Grittier. More real.'

'Eddie still the editor there?'

'Of course,' I said. 'They'll carry him out in a box.'

'I love Eddie,' Lily said. 'Such a great guy.'

'Yeah, he's a great boss.'

'I don't know Eddie,' Pierce said through a ghastly, insincere grin, 'but I hear he's great.'

Lily strafed us with another smile. Mention of Eddie had melted her reserve. 'Come through,' she said, letting us pass.

Half of the second hut was occupied by a miniature lecture theatre, with a dozen folding chairs facing a white projection screen and a podium. Behind the screen was a small office area, comprising two desks facing each other, a photocopier, a fancy-looking printer and a large wall-mounted TV. Lily's clone sat at one desk, and the other was presumably Lily's. Roles attract types. I thought of the two Rays at work – basically identical sub-editors, the same individual, apart from the fact that one was a white man and the other an Asian woman – and smiled. I thought of them fact-checking my Pierce profile and the smile faded. For that to happen, the draft would have to exist, and it was still very hard to imagine the act of *writing* it.

'I remember Eddie from a trip to Miami Art Basel, must have been a couple of years ago,' Lily said. 'When I worked for Peloton Public Relations. Such a laugh. Please, have a seat. Can I get you anything to drink? Water, tea, coffee?'

Yes, a drink, but none of those. The Need had been building up since we had left the train, and now I felt a horrible rush of it, a geyser erupting deep within. I was far from the pub, far from the opportunity to slip away, far from home, and the fridge at home was empty. What was here, where I was, didn't even feel real any more, only a ghastly succession of obstacles placed between my shade and being able to see and feel without pain.

'Water, thank you,' I said, trying to smile. Lily went to a water cooler in the corner of the office area and filled two small plastic cups.

'So you used to work for Peloton?' Pierce asked. 'And now . . . the police?'

'Yes!' Lily said, as if she could hardly believe it. 'On the media side, handling things like this.'

'So this fire is a PR problem, is it?'

'No problem at all,' Lily said, easy and relaxed. She handed me a cup of water, smile unfaltering. 'Our support is there to free up police and fire personnel so they can keep on keeping us safe, and that's what's really important, isn't it? But we prefer to think of ourselves as working on behalf of the event itself.'

'The fire?'

'The event. We prefer to see it as an event like any other kind of event we might handle – just like a product launch or an exhibition, for instance.'

'It's a fire,' Pierce said, with a disbelieving half-chuckle. 'A big fire. Not a . . . gallery opening or a new magazine.'

'Ha ha, yeah,' Lily said cheerfully. 'Well, we're not *promoting* it, as such. We're not saying, "Hey, come and look at this." Because you shouldn't. The advice is to stay away. But asking people to come to something and asking them to stay away aren't so different. It's all about managing perceptions of the event. Promotion isn't the sum of what we do. We're also here to make sure that the event is portrayed accurately and fairly – to dispel myths and calm fears. To put the event in the right light.

'Because,' she continued, 'it's more than a fire, isn't it? There's the spontaneous early combustion of a quantity of petroleum products, sure – and, about that, it's important to be clear, they were always going to be combusted, it's all a matter of context and scheduling. But the event also includes the vital, *vital* work of our emergency services, and the economic ramifications, and the contribution presently being made to London's atmosphere.'

'That's the part I'm interested in,' I said. 'The smoke column. Is it dangerous?'

Lily's smile was indulgent. 'Londoners have absolutely no reason to be alarmed.'

Pierce leaned in. 'That's not a "no", though, is it?' he said. 'If it wasn't harmful, why should people stay away? Why would it need a PR team?'

The gearshift in Lily's attitude was barely perceptible, but it was there. Outwardly, she smiled the same smile she had been smiling the whole time, a smile that seemed directly connected to a deep pool of honesty and compassion. But to me it had been reassuring and, perhaps, a little condescending – a sales or service smile. To Pierce it was less mollifying and more engaged – a smile of respect, of professional speaking to professional.

'I know where you're coming from, Oliver. We tend to avoid "totemic" words like "no" and "yes" because they are in fact more open to interpretation and inaccuracy than you might imagine. If I say "no" or "yes" I am confirming or denying the content of your question, and your question is open to interpretation. Indeed, I don't know exactly what you might mean by your question, what you might mean by a charged and flexible word like "dangerous", so a crude answer like "yes" or "no" risks all kinds of semantic pitfalls. However, an answer such as "Londoners have no reason to be alarmed" is precise and useful.'

'But it doesn't answer the question. It doesn't say if the smoke is harmful.'

'It does more than that. It *makes* the event less harmful. No one should go out there and stick their head in the smoke. Police and fire service advice is to stay away. We're clear about that. But do you know what could cause more harm? Much more harm? *Worry*. Worry can impact your health in a dozen ways. Worry can shorten your life: Worrying about this event is much more likely to cause us harm than the event itself. By reducing worry, we are directly reducing the harm associated with the event. What if someone is concerned by the air quality, so they stay at home and miss a day at work? That's unnecessary economic damage, unnecessary concern, unnecessary *harm*. This is precisely what I meant by our role in managing perceptions of the event: we are not concerned with the cloud of smoke as much as we are with the cloud of psychological consequences the event has created. The emergency services can deal with the combustion incident, while a public relations department can address the action of the event on the minds of the public. We can change the nature of the event for the better. We can do good that way. Our intervention here is essentially *therapeutic*.'

The atmosphere in the cabin had become stifling. How did they stand it? The reek of smoke was everywhere. The back of my mouth tasted like a petrol station forecourt and a space in my head had been surrounded by hoardings promising that a tremendous migraine was coming soon. As we left, Lily gave us both a tote bag containing a press pack, a couple of police and fire service leaflets, a squeezy fire engine with tips for preventing house fires written on its side, and a pen and USB drive bearing the Metropolitan Police emblem. She thanked us for stopping by, and for our interest in the event, and took my business card, promising to sign me up for an email.

Pierce held the cabin door for me.

'Patricia Highsmith,' the policewoman at the desk said.

'Excuse me?' I said.

'Patricia Highsmith,' she repeated. 'I enjoy a good Patricia Highsmith. In case your friend thought I didn't read anything.' She nodded towards Pierce.

'Patricia Highsmith,' Pierce said. 'Me too.'

Colourful hieroglyphs on the pavement, spray-painted by contractors, arrows and boxes limning the subterrain: *Blocked*.

No signal. By now I should have been deep in the bosom of Alexander De Chauncey. I didn't want to look at my phone, to measure the fallout of my cancellation, but my conscience was able to briefly overpower my other inhibitions and I looked. There was an email from his PR. Three minutes after I sent mine. 'Very inconvenient . . . Time very limited . . . Difficult to reschedule at this notice . . .'

Bad. Not maximum bad, and no worse than I could reasonably expect, but bad. Would they go straight to Eddie and complain? That might be the end for me. But there were no emails from Eddie or Polly, nothing else out of the ordinary. Would they email about something like that? Unlikely. It would be a phone call.

My phone sprang to life in my hand, throbbing with an incoming call, and almost flew out of my hand as I spasmed in surprise. Adrenalin thumped through my system. The passing chemical blitz made me woozy, and I felt the blackout grey crawling in at the corners of my vision.

Withheld number. That could mean one of the phones at the office.

I swiped to answer, thumb skidding on the drops of drizzle that had clung to the phone screen, little pinpricks of rainbow.

'Jack Blick?' said an unfamiliar voice, a confident drawl.

'Bick,' I said. 'Yes. Hello.'

'Alexander De Chauncey.' He savoured every syllable of his name.

'Mr Chauncey, Mr De Chauncey,' I began, already stumbling. I was completely on the wrong side of this conversation, the one who needed a boon from the other, and the one who had just done wrong by the other, a double supplicant, and De Chauncey didn't sound as if he was on the wrong side of anything, ever. 'I'm so sorry about this afternoon, I had another interview and it has—'

'Where are you?' De Chauncey asked, drawing out the words again, a note of bemusement in the question, as if there was nowhere that I could reasonably be.

'Er, Barking, as it happens,' I said. He could probably tell that I was outside, and hear the wind against the phone mic. 'I left a message with—'

A soft cluck or tut came over the line – perhaps no more than the sound of a man turning a Polo mint over in his mouth. 'We were supposed to be meeting,' he said. 'The girl from the magazine said you were coming over this afternoon.'

His girling of Polly, my immediate manager and a terrifying force in my life, triggered conflicting emotions: a crackle of righteous anger on her behalf, a spark of amusement and delight. 'As I said in my email—' I began.

'It's difficult this week,' he said with a sigh, as if I should feel sympathy for him. 'Not a sliver of daylight . . .'

'I appreciate that, and I really am sorry,' I said. 'I promise it won't take long, if you can possibly spare just half an hour in the next day or two.'

'Well, where are you now?' he asked, as if I hadn't just told him. 'If you can make it over here in the next hour or so, we could still do it.'

I swallowed. 'It might be tricky, I'm quite a way out.'

A sigh. I was pushing my luck. 'It's best we get it done today.'

'OK, I'll get moving now,' I said. There was no reply, no closing acknowledgement. The call was over. I put the phone back in my pocket with quaking hands.

'We should get moving,' I said to Pierce, thinking more about my empty fridge, cold fear twisting inside me. Even within me, in my innermost core, there was a lie – that I would make every effort to get to De Chauncey's office in Shoreditch – and, deeper, the truth – that I would not, and was already planning the heavy session I would need to anaesthetise myself against the consequences of that, and the rest of today's events. I wanted to believe the lie. It would be a really heavy session. 'This weather . . .'

'There may be another way around,' Pierce said. 'We might be able to get a better view, even if we can't get much closer.'

I looked up at the plume. A helicopter clattered overhead, tufting and tugging the sides of the column. Was it weakening, or simply losing contrast as the sky around it descended and darkened?

'Light's going,' I said.

'That might make the effect all the more dramatic,' Pierce said. 'There was a turning, back the way we came – if we go along there, we'll be able to find another way back down to the river and the fire.'

'No, I need to get back – that call . . .'

Pierce shrugged. 'OK, let's get back. It'd be good to get out of this.'

The puddles alongside the road had deepened and widened and the lorries, headlights on, tyres hissing, had sped up in the wet. To avoid getting drenched, we had to wait more often, and longer, and sometimes had to sprint.

'It's a shame to come out here and not to see a lick of flame,' Pierce said.

'Looks like they've got the place locked down tight,' I said. 'I doubt we'd be able to see anything.'

'Keen to get back?' Pierce asked, his tone a trace loathsome. I had forgotten that he knew about the drinking, and I disliked the possibility that he might be needling me about it. 'It's typical, though, isn't it?' he continued. 'We come out here wanting a brush with disaster, something real, and end up being fed a bunch of bullshit by PRs.'

My irritation with Pierce jagged upwards. So I wanted to get back and drink, true, but he had no right to say it. Or imply it, anyway. Knowing about my problem didn't mean he knew me. Perhaps I felt a little guilty – I was the one cutting the *dérive* short, even though it had been my idea. Perhaps these thoughts were all facets of the same general dismay about the way the day had turned out.

Anyway, hurt, I aimed for a spot on Pierce that I knew would hurt back.

'Isn't all this fussing over "authentic" urban experience a bit try-hard?' I said. 'A bit hipster-ish?'

'*Hipster*-ish?' Pierce said, and I was pleased at the affront in his voice. Bull's-eye. 'I'd say it's the opposite—'

'But it isn't,' I cut in. 'It's as anxious as the flannel shirt and the vinyl collection. An obsession with status, with defining yourself through experience. Getting mugged as some kind of artisanal treat. A pop-up that gives you something to Facebook about, something to define yourself to your friends. A marker of status, victimhood and depth.'

Pierce was glaring at me, but he didn't respond.

'When I read *Night Traffic*,' I continued, 'I loved it because I could relate it to my own experience; it took my memory, my trauma, and, without diminishing the ugliness of it, stripped away its *ordinariness*, gave it qualities I could appreciate.'

'That's exactly the kind of self-help bullshit people want from writers,' Pierce spat back. 'Exactly what I wanted to avoid. This idea that autobiographical writing has to inspire, which means everything becomes a lesson, so "how I got over this trauma" gets the unspoken addition "and you can too" and everyone's lived experience turns into a Victorian lecture on moral fibre and self-improvement.'

'But you didn't live it! You didn't overcome anything! It wasn't autobiography, it was fiction!'

'Nevertheless—'

'No! There's no nevertheless! A forged bank note isn't worth half of its face value, it's worth nothing!'

For the first time in our acquaintance I felt that something I had said to Pierce had really affected him. The indignation and pride that he had displayed moments earlier were gone, and he had the same haunted look he had at times when we first met, when he must have been weighing up the confession he was about to make. The squareness and bulk of him was unchanged, but now appeared baggy and tired, not a reservoir of force. I knew what it was: he wanted to salvage something, to retain some of his reputation as a writer, some of *Night Traffic*'s renown as literature. And he was seeing that it might not be possible.

'If you want to go ahead and come clean,' I said, 'you're going to have to get used to this kind of reaction. Worse. People won't want a sympathetic interview. They will want me to beat you up on the page, and if I hold back, they'll do it themselves. The days of good faith are *over*, my friend. Everything you did, it won't just be considered a sin, it'll be considered an insult, and that's so much worse.'

My innards lurched. Not nausea, though that was coming – an instinct I had gone too far. However long and wrong this day had been, I still had to get a feature article out of Pierce. The truly great interview I had seen shining before me was still attainable, unless I drove Pierce away. He might simply decide to clam up; worse, he might decide that there was no value in having this pet magazine journalist if he wouldn't even follow instructions, and go to one of our rivals, or a newspaper.

'You *do* want to go ahead?' I asked gently. We had reached the overgrown base of the stairs up to the footbridge. As we ascended, Pierce kept his head bowed, thoughtful rather than humble.

'I do, I do,' he said. 'I have to. Quin, remember? And I have to get on with my life. There has to be a way to do it that minimises the backlash.'

This struck me as delusional, but I admired his commitment to the idea. Maybe it was just denial, or a natural but misplaced desire to weasel out of the full consequences of his fraud. However I thought there might be a little more to it than that: an urge towards literary experimentation. Pierce wanted to take an established prose form, the confessional interview, and screw with its boundaries and conventions. And, truly, I wanted to enable that in any way possible, even if it meant being a passive enabler of what he had in mind. What I did not want was for him to take fright and decide to do it the normal way with the *Sunday Times*.

'You have to understand why people will be angry,' I said. 'It'll be seen as romanticisation of crime. Genuine victims of crime will be angry, especially if they read the book.'

'You're a genuine victim of crime,' Pierce said with a drop of acid. 'What makes you angry about it?'

'Well, you lied your way into my trust, which is a betrayal,' I said. 'Reading something like that is a two-way process: you, the author, are opening up to the reader, but in turn the reader feels as if they're sharing something with you. Regardless of how adeptly you did it, you were taking a creative holiday in my misery. That's as bad as fraud, really, because there's this implication that you *wanted* to experience an attack; rather than merely finding the good in a terrible experience, you were making that case from nothing. And you really don't want to experience an attack. The second time I was mugged, it . . . well, it really fucked up my life.'

We had reached the top of the stairs, disturbing a skulking pigeon. It fled up and out in an explosion of wings and scrambling claws. But before I clocked that it was a pigeon, I saw the pale burst of escaping feathers and a shining avian eye and imagined a rarer bird had been waiting for me.

'Can you tell me about it?' Pierce said. 'That second time?'

No, I realised – it wouldn't make sense and he wouldn't understand. It was too open to interpretation, and might not obviously support what I had been saying. 'I don't think I can,' I said. 'I'm sorry. Not now, or here.'

The encroaching gloom had made the footbridge a tunnel through Hades. Its few lights revealed enough of its slick, foul surfaces to make the threat clear. Another stunted winter day giving up. Coming through here alone, at night, was as unimaginably unwise to me as trekking solo through a crocodile swamp.

'We know getting mugged is horrible, Pierce,' I said. 'You don't have to go through it to know that. The fear of it spills out, infects the city. Places like this. It shuts down parts of the urban circuits, corrupts the operating system.'

'I think you'd be pretty safe here,' Pierce said. 'No one in their right mind would have a good reason to come here at night. Not even muggers. I hear what you're saying. But fear isn't a good measure of a situation. We fear lots of things that turn out fine. And there are lots of other things that we should fear, but don't.'

On the platform, huddled out of the steady, heavy almost-rain, we talked briefly and ambiguously about what would come next. I said I'd be in touch the next day. Pierce said he'd think about it. The pub excursion we had originally sketched out was forgotten. The pub is useless for determined drinking. I needed quiet, and privacy. The fridge had to be restocked. I needed to be away from people, all people, but especially Pierce. I needed the kind of clean that alcohol gave me, the dreamless sleep. Peace, alone on the sofa, a kebab or a box of chicken, that first beer, that *n*th beer. I could taste it – worse, I could *not* taste it, not yet.

Was there material to write a feature? Of some kind, sure. If 2,000 words could be woven out of fifteen PR-supervised minutes with a distracted celebrity in a hotel room, there'd be no trouble getting it from this sprawling wreck of a day. We had talked for hours. But at the same time I felt that he had told me very little. Most obviously, he had not even hinted at *why* he had faked the book. This waffle about 'authentic urban experiences' was not entirely convincing, not least because it contradicted itself. It had the smell of a smokescreen thrown up to obscure something else. Perhaps this was genuine journalistic instinct on my part. It hardly mattered because as I was thinking this, he stood beside me – jacket collar pulled up against the cold, hands crammed into pockets – and I didn't ask him. Getting away was more important. The minutes creaked by. No device is slower than the orange-lit information display in an unimportant station. Out at the edge, among the hubs.

For the rest of the journey we spoke very little, and it wasn't a long journey. Pierce got off the train at Barking in order to get the Tube back to Bow Road. I stayed on, aiming at Fenchurch Street. The train moved with little urgency, as if it could feel the rush-hour pressure building up in the city at the end of its line, and feared that approaching too fast could cause the whole place to rupture.

I checked my phone. More emails. I skimmed the senders

and subjects: there was an email from Polly but it was routine office stuff, no sign that De Chauncey or his press person had gone crying to Eddie. A couple of Twitter notifications, people favouriting things said by other people that happened to mention me. I hadn't said anything worthwhile on Twitter for days. Just empty I'm-alive, Is-it-lunch-yet stuff. What would really set my feed alight would be to tweet something like: 'Just spent day with @Oliver_Piercing. Major interview coming soon.' But that might inspire other journalists to get in touch with Pierce, seeing that he had decided to 'break his silence', and he might talk to them. I could tweet a tease: 'Spent amazing day with next interview subject. Rarely speaks with press. Going to be a big one.' But that's just annoying, isn't it? Perhaps I could layer the tease with some ironic distance, serve it backhand: 'I hate those teaser tweets, "secret meeting today, big story coming soon", but today I really want to do one!'

But that just made me hate myself.

This is what I tweeted: 'I am on a train. It is moving very slowly.'

Which was no more than the truth. I tried to bring up the @Oliver_Piercing feed, thinking – fearing – that Pierce might be coming out of his hole. But it was still blank, an error message.

Polly was in my notifications. She had favourited something I said about interviewing Bill Nighy back in early 2014. Why would she do that? Was it a deliberate message of some sort? Or just an accident, a slip of the finger? Either way, she was rooting about in the deep past of my timeline. Why? Looking for something? Evidence? She was unlikely to find anything. My online persona was a work of art. Modest, but without disingenuous self-deprecation. Always out doing interesting activities, but never boastful about them. Occasional wry jokes but no clowning or waggishness. Worldly without being jaded. Warm without being syrupy. Humane without being preachy. I liked to think that even my silences had a particular quality to them.

Not much was happening on Instagram. I took a photo of my copy of *Murder Boards* sitting on the stiff, worn fabric of the train seat next to mine, taking care to show its beard of bookmarks. That hit the right note. Literature. Work. Research. London. On the move somewhere. But not first class, oh no. Maybe the slightest hint at what I had been doing all day. Nothing that might contradict any later lies I might want to tell about missing the De Chauncey meeting. Perfect.

I had Tamesis notifications. Information for Fenchurch Street, as it had guessed in its spooky way that I was on a train heading there. A message from Kay.

Where are you?

I replied: *Been out & about w Pierce. Heading back now.*

Was she checking up on me as well?

The Tamesis screen flickered and refreshed, refilling with streets and labels and tags and coloured heat. *Travel Alert*, it warned. *Delays to C2C services into Fenchurch Street. Avoid if possible. More details / Show me other routes / What people are saying / Dismiss.* I dismissed the warning. It might have been possible to avoid C2C services if I wasn't sitting on one.

Twenty past five in the afternoon and as black as night on a viaduct snaking through Limehouse. I raised myself in the seat to look around the carriage. There were only a couple of other passengers. By now the train was at least thirty minutes late.

In the darkness, graffiti on the side of a new apartment building:

BUILD ROBOTS
DESTROY RENT
AND
TAKE THE REST OF HISTORY OFF

An electronic *tok* emitted from the train's public-address system, and it crackled softly as if an announcement were about to come, but nothing happened. The crackle, a machine breath so gentle it was barely audible, continued – the sound of expectation, of something about to happen. Anything coming over? No.

Updating London . . . said Tamesis, the Bunk emblem spinning. East London unfolded on the screen again, with the rail line into Fenchurch Street an angry red and the District and DLR baleful orange. The map pulsed with markers. *Fenchurch Street: Overcrowded. Avoid if possible. Tower Hill: Overcrowded. Avoid if possible. Bank-Monument: Overcrowded. Avoid if possible.* Breakdown rippling outwards. *Are you affected? Please tell Tamesis. We might not be able to help, but we love to listen!*

From Kay: *U in east? Drink?*

I replied: *Trains all ducked up.*

The little Bunk-star under my words turned from grey to blue, indicating that she had read my message, but it did not pulse – she wasn't typing a response. Nothing coming over.

Restlessness was mounting in me. The window that De Chauncey had left open was closing, causing a familiar churn of emotion: foreboding, and sickly delight. Even if I had wanted to hare over to Shoreditch and meet the man, the trains were now preventing me. I was obliged to go home and drink, boo hoo. It was perfect, and I started composing an excuse-filled email to the PR, hope that the disruption was severe enough and widespread enough to be news, to get into De Chauncey's bubble, and keep intact the illusion that I had made every effort to reach him in reasonable time. But there was still that fore-boding. Even if he accepted that there were real train problems, it didn't clear up his schedule, or his disinclination to help me out. That thought needed dousing in lager until it went away. Tomorrow had to be obliterated. That was the only job on my to-do list. And the train was keeping me from that, as well. Every minute I spent sitting in this inert train was another minute I could be safely back home annihilating the future. What had promised to be a long evening of drinking was receding into being a standard-length evening, or even a short evening. My insides crawled with dissatisfaction. Never enough time to waste. At least I would be home all day tomorrow. But, in theory, working – I had promised Eddie. What were the odds of getting a draft done? I needed one, even an 'unauthorised' version. I might be able to brazen out the De Chauncey situation if I had something really explosive to show Eddie, even a (carefully edited) transcript. But it didn't seem likely. Not with all the drinking I had planned.

The train lurched, and stopped again. Its halt had a more permanent quality this time: the engine sound dropped out completely and the lights flickered. I expected an announcement – I wanted an announcement – but none came, and the unre-solved possibility poisoned the air. Clicks and pings came from below, components cooling. I thought about the becalmed freight cars in their Dagenham sidings, weeds growing up around their axles. We were probably only metres from a station. A more serious problem? A bomb, gunmen on the loose? I took a look at Twitter and Tamesis again to see if bad news, awful news, was breaking. It wasn't. But Tamesis knew that something was up. Its real-time experience rating of Fenchurch Street and all other City stations was *bad and falling*.

On Tamesis, there was another message from Kay: *Do you*

want to meet up? I liked Kay, but this was horrible, horrible, my evening, she was crashing my evening. Which was, in any case, trickling away minute by minute on this *fucking train*.

Who was I kidding, thinking that Pierce would go ahead with the interview? He'd be home already, deciding obscurity was better than infamy, or on the phone to the *Sunday Times*. I'd be left with nothing, or an angle piece about how I almost had the story but let it slip away – which would probably have to involve coming clean about my own problem, if I did it at all.

What was wrong with this *fucking train*? It was serious, evidently – either that, or the heaters were on the blink, as an acrid smell was filling the air, beginning in the pocket of membranes at the back of my mouth. I rocked in my seat, and craned up again to see if I could detect any panic among my fellow passengers. No obvious alarm. One young woman was hissing a lengthy complaint about the situation into her mobile phone, but the others gazed without focus and did not frown or sniff as toxins misted the air.

'I've got to get out,' I said, gathering my things into my bag. There was no way off, of course, the carriages were sealed tight, air thickening and fouling, vents coughing fumes, but on a superstitious level I thought I might be able to jog the train into movement by acting as if arrival in the station was imminent. Also I simply had to move – to stay still was to be stifled, to invite paralysis and collapse.

My legs dissented under me. I found myself swaying against seats, attracting wary glances, being assessed for drunkenness, criminality and mental illness. Yes, yes, I'm sorry. No. I fear so. Again the speakers of the PA system clicked and crackled, but no words came over. The train *did* move, it shuddered again like a great beast dying but instead of dying it lived and *moved*. I looked through the window, seeking a familiar landmark to orient myself, only to see my own reflection, low-res in the smeared, scratched glass, eyes dark pits. I squinted and focused as the train gathered speed, and saw a line of white lights or reflectors beside the track. Except they were not reflectors or lights. They were birds, lined up on a wire fence, watching the train. Cockatoos, white cockatoos, not watching the train, watching me. They knew me.

At Fenchurch Street I had to physically shoulder through a crowd of irate City types, and one of them called me a 'fucking cunt', and I sincerely hoped they all got trapped together on a stinking train. Gulping the damp, cold air in a brick arch outside the station, surrounded by hunched and angry private misery, I realised that the District Line would be as bad or worse. I just couldn't face it. So I looked for a pub.

SIX

I've given some advice on how to write profiles. Here is some advice on how to be profiled. One piece of advice anyway, but maybe the most important: bring the interviewer close to you. The closer the better. Some people are wary of interviews and keep their distance, assuming that distance means safety. So they'll want to do the interview by phone, or – horror – by email, not in person.

This is a mistake, a big mistake. Distance is safety *for the interviewer*. It insulates them against feeling for their subject, and silences the scolding of their conscience.

Instead, draw the interviewer close. Meet them in person. Even better, meet them in your office or home. Make them tea. Make them a sandwich. Introduce them to your partner and your children. Clear the toys and phone bills off the couch so they can sit down. The journalist will snoop a bit, but your cooperation will give them a warm feeling inside. More important, they will have looked you in the face and drunk your tea. Their conscience works for you now. The guest–host obligation is still very strong, instinctive, hard to shrug off. It's an ancient, beautiful, sacred part of the human experience. Exploit the hell out of it.

(Of course, none of this will work on the turd-hearted soul-gaps employed by some tabloid newspapers. Nothing will work on them. Remember that they are scripting an entire alternative reality. You are, to them, nothing but substandard copy, and the facts of your life will be edited to suit. This is the price of briefly featuring in the imagination of a rapacious billionaire. But for the profile editor of, say, a modern urban lifestyle magazine, this approach will work fine.)

I can't remember what my earliest job title was, back on *Divider* – as I say, today it would be 'intern' but back then, only a fraction more than a decade ago, it was 'junior editor' or 'features assistant' or similar, and paid actual money. Which was welcome, because the role included one of the most hated tasks in the office: gathering 'vox pops' for a page on which 'normal people' (like you and me!) said what DVD release they were most looking forward to. I would go to Covent Garden, or Brent Cross, or Camden Lock, with a photographer and we would accost people. No one wanted to know. I got told to fuck off more times than I can count – bright points of human contact in otherwise total invisibility. Naturally the magazine was only interested in pleasant-looking people aged eighteen to thirty-five, because those were the only people that advertisers were interested in, so a lot of people were invisible to us as well. Of the small minority who did meet the demographic requirements and who did stop to talk about DVDs, many had inadequate English, or were keen to explain that Hollywood was SATAN'S

REALM, or they wanted to show off about going to see a Todd Solondz film in the 1990s. Respondents willing and able to answer our questions mostly didn't have the slightest idea about what was about to come out on DVD. (Think about it – do you?) Eventually we started taking out a cheat sheet, a list of prominent releases due in the next couple of months, to jog memories and maybe prompt some useful answers. All this work to produce a dozen headshots and priceless insights such as 'Can't wait for *The Polar Express!*'

It was never easy to approach strangers and ask them questions. Every time, I felt as if I were rucking against basic social training. And for no good reason. Those days would have dark evenings. After the Christmas mugging, I discovered that I simply could not do it any more. A photographer and I had gone to Greenwich for the day, and the weather was against us: scathing wind off the river, hail-hard drizzle. I approached a couple of people and was rebuffed: no time, no way, no English. My brain was prepared, once more, to put duty over taste. But my body was launching a protest. A cold, acrid mass of resistance was building in my chest, heavier with each passing moment. It waxed especially massive when I reflected that I was obliged to gather at least twelve usable responses before we could consider calling it a day. After twenty minutes or so I felt anchored to the corner, unable to move, almost unable to breathe from this leaden, freezing obstacle deep in my core, a pillar of misery, my mind struggling to think of ways to justify my body's total refusal. Could I claim to be ill, or fake a crisis phone call that would summon me away? As it happened, the photographer picked up on my private hell. I can only assume that it wasn't as private as I thought.

I told her about being mugged, and she was sympathetic, very sympathetic. We went to a nearby pub to warm up and have a drink – a pint, before noon. At once the glacial obstruction dissolved.

'Tell them,' the photographer said. She had ordered a bloody Mary, which had the poster-paint look of long-bottled tomato juice. 'They can't expect you to go out and do these interviews after something like that. Tell them you won't do it any more.'

'I don't know,' I said. This was my first real job and I felt I was in no position to be making demands.

'Then let's fake it,' the photographer said. 'I'll snap the first twelve people who come along, and you make up the quotes. We'll be done in half an hour.'

I was shocked by this suggestion. What if we got caught? She pointed out that the odds were steeply against discovery. The magazine was read by a few tens of thousands of people, ABC audited. That sounded like a lot, but it was nothing against the national population, and we would probably be photographing tourists anyway. They'd be back in Houston or Milan by the time their picture appeared next to a heartfelt endorsement for *Saw II*. And even if one person did discover their picture was used without their permission above an invented quote, where's the harm? It was a memory-card mix-up, nothing more. Big deal. A one-line apology in the next issue, if anything. My qualms about this amused her, and she told me about some of the sleights-of-lens she had been asked to do for other magazines. For my magazine. It was eye-opening.

'Look, I'm under no illusions,' she said at last. 'I'd really love to be doing Diane Arbus, Kevin Carter stuff. I can take a great photo. This isn't photography. This is the coloured sludge used to stick adverts together. It doesn't matter.'

Nevertheless, I couldn't do it. However safe we might be from discovery by readers, our bosses might suspect wrongdoing. That would be more serious.

So, after a couple of pints, I sent the photographer home and went into the office. There, I gave my section editor and the overall editor a straight account of what had happened, that the mugging made it impossible to do this assignment. They were formally sympathetic, making such gestures of fellow-feeling as social obligation and their legal responsibilities militated, visibly restraining their frustration that such a miserable and hated job was back in circulation, while still being sure to let some of it show. I was of course to be excused the task – that was what basic courtesy demanded, backed by the helpful shadow of human resources problems down the line. Their hands were tied. The only price I had to pay for playing such an immediately winning card was some discomfort of my own, of being made to feel that I had somehow conjured this hindrance to the smooth running of the magazine out of nothing.

A discussion of options followed. A couple of junior members of staff floated into the frame but were disqualified; there was talk of giving it to an intern. (The magazine industry at large was just waking up to the potential pool of free labour offered by internships, and was oblivious to the harm – they had struck oil in the basement of a burning house.) A day of photography made the page relatively expensive, I discovered.

At last the decision was made: they would fake it. The page would remain my responsibility, but I would use photographs from the vox pop archives, and invent the quotes, with an emphasis on films that would please our advertisers.

And so it was, for four months. I was certain that the ruse would be immediately exposed. It never was. What really stayed with me was the insouciance of my superiors. As if this sort of thing was nothing new. As if it happened all the time.

My point, such as it is, is that all interviews are acts of intrusion. Whether it's a sleeve-grabbing ten-word vox pop, or a lavish

5,000-word *New Yorker* piece, intrusion is the art, the craft of it. Social boundaries will be crossed. It's inevitable. Done well, no one is unhappy. No – not quite, not always. If an interviewee is delighted with an interview, if they think it's the most marvellous piece of writing ever, the interviewer is left feeling a little sore. A little cheated. It's even worse if the subject's PRs are ecstatic. Because you could have gone further. No boundaries were pushed.

You don't want the subject to be happy. You don't want them furious, either – Quin-level furious, editor-phoning furious. You want them to be grudgingly pleased, with maybe just an aftertaste of having been used. You want them to use words like 'fair' and 'close to the knuckle'.

There's an acceptable level of intrusion. An acceptable level of truth-telling. There's even an acceptable level of treachery. Think about that. An extent to which you can misuse a subject's trust without losing their cooperation and gratitude entirely.

And there's an acceptable level of snooping. That's what the interviewee consents to when they invite the journalist into their home – a certain amount of bookshelf-browsing, furniture-price-deducing and family-photo-studying, in return for a little more obligation and sympathy.

It's a deal, a contract. And you broker it as you go along, mostly, without very much being explicit. There are parts to show and parts to hide. There are comfort zones, and they are not bounded by neat, hard lines but by fertile zones of possibility. The discomfort zones, the border areas before one reaches the no-man's-land of broken trust and inexcusable breaches, are where the interviewer does business.

Pierce had brought a loaded gun to the negotiation. The contract with him was truly, uniquely, symmetrical: if I revealed anything he didn't like, he would reveal some truths about me. He had hacked the deal.

A line from Quin floated into my mind: 'People know they shouldn't feed so much information into their apps. But they do it anyway. Because they like the way it feels. They like to trust. And they know, the more we know about them, the more we can help them.'

Where had I heard that? Was it from the interview, a line only just bubbling to the surface now? Or had it come from somewhere else? Everything Quin said was TED-toned, rehearsed, audience-ready. No beta utterances. But this felt like something he had said to me in person, face to face. Where? When?

When I first felt the obstruction, the resistance, in my stomach after the abortive vox pops, I thought it was no more than a consequence of trauma, and that it would weaken and dissolve with time. Wrong. It strengthened and grew.

I've called it the Need. That's not quite right. It's difficult. These are sensations that taunt and neuter language. Something inside is screaming, and it doesn't use words.

But it can always use a drink.

The Need wasn't about drink, it was about everything. It existed before the drinking really started, it was already there. It did not elevate drink in my mind, or draw me towards it – what it did was shut down everything else. The drink was just what it left behind, the only respite. The Need blacked out the laptop, the clothes on the floor, the phone, the shower. Even looking at the laptop, and thinking about a day's work, was impossible without my guts and lungs clenching up. It foreclosed all other options. All it left clear was the path from the bed to the fridge. The Need filled every other corner, it was in me and choking me, like smoke.

The flat was cold, the tiles of the kitchen floor icy under my bare feet, but the Need didn't care about that. I took a can of

Stella from the fridge, cracked it open and sipped. The world opened a little.

No warmth came in with the thin grey light that filtered through the branches of the neighbour's tree and the filthy glass roof of the kitchen extension. It was too cold, colder than it should be. I put my hand on the radiator – it was almost as chilled as the aluminium can in my other hand. My first thought was to fire an angry email to Dave, the landlord. But then I looked at the clock: half past eleven. The central heating had turned itself off three hours ago.

Next door, the drill started up, battering away at the foundations. The tiles vibrated, my teeth vibrated. Was it just starting now, or had they been going since first thing? I didn't know. Either way, it hadn't woken me. Eleven thirty . . . I went back to the fridge. There was a plastic-banded four-pack of Stella in there, untouched, and a second band with only one can left in it. And the can in my hand. Six cans. Had I bought two four-packs last night, and drunk two cans? Or had I bought three, and drunk six? Whatever had happened, it had been enough to really knock me out.

Figuring the question, standing in the kitchen in my underwear, lager in my hand, I came up against the edge of something. An absence, a ragged hole in my memory where the previous evening should be stored. What time did I get home? How did I get home? It was before the corner shop closed, as I had bought cans . . . I tracked back, trying to find the end of the Sellotape. I had been with Pierce. We had parted company on the train. I had been on the train alone. It had been a bad journey. Then I went home.

No: I went to the pub.

Pubs make dim memories, by design. Light comes fourth-hand in a good pub, through dusty lampshades, frosted glass, glinting brass and bulging optics. Someone had shoved me at Fenchurch Street and I had been upset. I had a copy of the *Evening Standard* – the plume was on the front page again, with the headline 'Met Admits Drone Loss'. That was all quite clear. I had found a suitable pub. I had bought two pints of Stella. Both for me. That little memoroid, as it came bubbling up from the foamy depths, made me squirm. Two pints. I had been on a mission, a speed run to painlessness, and I didn't care how it looked to the barman or to anyone else. I used to dabble in spirits for that, quick results, but a couple of terrifying blackouts last year meant I now stuck to lager for my own safety.

Around here, my memory failed. The video stalls, the 'buffering' symbol spins, the image smears into nightmare blocky garbage. I shivered. It was cold in the kitchen, and all over the flat. I took my almost-finished can back to the bedroom to get dressed, trying to ignore the chaos of empties and unfinished fast food in the living room, and the atrocious state of my stomach and head.

I should do some work, I thought. I really should do some work. After I dressed I opened a second can of Stella and started gathering the empties from the foot of the sofa. Six cans were on the floor, one of which, I discovered, was nearly full. So I had drunk a little more than five. Not an excessive amount for me, far from it, although I had no idea how much I had drunk in the pub before then.

Blackouts were nothing new. Every night is a blackout, really. I rarely have any memory of either falling asleep on the sofa or of making my way to bed later. If I had been out drinking alone, a blackout was not uncommon. I avoided one of the pubs near home because the landlord had taken against me after a couple of incidents. Nothing violent or disgusting, just pathetic. One time I had simply fallen asleep, and it had – I was later told – been difficult to rouse me. Another time I had become rigidly drunk, literally paralytic, mannequin drunk, and had to be guided from the premises by the proprietor with a degree of physical exertion. Spirits had been involved. Then, some time later, one of the regulars clocked that I was still outside, rooted to the same spot on the pavement where I had been deposited, staring up into the sky, or at the tall Victorian houses all around, 'as if you were waiting for your fucking space ship to come back', the landlord observed, without amusement.

A man can get a reputation that way. I never liked that particular pub: under-populated, over-lit, sinister. Suspiciously durable furniture. A man can get a beating that way. A proper pub beating must be coming, there's an inevitability to it. I had done well to avoid it. Shortly after that second incident, a couple of hundred pounds was stolen from my bank account. It's impossible to be sure how or why this happened, but I believe my card details were taken that night in the pub.

I am more careful in the pub at the end of the street. I keep my patterns there conspicuously normal. A pint, maybe two or three, over the Sunday papers or after work. Never a really heavy session.

Often, an alcoholic will go to considerable effort to avoid being seen drinking. Before I became a drunk, I used to go out and get drunk with work colleagues. It happened often. Now, I might go out after work, but I will never get drunk. I will drink conspicuously little. I can't take the risk of letting go. Indeed, I don't like to go out with people from the magazine, because – a few sniffs aside, a bottle or three, barely enough to blunt the edge – I'll essentially have to abstain. So I refuse, or leave early. A few of them must regard me as a lightweight or a bed-by-

Newsnight sort. In fact I am going home to get the evening started.

I really should do some work. I took the full can I had found on the floor and used it to refill my fresh can. I did this over the sink, not risking more damage to the carpet, and felt very thrifty and houseproud. A little foamed over, and I carefully ran a tap over my hand and wiped down the can to avoid stickiness.

Turning, I saw the cockatoo again. It was in the oily branches of the neighbour's tree, shocking white through the sooted glass, lazily stretching out its wings, letting me know that it had been there a while, watching. Watching this whole time.

You can't just drop an unbelievable detail into an otherwise straightforward profile. It jolts the reader, jolts them out of the belief that you are a faithful conduit of the truth about the subject. If something unbelievable presents itself – the noted barrister used to be a shark-wrangler and is missing two toes from her right foot as a consequence; the acclaimed author is a fabulist who invented the meat of his bestselling non-fiction book; the promising journalist is a secret drunk who has padded a dozen recent interviews with recycled material and is being stalked by a vengeful cockatoo – you must take the reader's side in their disbelief. Confirm. Ensure you heard correctly. Ask for corroborating evidence and explanatory background. And account for the reader's likely reaction in the text itself: 'Unbelievable as it might sound . . .'

The cockatoo sounds unbelievable, I know. I have to account for it. For a second, long enough for the wet, heavy can to slip through my wet fingers and fall to the tiled floor, producing a spume of foam, I thought I saw the bird. Then I saw the truth: it was a plastic bag, caught in the branches of the tree over the back garden, exactly the same bag on the same branch as produced the same shock yesterday morning. Yesterday, on the bridge, it had been a pigeon, nothing more exotic than that. On the train – well, I don't know what that was, a line of reflective stripes in the darkness perhaps, but I do know that it was not a posse of malign avians. There is no cockatoo and there never was. I know. But every now and then, for a moment . . . I have to describe it as I see it, whatever it is, a mild hallucination, a recurring perceptual glitch, an outward manifestation of a kink in the psyche.

This particular kink isn't even discreet enough to be properly repressed. I know exactly what it refers to. It's so transparent it's embarrassing.

It relates to a lie I told. Not 'my first' lie. Who remembers their first, anyway? Little children have elastic standards of truth: to say something is to make it so, because the past disappears so quickly for them and the future is impossible to imagine. All that matters is the eternal present, in which – literal hand-in-the-biscuit-barrel stuff aside – the lie is the only thing that is real, and is therefore the only thing that can be considered true. Many little children are natural moral philosophers with bright careers ahead in politics, public relations and marketing.

No. This was the first time – I believe – that I invented a story for the entertainment of my classmates, and to make myself appear more interesting. A school friend of mine had been to visit his cousins, who had chinchillas. These animals lived in a big, complicated cage and were let out to be petted and to climb on my friend's shoulders. As he described visiting the chinchilla-cousins, and the fun he had had there, I saw the attention he was getting from our mutual classmates, and I wanted it for myself.

So I invented my own story. If it was exotic pets they wanted, that was what they would get. I said that an uncle of mine had a cockatoo, a white parrot, and that it had come to visit us. It sat on my uncle's shoulder, making him look like a pirate, and ate pieces of fruit from my hand. I don't know where I got the cockatoo image from, why that in particular and not a monkey or a ferret or a snake. But it worked. Some of the attention I coveted came my way. My friends even debated which was better, cockatoo or chinchilla, which annoyed chinchilla-boy no end. Graciously, I sat out this debate, proffering no opinion of my own, and secretly rejoicing that in some eyes my fictitious bird trumped his stupid rodents. It was so easy. It resembled magic – my brain had improved reality and captured the admiration of my peers, at no cost and with very little effort. Of course I would do it again.

A few lies down the road, I realised there were costs and hazards. I had to remember all the details of my edited reality and keep them consistent. If this uncle had come to stay with us, where had the cockatoo slept? Did it have a portable cage, or a perch, or what? No one had the knowledge to gainsay what I said, but I had to 'know', to invent, a terrific amount of supplementary knowledge to answer their questions, and I had to remember it. The more invention, the greater the risk. Other times, I stumbled into areas my classmates *did* know about, which was dangerous. One Monday morning, on a whim, I said that I had been taken to Thorpe Park at the weekend. But a friend of mine had been to Thorpe Park, and recently, and quizzed me about what rides I had been on and which were my favourites. My vague half-answers made him suspicious. He didn't openly challenge my story, but I could see him doubting it. This close shave should have stopped me – I can remember swearing to myself to stick to the truth – but in the end I was simply more careful, I put more thought into lies and deployed them with more caution. I refined my craft.

In any case, I couldn't draw a line and swear to the truth, because so many lies were in circulation already. If the cockatoo came up again, I would have to stick to my story. It wasn't easy to keep track of the lies, but I found myself well suited to the work. More troubling, in the long run, was the solvent effect all this invention and embroidery had on my memory. I had regarded the truth as solid and substantial, and the lies as very different, bright little additions to that edifice. Baubles on the Christmas tree – you know what's glass and what's conifer. But it wasn't like that. Memory proved more liquid than solid. Everything ran together. I found myself thinking that the cockatoo was real, that it had existed and that it had come to our house. The story had become so detailed and vivid, and had been repeated so often, what was the difference? In my mind, it was now being treated as memory. Stranger still, real incidents in my past – events that I knew had happened, that I could confirm – took on the taint of fiction. If the past could be endlessly rewritten and adorned, then none of it mattered, none of it was really real.

Thus, the cockatoo. I had made it, it was mine, it would not leave me. And it was not truly 'there', out there. What was out there was a white plastic bag, snared in the branches of a tree.

That, at least, was easy to deal with. Having picked up the dropped can from the floor, I left it on the counter so its remaining contents could settle, and wiped up the spill. I then opened a third can and took a single, contemplative sip as I planned my approach. Then I put on my shoes and coat, unlocked the back door and went outside.

It was still raining – it had rained all night. The tree might be in the neighbour's garden, but its branches spread out over my garden (Dave's garden). It was a lime tree, and as the rain dripped through its branches, it picked up a sticky secretion. Everything in my garden (Dave's garden) – a white plastic picnic table and a couple of chairs, a rusted barbecue, a couple of empty plastic planters – was covered in a thin layer of this vile, tacky substance, which never washed away or dried. Instead, it attracted grime from London's air. The once-white walls were streaked with black, the glass of the kitchen extension was dimmed by dirt, the plastic chairs adhered to you and left smutty marks on your clothes.

I hated few things like I hated this tree. Blocking my light was bad enough – did it really have to piss filth as well? I had once heard that trees could be killed by hammering a copper spike into their trunk, near the base. Since then, I had harboured fantasies of assassinating the tree. A moonless night, a stake to the heart, an ancient evil slain. When the neighbour's rebuilding plans emerged, I thought that the one bright side might be the removal of that damned tree, but it was apparently protected. A fully grown tree in Zone One – there are, I am told, many rules. Another indignity: its residence was far more secure than mine.

The bag appeared to be knotted onto the branch, and I didn't fancy my chances of being able to knock it loose from the ground. It was beyond the reach of the kitchen broom, as it was over the kitchen extension and I couldn't stand directly underneath it. However it was only a couple of feet above the glass roof of the extension – if I climbed onto the garden wall, and over the roof, it would be in easy reach.

Reluctant to spend long in the rain, I pulled one of the plastic chairs against the wall. To prevent it slipping away when I climbed on it, I dragged a rainwater-filled plastic planter over as well, jamming it against the back legs of the chair, trying to anchor them in place. Then I climbed up onto the chair. Grabbing on to the top of the wall, ignoring its freezing gritty wetness, I pulled myself up, using the back of the chair as a foothold. The plastic yielded in an alarming way, protesting its inability to support my weight, but I only needed its help for a second. With the top of the wall under my belly, I was able to get my foot onto the roof of the kitchen, and from that firmer foundation I could heave myself further up, and ultimately to straddle the garden wall.

From the top of the wall, I had a clear view into my neighbour's garden. I emitted a low curse – not pain or anger, but surprise. Awe.

I hadn't spent more than ten minutes in the back garden since the autumn. Why would I? Even in the summer it wasn't a particularly pleasant place to be. So I had not seen the house from the rear, not for a while. I knew, from the front, that much of the interior of next door was gone. The street-facing windows, their sashes replaced by Xs of wooden bracing, showed sky above. Now, from the rear, I could see exactly how much of the house was gone.

All of it.

The street facade was all that remained, held in place by a wooden framework. Thick black plastic covered what had been the 'inside', and the walls of the neighbouring properties, including my house. The whole effect was medical, a body bag. But where was the body? Everything was gone. No interior walls, no floors, no ceiling. The gap in the terrace was spanned by some props at about the level the floors should have been, stopping the rest of the street from simply falling into the hole.

And what a hole it was. The house hadn't been demolished down to the foundations – the foundations were gone too. The tree, which stood towards the rear of the back garden, was on top of a steep-sided little hill all its own, skeletal limbs of root sticking out from the slopes, washed clean and ghastly pale.

Apart from this hillock, the garden had been excavated to a depth of three or four metres. The digging had gone deeper under the house itself, or where the footprint of the house had been. A rough earth ramp, kept in shape by steel coffers, led down from street level into the pit, which was at least a storey deeper than the floor of my own basement flat. It was hard to tell precisely how deep, as the pit was part-filled with gravy-coloured water. An orange digger and a generator were sinking into the mire, like forlorn relics from a mechanised trench war.

I found myself fearing for the safety of the wall I was sitting on. What was holding it up, a lip of dirt, mere habit? Looking down – a swill of vertigo – I saw heavy steel sheets pressed up against its base, supported by props sunk into the mud. Would that be enough? No workmen were on site – today's drilling was coming from the other side, where similarly ambitious works were under way, and in half a dozen different places in a two-street radius. The council had tightened the rules and there had been a rush of project approvals ahead of the deadline.

It was madness. My extortionate little cellar had sometimes felt like a dungeon or a mineshaft, a hole in the cold, pressing earth. Now I could see it was a tissue box, exposed on both sides, and fragile. Home.

Not wanting to risk the wall much longer, I inched towards the bag. All the time, I was able to feast my eyes on the works next door, on the totality of my neighbours' 'renovation'. And I felt dizzy anger stirring up inside. I had to email for permission before hammering in a nail to hang a picture, and God forbid a pipe should burst. And next door, where they had a whole house, it had not been enough, they had given up trying to squeeze more out of the Victorian structure and had swept it away in order to build something that better matched its vast price tag – and pushing that value even higher in the process. Far beyond my means, of course. Even this hole, this puddle they had made, would be worth far more than I could ever imagine possessing, on the dream of the house that might appear here. Nothing but a number floating in space, a price tag with many zeroes attached to one big zero, an IOU for one house, a transaction, and everyone agreed it was too much for me. What was wrong with me?

I was above the glass roof, and within grabbing distance of the bag. I grabbed it. It spilled a trickle of freezing water down my wrist to the elbow, a treat stored up in its folds. But it was firmly in my hand and I did not intend to let go. I pulled at it but it didn't come away from the tree. I pulled again, harder, loosening a cold shower of drops. I lurched to one side and had to clamp my legs together to avoid sliding off the wall. For a ghastly moment I imagined myself falling into the neighbours' pit, hitting my head and sliding into the scum-lined pool at its bottom. Maybe my body would never be found – the concrete would be poured and I would end up interred beneath their home gym and wine cellar, a sacrificial victim to the success of their investment. It could be the closest I came to home-ownership – a deposit on someone else's property.

Regaining myself, I looked up into the branches of the tree, trying to see if there was an obvious way to untangle or unhook the bag. But it was not the bag that caught my eye this time, or anything that the neighbours were doing, but a familiar, dark shape, distinct even against the low, clay-thick clouds. The plume.

That I could see it from here was a surprise; that it was still there to be seen, an even greater surprise. Could it really be the same column of smoke, from the same fire? A second giant, skyline-swamping blaze in one week was hardly likely – it must be the same fire, still going after three days. Or was it? I wasn't sure about its location in the sky, not quite the direction I would expect Barking to be, more to the south . . .

But the deeper levels of the spine and the gut knew exactly what they were looking at. The plume's silent movements, that python swelling and squeezing, was just for me now, the menace of the quiet youth in my path who has made full eye contact and is holding it. For a moment I fancied that it had followed me home.

I had to get off this wall. Again, I pulled at the bag, hardest yet, and the branch buckled. Once more I pulled, gripping the wall as tightly as possible, and the branch broke, not cleanly, a nasty diagonal tearing-split that left it attached by a strip of bark. But I had it now. I stopped working on the bag and yanked at the detached section of branch. It tore away without too much effort and I threw it, and the bag, down into the next-door chasm.

Reversing myself along the wall was harder than I imagined. The cold cut the feeling from my hands; the damp made every movement unpleasant. Dizziness was setting in, an after-effect of the vertigo. I wondered if I was about to be sick, and the idea was briefly pleasing – not only a way to purge myself of the curdled remains of last night, but also my way of paying a tribute to next door's work. Swinging around, I pictured myself falling through the glass roof, into the kitchen, landing on the table among the empty and half-full cans in a snowglobe of shards – I had seen it so many times in movies, always so beautiful, often funny, but not something I wanted to try for myself. I imagined bad falls, bad landings, arteries severed, bones snapping like the branch, spinal fluid spilling, paralysis, slow painful death. My numb fingers tightened on the top of the wall.

Perched like a burglar, I reached out a foot to the chair-back I had used to climb up. Why had I positioned it away from the rear wall of the kitchen, widening the gap I now had to span?

Even with only a little weight on it, the chair-back flexed unpleasantly. But I had another problem. My other leg, still on the roof, was oddly wedged, knee bent at a harsh angle, with none of the slack I needed to swing it round and down to the chair. I tried taking more weight through my arms, hooking my elbows over the wall, but this just spread the discomfort to other parts of my body, and caused cold water to seep into my armpits.

Whatever the way forward, I had reached the point of no return – I didn't have the strength to heave myself back up again. I started trying to inch my leg off the glass, finding that my biggest obstacle was the plastic gutter at the edge of the roof – I couldn't lift my leg over it, and I didn't like the odds of it taking much weight.

Frustration flared up in me. All the softly-softly approach had achieved was to contort me into this ridiculous position. One strong, swift movement was needed: push up with the arms as hard and as far as possible, swing out the trapped leg, and bring it down to the seat of the chair. Up, and down. And dismount.

Not quite one movement, as it happened. An assortment of movements, mostly not deliberate, mostly graceless, mostly downwards.

My foot, as expected, caught on the gutter, which sloshed a cold soup of decomposed leaves. Panicking, I tried to pull myself up on the wall, but this action instead led to me putting a lot more weight on the back of the chair. The chair slipped, bending out from under me. My arms slipped too, moving from an uncomfortable position to an intolerable one, with my face now pressed up against the top of the wall. My panic went into its second act, developing its themes with gusto. The gutter pinged away from the roof with a great arc of slimy water, and my arms lost their struggle with gravity. I fell the rest of the way – not a straight, hard, bone-snapping fall, but one of those falls that takes a surprisingly long time, in instalments, through varied terrain, with a lot of scraping contact along the way. My crotch and the inside of my right leg had a long involvement with the chair, my face and right arm remained in close communication with the wall, my left hip crunched against the glass wall of the kitchen, my left foot – eventually, after much time – landed in the water-filled planter, which tripped me, sending me all the way down to the patio.

A drunk's fall, long-drawn-out, no drama, all ghastly farce, slow but unstoppable, a cringe to watch. The reason long-term, fatal drunks look so physically battered. The kind of fall that doesn't kill you the first time, or the second time, but will one day.

Hitting the ground, all the breath was blasted from me, tearing at my throat and lungs on the way out. I had banged my head, front and back – the blow to the back frightened me at first, until I realised all the pain was coming from the right side of my face, which had made grinding contact with the wall. Ringing metal pain, all the way through the cheekbone, the upper jaw and around the eye socket, back to the ear. Everything felt twice as large as it should be. Pain elsewhere too, but nothing more than I deserved. I was soaked, and filthy, and lying on the soaked, filthy paving of the back garden, but it felt like the right place for me. Above, through black branches, the pulsing shape of the plume.

And Quin's face. That fierce but honest face, a shining bald head.

'I used to hate beta testing,' he said. He had said? When? To whom? 'The beta – when things broke, or went wrong. I just wanted everything to work. But now I love that stage. You learn so much. When things break, that's when you see how they really work. You have to stop pursuing the ideal and respect the real, what's on the table in front of you. Broken machines, broken software, broken cities, broken people. You can work with them. So much potential.'

Where had he said this? In the pub? We didn't go to the pub when I went to interview him. It appeared he had said it to me, in person, I could see his face saying it to me, in person, in the pub. An unattributed quote.

Back indoors, I intended to strip off my ruined clothes, take a hot shower, dry off and settle down to some work. But the Need had spread out again, filling every corner of the flat, apart from the path to the fridge. A can first. I had been through a lot. I deserved one. Only two were left in the fridge, somehow. I drank. The top of the can came away from my lips smeared with red.

I slapped my hand to my face. After coming in from the wintry garden, I was cold, very cold, but my cheek was scorching to the touch. My hand, when I took it away, was painted with blood.

The face that appeared in the bathroom mirror seconds later had hurried from the set of a horror movie, not from the kitchen. A Twombly of blood and dirt was spread across my right cheek, streaking gore around the lips, back to the ear, up to the eye, down to the line of the chin. I soaked a flannel and started to wipe, fearing that my addled body had sent out the wrong signals, that I might be severely hurt or maimed, scarred for life. A big step towards being the human wreckage shivering in the corner of the pub or on the park bench, the perma-wounded, in a relentless downwards spiral of needless trauma.

But once I had splashed cold water on the mess – delicious, clean pain – I found it wasn't so bad. It wasn't good, but it wasn't hospital-visit bad. A nasty scrape – really a dozen or so scratches, a couple more like gouges, in an area of raw skin the size and colour of a slice of supermarket chorizo. Around this was a zone of thump scarlet, which I expected to bruise nicely. It was ugly, and dumb, and would need a few lies ready-prepared to explain it to people, but that was all.

I showered. Normally I wouldn't bother, facing a day alone, or I'd spend the day intending to, but never get around to it. But I ached, I was freezing, my clothes needed changing, and even I can't sit comfortably and drink through that. None of my other pains gave me cause for concern, although the pain in my head was atrocious – one of those headaches that resided in the roots of the teeth, in the knot that binds the spine to the brain, in the dark recesses under the eyes.

The shower gave me a terrific sense of achievement. Something achieved – two things, if you counted the plastic bag! – and the day only a little more than half done. Wearing my dressing gown, I started work on the next priority: consolidating the assorted empty and half-finished cans I had hanging around, yielding about two cans-worth of lager. Having thus set things on a solid basis, I put one of the open cans in the door of the fridge, sat down on the sofa with the other, and turned on the TV.

I really should do some work. But I had done a lot already and had earned a sit down.

My phone was jammed between the arm of the sofa and the cushion. Plucking it out, I stared at it. Much unpleasantness might be stored up within. My absence had been agreed in advance, at least. Here I was, 'working from home'. And no missed calls – that was good. But there would be consequences from my failure to meet De Chauncey. At best, another time would have to be arranged, something I could take to Eddie and Polly to show willing. At worst, De Chauncey and his people would be full of umbrage, there would be no later appointment, and Eddie and Polly already knew all about it. Yesterday I had been fairly sure that a strong Pierce interview would let me ride out those repercussions. Today I felt less sanguine. Deliberately defying Eddie's express wishes might cancel out any credit accrued from a genuine Pierce scoop.

But it was still possible that I might just be able to make another time with De Chauncey and glide through the whole situation. I found a relaxing programme on one of the factual channels, a man in a windcheater learning how to make a coracle, and settled down. Eyes shut, I opened email.

It wasn't so bad. A peck of nagging from Polly – a passive-aggressive 'Hope it's going well today!', a sinister 'Can't wait to hear your ideas!' and a quietly threatening 'See you tomorrow!!'. A one-liner from Eddie: 'How did it go with Alexander?' For a moment I feared that it might be a trap, that he might know everything and was trying to tempt me into a barefaced lie. That wasn't really his style, but it was possible. I didn't answer either of them. I did, however, compose a genial email to De Chauncey's PR, to see if time could be found later in the week. Nothing else of consequence. Office email successfully fielded. My glow of achievement gained lustre.

I moved on to other notifications, for Twitter, Instagram, Tamesis, Tumblr. My blood froze.

Tamesis was on, for a start. Generally I tried to disable it before a heavy session outside the flat. It wouldn't reveal my location to people I know, that wasn't how it worked. But it might, possibly, steer somebody – a workmate maybe – into the pub I was drinking in, and that was dangerous. It was too easy to imagine: Tamesis whispering in Polly's ear, 'Hey! Why not try the William Blake this lunchtime?' and a gang of my colleagues finding me there, chewing my second or third pint on my own.

I had switched Tamesis on when I was with Pierce, and had left it on. And when I had got to Fenchurch Street, not knowing the area, I had asked it for the location of a quiet pub. I had never switched it off. And now it was full of messages and alerts. Hundreds of them.

I am extremely careful with social media. I know the risks. One of my greatest fears – held in the folder 'career death / social endgame' – is that drink and self-pity suck me into a bout of horrible honesty on Twitter or Facebook, which of course I then do not remember. The way I find out about it is like this, in the morning, checking my phone. Because it could happen any night, every morning is marred by the fear – the fear that I have gone viral. If there's one thing people enjoy, it's watching a stranger's secret shame explode in real time.

With this in mind, the most chilling sight in the world is an app icon stamped with a very high number – 99+ notifications on Tamesis, the number was maxed out, and relatively high numbers on my other accounts too.

Feeling faint, feeling the grey creep into my peripheral vision, muscles slack in the hand and wrist, I thumbed into the app and tried to find out what had happened. This was not normal, this was 'racist rant' not normal.

But it was all good. Dozens of people wanted to be my Tamesis contact. People I had never heard of before, people I *had* heard of, but who couldn't have heard of me. Prominent journalists, tech people, people whose name I knew from TED Talks and *Wired* articles, Bruce Sterling, Warren Ellis. There was a lot of other activity too, mostly people liking or responding to an update from last night that mentioned me.

It was F.A.Q. Of course. Quin and me, in fact, in a selfie – no, not a selfie, a picture taken by someone not in the frame. He looked as composed as ever, wealth-casual. I looked a bit bleary and wary but OK. In the pub. It was fading back in, now, maybe thanks to the rising alcohol level in my blood. Quin appeared in the pub with someone else, a colleague maybe, and had joined me at my table without any noticeable awkwardness or hesitation. Quin's companion – I had the impression he was a subordinate – had bought a round of drinks, and almost immediately disappeared to take a phone call. When he came back he made an excuse and then disappeared for good. Even in my reduced state, it had seemed a little convenient. I was left alone with Quin. He wanted to talk about Pierce.

I could remember the picture being taken, the way Quin told his colleague to take it and didn't ask my opinion, total confidence, the warm arrogance of it.

The caption read: *Great to run into interviewer supreme Jack Bick, always a T-plus – speaking truth to power!*

Then a load of tags: *#influencer #thoughtleader #Tplus #socialvelocity* etcetera etcetera. In Quintalk this was glowing praise. As founder of Bunk and the creator of Tamesis, Quin had a terrific amount of juice within the app's user base: he might not have more contacts than anyone else, but he was in the top twenty. That kind of recommendation, magnified by that kind of reach, was an immense boost to my Tamesis profile, making me appear far more important and interesting than I really am. The spike in my numbers was astonishing, and was mirrored by bumps on my other social media accounts. This in turn had prompted a flurry of interest and envy from people already in my networks.

A couple of pieces I've written have had a few days of intense popularity online, and you could say they had 'gone viral' in a small way. Nothing newsworthy, just a few hundred people taking notice all at once, maybe low thousands, not the hundreds of thousands or millions of true virality. Maybe it doesn't even count. But you only need a few hundred shares or interactions to make it feel as if you are being constantly bombarded with notifications and messages, and it's possible to see the vortex of interaction start to sustain itself, attention breeding attention, as if it might never stop.

Magazines and writers want this kind of feverish attention, and consultants earn handsome fees telling publishers how to get it. It should feel good. But it doesn't. It feels horrible. You are no longer in control of something that you have made – it has a volatile life of its own. There's often a nasty edge, people saying they hate your work or that you're wrong wrong *wrong*, or that they simply don't see what the fuss is about. But even without that, going viral feels horrible. Eyes and minds in the hundreds, come to join you. Hello, here's a crowd, in your head. Every word, every decision, every silence, up for view. Something big, something much bigger than individual net users, stirred and skulked behind all those screen names and icons; it had noticed you and you didn't really want it to notice you and you couldn't take anything back.

Print didn't feel like this. But in the office, the digitisation effort quietly advanced, scanning, transcribing, proofreading. Every mistake, every bad decision, every borrowed line, brought into view of the unsleeping search, the giant.

After a lull, the drilling started up again next door. The vibration it sent through the fabric of the flat made the woodwork click and buzz and produced a tinny rattle from two cans touching each other on the side table. I moved one, stopping them clattering together, feeling the fillings in my head, the maturation and glory of my headache.

What was Quin playing at? Building me up higher, so I had further to fall? But surely that would rebound on him – he'd look a fool if he turned around now and said, 'This guy Bick, this #thinkfluencer, he's an incompetent drunk.' Perhaps it was just head games, designed to produce exactly this confusion and angst. Perhaps it was entirely innocent and he really thought I was a #brainleader and so on.

Improving the connectivity of the human network, Quin said about Tamesis – setting up chance meetings and happy accidents, boosting social capital and creative collaboration. It was all in his TED Talk: Steves Jobs and Wozniak are introduced by a mutual friend, Lennon meets McCartney at a church fête. 'You could call it fate,' Quin puns, strutting around on the stage. Pause for laughter. 'I call it the connectivity dividend. A day without an unexpected encounter is a day wasted. Loneliness, isolation, exclusion – that's the noise in the human network. We need to boost the signal.'

Well maybe, Quin, but in my experience connection caused plenty of noise of its own.

Another Quin aphorism: 'The only sure way to predict is to make things happen.'

Make things happen. I found Alexander De Chauncey's Tamesis profile and added him as a contact. Then I had second thoughts: if he looked at my Tamesis profile, if his account wasn't handled by his PR, the first thing he would see would be that Quin post. What I was doing the previous evening, instead of seeing him. Did that look rude? Or did it look . . . high-powered? Might it raise his opinion of me?

For good measure, I T-plussed him. That wouldn't have any effect unless he followed me back, but if he did follow, I would be ready.

Another Quin quote: 'We rely on chance – why not make it reliable?'

I really should get some work done, but I was down to my last can and I feared that if I didn't go to the shop, my anxiety about the fridge might impair my productivity. And I couldn't go to the shop without getting dressed, so for the time being I was staying put. My phone was beside me. Notifications still came in from time to time, new contacts on Tamesis, new Twitter followers. It was on vibrate, so when it was down the side of the sofa I had hardly noticed it in the din of power tools from next door. I might have missed Pierce's call altogether had I not been holding the phone in my hand, dismissing notifications, when it rang.

'Jack.' His tone was business-like, unpromising.

'Hi.'

'I've come to a realisation,' Pierce said.

Here it comes, I thought. I wondered if I should be recording the call, in preparation for a more hostile unauthorised article, or even to protect myself in court. This thought made me remember my voice recorders – and I was again skewered by panic. Had I laid eyes on either of my DVRs today? I had not. Where were they, post-bender? Where was Pierce's confession? A wisp of data on an inexpensive storage device in a bag lugged about town by an erratic drunk – that was all that was supporting my career.

'Go on,' I said, dizzy once more, the grey curling in.

'Well – first of all I want to apologise,' Pierce said. His words, these and the following, sank in slowly, taking time to deposit meaning in me. 'I behaved pretty badly yesterday. Rude, I mean. Putting you on the spot like I did, all that . . . I don't know . . . I don't want to say blackmail. It's not like that. But I put a lot of pressure on you.'

'Uh-huh,' I said.

'I'm pretty stressed about all this,' Pierce continued. 'You know, *Night Traffic*. Quin pushing me, messing with me.'

'Sure,' I said. 'Quin's, uh, Quin is . . .' But I didn't have anything to finish that with.

'The truth is, I really am determined to set the record straight, to come clean – Christ, why is everything about this such a cliché? I don't know – to *confess*, to tell the truth, to make amends – to *atone*, that's it, that's the literary word. I want to *atone*. And I think you're the guy to tell that story.'

'OK,' I said. I felt as if I had to clear an obstacle course in my head to get a full sentence together. 'That's really great to hear.'

'Something you said yesterday really stayed with me,' Pierce said. Again he had the practised manner that I had noticed during our interview; he had thought through what he was saying, rehearsed it. 'You said that when people find out about *Night Traffic* they're going to be angry – they'll want to see me get beaten up.'

'Yes,' I said. 'I mean—'

'That's it exactly,' Pierce said. 'What I was avoiding – the part I can't avoid. So let's do it. I can balance things out, show that I understand what I did wrong and that I want to put it right.'

A weird thought occurred to me as I tried to figure out what Pierce meant by this. But it couldn't be right.

'I need to get beaten up,' Pierce said.

I had been right.

'I'm going to get violently mugged,' Pierce said. 'The worse the better. And you're going to watch.'

SEVEN

It all rested on Pierce's confession. No: it all rested on my recording of Pierce's confession. That was everything, my muscle, my back-up, my leverage. Without the recording, the confession was inconsequential. It might as well have never happened. It would be his word against mine, a proven liar accusing an unproven liar. A *degenerate, desperate drunk*, accusing an *acclaimed author*. I had two recordings of the interview, but only one included the confession, and little else mattered. Or rather, I assumed it included the confession. But I had blacked out. Had I lost or damaged the DVR? One evening a few months ago I had spilled most of a can of Stella into my then-laptop. What my reaction had been at the time, I don't know. Maybe I hadn't even been aware. I discovered the accident the next morning, confronted with a soggy, sticky keyboard and a black screen. Hundreds of documents, hundreds of photos and hundreds of pounds, gone.

The other danger was that the recording had never happened. I was habituated to fuck-ups with interview recordings – it had happened with Quin. Button not pressed, wrong button pressed, low or dead battery and no spare, low memory, background noise, microphone in the wrong socket . . . In recent months I had made a comprehensive survey of ways to fail to do this essential part of my job.

And there was . . . a fear. I had not laid eyes on the DVRs since parting from Pierce. I needed to check the recordings. But the other Need had me. I could not do it.

It's hard to explain this incapacity. Why not just look, find out? Because if I had fucked up, but I didn't yet know that I had fucked up, the fuck-up had not truly happened, not yet. Drink helps see things this way – the drink, the Need, means that I can sit here on the sofa, paralysed with low-grade anxiety and fear, but able to deal with those problems because I have drink. Meanwhile the disaster, the possibility of disaster, is all conditional and abstract and positioned safely in a range of possible futures. It's susceptible to the kind of anaesthesia that drink provides.

What alcohol provides to the alcoholic is delay. It doesn't make your problems disappear, but it does defer them – it delays the point at which you will have to care about them. The price of this service is steep, but it always looks like a good deal at the time. 'At the time' is all that matters. Addiction is a kind of time travel, or the opposite of time travel: the obliteration of all the bad decisions that have led to a moment, and all the possible consequences and horrible unfoldings of that moment, so that only the moment exists. The past is soothed and the future postponed.

But this whole magical process only worked as long as there was beer in the fridge, and there was none left. The precious moment was dissolving. I would have to act, I would have to get up and go to the corner shop, and I would have to go out and see Pierce, and I needed to check the recordings of the interview. The commitments I had made were fading back in, a growing racket.

The shoulder bag I took to work was in the living room, leaning against the seldom-used armchair with the poor view of the TV, the one heaped with dirty laundry. It troubled me, the bag. Its shape troubled me, its poor posture. It was guilty. Something had happened. An ill odour clung to the thought of the DVRs.

I stood and – not thinking too much, trying to silence the awful thinking that was coming in now that I didn't have anything to drink – picked up the bag. Then I returned to the sofa and sat with the bag in my lap.

I stayed like that a while. Then I opened the bag.

It looked pretty good. There were my notebooks and assorted pens, and my copies of *Murder Boards* and *Night Traffic*. My laptop was there, safe in its padded side-pocket. The other worthless bits and pieces that float around in my bag were all present: a comb, a couple of memory sticks, a USB cable. There were no DVRs.

The bag's lining was black and quite loose, and it can be easy to miss objects. I took it through to the kitchen and started to methodically remove every item from the bag, laying them out on the kitchen table. There were no DVRs.

I ran my hands around the insides of the bag, feeling every seam and pocket, feeling the whole thing in its unusually light and empty state – it's never empty, this bag, never. I squeezed it, exploring if something might have slipped in between the lining and the fabric of the bag itself. There were no DVRs.

They were gone, both of them. I had lost the recordings of my interview with Pierce.

A period of numbness followed. I went to the corner shop and bought twelve cans of Stella. I smiled at the man behind the counter and said 'cheers' when he gave me my change. I walked back to the flat and put the cans in the fridge, except one, which I opened. I looked at the kitchen table, where the contents of my bag were still neatly laid out. I did not feel despair, or anger, or depression. I didn't feel much of anything at all – just emotional tinnitus, a rising, meaningless clamour within, drowning out any effort to put together a coherent reaction. I did not feel that all was lost: on the contrary, one of the sickly aspects of alcohol's deadening of consequence was that there was always hope, deluded hope – not hope at all but hope substitute, hope methadone, the dull synthetic buzz that left you thinking that perhaps you still might be able to turn around that 2,000-word profile that was due first thing in the morning, when it is already nine thirty in the morning and not one word has been committed to the screen. Not hope, then, but a continued flight from the implications of what had happened.

One ugly truth: I was now obliged to go out and spend the evening with Pierce, on the possibility that I might be able to do something to recover from the loss of the recordings. I could get his confession again, maybe, or at least a couple of quotes that I might be able to use. Some shreds of a feature that I might be able to take in to show Eddie and Polly on Thursday, or Friday if I decided to go to ground tomorrow. Even as alcohol shuts down my ability to understand anything coherent about the future, it has the extraordinary effect of stretching out that future, so that the eighteen or so hours between now and my appearance in the office tomorrow might be for ever, enough time to do anything, to achieve anything, to right all the wrongs and mishaps that were piling up around me.

Pierce had explained his plan to me over the phone. He wanted to recreate the circumstances of his invented mugging for real, in the hope of being attacked for real. The long, terrifying ordeal he had invented was unlikely to be replicated – or *enacted*, as it had never taken place – but he might at least get threatened and robbed. Maybe even roughed up. That, he figured, was enough: enough to show remorse, enough to show a willingness to atone, enough to show that he understood the reality of what he had created in fiction. What about the risk of more serious harm, I asked – what if he got himself stabbed? Well, it's a risk, he said, but not very probable, especially with a witness there. Meaning me. He didn't sound concerned. Indeed, I was left with the impression that he welcomed the risk. Did he want to get stabbed? Probably not, but he wanted the risk, he wanted it to be a real possibility. He wanted to put himself in the way of the blade.

What I did not understand was my own role. In *Night Traffic*, Pierce had been alone when he was attacked; this time, I would be with him. That must affect the likelihood of becoming a victim. He dismissed my concerns with a 'We'll see, we'll find out.' I don't want to get mugged again, I said. Fine, said Pierce. Run. But not too far. I need you to witness.

That was the important part. He needed a witness. There could be no ambiguity about the facts. He needed proof. And so did I.

'Anything I need to bring?' I asked.

'Your phone?' Pierce said. 'There might be a chance to document

– you know, to film or something. Or photos, afterwards, of injuries.'

This made me think of my scraped face. 'Won't they take my phone? If it happens.'

A thoughtful pause. 'Yeah, I suppose. Back up your files. You have insurance?'

'I think so.'

'Then you're fine,' Pierce said merrily. 'You get a new phone. Sorted. Everyone wins. Oh, and dress smartly. Jacket and tie. Like you've been to a posh party.'

The fabrications in *Night Traffic* were set against a background of established fact. Pierce had been to a party, the launch of a friend's book, and had drunk a good deal. Not as much as me on an average night, but a good deal for a civilian. Another friend, who lived further east, out in Leyton, had called a minicab, and had offered to drop Pierce along the way. They had expected to leave the centre via Whitechapel Road, which would ultimately pass by the end of Pierce's street. But the driver had instead chosen Commercial Road. It had been a warm night, and rather than argue and demand a detour, Pierce had asked to be dropped at the bottom of Burdett Road, a long connecting street, intending to walk the rest of the way home. He was cheerful from drink and friendship. I remembered nights like those. Halfway, he deviated from the main road into a side street, trying to shave a minute or two off the walk.

This much was real. The party had happened, the cab-ordering friend was real, the cab was real, the chronology to that point was easy to verify and check. So that was what we would do.

I napped for a while before going out, the fog of horror at the loss of the recordings having manifested as a terrible tiredness.

The alarm on my phone woke me at seven, and I was sure that I would have slept on without it. Changing into the jacket and tie that Pierce had mandated was an ordeal of heavy, aching limbs. Everything had frozen in place on the sofa, held with an aching frost, and moving shattered me anew. In the mirror, I studied the damage to my face. It had lost some of its delicatessen rawness and was adding smoky purple bruising at its edges and in the lower pocket of the eye. Tomorrow morning there would be some explaining to do in the office, if I made it in. The shirt and tie made it look worse, somehow. A bookie's clerk on the wrong side of a gang, a low-rung City sort after a fracas in an Essex nightclub.

I took some Stella on the Tube, poured into an aluminium water bottle I used to take to the gym. It held almost two cans, good for most London journeys. Anything to clear the sluggishness, the soggy fatigue in my bones.

Pierce was waiting for me in a pub beside Limehouse Station – almost underneath the station, beneath the elevated line I had spent so much time on yesterday. He greeted me like a friend, springing up from his seat, gripping my hand, patting me on the shoulder. Just thirty-six hours earlier, this would have delighted me, but now it was disquieting. Energy crackled around him, a bright photo-negative to my lethargy. He was on edge, volatile, and I wondered if he had taken something, either licit or illicit. It could simply be adrenalin.

'What happened to your face?'

I decided to give the truth a go. 'I was trying to get a plastic bag out of a tree in my back garden, and I fell.'

'Last night?'

'This afternoon.'

Pierce examined me. 'I thought maybe Quin had beaten you up.'

This stopped me. It was said without malice, but the fact that Pierce knew about my encounter with Quin meant I had to adjust the pieces on the game board in my head. If, that is, he did really know – could this be a joke that doubled as a lucky guess? I had assumed that Pierce's disappearance from social media meant that he no longer looked at it, but that was not necessarily true. My accounts, and Quin's accounts, were all public, anyone could see them. Pierce might have anonymous accounts of his own for quietly keeping tabs on things. I thought of that rush of unfamiliar followers over the past twenty-four hours.

'You saw that?' I asked.

Pierce nodded.

'I ran into him,' I said, trying not to sound guilty. On a technical level, I was pretty sure I had nothing to feel guilty about, but guilt came anyway. 'I went into a pub for a quiet drink on my way home, and he came in a few minutes later.'

'What an amazing coincidence,' Pierce said, eyes wide, cartooning innocence. 'Tamesis knew where you were, I suppose?'

'Yes, I used it to find the pub.'

Pierce stared at me, smiling, knowing. I had put together these 'coincidences' myself. I could readily imagine what Quin had done, but I still could not quite face the reality that he would misuse his own software like that. Why I couldn't, I don't know.

'Happens a lot around Quin,' Pierce said, 'that kind of coincidence. If I was still writing journalism I might be more interested in that.' He gazed deep into his bitter.

'Perhaps, in the piece, we can expose some of Quin's involvement,' I said. 'Since he'll no longer have any hold over you.'

'Perhaps,' Pierce said. 'I don't relish the idea of making an enemy of him, mind. What did he want to talk about, anyway? Me, right?'

Partial truth. 'I don't remember. But yeah, a bit about you. I think he might simply have been trying to mess with me.'

Pierce smiled. 'That might be 90 per cent of the reason he does anything. All the personal data he has amassed from his various projects gives him power, but . . .' Here, he frowned. 'What's strange about Quin, for someone so successful, is that he's terrifically angry. Maybe that's not strange. I had success, I was celebrated, and it did weird stuff to me. Anyway. He's made a lot of money. Millions, tens of millions. Maybe he thought that would give him the power to do what he wants. Not super-villain things, just . . . When we first met, he just raged about the city, about London. The cost of housing, how his staff couldn't afford their rent and had to commute for hours, the expense of that building in Shoreditch, how money was killing everything. He'd go on and on about the 1980s and 1990s, how great it was, empty buildings everywhere, artists, designers, squats, crime . . . No wonder he was a fan of mine, no wonder he liked *Night Traffic* and *Murder Boards*; I suppose it was a link back to that kind of grungy, squatty stuff.'

'Before my time,' I said. I hated to think about it. Soon the city would spit me out, dead, half-dead, or alive. Without my job, it was over. And then what? No other job, that was for sure. If people like Quin couldn't make it work, then . . . It made me angry, too. With Quin, as much as anyone. 'I would have thought he was responsible, at least in part; he's been the face of trendy Shoreditch for so long, him and his dazzle-pattern building and apps to help you find a good cold-press place and share photos of your ostrich burger.'

'Yeah, and you're a feature writer for a glossy magazine on Old Street, and I'm a *Vice* writer, a lapsed *Vice* writer anyway. We're all to blame. Christ, what was the name of the guy who founded your magazine? Aaron . . .?'

'Errol,' I said.

'Well, there you have it,' Pierce said. 'Didn't he do the first pop-up shop?'

'There's some dispute about that,' I said. Errol certainly believed he was the first, never having heard of market stalls or car-boot sales. But this didn't seem an appropriate fact to bring into the conversation.

'What's he doing now?' Pierce asked.

'He has a creative consultancy,' I said, fearing I was letting the defensiveness tell in my voice, and wondering why it was there at all. I revered Errol. His eye for the new, the pre-popular, was without parallel. He could make a magazine sing with metro-politan desire. He *was* the modern urban lifestyle, without doubt, and without visible effort. Eddie didn't encourage the Errol cult too much, which I could understand. They had been difficult shoes to step into. But sometimes, when Kay or Freya or I were convinced an idea was interesting and could not be dissuaded, Eddie invoked Errol. *What would Errol make of this?* He was more than the first editor: he was the first reader, the perfect reader, the one we had to please.

But when this had to be explained to an outsider, it could sound stupid. What would Errol have made of Pierce?

'And he publishes a magazine, *Networth*, for, uh . . .'

'Very rich people,' Pierce said. 'Yeah, I know it. They asked me to write a piece about Hackney Wick just after the Olympics. "London's Meatpacking District" or something.'

'What did you say?'

'I said yes, what do you think?' Pierce chuckled. 'Pound a word, fucking phenomenal. It was funny. "So you want me to sell the place?" I said. "Make it sound good?" No, no, they said. Make it sound dirty, *edgy*. That's what'll sell it. Like it's got *potential*.'

'Quin said something similar,' I said, not loudly.

Pierce drummed his fingers on the table, an impatient look coming over him. 'Honestly,' he said, 'I thought you'd be more excited about this. Great colour for your piece, isn't it? Better than a trip to Dagenham in the rain.'

Perhaps I should fake some enthusiasm, some crackle and verve, to make the excursion into the kind of zany adventure that I had once wanted to write about. But I could not. Since the loss of the recording, it was no more than an uphill slog, a Quixotic errand on the road to maybe avoiding losing my job. 'It's difficult for me,' I said, choosing not to share those musings, and use my victimhood instead. 'I really don't want to be involved in another mugging. Even to watch. That's assuming that it happens, and I don't think it will.'

'You don't have to worry,' Pierce said, without much sympathy in his voice. 'You'll be fine. I'll make myself the focus. You can – I don't know – recede. Not too far, though.'

I frowned. Pierce's conception of what would happen clearly resembled a chat with a charity fundraiser or an encounter with a street performer, not a terror-based robbery. If it happened – if! – I sincerely doubted that it would be something I could just step back from. The whole art of mugging was to shut off the exits, to enclose the world and charge for readmission.

He thought that he would have some kind of control over events. But that's what the attacker steals first, your control. And they never really give it back, even afterwards.

'You're very confident this is going to happen just the way that you want,' I said.

'Yeah, I've got a good feeling,' Pierce said, still with that bubble of energy. 'Really good feeling. I can see it perfectly.'

'It's not like imagining a scene,' I said.

'Well, it has happened to you twice,' Pierce said. 'It happens.'

'Not on demand,' I said.

Though the self-assurance in his words had hardly changed, Pierce had seemed diminished by my mild scepticism. But now he recovered, taking on that lecture-hall manner again.

'When I was writing *Night Traffic*,' he began (and I expected him to look from me to a spectral audience, as if we were on stage at Hay-on-Wye or Cheltenham), 'I came across a brilliant essay by David Freeman about muggers in New York in the early seventies, real behavioural sink, *Panic in Needle Park* stuff – do you know it?'

I did not. I shook my head.

'Anyway, there's two of them, man and woman, Hector and Louise. They work as a team. Louise acts like bait. She walks down the street, and when someone tries to chat her up, she steers him towards Hector, who puts a knife to his throat.'

If this information had any relevance to our situation, it was impossible to see. It might as well have been a tale of knights and chivalry, or cattle rustlers in the Old West.

'Yeah, but that's New York in the early seventies,' I said. 'Not . . .' I sat up in my chair and stretched out my arms, a gesture that took in the pub around us, the busy, bright, gentrified East End pub. After-work drinks that had turned into deep sessions, young flat-sharers enjoying midweek mini-breaks, sport on the telly, music. Maybe Pierce didn't see it, but I meant to take in the wider city: its intense inhabitedness, its unaffordable dormitory towers filled with fair folk watching TV and heading to bed.

'I know, I know.' Pierce looked deflated – perhaps even disappointed. 'It's a horrible story, anyway. Cockroaches, miscarriages. Another pint? Before we set out.'

It was a gloomy prospect for me, as well, this pub. Too many young couples, not married yet but not far off, talking about their work day before heading back to a building with two or three front doors. They'd have something waiting in the fridge, the rest of a big batch of chilli made at the weekend, perhaps, or a couple of M&S ready meals for the microwave. Maybe that would seem like a bit much effort, and he'd suggest, all sly, they get something in, and the phone would come out. And in half an hour they'd be unloading tinfoil trays from a sweaty white bag.

I had done that. Elise and I left *Divider* within a couple of months of each other – her for a recently launched news and opinion website, me for the job I have now. There was a leaving party every other week, it seemed, as the financial crisis raged and anyone with prospects headed for a lifeboat. And we both had prospects. Her website was the UK arm of a fabulously well-resourced US institution, a name that brought eye-rolls among print journalists, but with tycoons lined up behind it. The print journalists don't roll their eyes any more, and most of them aren't journalists or in print any more. Meanwhile I was headed for the reading choice of the taste-makers, one of the few physical magazines that looked certain to weather the eschaton of the analogue, because business-class lounges would always need something to go on their Noguchi coffee tables. Our combined departure brought urgency to our long-running discussion about maybe getting a place together, and we did it. Pooling our resources meant we could afford a small place that was fairly central – Pimlico, near Victoria Station, a reasonable midway between her work in Hammersmith and mine in Shoreditch.

It felt like the start. Excellent new jobs, a comfortable flat on a side street that was just for us, savings and mortgages and marriage possible soon. In the meantime we could enter the dress rehearsal stage of adulthood, where you do all those things that adults do, with just a little too much awareness. Doing the generous, laid-back adulthood that I never saw my parents do, which I assumed was the stage before their stolid permanence. Grown-up extravagances like ordering in food, which my parents did not do, but the adults do on TV. Going to the pub after work and talking about your day. Every day. Having wine with dinner. Every night. Not getting drunk, not really, just merry. But every night.

'Just . . . act happy. Drunk, merry, off guard. A soft target. Well-off, privileged. We should have our phones out, maybe. Definitely.'

Acting merry was less of a problem than I anticipated. To my surprise, I was a little merry. Pierce's fizzy enthusiasm had spread. Maybe my disco nap earlier was helping. Maybe it was my certainty that nothing would happen, that we were entirely safe, and I could simply observe Pierce, capture his erratic behaviour, and report it all.

Looking well-off was more of a challenge. My recent gaunt-ness comes as a nasty surprise when I happen to see myself reflected. Today's damage to my face didn't help. Pierce was little better. He did not suit a suit – it was not a question of build or fit or cut, it was a problem at the level of mien that left every part of his outfit looking wrong, a beach inflatable in the back of a car. If we rolled along looking jolly, I suspected that the impression would be more threatening than vulnerable, precisely wrong.

I had, perhaps, put my fingers to my scraped cheek as I thought about it – in any case, Pierce picked up that I was thinking about it.

'So how did that happen, really?'

I frowned at the implication. 'Like I said. I was trying to get a plastic bag out of a tree, and I fell.' Sometimes self-deprecation sweetens belief; why would you invent a story that puts you in a bad light? It worked well with lies, and it was disappointing that it did not work better with the truth. 'It was stupid. The drink, I suppose.'

'Why were you trying to get a plastic bag out of a tree?'

I hesitated. 'It was bothering me.'

'How?'

'It kept catching my eye.'

Pierce smiled. 'Well, that is pretty stupid. It wouldn't work in fiction. People expect nice clear chains of cause and motive. In life, of course, stupid stuff happens for no reason. Or it only makes sense for a second, not before, and certainly not after . . .'

I felt the cheek under my fingertips – the skin unfamiliar, rough, hot. Pain from touching, the odd moreish pain that can be controlled and savoured. Once again, I resented being interrogated by Pierce. He could not help himself.

'I have a question for you,' I said.

'Go on.'

'What really happened that night?'

'What night?'

'The night you didn't get mugged.'

Pierce frowned. 'I got dropped off by the cab around here' – we were on Commercial Road, under the spire of the Hawksmoor church – 'and I walked home, exactly the way we're going now.'

'That's it?'

'That's it. Nothing happened.'

'When did you decide to invent the mugging and write the book? Was it on that walk? Before? Afterwards?'

My main intention in this line of questions had been to shift the subject away from me; I also wanted to guide Pierce into saying more about his fraud, in the hope that I might be able to jot down some relevant quotes, or perhaps even record something useful on my phone, some indisputable proof that he had invented the story. I was surprised to find Pierce's manner becoming prickly and guarded – more than I would have guessed, given that he had already confessed, and I knew the truth.

'I'm not sure I remember,' he said, not with much confidence. 'What do you mean?'

'When did you decide to write *Night Traffic*?' I asked, and I realised that it was the question I should have been asking all along. It was a remarkable thing to do, to commit a fraud like that, to sculpt such an enormous lie. It was not a project one embarks upon accidentally or innocently; there must have been a genesis, a moment of inspiration or decision, an intent. He might say that people did stupid things for no reason, but this wasn't a drunken misadventure or a moment of madness. It was a book. It was 60,000 words of artfully constructed deception undertaken with total commitment. When? Why?

The longer I thought about it, the more vexing the chronology became. In the *Night Traffic* version of events, Pierce was traumatised by the attack and spent days and weeks shut up in his flat before deciding on using writing as a form of therapy. This period of seclusion was, again, verifiable fact: he had vanished from social media and stopped answering emails, a dry run for his later deliberate hermitage. The plan must have formed on the night, because he was already acting the role he had chosen the next morning. But the confusion with the minicab – that appeared to be genuine bad luck, a random event. Impossible to plan. Possibly the idea was already fermenting, and then fate proffered the perfect night . . . Nevertheless, it wasn't clear.

'Had you already had the idea to invent the attack? Or did you think of it while you walked this way?'

'I mentioned . . .' Pierce began, then halted. 'I said . . . about being unhappy with the kind of work I was doing, the kind of writers I was being bracketed with. That was before.' He was avoiding eye contact, thinking it through – or coming up with a plausible lie.

'And then you had the mugging idea on that evening?'

'Yes,' Pierce said uncertainly. 'The idea . . . Before that night, I wasn't going to write the book. Afterwards, I was.' He scowled.

'So what gave you the thought?'

'"Where do you get your ideas from?" Is that where this is going? I honestly . . . creativity really isn't like that.'

Curious. 'Even if nothing happens, it'll be good to see the, uh, the scene of the crime,' I said. 'You might remember something. Besides, it's on your way home, isn't it?'

'Yeah,' Pierce said. 'Like you say, I'm sure nothing will happen.'

Maybe not. But I saw it now: within the unravelling of Pierce's big lie, another lie was being revealed.

I had thumbed through the streets on my phone while we were in the pub, and I had a rough sense of where we were, a pointer moving on a mental map. Commercial Road was an unloved artery lined with architectural hulks left over from the time of the docks. Even this late, traffic on the road was constant and the pavements not empty. Ahead was the lighted citadel of Canary Wharf, the watchtowers of the banks. Behind that – and for the second time that day I felt a queasy kink of surprise – the plume.

The sight of it caused me to miss half a step and scuff my unfamiliar smart shoe on the pavement. It was not the smoke column itself, although it had the baleful presence I knew well;

this time, at least, it was where I'd expect it to be, maybe a little larger, a little wider, which gave it the illusion of being closer. No, it was the fact that I could see it at all against the night sky, against the solid dome of low cloud. It had the curious quality of being lit from below, perhaps by the ambient light of the city, perhaps by the fire itself. Perhaps it was a quirk of the atmosphere, an optical illusion – the plume could almost be somewhere in Canary Wharf itself, a towering inferno among the skyscrapers.

'Still burning,' I said.

Pierce had stopped a pace ahead of me. He glanced towards the towers and the plume. 'The lights stay on all night,' he said. 'I was once at a party with someone who worked for one of the big Square Mile law firms, and he said that if they turned off the office lights, even in the wee hours, they got complaints from clients. Not giving it 110 per cent, you see, not burning the midnight oil.' He shook his head. 'It's fucked up.' And he kept walking. I followed.

We turned left, north, onto Burdett Road. If you had a paper map – the large one on Pierce's wall, for instance – and a ruler, and you drew a straight line from the place he had been dropped by the cab and his house, you'd find that no roads came close to following that line. There were topographical accidents in the way, most significantly two canals. But we were also cutting across the grain of the East End, the main roads radiating out from the centre of London, the spider-web connections traced between those spokes. This urban rhythm, this warp and weft, was against us. By main roads, a lightning-strike zigzag, a steep backwards N, was the only path, and this turn took us onto its middle stroke. Pierce's shortcut – if it had happened as described – had been an effort to shave some of the distance from the zag.

My provincial childhood furnished me with memories of deserted midnight streets, sodium-sterilised, which gave a fugitive air to any lone cars that sped through, high above the thirty limit. Why linger? The last bus was at 11.08 and after that the place was a husk. The four city sixth-forms took it in turns to host the annual tragedy, two or three of their headcount lost, a sporty hatchback gift from Dad overturned between hedges, beaten into a ball of tinfoil, trails of fluid along the scarred road surface, special assembly. The title of Pierce's book, *Night Traffic*, used 'traffic' to mean business, transactions, trade, human traffic. But there was traffic at night in London, car traffic, as my suburban soul had been startled to discover. Who were these people? Where were they all going?

Not long after I arrived in London – especially after the Christmas robbery – a place like Burdett Road might have scared me. The canal, gloomy terraces, slab blocks on both sides of the street, and our pavement passed between a high brick wall and a screen of trees. Fly-tippers had called between some of the trees, leaving odd little heaps of ungainly rubbish: crushed baby-buggies, black bags of polystyrene packing, bed headboards spattered with peeling Care Bear stickers. Blind alleys punctured the wall.

Today, however, I saw the security lighting, the bike hire racks, the cranes over it all, unsleeping red demon eyes to ward off low-flying aircraft. We passed a modern church, a divine electricity substation. 'This is the Gate of Heaven,' claimed the red letters set above its porch. Crossrail had swallowed a site on the far side of the road, giant machines behind glossy hoardings. *Helping you make the great escape. Whitechapel to Heathrow in 36 minutes.* I remembered a nugget from Pierce's book: Burdett Road, one of the tower blocks along here, was the subject of Pulp's song 'Mile End' – all squats and squalor, fights, burning cars. When was that, twenty years ago? Had it ever truly been like that? No doubt, but now it was hard to believe. It was before the colourful glass balconies had been added to these long, low blocks, that was for sure, before they sprouted the smart black railings and neat landscaped lawns, scattered with those tidy boulders that urban renewalists leave behind – regenoliths.

'This is where I turned off,' Pierce said. It wasn't really a turning, more a continuation of our current course – it was Burdett Road that veered away, hugging the park to our left. The street narrowed and sprouted car-obstacle humps and islands. The traffic disappeared. It was quieter and darker, a patchwork of truncated pre-Blitz leftovers and uncharismatic post-Blitz reconstruction. Names I remembered from *Night Traffic*: Eric Street, Ropery Street.

'So what did happen that night?' I asked.

Pierce shrugged. 'You asked that already. Nothing. I walked up here. The main road, Mile End Road, is just up there.' He gestured north, and I could see the street ended about a hundred metres further on. A twinkle of passing cars, the blue interior light of a night bus. 'It's five minutes to my house from there.'

We had come to a recess where purple dumpsters were parked, the recycling point for the surrounding housing estate. It was enclosed on three sides by high walls of windowless brick. The surrounding street turned its back on the spot, hemming it with clutter: car parks, playless strips of grass, a concrete cow.

'This is where it happened,' Pierce said. 'In the book.'

The architecture was right enough – it made a good spot for a group to loiter, mostly unseen, a dark harbour in which to surround and intimidate a passer-by. But there was no group here. And even past midnight, the mental weather was wrong.

'It doesn't feel very threatening,' I said. I wasn't sure. Maybe on my own I would feel differently. If I were another gender. So many personal factors bear on the complexion of a place, quite apart from its physical structures.

'I'll show you some of the places I mention in the book,' Pierce said. 'We'll see how bold you feel in the cemetery.'

Down Ropery Street, pastiche Victoriana on one side, and the real thing on the other, a fortress-like National School behind eroded brick walls. Halfway along, the street doglegged, a printer-jam kink without cause, and the pastiche was succeeded by authentic terraces. Further along, another abrupt dogleg, adding to the sense of a maze of nineteenth-century *ad hoc* building.

'This is a bit more like it,' I said. 'Real East End.'

'Yeah, a bit gangland,' Pierce said. 'It's actually lovely during the day. Quiet and pretty. That's where I bought the desk.'

Pierce's 'desk' was a sturdy, wide slice of mdf slung between two filing cabinets. He had bought it from a timber yard up ahead, where the street took a sharp turn right. It would be easy to miss the yard, a modest wooden gate on the outer elbow of the turn. It had featured in *Night Traffic* as the only time Pierce had previously visited these streets: to buy the surface he wrote on. Was that the connection he made when he decided to invent the attack? A sheet of engineered wood, bought on a crooked street, making a work of engineered and crooked biography? I had to remember that he had not walked the streets exactly as he had described: it had all been a later invention, a tour as contrived as the one we were on now. More so. I pictured him sitting at that desk, Google Streetview open on the computer screen. Or standing on this corner on a quiet and pretty day, camera in one hand, notebook in the other, not revisiting a trauma at all, but smiling at his cleverness, at all the observations and linkages he would put into *Night Traffic*. It made me angry. Why, I don't know. Was I a victim, really? A victim of fraud and deception? I had been cheated by Pierce, made to feel things under false pretences, impersonally lied to.

'You still haven't answered my question,' I said. 'Not really. When did you decide to write *Night Traffic*? To invent all this? What made you do it?'

Maddeningly, Pierce ignored me again. None of the street's weak orange light reaching him, moonless introspection. How he was able to do this, I don't know. Maybe people just accepted it – a novelist's privilege, to be moody and inconsistent and elliptical.

'That's the cemetery,' Pierce said.

Aged trees rose in a crowd behind the terrace, bare black branches untouched by light. A pool of blackness in the city.

To briefly recap *Night Traffic*: walking home on Eric Street, our hero is accosted by a gang of youths. Cheerful, reeking of skunk and violence, multi-ethnic. (Another stab of anger. I thought about Pierce composing the very balanced racial make-up of the group, being careful to include and not offend. A complete rainbow of bourgeois fear, no one left behind.) Once the group has impressed upon Pierce the seriousness of his situation, he is taken to the cashpoint of a nearby newsagent to withdraw his ransom. But the cashpoint is not working. So he is marched through these quiet streets in the direction of another. They are heading to a small Tesco across the road from Pierce's own street – his own suggestion. But on the way, they detour into the cemetery to make a more thorough stocktaking of Pierce's possessions and removables.

No ordinary cemetery, this. Tower Hamlets Cemetery Park had not received the dead for more than fifty years – the vast Victorian necropolis had been given back to nature, and thick forest had grown up within it, with narrow muddy paths running through deep brambles and fallen, upheaved lumps of crumbling memorial marble. By day it was quiet, wild, gothic, eerie. By night – I did not like to speculate. It radiated darkness, as if the night itself was made here, and here was its signal clearest.

Pierce had been right. The boldness was gone from me.

'Seems more like a place to get murdered than mugged,' I said. 'I can see why you put it in the book.'

'Yeah, it's, uh,' Pierce said. His voice cracked and he swallowed. 'It's atmospheric.' And, in his hands, it had made for atmospheric writing – violence among the tombstones. Chthonic horror. Chthonic, relating to the underworld; I knew the word from Pierce's book, from that scene, the one all the reviews quoted, the one in the cemetery, and here I found it applied.

A high wall separated us from the jungle, and we skirted it in silence. The entrance lay on a crossroads corner; just within, a war memorial, a brightly painted community centre, and an Edwardian keeper's cottage, then a curtain of ink. Above the skeletal trees, the plume, squeezing and rolling, still with the source-less inner light.

'I wish that thing would go away,' I mumbled.

'It's mostly just kids snorting nitrous and trying to scare each other,' Pierce said. His attitude had entirely changed – the energy was back. 'I reckon you're right, it's not going to happen.'

'You don't want to go through with it?' I said. I had not expected this, not at this moment anyway. 'The mugging? Because if there was anywhere it could happen, this seems most likely.'

'No, no, I do, I do,' Pierce said. 'But not here. I'm just not sure it's going to happen. Feels too contrived.'

I weakened in the knees. Disappointment at another failed outing, another so-so bit of uneventful colour for the piece, contended for a moment with epic relief, before being washed away by it entirely. I could return home, I could drink, I didn't have to go into the cemetery. Without prompting, I looked towards the far glimpse of Mile End Road, and its passing night buses.

'Contrived, OK,' I said. This was a weird thing for Pierce to say – of course it was contrived! – but I didn't want to argue, not when the fridge was calling me. 'Contrived.'

'Yeah. Inauthentic. Look at us. This is ridiculous. We need to think it through. New plan.'

A whoop rose up from the cemetery park, a multiple shriek of joy, blunted by the trees and distance, but sudden enough to make us both start.

'Kids,' I said.

'Kids,' Pierce said.

We walked towards the main road. That was the end of the experiment, then – there would be no mugging. But neither of us said anything to declare the episode closed.

'It's not even eleven,' Pierce said. 'That's the trouble. We're too early. It was later than this.'

In the book, I thought. It had been later than this *in the book*, the crime that you had invented. I just wanted him to acknowledge that.

'We should try somewhere else,' Pierce said. 'No sense giving up now. How about those big housing estates south of the river? Elephant and Castle. They were always a byword for mugging when I was growing up. I would never have gone there at night.'

I grimaced, which Pierce saw, and he tutted at me. 'Come on, you said you were up for an expedition. We've got to do this properly, give it a proper try.'

'Round here is one thing, but going all that way . . .' I began, heeding the siren call of the fridge.

'It'll be fine,' Pierce said. 'With two of us I'm sure there'll be no real danger.'

'Then why . . .'

'Just the right amount of danger, then. Come on. I'll call an Uber to my flat, we can have a quick beer while we wait.'

I sensed that I was being bought off. But Pierce got something out of the deal as well – he didn't have to walk back alone.

EIGHT

Pierce's flat was three minutes away. That was one of the sympathetic details in *Night Traffic*: that the attack had happened so close to where he lived, in a neighbourhood he thought he knew. Again, that pang of rage at the calculation that had gone into the deception. We walked back together. Pierce had already summoned an Uber driver, but he would be half an hour. It was peak time for cabs: the pubs and parties emptying out, people on the move – peak time for muggers, too, perhaps.

Three brown bottles of cold Czech lager reclined in Pierce's fridge. It was, I suspected, the same beer that had been there the previous day, and I marvelled at people who could do that, who could keep beer in the fridge without touching it, without even thinking about it, for days.

When I first lived with Elise, I could toss four cans or six bottles into my shopping basket, and one or two of them would still be there two or three nights later. Wine, too. We'd have wine with dinner, like grown-ups, and there'd be some in the bottle the next morning, the next evening. We could get home from the pub and find there was nothing in the fridge or no bottle on the side, and wouldn't give it a second thought. There must have been tiny firsts, too insignificant to have noticed at the time, too insignificant to remember now. The first time I felt the drop of fear in my gut upon discovering there was nothing in the house. The first time I went, 'just nipping out', to the corner shop to get a can or two to cover that hole. Or four cans. The first time I stopped by the corner shop on the way back, just in case there was nothing in the fridge. Nothing special, no deliberation. No fanfare. No awkward questions, no guilt, doing nothing wrong.

And then, later, the first time I got the tilt of the head from Elise. The first time I got the 'Really?'

Curious to know if Pierce's instincts about south London were reasonable, I took out my phone and opened Tamesis. *Best place to get mugged*, I asked it. The Bunk logo spun as Quin's servers pondered the question.

Did you mean: Best places to buy mugs. Best places to get mugs printed. Best places to get mugshots.

Where in London has the worst street crime? I asked, trying to tailor my question into something the algorithm was equipped to answer. The screen took breath and began to fill with colour and information. Street crime offences by ward, 2010–2015. Data source: Metropolitan Police. I tweaked the screen, zooming out. The familiar matrix of streets twitched and resolved. The river scooped up the neighbourhood. The broader shape of London cohered, the parks, the Thames's turns. But the data overlay was confusing, a marbled mash. My own borough, Westminster, stood out as being particularly bad, which puzzled me until I remembered the West End, all those drunks and tourists. That was where I had been mugged, the first time. Kensington and Chelsea – rich, rich, rich – also appeared more dangerous than I expected, but I didn't like the chance of it happening to us if we tried there. Everywhere else was a mélange, with pockets of danger mixed in among stretches of relative safety; the central boroughs appeared slightly worse than the suburbs. But there was no definitive answer, no no-go zone. Just noise. And this, I supposed, was just the view from the statistics, not the real picture at all.

'Honestly,' Pierce said, 'I don't know what happened that night.' He had been silently tilting his beer while I fiddled with my phone, deep in thought, and this announcement came without preamble. It had been on his mind.

'Describe it to me,' I said. I still had to get the material for an interview, somehow. I needed to know.

'You recording this?' Pierce asked, nodding at my phone, which was cocked in my hand, screen lit.

I wasn't, but I realised that I should be. More than the basic raw materials of the interview, the quotes, I needed proof of the fraud – I needed a recorded acknowledgement of the fraud, if not an outright statement of guilt. Pierce describing the actual turn of events, and how he decided to construct his tale, would do very well.

'May I?' I asked.

He rubbed his face with his free hand, pulling at the skin, like a man trying to rub away his tiredness.

'I'd rather you didn't,' he said. Seeing my expression change, he added, 'I know, I know, it's just hard . . . it's good to get this out in the open, but hard to . . . commit to it.'

As exhausted as I was by Pierce's prevarication, I had some

sympathy for the difficulty the truth could cause in a mind accustomed to deception and delusion.

'You'll have to commit eventually,' I said. 'If we're going to do this, I can't have the possibility of you turning around and saying *this* didn't happen.'

Pierce was nodding. He had started nodding before I finished speaking. It was the kind of nodding that could be read as meaning: Yes, yes, shut *up*.

'Honestly, I wish you'd trust me a bit,' he said.

I wasn't going to allow that. 'You tried to blackmail me to get the story you want. Yesterday. You were sitting right there and I was sitting right here and you tried to blackmail me. In fact, I *am* being blackmailed, aren't I? There's still that threat? Just so we're clear. Let's not talk about trust.'

Pierce slumped. 'Just trying to protect myself.'

I drained my beer. It had not lasted long.

'*Are* you recording this, though?'

'No.'

'OK. Please don't.' He sprang out of his chair, walked over to the map on the wall, and started to pick at it, tweaking and adjusting its hide of notes and clippings as if grooming a pet. 'Like I say, I don't know what happened that night. I mean – on a crude, sensible level, I do know. I walked home. Nothing happened. I went to bed. But when I woke up – I couldn't get out of bed.'

He turned his attention to the stack of foreign-language editions of his books that crowned one of the filing cabinets. The same basic imagery, reiterated by different graphic designers for different markets: London, violence, police.

'I had been at this lovely party, this book launch,' Pierce said. 'Another clever little novel, by someone I know. It's here some-where. I blurbed it. People I know, authors, friends, publishing people. They were all very full of praise for *Murder Boards*. How real it was, how important it was. The London novel they wanted, they needed. And I was lapping it up. I loved it. To be considered . . . I don't know, in touch with a particular kind of realness, *grittiness*, *authenticity*. I know I keep coming back to that word, but . . . And the next morning . . .'

He took a swig of his own beer, and it foamed energetically in the bottle. 'The party had been in the upstairs room of this pub, a refurbished pub, walls all painted this rich green-grey colour probably called "snail tongue" or "wax jacket twilight" or something, this big industrial clock on the wall, blackboards everywhere, steel furniture made to look like it's spent forty years in a machine shop but you know it's brand-new, bearded blokes in plaid shirts on either side of the bar. I mean, don't get me wrong, a nice fucking place, but a fantasy, yeah? An utterly conformist effort to look original. And when I woke up, I thought: I am that fucking pub. I'm a fucking fraud. I'm producing a simulation for a few coddled readers to feel like they're getting something real.'

It made sense. But it also did not make sense. 'So you decided to be a fraud?'

Pierce's face twisted into a pained smirk. 'Yeah. I suppose that's about the measure of it. I wondered what would constitute something real. Then I decided to invent that.'

'Was it a kind of revenge?'

'No. No! On who, the readers? Publishing? Those people? No. I love those people. I am those people. That's not it. At least they're looking for it. The trouble is, they want it so bad, they see it everywhere, where it's not. There are two kinds of reality, yeah? More than two. Occupying the same space.' He gestured at the map. 'Layers. Heterotopia. The same environment, experienced completely differently by different people, in different circumstances, at different times of day. And night. There are

other people out there. We didn't used to have much contact
with them. But now, we can hardly even see them. That's how
we have reshaped the city, how we have structured our mental
environment. Sitting here writing about the other people, I might
as well be writing about knights in armour. It's imagination. And
they are right there. Right! There! But the walls of the bubble
are so strong . . .'

'It sounds as if you were depressed,' I said. 'Are you?'

Pierce shrugged. Or rather, I thought he shrugged, but in fact
he was pulling his phone from his trouser pocket.

'Our ride is here,' he said.

Where am I most at risk from street crime? I tried, as we were driven
through the dark, hissing streets.

Tamesis came up with advice for avoiding street crime. And
it was what you'd expect: stick to busy, well-lit areas, use licensed
cabs, don't go alone. That was what was said about victims of
crime – it has been said about me, to me: 'In the wrong place
at the wrong time,' as if the crime were spring-loaded and waiting
to happen in a particular location, like a mousetrap. Actually
hunting for that location revealed the notion as absurd. Could
we invite the crime, somehow attract it? I realised how this whole
enterprise would take on an entirely different complexion if one
or both of us was female. Or if we were a gay couple, holding
hands. Those were the sections of the population who were
skilled at making crime happen, out of thin air, to themselves.
The crime whisperers. I realised that there was simply no way
that we would be doing this if either of us was a woman. And
the entire endeavour seemed abruptly more foolish, even
grotesque: a peacock display of privilege. Look at us, male and
white and hetero, from good-enough neighbourhoods – we can't
even get mugged in this town.

Did Pierce get that? I doubted it, though he was sensitive to some of the delicacies around the subject. In *Night Traffic* he had been scathing about the asking-for-it myth: You're never a victim-in-waiting, nothing is preordained. You don't have it coming. I was in no mood to give him credit, but this was one thing that Pierce got dead right in that book: the alchemy of it, the near-random collision of factors that transmuted part of the mostly benign city into a moment of terror.

Pierce was sitting in the front passenger seat, chatting with the driver. More than chatting: bonding. They were roaring away like old friends. The driver was Estonian; Pierce had been to Tallinn on a British Council jolly a couple of years before. I suspected that if I tried to impress the native of a place with impressions of their home picked up from a six-day jaunt, I would crash and burn in a firestorm of condescension and naivety, but of course Pierce was navigating it beautifully. They talked about the British stag parties that had besieged the city, and then they moved on to the Baltic ferries used by Swedish teens to get shitfaced, and of course Pierce knew a *Vice* writer who had been on one of those, and he had stories, and the driver snorted and yelped with laughter so much I feared we might come off the road. I hated them both.

The Uber took us to the road junction at the heart of Elephant and Castle. This was as far as Pierce's instructions went – for here we would be on foot, and in theory vulnerable. We were dropped on a peninsula of pavement on the south side of the doomed hulk of the shopping centre, and the scene was promising enough: walkways and underpasses, railway arches, patchy street lighting. But the junction pounded with traffic and buses, and the pavements were busy. Too busy, really, and I wondered why.

'It'll be quieter away from the centre,' Pierce said. 'Better.'

And we both knew what he meant: more dangerous. The concrete labyrinths that had loomed large in the London of our youths, the loci of all provincial middle-class fear.

But we had made a mistake: misremembered it, given the driver the wrong destination, replaced one memory with another. We crossed under the railway bridge, expecting dripping shadow and mute monoliths, a place taxis won't take you. The first thing we saw was a line of taxis, orange lights on, waiting for trade. Behind that, carnival brightness and music. Galvanised security fences screened the boundary of the estate, but it was not deserted or closed. The fences were strung with fairy lights and bunting, and in front of us was a scaffolding arch bearing a name spelled out in weathered letters reclaimed from older signs: WINTERZONE. Beyond the arch was a prim favela built from shipping containers that had been painted in acid colours, a miniature city on a bed of playpark woodchips. In the distance was another splash of coloured lights, machine movement, crashing and cheering.

'What is this?' Pierce said, horror in his eyes, upturned face bathed in light.

I knew: I had heard of Winterzone, people had been talking about it in the office, and there had been a brief piece about it in the most recent issue of the magazine. A ground-breaking experiment in interactive urban renewal, urbanism as entertainment, shopping, music, film and street food. Nowhere does food indoors any more, it's all street food. I just hadn't realised that it was here.

The gates were guarded by a line of glittery young people in black North Face, each bearing a tablet computer. They smiled and reassured us that entrance was free if you accepted the shared-space conduct fist bump, and I think my bruised face drew a suspicious look. We each bumped fists with one of the pad people and agreed that our conduct would abide by the terms and conditions that were laid out on the website accessible from the URL found on the wristbands we were issued.

'Isn't this where the big council estate used to be?' Pierce asked one of the gate guardians, a bright-eyed girl with pink spiky hair.

She raised both eyebrows, pleased by the question. 'Right here!' she said. 'You're looking for the Renewosaurs? They run till midnight. You can catch them next to where they're projecting the film.'

She gestured across the container village, where the site was bounded by a giant advertising hoarding, several storeys high and several streets long. But although it was covered in advertising, it was not a billboard, but one of the slab blocks of the estate, mummified in a taut white plastic wrap. Slogans were splashed across the giant canvas:

WINTERZONE brought to you by CASTLE PARK.
YESTERDAY . . . TO THE DAY AFTER TOMORROW. A
state-of-the-art development of new homes to own or rent.
JOIN US and TAKE PART in a vibrant celebration of the transfor-
mation of URBAN RENEWAL.

And much more of the same, alternating with a tasting platter of corporate logos: the local authority, property developers, building contractors, a hedge fund, a Singaporean pension fund, Wolfe / De Chauncey and others.

We wandered onto the festival site, numb, staring, our plan temporarily forgotten. In the distance were the amped cries of Sam Neill and Laura Dern battling dinosaurs against a John Williams score, and another splintering crash, which brought a round of applause. The crash was not part of the film. Closer at hand, the music was familiar wispy female vocals over a twangy banjo, and although I knew it and had heard it in adverts, I couldn't place it. Shopfronts in the shipping containers dispensed artfully sloppy burgers or cashmere sweaters. A spoken word poet was denouncing austerity to an audience of five people reclined on velour-covered cushions in a yurt. Visitors milled around us, a crowd heavy in beards and caps and stiff vintage military overcoats. The women had mastered the miraculous balance of dress that would work just as well pitching a phone game to venture capitalists in Dalston as it would at one of my mother's WI meetings. It was eleven-ish at night but the shared space conduct fist bump was holding effortlessly – no one was visibly drunk, though most held bottles of microbrew, many swaying them casually from the barest contact of index finger and thumb. I saw two buggies with babies slumbering peacefully inside.

'Fucking . . .' Pierce muttered, but he couldn't even bring himself to finish his profanity. He had not closed his mouth since we arrived, and appeared distraught.

'What's this music?' I asked. It was bothering me, so obviously a song I knew, but just out of reach.

'"Sweet Child O' Mine",' Pierce said. 'Cover.'

On the inside, I was rejoicing. I shared Pierce's disgust at this Mumford-infested travesty, but it had at least shut down his bizarre plan to get attacked. I might even be able to get a drink. We could sit down, and I could record a few essential quotes on my phone, and I might even be able to write a few lines tomorrow, enough to get Eddie and Polly off my back, some red meat to throw into the Monday meeting on Friday.

'Not much risk of getting mugged here,' I said, trying to conceal my relief. 'Robbed, maybe, if we buy a beer.'

Pierce came to a sudden stop, feet scrunching on the woodchips.

We had reached a clearing in the midst of the shipping containers, surrounded by boutiques, bar fronts and Brazil-themed fast food outlets run by ex-financiers. Cumin and turmeric wafted through the night air and there was a burst of sizzling as something was flipped on a grill. A nearby group burst into educated laughter, making a big physical display of it, slapping legs and patting each other on the back. One, over-come with mirth, took off his flat cap and scratched his shaved head.

'When I was younger, in the eighties or nineties, this place was . . .' Pierce began. 'You wouldn't come here.' He waved his arm at the banner that dominated the clearing: *VILLAGE GREEN @ CASTLE GARDENS. Community will be at the heart of everything we do.*

'Let's get a drink,' I said. 'Talk.'

'Yeah, yeah,' said Pierce inattentively. 'We will, but I want to see . . .'

We crossed the clearing. Chalkboards advertised henna tattoos and curried goat burritos and wildstyle graffiti masterclasses from street art professionals. Under a thicket of patio heaters, a young man in a pork pie hat had stripped down to his string vest and was languorously grooving to the music, as if this were London Fields at the height of summer.

'What is this music?' I asked Pierce. It was the same artist, or similar, lisping and strumming away winsomely.

'"Lithium",' Pierce said. 'A cover.'

Before, our view of the far half of the long slab block of flats had been obscured by a tower of scaffolding, which supported floodlights, speakers and a climbing wall. The container-street spread out into another large open area, larger than the 'village green', thinly filled with a crowd lounging on branded picnic blankets and deckchairs under additional groves of patio heaters.

Many were sitting on the stumps of fallen trees. Above them, projected onto the skin of the shrink-wrapped council block, *Jurassic Park* was into its final half-hour. But the crowd's attention was divided. Although many were watching the film, more were focused on where the plastic dermis of the block ended in a ragged, twisting line.

Behind a cordon of polished hoardings, under spotlights, two demolition machines were tearing at the slab block, ripping it down piece by piece. Their long jointed necks were wrapped in strings of coloured lights, and the hydraulic jaws that were chewing through ferroconcrete were painted to resemble dinosaur heads. A window popped from its frame and smashed onto the hillock of rubble below, and some in the crowd whooped; with a snap and a twang, a section of floor broke away, bringing down a strip of facade as it slumped, and the punters roared.

The hoardings around the demolition site were covered in images of lush primordial greenery, overlaid with further inspiring slogans: *SAY FAREWELL TO THE OLD . . . CELEBRATE THE NEW. Castle Park is coming. The next era in urban evolution. Register your interest today.*

One of the Renewosaurs was worrying a structural support loose, tugging it back and forth to splinter the concrete away from the steel rebar underneath. The slow, cracking action made me run my tongue over my teeth. My mouth was dry.

'I can't fucking believe it,' Pierce said quietly. 'This is . . . This place always seemed, I don't know, indestructible. Like it would always be there, good or bad.'

'You never wanted to come here,' I said. 'It was terrifying to you.'

His jaw muscles tensed. 'Yeah . . . But it was part of the city; it was real, not like . . .' He nodded towards the throng of beards and checked shirts.

'This lament for the dirtier, more dangerous city of thirty years ago was familiar Pierce territory, echoed in all his books and *Vice* pieces. And I was sympathetic to those angry, melancholy swipes against the rising tide of glass and waistcoated private security and Byron burgers. They had made me a fan of his. I *had* been sympathetic, before I knew the truth about *Night Traffic*. But that city had been before my time. I had been a child, growing up two hours away (by the faster train), where the whole of London was an exquisite, hazardous mystery. I was fascinated by a prior London I had never seen myself. I thought I was angry about that London disappearing – as angry as Pierce. But what if I was not? What if I was angry, and sad, about something else, and London was no more than a setting?

'You think they should have kept the estate as it was?' I asked.

'Why not?' Pierce fired back. 'I bet the buildings were sound. Beautiful, in their way.' He turned his gaze to what remained of the slab block, stretching back to the entrance of Winterzone.

'But it was a sink estate,' I said. 'Crime. Neglect. Uninhabitable.'

'People lived here, though, didn't they?' Pierce snarled. 'And where are they now? Not fucking here, that's for sure, not in this fucking crowd.'

Resentment smouldered in the pit of my being. I had blundered onto the wrong side of an argument, or had been manoeuvred there, and it wasn't fair. I desired, in a flash, to tear off Pierce's mask, and savage him in print, like one of the demolition machines that were methodically going about their business above. I wanted to gouge into his facade of authenticity and concern, and show that it wasn't as solid as it appeared. But I distrusted my motives. My revenge-lust was genuine enough – but I would also be playing the social-media takedown game, whereby if I could explode the myth of someone like Pierce, I would set myself up as being even more authentic and concerned than he ever was. I would absorb his stature and make it my own – while being no less a fraud.

More than anything I wanted to sit and drink. It had been a while, even with the refresher in Pierce's flat, and my legs were getting shaky. I wanted to be back across town; the fridge was full, but time was still an issue because a certain amount of drinking had to be done before I could go to bed. I don't go to sleep, not any more – it was a matter of scheduling my blackout.

But I couldn't leave, and I couldn't tear Pierce apart – not without a recording, or some kind of leverage. I needed Pierce on the record.

'Let's get a drink,' I said. 'I don't want to watch this.'

Pierce gave me a look, and I ignored it. I had indulged him long enough. I turned away and began to walk, and (to my mild surprise) he followed. A particularly energetic crash came from the Renewosaurs, and the crowd gibbered and yelped its pleasure.

Laura Dern's face filled the screen above. 'Run,' she said, through gritted teeth.

We returned to the 'Village Green', where the bars were concentrated. We sat on stools made from fresh-cut sections of tree trunks – 'upcycled' from the mature planes that had grown on the estate, and available for sale, a label said. The table was an upended barrel cut in half at the waist, and everything was low down, like furniture in a primary school. Pierce went to fetch the drinks. The crowds were slackening, going home. Men in baseball caps and hi-vis vests – a look completely out of step with the woodsy, casual vibe – were emptying litter bins.

Waiting for Pierce to get back from the bar, where tattooed artisans pulled plastic pints using pumps fashioned from the handlebars of Chopper bikes, I took my phone from my pocket.

I wanted it ready to record a confession. I was still turning over the loss of the DVRs, more in the gut than in the mind, a physical sensation, churning beneath the sedative helplessness that paralysed useful thought about the problem. How could I have been so stupid, so negligent? I was accustomed to regarding myself in the worst possible light, but even by my low standards this lapse was difficult to countenance. How had it happened? How could it have happened? It was perfectly natural that I, a walking disaster, should suffer such a calamity, but putting aside the moral and chemical shortcomings that had permitted it to happen, what were the simple mechanics of the disappearance? Since I had discovered the loss earlier, an obsessive part of my back brain had been relentlessly milling the question, and only producing more questions. Fallen from my bag? Improbable. Taken by an opportunistic thief? Doubtful, when a perfectly good laptop was right next to them. Had I taken them out of my bag for some reason – to show Quin?

Quin had been there. The more I sifted through the murky memories, the more his presence felt connected to the absence of the DVRs. Had I told him about the interview, about the recordings? We had talked about Pierce. Had I *given* him the DVRs, or somehow invited him to take them? Had I wanted them to disappear?

There wasn't much sense to that, but it would fit with another mystery that was stirring within. Why wasn't I more upset? I should, by rights, be paralysed with despair. It took so little to make me want to give up everything, to surrender and die. If I missed a Tube I found myself wanting to jump in front of the next one. I was coming to the end of the week almost empty-handed, with no De Chauncey interview and precious little to show from the Pierce interview. In less than thirty-six hours I would have to account for myself and I had nothing but lies and allegations. But here I was, coasting along, letting Pierce amuse himself.

My phone was enjoying Winterzone, at least. Google wanted pictures of it, and had travel and weather information. Tamesis was alive with reviews and suggestions and sponsored content and requests for feedback. This was exactly the kind of young, connected, well-off crowd that would use Quin's social-mapping system and it was busy grinding its gears, trying to make connections. People I know had been here earlier, it said, and I saw Freya and Ilse among the names. And Alexander De Chauncey. He had added me back. Would I like to invite my T-Plus list? Would I like to make my presence public? Would I like to add pictures or reactions to the event T-cloud?

I would not.

Pierce returned with two bottles of beer. They had been immersed in ice water, and their labels were askew, glue dissolved. Sloughing off like reptile skin. Fluorescent labels, covered in Smileys: 'Madfer Pils' by the Brilliant Balham Brewing Bros, a microbrewery.

I tapped my phone. 'I need to get some quotes,' I said. 'It's time. You have to tell me about *Night Traffic*. How it happened. How it *didn't* happen.'

Pierce grimaced. 'Didn't you get enough quotes yesterday?'

'No,' I said. The secret recording was gone, now, so the truth and the lie were the same. 'You asked me to turn off my recorder, remember? Keep it off the record.'

'Yes, of course,' Pierce said unconvincingly. He had known this full well, and was simply trying to wriggle off the hook. 'Can't we keep it off the record?'

'We're out of time,' I said. It was time to push hard, as hard as possible. 'I have a deadline. I need it on the record.'

'Why?' Pierce said, squirming like a child, slipping the label of his beer around with his thumb. 'You know the truth. I invented the whole story. It's fiction. You know that from yesterday. Why do you need me to say it on tape?'

'I need quotes. I can't report a whole conversation from memory. A lot happened yesterday. I need it in your words, specifically about the fraud.'

He winced at that last word. 'What you want is blackmail material.'

Another ugly word, but I controlled my reaction. Blunt was good. 'I need material I can take to my editor, yes. Something that can stand up to lawyers. Something that stops you from going back on our deal and denying everything.'

'Our *deal*,' Pierce said, dragging out the word, mocking it. 'I wasn't really aware we had made a *deal*.'

I took a deep swig from my own bottle, washing away this petulance, then woke my phone and brought up the voice recorder app. A wavy line jigged on the screen, picking up the merry noises around us, the chirpy music, the scrunch of Converse on woodchip.

'Why did you decide to invent the story about being mugged?'

'I don't know what you're talking about,' Pierce said. 'Everything in *Night Traffic* is 100 per cent true.' He stared at me, expressionless, defiant.

I stopped the recording. 'You have to go on the record.'

'No, I don't.'

'What's it going to take?' I said, feeling anger flash up inside me. 'I could just write a story without your cooperation.' Pierce raised his eyebrows at this, taunting, daring. I felt the scorch in my lungs, in my throat. 'I could go to Quin,' I said, not really thinking, but I was rewarded with an immediate change in Pierce's whole demeanour. 'Yeah . . . Quin knows something, doesn't he? He has information.'

Pierce blanched. 'Don't do that.'

I had no actual desire to go to Quin, and ensnare myself further with him, but I realised that Quin's Tamesis post about me had materially shifted the balance of power between me and Pierce, and Pierce knew it. It was satisfying, at last, to have some traction. 'What does Quin know, anyway?' I said. 'How did he figure it out?'

'He didn't,' Pierce said. 'I'm sure he would have – he was quizzing me about what happened. I don't know. I told him the truth. I couldn't stand it any more.'

The patio heater was enough to make me uncomfortable in my winter coat, but Pierce shivered in his. His eyes flicked from point to point, mostly downwards: ground, barrel, bottle, phone. 'It's become so complicated in my mind,' Pierce said. 'I thought that a single night could be kept separate from everything else. That what I put there could be sealed up. But it has spilled, and it keeps spilling out, everywhere . . .'

Like the plume, I thought. An uncontrollable reaction, spewing poison into the air, into the water, toxifying all it touched. And instinctively I searched for smoke in the dark sky, and there it was to the east, a rolling wall of mobile night, tanned by ten thousand streetlights. Closer, again? We had travelled a good distance west as well as south when we came here, away from the fire. And yet, if anything, I could have sworn it was closer. But London is curved: the bends of the river, the scoop of its wide valley, have distorting effects, so that what you imagine to be east is to the north, or two areas you believed to be far apart are in fact close together.

No need to share any of this with Pierce. 'I've found the same thing,' I said instead. 'Tell enough lies, or a big enough lie, and the truth gets corrupted. The boundary gets lost, it rots.'

Pierce narrowed his eyes at me. 'Right,' he said. 'So the

falsehood corrodes what's true. The true feels false. But what happens to the lies? Does their nature change as well?'

I tried to look attentive and sympathetic – an interviewer face – but I didn't follow what Pierce was saying. I let the silence open up, hoping he might elaborate.

'I've had to pretend that the attack was real for so long, that it has begun to feel very real to me. It wasn't really a perform-ance, when I was talking about the book to people – I believed it. I inhabited it. So when I try to account for the lie, to trace it back to its beginning, like you keep asking me – it's a blur.'

'It can be very difficult to tell where an idea came from,' I volunteered. 'But there must have been a moment when you chose to commit to it, to write tens of thousands of words . . .'

'That night,' Pierce said. He looked exhausted. He had appeared tired earlier, in the pub, but that had disappeared during our stroll when there had been bursts of energy, and he had a brooding focus about him. That had expired, and I could see the dark crescents under his eyes, the unhealthy sheen of his face – he was starting to resemble me. How much sleep was he getting? What kind of pressure was he under?

He reared as if trying to keep himself awake, and rubbed his stubbled chin with his knuckles. 'What I've realised is that it was completely improbable,' he said. '*Night Traffic*, I mean. That kind of attack. I don't think it happens any more. It's incredible that people believed me. I mean, look around.' He cast out his arm at Winterzone. The whispery, plinky music was now a cover of 'Debaser' by the Pixies. Amid a constellation of corporate logos, the property consortiums promised *All the grit, none of the grime . . . Bringing London's vibrancy to a world-class residential destination*. 'The city's changed.'

'People *did* believe you, though,' I said. 'So it must have been realistic.'

'People wanted to believe,' Pierce said. 'But it's mopeds now, or identity theft. Fast. Not lingering. Not personal.'

'It does happen,' I said. 'It happened to me.' *Twice*, I didn't add.

'Because it's part of the illusion. The frisson. All these wankers playing dress-up in the ruins. Acting out a kind of city that's gone. And the people who lived here, where are they now?'

Again, I felt the heat rising in me. 'What, the people you want to get mugged by, as part of your Authentic Urban Experience? Fucking hell. You should take a look at yourself.'

'Trust me, I have taken a long look at myself,' Pierce said. 'So we had a deal – I seem to recall that the deal involved recreating the mugging. We haven't done that yet.'

I sighed, almost a gasp of frustration. 'It's not going to happen,' I said. 'Not here, anyway – probably not anywhere. Not when there's two of us. What do you want to do, pay a bloke in a pub?'

'No, no,' Pierce said. I knew his tone, I knew his whole stance: a writer in the Monday meeting whose pitch is bombing, and they're trying to talk it back to life. 'It has to be—'

'Real?' I said, and I didn't edit the contempt from my voice.

Pierce didn't respond. He was gnawing on the problem, pinching his top lip, scowling at the eroding crowd. The T-Rex had made its final appearance in *Jurassic Park* and people were drifting home. One by one the shipping container boutiques were closing, doors clattering. 'Maybe the streets around here,' Pierce said. 'I mean, they must be a good hunting ground, right? With all these . . .' He stopped, groping for the right word.

'Mumfords,' I supplied, drawing a wolfish smile from Pierce.

'Mumfords, yeah. The Nathans. If anyone deserves to get mugged—'

'No one deserves to get mugged,' I said sharply.

Pierce cocked his head. 'I know it's a delicate subject for you, maybe *you* didn't deserve it, but – no one, really? You sure about that?'

I frowned at him.

'Not even me?' he asked.

I was stopped. I had something ready, some remarks on how I wouldn't wish street crime on my enemies, Twitter-scented piety. But I was stopped.

'I lied about being attacked,' Pierce said. 'I profited from that; quite handsomely, I might add. Wouldn't it be fitting if I was mugged?'

Although I wanted to disagree, I could not.

Pierce leaned in to me, eyes dark and filled with conspiracy. The old Pierce. The man I had wanted to meet, and to interview. 'If I deserve it, there must be others, right? You know there are. This is important – this is what I wanted to say in *Night Traffic*. The crime might be horrible in individual cases, but in general – in general it might be important, it might even be vital. The city needs it. It's part of the ecology. The city needs fear. It keeps the balance, it stops the wrong sorts getting the upper hand. It stops the Mumfords taking over. And we've lost that.'

'But it's not the "wrong sorts" who get the worst of it, is it?' I said. 'It's the terrified little old ladies in council flats, getting their jaws broken for two quid. It's poor kids who know they won't get a bike for Christmas because it'll get taken off them while the tree's still up.'

Pierce closed his eyes, as if impatient with this objection. 'Yes. Yes. And I said the same to Quin.'

To Quin? Why was he talking about this to Quin?

'It's good that those people are less in danger now – that's good. But the trouble is that it let the Mumfords off the hook; they can buy up the neighbourhoods, they can exploit places that had a reputation for crime to make a profit on the property market without ever fearing that crime themselves, and they can walk around at midnight, braying and accumulating. And the little old lady and the poor kids get robbed another way.'

'What are you saying?' I said.

'Why did you buy my books, read my essays?' Pierce asked. He didn't stop for an answer. 'Because you saw the city the same way I did. Just like a lot of other people. You're angry too. That's what I've been describing: the city out of balance, lost to the rich, the oligarchs, the hedgies, the trust-funders.'

I thought of Pierce's flat, bought with his inheritance, and I stayed silent, because being angry at Pierce was futile. He was a hypocrite, of course – and so was I, working at the magazine, paying my rent, peddling the modern urban lifestyle, taking part in the whole ghastly orgy of property and consumption even as it drained my pockets and my hope. I should just get out, fuck the lifestyle, but I wanted in, I wanted in so very much, I wanted to be one of the guys cheerfully necking one beer to wash down a £15 burger at 11 p.m., talking about boxsets and exhibitions; I wanted that so much, it had destroyed me. It made me hate them so very much, the ones who were in, the owner-occupiers, the owners, the occupiers, the ones who had raised the bar so high that only daughters of Russian gas tycoons could enjoy themselves, and even they were chasing around after a city that was dying, even as the developers raised parodic imitations of it for their amusement. So was Pierce right? Was fear all it needed?

'You talked about this with Quin?' I asked. 'How did this come up with Quin?'

'It's like I said,' Pierce said. 'No one's angrier than Quin. I think he's trying to do something about it with Tamesis, but I can't tell what. Are *you* angry?'

I thought of my flat, and the dust that filled my mouth with every breath, the pulverised waste of my neighbours' dedication to hammering every last pound of value from their plot. Sixty per cent of my salary went on that flat, and I couldn't even repaint it to cover the hairline cracks that multiplied through its plaster. Yes, I was angry. Of course I was angry. But what was the remedy? Even if fear was needed, what did that mean in practice?

'What are you getting at?' I asked.

'If it could be correctly targeted,' Pierce said, 'perhaps a little more street crime wouldn't be a bad thing.'

I stared at him. My beer was gone – I didn't quite know how that had happened, and I didn't like my chances of being served another, as a go-home vibe was building around the festival. And I wanted to go home, but first I wanted Pierce to finish his thought, to say what it was he was circling around, so again I let the silence talk.

'If we picked the right targets.'

'We?'

Pierce rubbed the bristles on his chin. 'We've been going about this all wrong. I've been trying to create this authentic experience – look, you can roll your eyes all you want, but that's what I've been saying all along, that's what I'm looking for, something real – but the city hasn't been cooperating. Because it's an experience with an active side and a passive side. And you can't actively be the passive side, the side it happens to. But you can be the active side, the one that makes it happen. That would be no less authentic, no less contrived, right?'

My voice dropped to a hiss. 'You want to go out and mug someone?'

Pierce nodded. 'Sure. Why not. We can see it from the inside, that way. And put a bit of fear back on the streets. Hey – it might even be therapeutic for you. Work out some of those demons, yeah? Getting mugged is one of the reasons you drink, right?'

On a very superficial, limited level that was true, but it was also untrue, a crass simplification. But I did not want to get into that.

'What about atonement?' I asked. 'What about making amends for *Night Traffic*?'

'I'm starting to think that atonement might, in fact, not be the right approach,' Pierce said. 'I'm entertaining alternatives. If the mob can't be appeased, perhaps it can be baffled.' He brightened, and tapped the barrel-top in front of me with his index finger. 'It'll make a great piece for you. I only wish I was the one writing it.'

I felt a scabbed scratch reopen with a jab of pain as my face contorted in response. 'I'm not taking part in this!'

'You're an observer, you're golden, blameless,' Pierce said. 'You've been manipulated by the devious Oliver Pierce, I don't know. If I could guarantee to you that the person we chose absolutely, undisputedly deserved to have the fear put into them . . .'

'Oliver, no.'

He jumped in, not letting me elaborate on my refusal. 'One attempt. Tomorrow night. And in exchange . . . A signed confession. For your editor, right? To put in the vault. I'll bring it with me tomorrow. Full cooperation. You can ask what you want, on the record, you'll get the exclusive. Signed and sealed.'

Tomorrow was Thursday. If I had a signed confession and a guarantee of cooperation in my bag on Thursday evening, I could take it to the meeting on Friday morning. It would be enough to appease the mob at work, for sure. And what would I have to do to get this guarantee? Spend another evening blundering about the streets with Pierce, observer to his increasing mania. Eyewitness to the unravelling. He was right, it did make for a great story. A real escapade. I was certain that no actual crime would take place. Tonight had been a fiasco. Did I have confidence that the stocky cult novelist before me could confront a stranger in the street and demand his wallet and phone? How, exactly? Nothing would happen.

Especially if I could make the pool of potential victims as small as possible.

'We need to lay down some rules first,' I said. 'Get the right target, yes?'

'Rules, yes,' Pierce said. 'Good.'

'No women,' I said. 'Men only. Healthy, able-bodied, adult men.'

'Absolutely,' Pierce said. 'Wouldn't dream of anything else.'

I fixed him with a stare. 'White men. You don't want a racial component.'

'I agree. Simple mugging. No hate angle.'

'On the same score, heterosexual.'

Pierce frowned. 'Well, that's hard to guarantee.'

'But if there's any doubt or possibility—'

'Well, now you're being prejudiced. There is no way of telling.'

'Fine. We'll put a pin in that. And they have to deserve it. They have to be the right sort.'

'This sort?' Pierce said as Winterzone's guests streamed past us towards the exit. The Renewosaurs had quieted for the night. 'The streets around here must have potential right now . . .'

I winced, feeling once more a shard of pain in the circuit of my right eye as the damaged skin around it stretched and wrinkled. It was a complicated crowd. As a group, I might detest it – there was the abstract entity causing the harm, cheering the purgation of the city – but as individuals it was less obviously malign. The two men sitting nearest us, for instance, one wearing a shiny Moncler jacket, the other in a conspicuously moth-eaten

Fruit of the Loom sweatshirt bearing the 1990s logo for Electronic Arts. What about them? Struggling artists or advertising executives? Private renters or owner-occupiers? And what if that mirror was held up to us? At least I didn't look the part, I thought, with my injured face and court-appearance suit, my underlying pallor and shakes and emaciation. I had a 200-hours community-service look to me. Unless that could all be read as ironic, a carefully constructed pose – the guardians of Winterzone had let me through with barely a twitch, after all, apparently satisfied on sight that I wasn't an ASBO graduate.

'No,' I said. 'You can't just charge off and try to get someone. You should have a clear idea of who merits the crime.'

'How do we do that?' Pierce asked, visibly impatient.

You don't, I thought. I didn't want to facilitate an assault, I wanted to put so many ethical hurdles in the way that it was impossible. But I did want to appear helpful.

'We could mood-board it,' I said. 'It can be a useful creative tool – make a wishlist of the best possible victims.' I opened my bag, took out my reporter's pad and laid it between us. 'Who would be ideal?'

Pierce frowned. 'I don't know. City types. Property developers. Estate agents, the big ones.'

'Alexander De Chauncey, for instance,' I said. 'He would be perfect.' I jotted his name at the top of the list.

'Who is he?' Pierce said. 'The name rings a bell.'

'He has a chain of estate agents,' I said. 'Wolfe / De Chauncey – you must have seen them?'

'Yes, yes,' Pierce said. 'He's ideal.'

'Obviously we can't actually do him,' I said, patting the pad, trying to make the nature of the exercise clear. 'We're just trying to get a feel. And I have dealings with him.' I crossed the name off, for emphasis.

I tried to think of more names. The culprits. I had never met my neighbours, and without names or faces it was hard to condemn them directly. I knew my landlord's name but nothing more about him, only the occasional elliptical email. Bella's husband Dan? He was horrible, they both were, but I didn't want them beaten up.

'Boris Johnson,' Pierce suggested, and I nodded enthusiastically. The mayor's name went on the top of the list. And so we went on, thinking of the most nauseating Londoners with the worst possible politics and the biggest slices of the pie. Former tabloid editors turned TV presenters, style gurus, right-wing commentators, think tankers. Pierce added a couple of obnoxious writers he had feuded with: Mike Butcher, the bestselling self-help novelist; Hugo Pleasance, a pop-sociology twerp, author of *Will This Do: The Surprising Science of Adequacy*; Phil Lothian, a critic and columnist for a liberal newspaper and the *Spectator*. It was an ugly list.

'A good start,' Pierce said.

'We've got the flavour of it,' I said. 'Of course you're not going to bump into these people. This is just the mood board.'

'And the mood is hatred,' Pierce said. 'Tomorrow, then. Signed document in hand. We'll do – whatever.'

'No signed document, no whatever,' I said. 'No more games.' Before, I might have balked at setting an ultimatum, fearing that Pierce would simply walk away. Now, I had nothing left to lose.

Pierce nodded. 'No more games.'

NINE

It *was* a game, though, all of it, that much was revealed as soon as a pneumatic drill split the shell of unconsciousness. The drill had become a mosquito whine, not the deafening, marrow-penetrating racket of previous mornings but an uncomfortable buzzing rattle, alternating with silence.

I awoke without having rested. It was as if I had bumped into an absent colleague's desk and nudged their mouse enough to wake their computer, showing what they had been looking at when they were called away. That was the thought left over from the previous night: it's a game. Or rather, it's a mockery, a pantomime of reality. Lists of victims, signed confessions? These were the props of melodrama, not journalism. I had nothing. Two days had passed with Pierce and I had achieved nothing.

In the dim, dilute light of the basement morning, I knew that I was out of time. There was no additional day to work on getting useful material from Pierce – or from De Chauncey, and remembering De Chauncey brought on a fresh surge of panic. For a vertiginous second, sinking into the sweat-damp mattress, I feared that the day might already have passed – that I might have so thoroughly medicined myself on Wednesday night that I had awoken on Friday morning. I entertained this thought long enough for its positive side to appear: at least there would be no more delay, not another twenty-four hours of sticky, desperate delusion as I imagined I might yet heave my career out of the fire. Cut straight to the deadline.

But I had not been spared, not that way. The realisation that I was out of time came from elsewhere. The sound had ceased in the few unpleasant moments I had spent wondering what day it might be – the flat was quiet, but for the bickering of the builders outside. I sat up, and swung my feet out of bed. The room was cold, the central heating off already, the only part of the house that kept up the ridiculous fiction that I maintained a normal work schedule. Atomised brick and cement had accumulated in the corners of my eyes and the recesses of my mouth. How much had I swallowed in the night – how much did I swallow every night, since the neighbours started their improvements? Was it building up within me? Was I saving that kind of deposit? How benign would it be? I thought of asbestos, and the myriad other horrors that lurked in old houses: fibreglass, mycotoxins, mould, spores. Should I email Dave? What good would it do?

The central heating had cooled to nothing. My bedside clock said it was 10.17, which gave me a nasty lurch. We were supposed to be in the office by ten at the latest, and it took forty-five minutes to get there, so I was at least an hour late. But I had already decided to skip the office and 'work from home'. True, I needed to dash off a quick text saying that I was working from home, and it would have been better to do that before nine thirty, showing that I was out of bed at least; Eddie had in the past emphasised to everyone the importance of this notification as a bare minimum. 'We do like to know where you are and what you're doing,' he had said at more than one Monday meeting. Then his indulgent expression would turn pained. 'Don't leave us guessing – it's just rude, for one thing.' And that was what always got me – I didn't want to be rude to Eddie, not when he was so willing to stretch the rules for us.

So, a text. But where was my phone? The closing stages of the previous night were a familiar blank.

I did not need to consider the question long, because the drilling sound started up again, that altered, distant, hollow drilling sound . . . not a drill. It was my phone, vibrating on the bedside table. I had left it on a bed of coins, so its vibrations had an unusual, metallic quality, and it was this I had heard earlier. And I realised why I had jumped awake with the certain knowledge that my time was up: I had been lying in my bed, not yet awake, listening to my phone pulse over and over again, the repeated sound of someone calling, getting sent to voicemail, and calling again.

The screen was alight as the caller tried again: number with-held. That meant the office. Outgoing calls through the switchboard never showed up. I answered, expecting – dreading – Eddie or Polly.

'Yep,' I said, trying to sound friendly, but also like someone called away from an important work-related task that merited my fullest attention.

'Are you still in bed?' said an unexpected voice. It was Kay.

'Nope,' I said. 'Up. Working from home.'

'Did you clear that with Eddie?' Kay said, her voice urgent but low. I could picture her, I had seen her make this kind of clandestine call before: she would be hunched over, elbows on her desk, free hand over her other ear, hiding behind dog-eared stacks of magazines. 'Because, listen, because they are *on the warpath* about you not being in, and you need to get here ASAP.'

'Right,' I said. So, it was the end. The ceiling was falling, the floor opening up. 'I'll leave right away.'

'Sooner than that, yeah?' Kay said. 'As a friend.'

The call ended.

I wondered how much time I might have, really. Enough for a can or two? I could do without a shower, just about, as I had showered the evening before, so perhaps I could just squeeze in a can. The usual drunk maths began to play out: how late was I? If I was not very late, then I could spare the minutes needed to fortify myself with a Stella, or even two. And if I was very, very late, then those minutes wouldn't make too much difference and I could afford that Stella, or even two. But there was a nasty little strip of no-man's-land between those two comforting trenches, when I was late but the damage was still escalating, and I needed to get moving. I feared I might be on that thirsty median this morning. Trouble had accumulated on my phone. I had missed three calls – how I hated the sight of that twisted red arrow. There were emails as well, of course, and texts, and other notifications, but calls were trouble. Missed calls were big trouble.

As if to confirm my worst suspicions, the phone started to vibrate in my hand, another incoming call. When I swiped to answer, my thumb dragged on the particles of grit that had settled on the screen during the night.

'Yep.'

'Jack.' It was Eddie. 'Where are you?'

'I'm on my way,' I said. There was nothing else I could say, but it set another clock ticking. No time for that can.

'It is' – there was a significant pause while he checked, probably from the lower-right corner of his computer screen – 'ten twenty. You should be here before ten. And you are still on your way. Are you still at home?'

'I'm sorry, Eddie,' I said, trying to sound as humble as possible without crawling. 'I overslept.'

'We talked about this.'

'I know, I know. I'm sorry.'

An exhalation came over the line, accompanied by rustling and bumping. Without being able to see him, I knew that he was running the fingers of his free hand through his curls.

'Find me when you get in,' he said. 'I need an update on your pages. Polly too.'

He was being stern to a positively un-Eddie-like degree, which terrified me. I had at last depleted his goodwill, and I was so frightened I put both feet into a hole. 'Sure,' I said. 'It's all good.'

'Great,' Eddie said. 'I look forward to hearing about it. I knew you'd get a good result with Alexander.'

'Yeah, absolutely,' I said.

'OK, see you soon. Don't get back into bed.' I could almost hear the smirk, the twinkle in the eye. The call ended. The old Eddie was back, but that was the old Eddie's way of issuing a warning.

My deceit was fully formed and disastrous. I should have said . . . almost anything else. I should have prepared Eddie for the bad news that I would inevitably have to deliver once I was in the office: no record of the Pierce interview; no interview with De Chauncey at all. But instead I had lied. I knew exactly why I lied: I wanted to enjoy a single second of normal, cheerful interaction with Eddie. To perpetuate, for the shortest time, the impression that I continued to function. To live in a way that was not simply waiting for disgrace, and death.

The white shirt and smart trousers I had worn the night before were heaped on the floor beside the bed, on top of a trampled stratum of older, dirtier laundry. That was good – I would at least look fairly presentable. But then I recalled the condition of my face, and to recall it was to crack the veneer of numbness like the crust of a crème brûlée and feel the pain again.

If only I could have that drink. The emergency ultimatum from the office overpowered even the Need's ability to keep me in place, but it would not give up. Opening my shoulder bag to check its contents – no DVRs, of course – I discovered the aluminium water bottle I had used to take beer on the train last night. It was empty, and a little sticky. Moving briskly, feeling efficient, I took it to the kitchen, ran it under the tap, dried it off and refilled it with two cans from the fridge. (Two of the three remaining – I had, it appeared, been industrious on my return, and the living room was mined with empties and not-so-empties.)

Another shameful first. Maybe there wasn't much material difference between drinking in the shower in the morning and drinking on the Tube in the morning; maybe there wasn't much material difference between drinking at lunch and taking drink into the office. Every daring transgression became every day in time.

A couple of years back – after I had started going to the pub at lunch, but before the morning cans began – I had sat next to a guy drinking a booze-hardened energy drink on the train into work. It was impossible to be entirely sure, but I was sure. The cloying chemical reek of off-brand energy drinks is a familiar part of the rush-hour bouquet, but he had added a few measures of harder stuff. And he looked the part, too, his shirt creased, trousers stained, eyes red and haunted, stubble undisturbed by a blade. Just about ready to give up the charade, or have it torn away from him. Not a sight to please a manager or any colleague. I hoped that lives did not depend on his work, that he was not on his way to direct aeroplanes or perform surgery. The sorry scene might have been salutary, but instead I drew a perverse lesson from it. I wasn't that bad, I told myself. I didn't have to worry too much. Here was living proof that there was much further to fall before the fall became final. And plenty of opportunities to change course entirely.

Bottle sloshing in my bag, I set off for the Tube.

A great heaviness had settled into my heart and my tread by the time I reached the office. I dreaded the attention my battered face would bring, the questions I would have to answer, even if they were kind. I did not have to lie about the essentials, at least. The effort to remove the bag from the tree was real and blameless enough, and I did not have to mention cockatoos or my blood-alcohol level. But I did not want to deal with people at all. I did not want anyone picking up the stench of decay from me. The prospect of the catch-up with Polly and Eddie was even worse. I had placed my last remaining hope in coming up with a convincing way to present the facts: figuring out, on the Tube, a way to tell the truth, but put an appealing spin on it. As it had turned out, all my creativity went into taking nips from my aluminium bottle in a surreptitious way while trying not to appear surreptitious. Agitated by the walk to the station, the bottle fizzed and spat in a conspicuous way when I tried to open it, and sent a trickle of foaming liquid over my knuckles. For a second I feared the whole thing might erupt in a geyser of beer, exposing my secret shame to the carriage. I had to screw the cap back on with a hard twist, and then try to release it very slowly, easing the pressure off, and it hissed and bubbled and generally made not-mineral-water noises.

The spilled beer made my left hand and wrist unpleasantly sticky and dirty-feeling, and I wanted to wash. But as I stepped out of the lift, I saw Mohit heading into the toilets, and did not want him observing me. For long seconds I stood in the lift lobby, half in the lift and half out, while an impatient electronic voice told me not to obstruct the doors. It was tempting to back into the lift and take it back down, to leave the building, go to the pub or return home, shut off the phone and head for unconsciousness . . . And ride out the consequences. The consequences would be very severe, but I could ignore them, until the money went, around the time of my next rent payment, or the one after.

The smell of burning was overpowering – I could taste it, thick scorched tar at the back of my mouth. Opposite the lifts were windows facing east, looking across the rooftops of London towards Barking and the smoke column. The view was identical to my first sight of the plume on Monday – that had been through the adjacent windows on the other side of the door into the office. And it was still there, the rising smoke, feeding a sky stained dark by four days of uninterrupted pollution. How could it possibly still be burning? What was left to burn? Why wasn't everyone gathered here like they had been at the start, saying, 'This is bizarre, this shouldn't be happening'?

I could swear that it appeared to be closer, and filled a wider wedge of the horizon. In the winter gloom it was difficult to be sure, but I remembered the stark, black column that we had all seen on Monday, how far away it seemed to be; that was part of what made it impressive, the fact that it was so obviously distant and yet so very prominent. It didn't match this sprawling toxic curtain.

The lift doors stopped complaining and began an electronic

hollering. I stepped out and the doors closed with an aggressive snap. My hand was still dirty, and I feared that I reeked, but I pushed into the office regardless.

Only Kay acknowledged my entrance – she raised her eyebrows at me, an exaggerated look of alarm, and then pointedly turned to the aquarium. Eddie and Polly were bunkered there, Eddie unusually stiff, sitting straight, Polly leaning forward with her arms crossed tight, hair behind ears, staring down at papers. Her legs were kicked back under the chair, crossed at the ankles. The whole scene was tense.

Outside the aquarium, the office was quiet. We were in the meaty part of the production cycle, when features start to come together, and my colleagues were out visiting places and meeting people and overseeing photoshoots. Test spreads had started going up on the wall behind Ilse – tomorrow these would be brought into the meeting and Eddie would pass judgement. I saw a couple of pictures of Pierce in the mix. Pierce standing with his back to the wall-map, arms crossed. Pierce on his tatty leather sofa, looking louche. Pierce pressed up against the wall-map, fingers running through the thick mane of psychogeographical trivia, ecstasy on his face, like a man lying in a meadow on a summer's day. This last was a particularly good photo, and triggered a pang of envy at the good fun Pierce appeared to have had with Alan, the photographer, while I was drinking my way out of panic in the Liverpool Street Wetherspoon's. One unwelcome emotion abruptly gave way to another: why be envious? Was I still besotted with Pierce? Did I still want to be his friend and peer? On Monday I would have been delighted with these photos, and what they said about the unwritten feature that was to accompany them – the feature I wanted to write, in all its glorious potential. Now it was all sullied and ridiculous.

I sat down and switched on my computer. Using my phone – more discreet than work email – I messaged Kay: *What's going on?*

I don't know, she replied. *Something.*

Redundancies? I asked. I watched as the message icon changed – Kay had read it. But she did not reply. I turned in my chair to look across the office at her, and she shrugged at me.

About me? I asked.

They weren't happy with you earlier, Kay replied. *What happened to your face?*

I fell off a garden wall, I said. *It's a long story. Not a funny one, sorry, just stupid.*

Are you OK? Kay asked.

I took a long time to reply. *Yes, fine. Sorry. Just got a lot on.*

We should catch up, she said.

I know, I said. *I'm sorry I didn't come out and see you the other night.*

That's fine. You could have just said you were with Quin.

She had seen Quin's Tamesis post. Of course she had seen Quin's Tamesis post. It would have lit up the sky across my contacts and T-pluses.

Sorry, I said, and left it at that. She did not reply, and I did not look around to see her expression.

Casual as anything, I opened my bag and took out my pad and my aluminium bottle. There was no further risk of an explosion, but the bottle still made an unwaterly *Psst* when I opened it. No one reacted. Mohit was back from the toilet and had resumed the interminable succession of phone calls that comprised his job. I took a gulp, but my movements were so self-conscious and awkward that I fluffed it and dribbled down my chin. At that moment, tilting my head to wipe my chin with the back of my still-not-washed hand, I became aware that I was being watched. In the conference room, Eddie and Polly had stopped conferring and were looking out through the glass wall towards me. When they saw me see them, Polly rose and came out of the aquarium in that slightly bowed, scuttling pose that comes instinctively when leaving an ongoing meeting, as if one is exiting a helicopter.

'Polly, hi.'

'Jack, hi. Can you join us a minute? It would be great to hear where you're at.' I watched her eyes flicker as she registered the state of my face.

'Sure.' I stood and grabbed my notepad, trying to look normal, and followed her back to the aquarium, both hands and chin smeared with part-dried beer. Eddie did not take his eyes off me, his gaze level, neither pleased nor displeased, but fierce, attentive. This might be how regular bosses look, and I didn't like it. I wanted the old Eddie, our friend, back.

I circuited the conference table, sitting on the side Polly had been sitting, but further from Eddie. I wanted to be able to see out into the office. Polly did not resume her former seat, but sat across from me, nearer Eddie. Me and Them. Confrontational.

'How did it go on Tuesday?' Eddie asked, without particular emphasis or inflection. But there was no hello, how are you, what happened to your face, and that spoke for itself.

The success of my lie would depend on what Eddie knew, and I started to do the maths. If he had called De Chauncey, or De Chauncey's irate PR had made a call, then Eddie would already know that there had been no interview, but he was keeping that information to himself. Or he was working under the assumption that the meeting had gone ahead, which meant that I was in a different kind of trouble, not quite so bad, but with further to fall. To put it another way, it was possible that my employment was already as good as terminated because

Eddie knew that I had ditched De Chauncey and then lied about it, in which case lying again wouldn't make things all that much worse. But if Eddie believed that the meeting had happened, then telling the truth would make a salvageable situation far worse, perhaps fatally worse. So there was only one answer worth giving.

'Fine,' I said. 'Great.'

'You got everything you need?' Eddie asked. He was giving nothing away. Was that suggestive of a man who had information that he did not wish to give away? Or was I being paranoid?

'Yeah, more or less,' I said. I was committed, then. De Chauncey had added me as a contact on Tamesis, I remembered. He had not cut me off. It wasn't much, but it was grounds for hope. I could make more calls, fix up another meeting. But my reply had been suspiciously ambivalent, so I added, 'I'm doing follow-ups.' That was always a good line.

'And Wednesday? Get much done?'

I shrugged. 'Transcribing. Yes. Absolutely.'

'Can we see?'

He wasn't going to take my word. 'Well, it's not quite done.'

Eddie cut me off with a sharp exhalation, and pushed his fingers into his hair, exposing a lined forehead. 'I thought you were going to have something for us to see,' he said, with distinct tetch in his tone.

Polly had not said anything yet. Her demeanour was, to my surprise, far less hostile than Eddie's. She was not staring me down, turning me into a wall shadow with her death ray. And she was not obviously gloating at my discomfort. Her clipboard was held lightly in one hand, its top resting against the table, tilted towards her so I could not see what was displayed there. Was that why she had sat opposite, so I could not see her notes? What was it? A typed and indexed dossier on me? And on that thought, I twigged why she wasn't joining Eddie in his cross-examination, why she looked sympathetic, even kindly. Her work was done. She had given all the facts to Eddie, built the case against me, poisoned his mind. Now she could relax, and it would serve her to appear neutral rather than vindictive.

'Jack?'

A thick, caustic substance was in my mouth, coating the interior of the cheeks, filling my throat. My hands felt unbearably hot and dirty.

'There's a lot to do,' I said. 'Two interviews. You know.'

Absurdly, I found myself riling up on the back of my own falsehood, indignant at the thought that I could have typed up two interviews in one day. I'm not a machine! That I had failed to attend one interview and had lost the recordings of the other did nothing to dim my righteousness. This was unreasonable! They were holding me to an unrealistically high standard! The fictional me that had coalesced for the purpose of this meeting was filled with thunder. I swallowed, trying to clear the bitter glue from the back of my mouth, and tasted blood. It was hot in the aquarium, too hot. The air was foul. How did they expect me to defend myself if I couldn't breathe?

'Uh, sorry,' I said. 'I was . . . trying to do both. I wanted to have both, for now. And I ended up not quite finishing either.'

Polly smiled at this – it nearly sent me unconscious, but she smiled, a pleasant little smile of alliance. Her duplicity turned my stomach.

Eddie picked up his pen and examined the flatplan that was laid on the table in front of him. 'That happens. We've assigned pages for both. It would be great to get a sense of what they talked about, the kind of tone you're going for. To make sure there aren't any conflicts. What did you talk about with Alexander?'

I puffed out my cheeks. My heart was doing about two hundred beats per minute. 'Phoo . . . lots of things.'

It was Eddie's turn to smile, a mischievous, conspiratorial grin. 'Sounds like Alex,' he said. 'One of God's talkers – I bet you couldn't believe your luck.'

'Well, er,' I said. It was true, I couldn't believe my luck – Eddie had not heard anything from De Chauncey and my lie was temporarily intact. And I saw an opportunity. 'That's why transcribing has been such a challenge.'

'Did he go into his background? That's all quite interesting.'

Success had made me willing to gamble. Alexander De Chauncey – what could be read into a name like that? 'I don't know if the readers would care all that much about all that rich-boy stuff, to be honest.'

Eddie's brows crashed together and his top lip wrinkled in disbelief. Error, error, abort, abort. 'I mean,' I said, 'De Chauncey is interesting because he's so different to that kind of story.'

The storm dispersed. 'That's what I thought. So what did he say to get your interest? What angle do you want to take?'

'Property,' I said, with a decisive little nod. 'The property industry. In London.'

Eddie blinked. 'Yes. Well, I should think so. But what in particular?'

'In particular,' I said, tasting the words, 'he was . . . very interesting on giving a . . . general overview, taking in a lot.'

Eddie was nodding. 'Top-down, eagle's-eye stuff? On the industry?'

'Yes,' I said. 'Where it's at. Where it might be going.'

'What did he say about that? Where it might be going.'

'He says . . .' I stopped. Coming up with convincing lies was one thing, it would get me through the next couple of minutes. But I was also running up a bill for the future, placing demands and constraints on an interview that had not yet taken place, that had not even been arranged, and might never take place. If De

Chauncey emailed today saying, 'Sorry, I'm off to Miami for eight weeks, let's do something in the summer,' then I was stuffed.

'It's not quite there yet,' I said, meaning to restrain the lie. It was getting away, pulling the boat. 'Like I say, I'm doing follow-ups.'

Eddie narrowed his eyes. 'What do you mean? I thought you said you had lots of material.'

'Yes. Yes. But I really want to refine his central point, make sure I got it.'

'What was that?'

'What was what?'

'His central point.'

'Well, as I say—'

'As you understand it.'

Both of them leaned in slightly, waiting for my reply. I feared my chair might somehow be on an incline, and could slip away from underneath me, sending me to the floor. The air-con needed a service, for sure, it was blowing out only hot, stale, monoxidey air, scented with hot electrics and smouldering dust.

'It's hot in here,' I said. 'Don't you feel hot?'

Polly and Eddie exchanged a glance. It was an interrogatory glance on Eddie's part, seeking a cue or confirmation from Polly. She bit her lip in response, uncertain.

'You look awful,' Eddie said with a sigh. His tone was not kindly. 'I got you out of bed, didn't I? You haven't washed. You're a mess. What happened to your face?'

'I fell down in the garden,' I said, suddenly aware how pathetic the whole story sounded, even if it was the truth. 'Hit myself on a wall.'

There was no sign of whether Eddie accepted this explanation. He simply moved on. 'Did you go out last night?'

'No,' I said. I thought I hadn't. I genuinely believed that I had not 'gone out' in any conventional sense. After all, while I was out, I had only had two pints, and a couple of bottles. If you didn't count the roadies on the train, which I considered an extension of my at-home drinking. There had been drinking afterwards as well, but that was also at home, not out. But it wasn't as if I had *gone out*, not in the accusatory way that Eddie meant it. 'No, kind of. Not out late though.'

'You were out on Tuesday. I saw on Tamesis.'

Yes, obviously. Everyone had seen that. But that was magazine business! In a way.

'Yes.'

'You're out every night, you're in a state, you're not getting the job done, you're not getting it half done . . .' Eddie sighed and cast his eyes downwards, breaking what had been a chilling stare. 'You're putting me in a very difficult position.'

The long-delayed moment had arrived. I had to play my last card.

'We should postpone the De Chauncey interview,' I said.

Eddie closed his eyes and axed his hand down on the flatplan, hard. 'As I have explained, more than once—'

'*Listen*,' I said. 'You'll want to postpone it when you hear what happened with Pierce. You'll want the pages.'

He reopened his eyes. Polly, who had been tense and straight-spined since Eddie's change in questioning, was staring at me intently, not with malice, but with interest. I had their attention.

'Go on.'

'The mugging book,' I said. I had spent a great deal of time thinking about this moment, but, I realised, had not rehearsed it. 'The bestseller, weeks in the chart.'

'Yes.'

'It's fake. He invented it. Made it all up. It's a fraud, a hoax. He's been lying about it for years and he wants to confess. To us. Exclusive.'

Polly was smiling. Her expression was one of pure avarice. I knew it well: she *wanted* the story. When you get that, you've got them. To want to hear it is to want to believe it. 'That's . . . incredible.'

'Unbelievable,' Eddie said. He wasn't smiling. He was wide-eyed, though. 'He exaggerated it, or . . .?'

'Invented the whole thing,' I said. 'From nothing.'

'That's a phenomenal story,' Polly said. 'We . . .' She turned to Eddie. 'Syndication. National pick-up, definitely. Maybe international.'

Eddie waved his hand, a *slow down* gesture. 'We have this?' he asked me. 'For sure?'

'For sure. Exclusive.'

'You've got it on tape? There's the legal side to consider. We need belt and braces.'

'Belt and braces,' I said, basking in the transformed atmosphere of the room. 'He said he'd sign something for us.' That wasn't even untrue.

'He said he *would* sign something?' Eddie said, ears pricking up. 'He hasn't?'

'He said he'd get it to me this evening.'

'I'd like to listen to the recording.'

I don't know what my face did, exactly, but it wasn't voluntary and it hurt.

'We don't want a repeat of what happened with the Bunk guy,' Eddie said firmly. 'Remember? Definitely not with a big story like this, where a man . . .' He stopped. 'Does he understand the seriousness of it? Pierce, I mean. There might even be legal consequences for him, who knows. We can't afford the slightest risk.'

'It won't be a repeat of what happened with F.A.Q.,' I said.

'I will need to see your notes, and hear the recordings.'

My instinct – an obscene, self-destructive instinct – was to smirk. What notes, what recordings? Hardly a word on paper, nothing on tape. Why did I find that so funny? Because of the gigantic trap I was setting for my apparent nemesis, the future me who would have to make good on these promises?

'Yes,' I said. Put the right spin on it and the word *yes* can be terribly non-committal. 'It's such a big story. I'm still amassing material. I'm seeing him again this afternoon – Pierce, I mean.'

Eddie darkened, but Polly spoke before he could reply. 'There's still tomorrow,' she said to Eddie. *Still* tomorrow? What did that mean? The meeting? But I knew what it meant: much as I might want to find myself delivered into safety, a load of wild promises in a meeting room wasn't going to do it, not alone. I did still have to produce the goods. The Jack of this instant might have evaded disaster, but not future Jack, that poor swine, who had more debts to his name than ever.

'It's a great story, Jack, really great,' she continued, to me. 'I'm excited. It's a cover, I'd say, possibly.' I was very used to phoney encouragement and enthusiasm from Polly, but this seemed to be the real deal. It was disorienting.

Eddie's less enthusiastic attitude was harder to explain. 'Yeah, a great story,' he added, without much heart. 'It's like I say – belt and braces.'

'Got it,' I said. 'Belt and braces.'

'And that means De Chauncey as well. Get the transcript ready for tomorrow. Just polishing to be done, right? A story in the bag, in case something goes wrong and it's Pierce we have to hold over. Belt and braces.'

'Belt and braces. Got it.'

Belt and braces. Belt and braces. Belt and braces.

I left the aquarium in a typhoon of emotion. Pulling me one way was the elation of having avoided certain doom – that would have been it, for me, that meeting, had it not been for Pierce's literary fraud. Pushing me the other way, back towards the abyss, was the certain knowledge that I had neither story and precious little time. To go back now and say, 'Well, I had the Pierce confession, and I lost it, and I never did the De Chauncey interview,' I would be worse off than ever.

Kay followed me with her eyes as I left the meeting, concern jostling with ferocious curiosity. But she did not rise from her seat. Eddie and Polly had remained in place, continuing their mysterious summit – I assumed that Kay did not want to be seen pouncing on me for gossip. The whole team was on edge, with redundancies in the air. I knew that when I sat down and checked my phone, there would be messages from her there.

I was right – and Mohit had messaged too.

What's going on? Kay's first message read. *You OK? That looked intense.*

Mohit asked the same thing: *What's going on?*

I glanced up at him and he gave me a half-smile, still buried in a phone call.

All fine, I replied to Mohit.

I'm fine, I replied to Kay. *It was a bit intense but basically just a catch-up.*

Lunch? Kay fired back.

Maybe later, I replied. *Got loads to do.*

But what could I do? I had neither belt nor braces, and my fly was open as well. Pierce couldn't be relied upon. I was coming to the conclusion that he was unwell. The burden of concealing his fraud had broken him – and fraud itself wasn't the work of a healthy mind. This bizarre obsession with somehow recreating a non-existent crime was evidence of a deep disturbance. There was a ritual quality to it, but what was the ritual supposed to achieve? Balm for his tortured conscience, somehow.

I wish I could say that my worry for him was pure human sympathy, but it was not. My main fear was that he was unravelling too fast for my story, and that his descent might not help me reverse my own.

The horizon kept getting closer, a blazing line of failure that would soon be under my every fleeing footstep. There had been a time when Pierce's welfare might have mattered to me, but it was just interference now, a dull hiss in the ears as I tried to keep myself ahead of disaster. Just as, at the time, I had hardly cared about the consequences of filling the Quin piece with recycled material. The present was a narrow, slippery strip of time, always sliding out from under my feet, and ahead lay the wall. Close, closer than ever.

As if in sympathy with these reflections, the office had taken on a twilight quality, at the height of the day. I looked up to the window and saw a thick grey sheet of incoming winter rain. Into this shroud belched the plume.

But that could not be. When the rain slapped a dome over the city, its edge was always just streets away, not as far as Barking or beyond. But there was the smoke, wide as a borough and taxi black against the grey of the sky. And I could smell it, even behind the office's triple-glazing and air conditioning. I could taste it, that low-octane, high-carcinogen tang, that bouquet of badly maintained gas appliances, dying cars and overloaded wall sockets. The scent of mucus membranes dissolving on contact with compounds not found in nature. It could not be the same fire – it was closer, wider, its pulse more insistent. But where was the concern? No one gathered at the window as they had on Monday. Could they have become somehow desensitised while the city burned out of control? They had their heads down, working.

I put my own head down, taking another slurp from my

bottle. The sight of the plume had disturbed me deeply. Just to be sure, I brought up Tamesis on my phone and checked for events and emergencies to the east of the office that might account for the smoke. There was no major fire. I thumbed the screen eastward, out to Barking, to see what was happening. No alerts, no warnings. The news stories were all a day or two old, apart from one about insurers.

Where's the fire? I asked Tamesis.

The Bunk logo spun in thought.

Where are you? Tamesis asked.

I looked at the Bunk logo. The all-seeing B.

Belt and braces.

I dialled a number. I had been so excited when this number had been sent to me, in an email months before. Another age – I had felt myself up against collapse back then, not knowing how much further I could stagger without falling. Were more months ahead of me? Not a chance. Getting this number, a direct private line, had been a great boon, a way of holding back the coming . . . whatever was coming.

'F.A.Q.'

'Francis, hi. It's Jack Bick.'

'One moment, Mr Bick.'

That's how you know you've arrived – having someone to answer your private direct line. Was that efficient male voice the young assistant who had been with Quin when they found me in the pub on Tuesday evening? His cover? Or could it be – the background noise had changed, a shift perhaps no more than the bearer of the phone moving from one room to another, or perhaps I was talking to a machine, a discreet piece of software that could screen calls on the basis of voice print and other inscrutable factors.

In any case, I was let through.

'Jack Bick,' Quin said, drawing out each word of my name as if I were an old friend and my call had prompted a rush of happy memory. 'What can I do for you?'

'Francis,' I said. 'I, er, wanted . . .' What did I want? What were my three wishes? Or one wish? Magic away my problems, oh genie of the app. No, the monkey's paw was more like it – there would be a price. 'I wanted to thank you for your kind words on Tamesis the other day. It was . . .' It was creepy and alarming and I was still trying to divine the meaning of it. 'It was generous of you.'

'Think nothing of it,' Quin said, in the same warm tone he had used to greet me. Even when we had been arranging his interview, he had not been this effusive. 'It was good to run into you like that. And to clear the air.'

I felt a flicker of anger. *To run into you like that* – like what? He knew like what, the mechanisms he had abused to find me, and I did not. And as for clearing the air, what had been done to clear it? It did not feel clear; what would that mean? A balance between us, a settled account? However it stood, it was not in my favour, I knew that.

'Yes,' I said cautiously. 'I've been using Tamesis a bit more lately.'

'That's great,' Quin said. 'You'll find that the more you put in, the more you get out. The more it learns, the better the results.'

'I've been a little suspicious of it in the past,' I said. I had a way to approach the topic, and I tried to keep it in mind. An interviewer evolves these skills. 'You know, it can be a bit spooky at times, like Google knowing where you are and what you're doing . . .'

Quin chuckled. 'Yes. But spooky is good! I count spooky as praise. Spooky means that it's working. Wrong isn't spooky. Unhelpful isn't spooky. Spooky is getting it right. I love spooky.'

'It knows so much . . .'

'It doesn't know, it deduces,' Quin said. 'Location and time tell us so much. You're in a restaurant at lunchtime, we can safely say you're eating there. You're on a certain street at a certain time of night, we can assemble the rest . . .'

Time of night? Why would he say time of night? Was he making an oblique reference to my walk with Pierce? It was troubling, but it was exactly the kind of snooping that I wanted to exploit. If he had meant my evening activities, he had not been able to resist mentioning that he knew – that unwise desire to flaunt his capabilities was what I was relying on.

'I was wondering if you might be able to help me with something.'

'I'm already helping you,' Quin said, amused. 'Don't you remember?'

I didn't remember. I had the sense of descending an unfamiliar flight of stairs in the dark, and believing I had reached the landing one step too soon: a sickening void and plunge where there should have been a footing, then a jarring impact. But what would it look like to admit to a blank spot in my memory? Could he be referring to something that I did know about? The Tamesis post? The decision to let my plagiarism slide? One of those. 'To help me with something else,' I said.

'Go on.'

'I need to find someone,' I said, lowering my voice. Mohit was engrossed elsewhere. I could not see Kay. I had come to the crucial moment, but found it was difficult to articulate what I needed. 'Alexander De Chauncey. I'd like to get an idea of where he is going to be over the next couple of days.' No. That wasn't enough. Push. 'This afternoon. I want to find him, and I don't know where he is. This afternoon, ideally.'

A breath on the other side. A thoughtful sound. 'I know

Alexander a little,' Quin said. Why wasn't I surprised? 'Interesting fellow. Busy. You understand, I can't just share location data from Tamesis. That would be a terrible breach of trust. Not to mention against the law.'

'Of course,' I said. I understood that there was another game to be played, a fiction to be co-written.

'But some information is public, or semi-public,' Quin continued. 'It simply resides with particular audiences, and not others; it has not been restricted, it has simply not been distributed. The delineations may be arbitrary. If we tweaked the audience of that information, fractionally expanded it . . . Well, you could call that *journalism*.'

'Well put,' I said. Again, I checked to see what the others were doing. They were preoccupied, but I softened my voice another decibel or two. 'And speaking of journalism, I know that you are taking a keen interest in my profile of Pierce, and if there is anything you want to contribute that might ensure its accuracy . . .'

'Accuracy is so important,' Quin purred. 'How is it going with Pierce?'

'Pierce is very committed to doing the profile his way,' I said. I tried to sound tired, which came easily.

'Yes,' said Quin, concern in his tone. 'I believe he would rather not do it at all.'

'I wish I could make him understand that interviews are not written for the benefit of the interviewee,' I said, choosing my words carefully. 'They are written solely for the benefit of the reader.'

'Mmm,' Quin murmured, hesitant, not confirming or contradicting.

I needed to make myself plain. 'I want to get the story right. Pleasing the reader is my only concern.'

'Well—'

'You are the reader.'

A satisfied exhalation was carried across the city's ether. 'Oh, I see. Well. That's good to hear. How can I help?'

'What proof do you have of Pierce's fraud?' I asked. 'He told me that you stumbled across evidence while uploading his research into Tamesis . . .'

'Not quite,' Quin said. 'I must have been close. We were looking at his notes relating to *Night Traffic*, that's true. Not prying – they were scattered everywhere in his files, no system at all. Pierce . . . it's a harsh thing to say about anyone, but his data architecture is simply *woeful*.'

'And you found inconsistencies? Evidence that he had invented the story?'

'No!' Quin said, with a laugh. 'Inconsistencies, that suggests intent, pattern, composition – no, Pierce's notes were simply garbled. Word salad. I was concerned and mentioned it to him, and he became very agitated and upset. Then he confessed. Told me the whole story. Said I was the only one who knew, apart from himself.'

My gut cramped. 'He led me to believe that you found out because of data analysis, punching everything into the Bunk mainframe . . .'

'I dare say we would have done eventually,' Quin said. 'We already had a lot of data relating to *Night Traffic* entered – "punched in", if you want to be antique about it. No killer proof, though. But it doesn't matter now, because of your superb work. You have the proof. It has all worked out.' Another stirring came down the line – a muffled voice, perhaps? 'Jack, it's been a pleasure, fantastic to hear it's all going so well, but some people are waiting for me. Let's later this. See you on Tamesis.'

And he was gone.

I lowered my phone. It was blood-hot and my palm was sweaty. But my insides were chilled. I had imagined that Quin had a grail, a smoking gun, an iron tabulation of Pierce's errors and inventions that I could use to back up my story in the absence of cooperation from the author. But perhaps no such dossier existed. Quin had been relying on *me* for proof. I had betrayed Pierce by promising that I would write the story the way Quin wanted, while lacking the proof needed to actually write that story, thus running the risk of betraying Quin. It was entirely possible that through my fumbling they would both end up furious with me. And all that was predicated on actually writing something, anything, and that didn't seem any likelier than it had earlier in the week. I had gone behind Pierce's back for nothing – possibly worse than nothing.

Unless. I woke the phone and brought up Tamesis. What I expected, I don't know. A glowing icon on the map showing the precise location of Alexander De Chauncey, like in a spy movie. Here's the arsehole, marked with a brown star to match the blue Bunk star.

Nothing like that. The screen was merrily filling with information: nearby cafés and restaurants in which I might want to have lunch. Nearby pubs. The city glowed hot around the office – multiple T-plus contacts in the vicinity. My colleagues. I thumbed over to Wolfe / De Chauncey's Shoreditch office, only a few streets away, but there was no tell-tale emblem or pulse there.

All the air was going from the room. I picked up my aluminium bottle, but it was empty. When had that happened? The last sip of beer had dried to glue inside my mouth. The meeting in the aquarium had broken up at last and it was empty, door open. Outside my bubble of misery, this had released some of the tension in the atmosphere, and the office felt busier and more relaxed with Eddie and Polly back at their desks, Eddie on the phone, Polly chatting quite normally with Kay. Already, it was lunchtime – I could sneak out and recharge.

But Polly was on guard. As soon as I left my seat and put on my coat, her eyes were on me; when I made for the door, she at once broke off her conversation with Kay and hailed me.

'How's it going?' she asked.

'Oh, you know,' I said. 'Getting there.'

But she hadn't meant *how's it going*, she had meant *where are you going*. 'It would be great if we could see something this afternoon,' she said. 'Ready for the meeting tomorrow. Going to lunch?'

She said it with a smile, but I picked up the implicit warning, and could imagine her making a mental note of the time for later addition to her clipboard, ready to be compared to the time of return.

'Uh, yeah,' I said. 'Just going to get something in.'

Kay had been watching this exchange, impassive. Hearing this, she returned her attention to her screen, a touch of coolness in her demeanour.

'Great. See you soon.' The threat lay near the surface.

I did not dare to go to the pub, not even for one, not even for a half. Instead I went straight to the sandwich shop, where I bought a BLT and a bottle of water to go. But the water was a depressing weight in the little brown paper bag they gave me. I needed a proper drink. I went to the nearest convenience store, a little hole in the wall I usually avoid for fear of running into someone from work. The cans were sold individually, each with a little luminous sticker bearing its steep price. I put the cans in a battered basket and added a couple of vodka miniatures. The spirits were OK because I wasn't drinking them on their own; relying on them, that was a slippery slope – I was just using them to fortify my beer. Two cans went into each outside pocket and the minis went into an inside pocket.

The aluminium bottle made all this possible – it really was proving a boon. I should bring it in every day. But my plan – plan was really too grand a word – had only come together in the sandwich shop, and I had left the bottle on my desk. Discreetly decanting the cans would be a logistical challenge.

It had started to rain. The thick cloud almost reached street level, but still the plume was there, a foul swatch of crisp, peristaltic filth against the opaque, even grey of the winter storm. No more ambiguity: it was closer. The question of why, or how, would have to wait. There were higher priorities.

I returned to the office, grimly aware of every clank and jangle that issued from my overweight coat, feeling like a cross between a poacher and a primitive robot from a 1950s movie. And getting into the office was only the start of it. Somehow I would have to get the bottle and decant the cans into it, when I was sure that my moves would not be closely watched. For the second time that day, I found myself stalled in the area between the lifts and the office, trying to figure out what to do next.

Fate came to my assistance. While I had been out, the lunch exodus had taken place. On a normal day I would have left before it started and returned after it had returned, so I had forgotten that it happened at all. But our part of the office was almost deserted – no Mohit, no Polly, no Rays, no Kay. Eddie was inside his stockade and Ilse was trying to burn holes through her vast Mac screen with a kind of focused horror. Neither was likely to pay me much heed. Keeping my coat on, I put the paper bag containing my sandwich down on my desk and picked up the aluminium bottle. Then I turned and left, going to the toilets, heart pounding in my chest. If I was discovered, explanations would be difficult and suspicions would be confirmed. Why take that risk? I did not have a ready answer to that – just that the unbearable pain of carrying on was, for today, better than the unknowable pain of stopping.

I had to use a cubicle, for privacy, and that presented more difficulties. The only flat surface was the seat, the cisterns were behind the tiled wall. The bottle would only fit two cans, so half of my purchase would have to wait until later, and I would have to repeat this whole ridiculous operation. I hung my winter coat on the back of the cubicle door and opened a can. The crack of the seal breaking seemed aberrantly loud in the confined space of the cubicle, and it hissed and spattered seething beer over the back of my hand. It had been bouncing around in my pocket, getting agitated, they all had, and I would need to be careful. Foam continued to well up, splashing onto the floor, so I put the can to my lips and slurped away the excess, desperate to stop the loss.

The cold beer touched me like a benediction, immediately banishing the vileness and dryness that had gathered in my mouth. But with its spreading, quenching coolth came fear. I had not checked the other cubicles when I came in. There were three. I had rushed to the end one, furthest from the door, considering it most discreet. But I had not checked the others to see if they were occupied.

I held still, listening for any sounds of occupation from the neighbouring cubicle – a sniff, a breath, a scuff of shoes on tile. Nothing came. The partitions had wide gaps at the top and bottom – I dipped down to see if I could see feet. Nothing. Safe, I was fairly sure. Fairly.

Continue. I poured the beer into the bottle, where it gurgled and frothed but behaved itself. Then I added the contents of one of the miniatures, before taking out a second can. This time I was more careful. I pulled back the tab with care. The beer began to push and spit through the small fracture.

The toilet door opened, and someone walked in.

The beer was still hissing and hawking, sounds that seemed deafeningly loud in the confined space. White spume was filling the lipped area on top of the can.

They paused, whoever it was who had come in. Were they checking themselves in the mirror, opening their fly, or pondering over the strange noises coming from the far cubicle? It was, at least, a plumbing kind of sound, the sound of a spluttering tap or a limescaled cistern trying to refill itself.

But the beer would spill if I did nothing. I put my lips to the circular white puddle that had formed on top of the can and tried to quietly drain some of it away. The spitting changed pitch. I prayed that the newcomer stayed out of the cubicles, but feared it made little difference.

Urine splashed into the urinal. I used the cover of the noise to slurp more greedily at the beer. The pressure within the can had eased and it had stopped its tell-tale whispering, but I couldn't pull back the tab all the way without an unmistakeable report in the echoing hush of the lav.

Whoever finished his business and washed his hands. Then he exited. Perhaps he had never known of my presence. I poured the second can into the bottle, but made the mistake of hurrying, so the foam rose up the neck and ran out over my knuckles. Sticky residue would be left everywhere – I would have to run the bottle under the tap. And I was not quite finished. There was a problem I had not anticipated: the empties, two cans and the plastic bottle of the miniature. I didn't like the thought of carrying them around in my coat pocket – they might be lighter, but they would rattle more, and drip and smell.

There was a litter bin in the toilet, a good deep flip-top bin, but I was wary of leaving the cans on top of the rubbish, in case they were seen. So when Eddie entered the bathroom, he found me digging around in the bin, trying to bury them, and although he saw nothing specific his nod of greeting was accompanied by a deep frown of obvious suspicion.

He went to the urinal, and I went to wash.

The cold water was too cold – I was shivering. Or rather, my hands, pale as blobfish dredged from the deepest ocean, were shaking. I turned the water to hot and squirted soap onto my palm, hoping the rubbing of one hand against another might steady the tremor and burn up the time until Eddie left.

Eddie joined me at the sinks and soaped his own hands, eyeing the energetic lather than I had generated.

'We never really finished our talk about Alexander,' he said.

Part of the flimsy scenery of my life came crashing down. The strength was going from my legs, getting sucked into an abyss of unconsciousness and collapse. I had eaten nothing in more than twenty-four hours, and the consequences were coming, the horizon was closer than ever.

'Didn't we?' I said.

'No. And I'd like to hear more about how it went.'

'I've been prioritising Pierce,' I said.

'Well, don't forget about Alexander,' Eddie said. 'I want to see some of that, too.'

'I thought we were postponing it,' I said, clinging to hope.

Eddie fixed me with a stern, patient look. He had finished his hands; I had not yet rinsed mine. 'On Monday,' he said slowly, 'we agreed that you would do both.'

'A lot has changed since then,' I said.

'Nothing has changed. What's changed?'

Well, I was dramatically more fucked up, but that wasn't worth mentioning.

'I don't see the problem,' Eddie said. 'You did both, right? So tidy up some quotes, write an intro, and bring it into the meeting.'

'Pierce is such a big story—' I began.

'So big,' Eddie interrupted, 'that we might need to hold it. If there are legal issues. We have to be careful. So you have work to do, yes?'

'Yes.'

'You're a senior team member, I shouldn't have to explain this.'

'No. I understand.'

'Good.' And he stalked away.

With his departure, my last supporting wire was snipped. My fingers slipped and jarred as I turned off the tap, and I slumped against the sink. My hands had probably never been cleaner.

Losing my job was one thing. I doubted my ability to get another, certainly in the brief window before financial disaster. The Need would thicken to fill every crack of every day, to fill every part of life, and that would be the end. But that was just a technicality. Losing the respect and friendship of Eddie, who was friends with everyone and supported everyone, Eddie who would do anything for his staff: that was so much worse. It was that that marked me as impossible to save – as unfit for saving.

Back at my desk, I checked emails for some kind of signal from Pierce, from Quin, from De Chauncey or his PR, from anyone. But there was nothing. What would they say, anyway? What was I expecting, or hoping for? What was the best case, now?

I looked at Tamesis. There were notifications, which I had assumed were the long tail of Wednesday morning's surge. And mostly they were, but for two: an event invitation, and confirmation of my RSVP.

I hadn't RSVPed to anything. But there it was, Tamesis had marked me as definitely attending an event this afternoon.

The Directors of Harbinger Homes and Wolfe / De Chauncey cordially invite you to celebrate the final phase of . . .

TEN

I bought a can-crusher. I think that was an important step.

Elise was unhappy about the cans. The empty cans, specifically. I did not keep large supplies of lager in the fridge, I bought the cans in fours, always trying to camouflage them with other, necessary purchases. I became very conscientious about doing the household shop. I went to the little Tesco three or four times a week. But although I would meet immediate needs, I would never pre-empt future shortages. I might remember that we were on the last dregs of Fairy Liquid just as I stepped out of the front door, and yet choose not to buy any, so as to have another reason to go out in a day or two. Lots of little trips, that was the trick. I don't know how much I thought of it as a 'trick', or thought about how the run of my life was beginning to bend around the cans in the fridge. Not thinking ahead was my way of thinking ahead.

Every time I went out, I bought four cans. Not too many – nothing to suggest that I had a problem. When I couldn't reasonably go to Tesco, I'd go to the little convenience store on the corner and get a couple of cans. Maybe a stick of gum or a Lion bar as well.

Elise became worried about the amount I drank. She saw the can before dinner, the wine during dinner, the wine and cans after dinner. She didn't confront me about it, that wasn't her way. She was forever fearful of nagging, of being shrewish. That wasn't her, she said; it didn't seem like a very grown-up way to handle a relationship, she said. I appreciated that, and the generations of male manipulation that have put these fears into the minds of thoughtful, caring women. She told me that she was worried that *she* was drinking too much in the evenings, and perhaps we could limit ourselves. Yes, of course, it was easy to agree. I didn't want her to worry, so I started being more subtle. If we were watching TV after dinner, I'd wait until she went to the loo before opening a new can. It wouldn't be obvious, as long as I kept a couple of empties on the table beside me. I discovered that it was possible to open a couple of new cans at once, and have both beside me. That way I wouldn't get the sideways glance, directed at the can as I carried it from the fridge. I knew that glance was connected to an unspoken tally. That it was connected to the presence, the growing presence, the unacknowledged and unspeakable presence, in the flat, in the relationship, in our lives. I didn't want her to worry, that was why I started to conceal.

The empties were difficult, though. A source of contention. A source of worry. I could replenish the cans every day, but the recycling only went once a week, and the empties would pile up, filling the small green kitchen bin. If the recycling truck didn't come, or we missed it, a real storage crisis would develop, and the silent presence in the flat would inch into visibility. It was the empties that caused the first real argument – the first time we stopped talking about the symptoms of the presence, and touched on the presence itself. Elise did not say that I drank too much, or that I had a problem; no doubt that was what she wanted to say, but she did not. It was presented simply as a household problem: too many cans.

So I bought a can-crusher. That was my solution. No more reproachful sentinels on the countertop. I knew what she meant when she complained about the cans, what she really meant. But I aimed squarely at the symptom, and my thought when I found the crusher in the hardware shop was: this will make it much harder to keep track. Not: there is a problem here that must be addressed. Not even: I must make an effort to keep the kitchen tidy. My only thought, when I brought it home and installed it, was concealment.

The cocktail wasn't very appealing once I got it back to my desk, but I drank it anyway, and without too much hesitation. Who was I trying to fool?

Quin had delivered, it couldn't be denied. He had inserted me into the guest list for an event that afternoon, and De Chauncey would be present. But I couldn't simply show up and start interviewing. I might not even be able to get close to the man. And leaving the office was a problem in itself. I was being watched. It would be very hard to explain to my jailers why I had to go to this event: as far as Eddie and Polly knew, the interview with De Chauncey was done already. That was the fiction that we were all role-playing, anyway: Eddie possibly knew the truth, or had suspicions, and was giving me the space to humiliate myself, to heap up lies until the whole edifice of deception collapsed with no way for me to escape from the wreckage. Tomorrow morning, it would come crashing down.

I sat at my desk, drinking from my bottle, planning my exit. The event began at 4 p.m., an afternoon tea, and it was close to the office, at Zebedee, a boutique hotel off Great Eastern Street. I could *Mary Celeste* it: hurry out wearing only my jacket, leaving my computer switched on with my pad and pen prominent nearby, my bag under my desk and my winter coat on the back of my chair. I might have gone to the toilet, or to make a sensitive phone call in the stairwell, which people did all the time. The chair was important: it mustn't be tucked under the desk, but left sticking out, turned to one side, as if I might return at any moment. By the time my absence was noted and it became clear I wasn't coming back, it would be the end of the working day. Easy.

Rain was falling in freezing sheets, and I wished I had my winter coat on, but it helped the illusion to leave it. Who would go out in this downpour without their coat? I pulled up my lapels, kept my head down and hurried along Old Street, sticking close to buildings. As I reached the steps down to the underpasses around the Tube station, I almost ran into a skulking object, and it responded with a burst of frenzied white wings. A cockatoo, taking flight! But no, a man rushing into the station, trying to shelter himself with a collapsing copy of the *Evening Standard*. I gave some thought to buying a cheap umbrella, but the damage was already done, and I feared the cumulative effect of the bruises on my face and my bedraggled, creased clothes.

'Always look the part' was another piece of advice my father had given me. Thinking about this guidance, I realised it had kinship with what he had said about deterring muggings by looking threatening. The world didn't check ID too closely – wear the right clothes and you'd get given the according role. Therefore we had a surprising amount of latitude to define ourselves; to say 'this is me' and be accepted.

This advice was deeply rooted in background, of course: white, male, middle-class, educated. Change any one of those characteristics and Dad's look-the-part ideology might not have carried him so far. And he had a further advantage in that he only aspired to a kind of provincial, professional stoutness, and nature had happily shaped him to that purpose. The suits he wore were not fancy or flashy or even tailored, but they looked like extensions of his very essence, so they fitted, in all ways they fitted. One time, in the buccaneering early days of home internet, he had found a site that would send you a hand-made suit from Hong Kong if you entered an extremely detailed set of measurements. Dad was extremely excited about this service, and its astoundingly low price tag, and after he and Mum had spent an hour with the tape measure, the suit was ordered. Seven weeks later it arrived, and my father tried it on. The cut was flawless, the material exquisite. But it was all wrong. It was too obsequious to the form beneath. It was too personal. What suited my father about suits was their anonymising, smoothing effect: wool blankness.

Both my parents saw the problem with the work of art that came back from the Far East. 'It's very smart,' said my mother, with a tilt to the words that made them utterly damning. He never wore it again.

By the time I arrived at Zebedee, I did not like to imagine the impression I made. The icy rain had given me a headache and my hands looked shockingly pale, like creatures dredged up from an ocean trench. The receptionist's smile was a technicality, and he directed me to the function room with a blend of relief and scorn: I was not a guest, but also not his problem, and I would linger only a while. He would not have to eject me, I was not one of the invisible people made shockingly visible.

The clipboard-wielding women in tight red skirts at the double door of the function room were more difficult to pass. They viewed my approach with open disbelief and dismay, and they checked their lists with obvious doubt. Order was restored to their universe when my name could not be found. No Jack Bick.

A flaw in Quin's mastery, a missing connection, an unfilled field? It was always possible – if the lists had been printed before he had worked his magic, for instance – but it struck me as unlikely. Another explanation seemed more probable.

I closed my eyes, terribly weary, head pounding. 'I might be down as James Bickerton.'

The ballpoints traced through the Bs again. Rubbery little smiles. 'Mr Bickerton. Welcome.'

It was only sensible to account for Quin's casual arrogance, his urge to flaunt what he knew, what he could find out. He would have his justifications, of course – discretion, perhaps, believing that I might wish to conceal my presence here. But the real purpose would always be to send a little message: hey, *James*. I found your real name.

How much of my life had been spent crafting myself for those moments – the moment the smartly dressed young people on the door stepped aside with a smile. But the day was coming when I would no longer pass. When no name of mine would be on the list and I no longer looked the part. It was close, now.

For now I was through, again. Into the discordant grandeur of Zebedee's main function room: plain breezeblock walls accented with touches of gold leaf, exposed metal ducts on the high ceiling, some of which appeared to have come free and were hanging by unsteady threads, their interiors blazing with white LED light. Postmodern chandeliers. Big screens and a stage at one end of the room, a bar and buffet table at the other. I was handed a glass of champagne and drained it – but it was not champagne, it was smoky and bitter, like cold fizzy tea.

'What is this?' I asked, spluttering.

'Assampagne,' the surgeon-suited waiter said. 'A sparkling tea blend, non-alcoholic, low calorie and high in antioxidants.'

'Delightful,' I lied. 'May I have another?' The awful possibility that the event might be dry had, thank heavens, occurred to me before I left the office, and I had taken precautions, picking up another couple of miniatures that I could use to Long Island this tea. Fortunately, I could see phalanxes of wine glasses being filled beside the food. The food was eccentric interpretations of the 'afternoon tea': a 'deconstructed egg and cress sandwich' that comprised a peeled quail's egg, an egg-shaped ball of white dough and a single stem of cress in an egg-shaped bubble of aspic. Pass. In the far corner of the room was a display that resembled a Gordon Matta Clark artwork: the disembodied corners of four rooms, providing the sample 'spec' of the apartments being launched, the materials used for floor and wall coverings, the look of the power sockets, taps and lights. In this small maze of room-shards I quietly slipped a vodka miniature from my pocket and added it to the Assampagne, taking care to do it over a sink – half a sink, anyway, sliced through the middle. The spirit didn't do much to improve the taste of the cold, bubbly tea but at least I knew it was doing me some good.

Thus fortified, I surveyed the room, looking for De Chauncey. Although I had seen pictures of him online and in the *Standard*, that didn't help. The expensive suit, the winter tan, the overall sheen of private education and attentive skincare. The glow of Ownership. There were four dozen people here who fitted that description, and a similar number of their female analogues. This wasn't an event for hopefuls looking for first homes, but rather the representatives of more significant interests, bulk-buyers, the agents of agents, varnished marionettes whose strings connected to immense bergs of capital. And people in the industry, wheel-oilers, for whom this was a social occasion, the chance to enjoy the beginning or the end of something, and to show off. And lifestyle journalists, industry journalists, people who did not naturally have the glow but who were good at faking it as part of their work. Just as I used to be. Journalism – this kind of journalism – offered unbeatable opportunities for aspirational role-play, the brief chance to pretend to be rich, to be inside the high-ceilinged room behind the clipboards, drinking the absurd drink, enjoying a premium experience. It was a life full of those tiny tastes, used to promote this or that, the five-minute helicopter rides, and it attracted (or failed to repel) the chameleon type. I used to be able to fake the glow too: I did have the one good suit and the two good shirts, and contrary to what my parents believed I could look the part; but there were other parts I wanted to look: the young writer, the edgy journalist, which was why James Bickerton had become Jack Bick, a name I thought was more *Vice*. That was what had made me such a fan of Oliver Pierce: he was doing what I wanted to do.

A short man with prematurely grey hair, not De Chauncey, took the stage and addressed the room with the assured nonchalance of the very rich. 'If you could all find a seat . . .' He recognised someone in the crowd and gave them a wave and a wink. 'We'll kick off in a minute or two.'

I dumped my empty glass at the bar and took a couple of glasses of wine – 'this is for someone', perfectly true, they were both for someone, I was someone – before finding a seat near the back of the room, but not so near the back that the bar staff would be able to see me drink both glasses. I was at the side, by the windows looking onto the street. It was dark already and the rain was hammering down. A filthy night, my mother would have said.

Once the company was seated, the short man again took the stage. 'Ladies and gentlemen, thank you so much for coming out in this beautiful London weather' – a public relations laugh from the room – 'to join me to celebrate as the final phase of YOLO Shoreditch comes to market. We're incredibly proud of these last 171 units, completing a development that is already one of London's must-have addresses. You'll be pleased to hear I won't speak long, I'm sure a lot of you are keen to get back to the bar' – a laugh – 'and maybe try some of those eggy things, that is if Charlie hasn't enjoyed them all' – a bigger, less polite laugh from a smaller number of people. 'We've got a short video for you in a moment, to give you a taste of this beautiful project, and then I'll be handing over to Alexander De Chauncey of Wolfe / De Chauncey, who is handling sales on YOLO just as he did so ably on Bling Battersea, Tribeca Catford and N.W. Wow . . .'

My phone was vibrating. It was silent, but not switched off. Eddie or Polly, wise to my escape and calling me back for a bollocking, that was my guess. It was bad. I couldn't answer, not in the middle of a presentation, and I didn't want to draw attention to myself by leaving the room. I had come here to see Alexander De Chauncey. I would listen to him talk and then maybe try to ambush him afterwards. He was here to network, to sell, I was sure he would work the room – it wasn't much, but it was something, and I was staying.

I slipped the phone from my pocket. It wasn't the office – it was Pierce. Calling, rather than emailing or messaging, struck me as being very Pierce: unpredictable, eccentric. But I had to thumb him over to voicemail. It would be about our plans for the evening – scrapping them, I hoped, in light of the rain. The wetter it got, and the drunker I got, the more appealing I found the idea of staying in, even if it meant no confession, no co-operation, no nothing. I could just try to busk past that tomorrow. Pierce's idea was scarcely workable even in fine weather, so he could hardly insist.

I had other notifications. Tamesis knew that I was at this event – it wanted me to post about it and tag in others. It suggested other T-plus contacts in the area: Alexander De Chauncey, Francis Quin, Eddie, Polly. Meet up, make connections. Build social capital, make the city smarter.

Sitting in a brightly lit room beside a huge picture window, I had the sudden fear that I might be very visible. From the street, I would be as prominent as an overpriced handbag in Selfridges' Christmas display, and a passing colleague might see me and wonder what I was doing. Nothing very wrong, as it happened, but I feared any line of questioning that attached to one of the loose threads of a lie. And there were plenty of lies and plenty of loose threads. I stared out of the window. The CEO of Harbinger Homes had wrapped up his introduction with a few in-jokes and we were on to the video: the towers of the financial district, hurrying crowds of commuters, shops and buses in the West End, beards and thick-framed glasses being creative in Shoreditch. Maps of the area that made YOLO appear to be the hub of the entire transport network. Computer visualisations of the project as it would appear when completed. The promise of Crossrail. Renderings of room interiors. Dashing young couples touching champagne flutes on balconies, the lights of the city before them.

I could hardly see the street. The moving lights of cars and the dim nebulae of the streetlights were the clearest, and splashes and smears of reflection. I hoped that the rain would wash the smoke from the sky and scour the hydrocarbons from every surface. The few passers-by had their heads down, cowering under umbrellas or sodden newspapers. But in the shuttered murk of the far side of the street, paleness stirred. Someone was there, a white face sheltered in a gateway, watching me.

A passing car disrupted the scene long enough for me to lose the face, or whoever it was moved away – but there was something else there, in the lake-bottom sludge, white forms like skulls. I leaned into the glass, wishing that I could wipe away the beating, racing drops that marred its outer surface. There they were, I could see them distinctly. Cockatoos, three of them, perched on the sill of a bricked-up window, sheltered under the arch above.

It could not be. Simply another manifestation of the odd phenomenon that had dogged me. I would hesitate before saying *hallucination*, still more before saying *vision*, but I was seeing something that I could feel sure did not exist as a physical fact. Not even seeing, really, just interpreting a shape in the gloom as a bird – three birds, in this case. What would it be this time? Rubbish bags stuffed into the slats of a ventilator, the hasty zags of a graffito, a family of albino pigeons? Not actual cockatoos.

I stared at . . . the source of the impression. Three birds, perched in a line, exactly opposite my window seat, stared back at me. I tried to unlatch the illusion, to break its spell and have the reality of the scene drop into place. It did not. The cockatoos remained. One tipped its head to one side. Another took a step sideways. Was it possible? I knew of the colonies of wild parakeets in London's parks, a whole population thriving from a few fugitive pets. But cockatoos, really? In midwinter?

The video presentation came to an end with a flourish of rousing music. White yuppies faded from the screen, replaced by the words YOLO SHOREDITCH on black, and PHASE 3 NOW AVAILABLE. The man from Harbinger Homes led a restrained round of applause as he retook the stage. But he did not stay: he was there to introduce a man who 'needed no introduction'. Alexander De Chauncey, who followed in a boyish burst of energy, came in for a power handshake with the Harbinger exec. The crowd clapped, and he clapped as well. There was no distance between how he looked in real life and how he looked in the magazine photoshoots – as if he had already been retouched, in the flesh.

'Thank you, thank you,' he said, acknowledging the applause, closing his eyes and inclining his head modestly, still clapping. 'Thank you. Let me tell you, it's such a treat to be involved in this *beautiful*' – he prolonged the word in a practised cockney drawl – 'project right here in Shoreditch, where I started my little business twenty years ago. And as we've grown, we've witnessed this area's transformation, and it's such a treat, ladies and gentlemen, such a treat to be part of a beautiful project like this, which is carrying forward that regeneration. What this is, it isn't just building, this is *placemaking*.'

I had taken out my phone and started recording when De Chauncey came on stage, and I looked down at the jittering heart-attack line on the screen as applause again rippled across the room.

'The beauty, for us gathered in the room today, is in watching the unfolding of this glorious natural process, regeneration. It's been going on here a while, turning a place where you wouldn't want to walk down the street at night into a world-class residential investment neighbourhood. In YOLO, we're seeing the latest stage of that process.

'First of all, you've got the artists, the cool kids, the people I call the *trendsetters*. Not a lot of dough but loads of savvy, yeah, like me back in the day. I love these guys, the pioneers, the early adopters, the shock troops. You know, scratch an artist, a creative person, and you'll find an entrepreneur, someone who can see what others can't, someone who can make something from nothing. And that's what they've done here. But, like I say, not much dough. What they do is bring in the businesses – the coffee shop and the bike shops, and the few investors with the vision to see what the artists saw. That's where I come in. You look at where the artists are going, and you follow. Shoreditch, Hoxton and Dalston yesterday, Peckham and Hackney Wick and Walthamstow today, Leytonstone and Canning Town and Tottenham tomorrow. You know, the funny part is, I don't know anything about art. But I love what they do in the property market. So you can call me a critic. A connoisseur.

'After the artists, the money starts coming in – the hipsters, the younger City guys, guys in advertising. People who want buzz, who want to live somewhere a bit edgy, a bit cool, who want realness and authenticity. They're the ones who establish the neighbourhood as an investment destination. That's when beautiful projects like this get unlocked, and that's where you come in, ladies and gentlemen.'

A friendly murmur of recognition ran through the room. I squirmed in my seat.

'Is there still value to be realised in Shoreditch?' De Chauncey asked. 'There assuredly is, ladies and gentlemen; every day we see handsome gain on new developments, especially when bold investors buy off-plan, as the first and second waves of regeneration give way to a stable third-wave ownership community. And Wolfe / De Chauncey is here to help you realise that value. I call it the no-key guarantee: you won't even have to set foot in your assets. We can offer end-to-end agency service, handling every stage of the tenant journey totally seamlessly. You'll hardly know they're there. What we offer is the investment dream: all the advantages of ownership and none of the burden.'

He paused, as if setting up a punchline.

'Of course, you might be looking to live in the property yourself. Whatever. I'm not here to judge.'

Laughter. Heads bobbed and I gave the backs of necks an executioner's eye. Groomed hair, sharp-edged: all had felt the warmth and gentle press of the barber's electric razor recently. Mine had not. Some of the necks were fat, folded, spammy; others tanned and gym-fit. White collars on coloured shirts. Gold chains. These were them, for sure, these were the owners. Pierce would want to be here – a room rigid with targets.

I finished the first glass of wine and began the second. The woman sitting three empty seats away from me turned her head, very slightly, precision electronics, keeping her glance discreet, but I still clocked it. I might have muttered something under my breath to draw her attention, an opinion of the people in the room, or she had noticed the chain-drinking. I turned to her and raised my glass cheerily. She turned away, stony. I didn't take any pleasure. I just didn't want to be seen.

De Chauncey's pitch had the cadence of words spoken many times, a funny story the teller is fond of telling, smooth and pretty as sea-glass. Like most self-made men, he enjoyed reflecting on his beginnings. The tale was given an air of humble, self-deprecating surprise, as if success had been the last thing on his mind, and he couldn't quite believe it had arrived. Curious that self-unmade men, like myself, had the same obsession with origins, but a harder job finding them. For De Chauncey's breed, there was always the good decision, the bold move, the happy partnership, the opportunity that others had missed, that spelled success. Whereas I skidded to failure on a smear of circumstances and decisions that hadn't even felt like decisions when they happened. Maybe it was the same for De Chauncey, really, but he had been able to rationalise it all in a way that I had not, to compose it into a neat story. Of course he would want to justify his success, and make it logical, laudable, only right.

The opposite view – that his ascent had been a pinball journey of luck and accident – implied that all our fates were simply random, that we were in the passenger seat of life, watching the scenery as we approached the Savoy or the cliff edge. No one wants that. I say that as a storyteller – it was my job to give lives meaning on the page. A narrative, an arc: that was what people wanted. The truth was only an accessory. What was a story but a *semblance* of truth, a flavour of truth, applied to a collection of details that may or may not be true? And to collect those details, to include some and not others, was to engineer the truth. Not to warp or undermine it – let's not be judgemental. But to organise it. To give it meaning. Otherwise it was no more than a transcript of a toddler's unchronological torrent of tear-soaked, dribbling confession: true, no doubt, but impossible to follow.

De Chauncey, for instance, was editing, as well he might: some colour about setting up his first office in Shoreditch before Shoreditch was Shoreditch, with junkies on the doorstep, and the deals that eased his rise – useful stuff for me, yes, and I could feel myself, without even wanting to, editing the edit to serve what I might want to write. But the story had all the omissions and elisions one expected. The money must always come from somewhere, and circumstances count. He had started just as the city began its long, blazing boom, the eruption of wealth that we were only now coming to the end of. His particular dealings were trifles against the stirring of the leviathan he had ridden for twenty years, which shattered the land and remade it.

He had moved on from the general spiel about himself and London – one good for any occasion – to the specifics of phase

3 of YOLO Shoreditch. Wolfe / De Chauncey's investment package for rental property came with the very latest in tenant management technology, thanks to a ground-breaking joint venture with—

I belched – a sudden upward rush of rotten acid was behind it. It was as if a switch had been thrown, and I had gone from feeling broadly fine to reeling with nausea and knowing, for a fact, that I would vomit, very soon, perhaps too soon to do anything decorous about it. Phase 3 of YOLO Shoreditch might at any moment receive an unholy baptism, right here in the Zebedee function room. I rose from my seat, not fully standing, doing that embarrassed stoop that we do when leaving a cinema during a film, and bumped into the row of chairs, clattering them together. De Chauncey's patter missed half a beat. Moving as fast as I dared, as if carrying a brimming container within me, I fled up the side of the room and out of the door, barely pausing to demand 'toilet?' from one of the clipboard patrol and receive in response a gestured, frowning direction.

I did catch the name of the company that was the other half of the ground-breaking tenant management joint venture. Bunk Innovation, of course.

I did not quite make it. Most went into the shining black bowl of Zebedee's lobby toilet, but some went on the rim, and on the toilet floor, and on the cuff of my jacket and shirt, and on my hand and wrist, which had been clamped over my mouth. I knelt on the hard tiles, panting, looking at the liquid mess I had made. The door behind me was unlocked, there had been no time, but was braced closed by one of my feet. I watched the glints made by the toilet's gem-hard LED lights on the black ceramic of the bowl and the oily black tiles, breathing hard, then stood. At the sink, I washed out my mouth and splashed water on my face. I rinsed the vomit from my cuffs and rubbed handsoap into them, then rinsed that. It was a fancy brand of soap, called Abattoir, and quite perfumed, but a better smell than the alternative.

My face was a discouraging sight in the mirror, but no surprise. Sweat and splashed water had made my hair cling to my brow and temples. The bruises and scrapes around my eye resembled exotic mould breaking through the faded wallpaper of my skin. The suit, wrinkled by rain and exertion, did nothing to make my overall appearance more salubrious or respectable – a candidate for embalmment, not a new job. Would I be able to find a new job, if the magazine gave me the push tomorrow? Perhaps I would be able to negotiate resignation or redundancy rather than dismissal, although redundancy seemed unlikely. Redundancy would be winning the lottery, in the overall span of possibilities, and no way would they want to spend money on me. It seemed utopian. Could I imagine myself pursuing other jobs, getting interviews, convincing employers? No, I could not. As soon as I was home all day, the Need would start to swell, pushing out everything else. It would devour the redundancy pay-out. Even if I did somehow get another job, I would never keep it. It was too late.

More people came into the toilet: three men in sharp suits, two of them conducting a loud conversation. The presentation had come to an end. The newcomers eyed me suspiciously and I wondered if there was any lingering odour. I gave them what I hoped was a dangerous look, and exited.

Duty remained. I might be able to get De Chauncey in conversation and claw a few printable quotes out of him. But where was he? The clipboard sentinels regarded me with obvious distaste but let me pass, despite my cadaverous complexion and damp clothes. They must have suspected what happened, having seen me leave in such a hurry. My sinuses burned – creeping acid at the back of the throat, or the smell of smoke? I kept my head down and pushed towards the bar. With the presentation over, the attendees had moved to that end of the room and were mingling excitedly. They all appeared terrifically satisfied with what they had just seen. The screens around the room had switched to looping promotional video. Near the door, two of the tight-skirted PRs were setting out rows of gift bags printed with the words 'You Live . . . You Love . . . You YOLO'.

No sign of De Chauncey. He must still be here, surely, this would be his element, his chance to hand-sell apartments by the dozen. I deviated towards the bar, looking for something to eat, regardless of the silly shape it came in; stripped back to its lining, my stomach was growling and writhing like an injured animal. But the food had been taken away. I took a glass of red wine instead – just the one, I needed to be more careful – and moved to the side of the room. My head throbbed. The throng was thick and noisy and I could feel its contempt for me. I hated them. I didn't belong here, and I feared that it had become obvious – and I considered Quin's chicanery in getting me through the door, and De Chauncey's mention of Bunk. Why was I even surprised? Bunk was everywhere else, worming its way through the city, plugging itself into system after system. It made complete sense that it would have a tie-up with a firm like Wolfe / De Chauncey, edgy, cool, app-using Wolfe / De Chauncey . . . What was strange was Bunk's enduring interest in me, Quin's seeming fascination with my life and the steady progress of my collapse. Just as he had been interfering with Pierce as well – were failing writers his kink?

Not that losing my free will was much of a threat – I was barely able to exercise it. Keeping control of the most basic functions was more and more of a challenge. My insides felt crushed, and the wine I sipped tasted bad, though it was undoubtedly excellent. I knew I needed food, but I didn't feel hungry, just weak, as if I might simply crumple to the ground. Seeking greater obscurity, better cover, I headed over to the corner of corners, the display of samples from kitchen, bathroom, hall. I could part-hide there, look busy and interested and purposeful. But it was not the refuge it had been before the presentation – people were there, looking at the taps and carpets and plug sockets as if they were priceless artefacts in the British Museum. And going that way took me closer to the windows. I could not resist looking out, trying to see if the cockatoos were still there. A bright security light had come on across the road, drowning out everything else, making falling raindrops into welder's sparks. It was not yet 5 p.m. and outside it was grimmer than midnight. No chance that Pierce would want to go out roaming in this foul weather – not even he could be so determined, and I would have to put my foot down if he tried to insist. I only hoped that he did have some kind of proof or confession for me, whatever it was. It seemed implausible, that he would just sign up with an incriminating sheet of paper, but maybe he would, and I would have evidence of my triumph to take into the meeting – my great achievement, which had fallen into my lap and I had done everything to throw away.

I turned back to the room and the action set off another tremor of nausea. I had nothing left to bring up, but my body wanted to heave anyway. My instinct was to dash out to the toilets again, but my legs now combined the least mobile characteristics of lead pipes and wet noodles. I managed two staggering steps, into the mock-up of the corner of a kitchen. Ahead was a sink and I slumped over it, clutching the tap, knees sagging. Not real, I told myself, not a real sink, no pipes, but my body clearly regarded it as sufficient. A belch erupted from me and something hot and vile came up into my mouth. With titanic effort I swallowed it back. The sweat on my brow broke surface tension and I felt a cold line run over my temple, coming to rest in an eyebrow. Another spasm raced through my innards and I belched again.

'Oh God,' I gasped. My vision swam, shining spots swarmed, and the grey started to crawl in at the edges. Might my body give out before my career did? It had not seemed possible before, but now I felt the hospital ward might be closer than the job centre. And it would be entirely my own fault, considering the cocktail I had mixed for myself today, on an almost-empty stomach. 'Oh, God,' I said again. 'I deserve this.'

'You really do,' said the voice of God.

It was a warmer voice than I expected, almost comforting. He was above me now, blocking out the light. I turned to look into his face. It was Alexander De Chauncey.

He had stolen up beside me while I was preoccupied. It felt like a sneak attack, but I doubted he had been sneaky. My visual range had shrunk to no further than the rim of the sink, and the blood was gushing in my ears. He could have been clashing cymbals and I wouldn't have noticed his approach. And here he was, satisfied smile across his well-upholstered face, close enough for me to smell his scent, all vanilla and woodsmoke. And he was judging me. How did he know what I deserved? He knew nothing about me. But I could not find a reply, not even a 'fuck you'. All I did was stare at him.

'Beautiful, aren't they?' he said, and seeing my face wrinkle with incomprehension he gestured to the sink tap, which was still clutched in my hand, the only thing keeping me from slipping slowly to the floor. I was drawing strength from the cold, thick metal. 'I saw the way you fell on them. You've got a great eye. Italian, made at this little family atelier just outside Turin, amazing little place.'

I didn't say anything. All those words were known to me, but it was difficult to juice meaning from them.

'That's the great thing about this project,' De Chauncey continued. 'It's the penthouses that get the attention, of course' – he motioned to another part of the display, where half a dozen suits were admiring a wall-mounted light – 'but there are really no low-spec apts at YOLO. It all has the same attention to detail and top-rank design. You *do* deserve it, is what I'm saying, what-ever price point you're at. Are you considering making a purchase in the building?'

I have never felt further from a human being. He said this so lightly, as if I could just reach into my jacket pocket and bring out the £800,000 for a one-bed in YOLO. And there were people here who could do that, who bought flats like I bought cans, four or eight at a time. De Chauncey was a pro, so it was possible that this question was merely polite, and he was well aware that the wretch in front of him could not afford a flat. If that were true, he did a superb acting job, and I saw a man who moved naturally through climates of extreme wealth and privilege, far more extreme than even his own. And I could tell, just by looking at him, by looking at his suit and his haircut and smelling his fragrance, that the bath in his house did not touch the wall, you could walk all the way around it.

'I'm a journalist, actually,' I said. Better not say more.

'Oh, right,' De Chauncey said. There was no suggestion of disappointment, but his mien shifted angle – from sales to marketing. 'What can I help you with today? Any questions? Don't get me started, though, I can talk and talk about YOLO, it's such a beautiful project.'

'Yeah, there is one thing,' I said, switching on the recorder in my phone. I had turned it off in the toilet, but not until after I had finished vomiting. That would all be on the first recording, crystal clear. 'I had to leave during the presentation . . .'

'I saw,' De Chauncey said, with no obvious reprimand. 'Everything OK?'

'Fine, yeah, I was just . . . I felt a little light-headed.'

'It can get a bit stuffy in a room like this,' De Chauncey said. 'You feeling better now?'

'Fine, fine,' I lied. 'You had just mentioned your joint venture with Bunk Innovation, but I missed exactly what it was Bunk did for you.'

De Chauncey raised his eyebrows, enthusiasm lighting his face. 'Right. Happy to talk about that. It's beautiful, actually. We've been working with them for years on tenant management software. Let me explain properly. Say you own property as an investment.'

'OK,' I said. Never going to happen, but I could allow myself the miserable dream.

'If you own – say – a gold bar, it sits in a bank vault and never gives you any trouble. It never complains. You don't have to repaint it every five years. It just holds, and maybe accrues, value. But the best asset class, by far, is residential property in London. Way better than gold bars, or stocks, or anything. Not only does the asset itself accrue value faster than any other possession, it also pays you rent. It's magic, as investments go.'

'OK,' I said.

'But it comes with all kinds of obligations: you have to find tenants, collect rent, kick out deadbeats, check for carbon monoxide, repair burst pipes, all kinds of hassle and cost. No one wants to be a landlord to deal with all that, they want the asset and the rent, right?'

'Which is where you come in, as a lettings agent,' I said. The conversation was making my stomach churn, but I put on a performance of supportive interest. I wanted to appear to be on his side. On the side of the owners.

De Chauncey raised a thick finger. I saw the glint of a thumb ring. 'Aha. Yes. That's what a lettings agent does, sure – manage properties on behalf of owners. But, you know, lettings agents don't have the best reputation. People have all kinds of prejudices about them.'

About you, I thought, but I didn't say anything.

'What people want – what tenants want – is to deal directly with a person, with their landlord. Even if the service is worse, or at least no better. It's just a more human experience than dealing with an agent, I guess, you know they have a stake. But, you know, a lot of landlords don't want that. You might be talking about a high-net-worth individual who owns fifty properties, and who's much too busy and important to worry about every dripping tap and speck of mould. You might be talking about a Far Eastern or Russian investment consortium that owns 200 properties without even seeing them. These are the entities we're dealing with. You know, they're not going to take calls from Colin in Camden whose boiler's making funny noises. But they do deserve access to the world's premier investment asset, arguably more so than some amateur with a spanner.

'But with Bunk's help, we've built software that solves this problem. We've been working on it for years, trialling it in the market, and it runs a treat, flawless. Basically, it's a machine landlord. Not a machine, a program – an algorithm. It can understand tenants' emails and reply to them, and it's all linked up to our job management software, so it can order repairs or whatever based on what they say. If – and this is the great part – *if* it decides that a repair is needed. It's a clever beast, it makes decisions, filters out the trivial timewasting stuff, and it does it all without bothering a single human being. It knows how often a tenant has asked for something, and it can monitor their word choices for anger or urgency and so on. It's beautiful.'

He glowed with enthusiasm for the machine, and I felt the bile rise in my throat again. The grey closed in. Houses for some, many houses; being ignored by a machine for the rest. It was no way to live. My brow was cold with sweat and I could feel the tremor in the hand I raised to it.

'Are you all right?' De Chauncey asked, frowning.

'Uh, yeah,' I said. I didn't know how much longer I could go on – I had to get home, to rest, above anything else. Was it home, though? What was it? It was a lash against my back to keep me working, a phantom of finance.

'Was there anything else?' De Chauncey asked, visibly anxious to get away. No more value could be realised from the conversation, it seemed.

'Yeah – yes,' I said. I had to go on. 'I should introduce myself – I'm Jack Bick, I work for—'

'For Eddie!' De Chauncey exclaimed. He raised his head and rolled back on his heels, reeling a little at the happy thought of Eddie. 'Love Eddie. You were going to come and see me, weren't you?'

'I'm sorry I couldn't make it,' I said. 'I've not been well . . . It's been a bad week.'

'You don't look too well,' De Chauncey said. 'Do you need to sit down? Glass of water?'

'I was wondering if you might be able to do the interview, if you could just spare thirty minutes . . .'

De Chauncey sucked his teeth loudly. 'Next week?' he said with a grimace.

'I've got to take something in tomorrow,' I said. I no longer cared how desperate or unprofessional I sounded. 'I'm sorry, I know that's not your problem.'

'Well, I'm impressed you came out here when you're ill,' De Chauncey said. It was disorienting that he was being so reasonable. Then he shrugged, palms up, a motion that took in the whole room around him. 'But, you know, it's an important night for me . . .'

I sagged. 'I understand.'

'I'll tell you what,' De Chauncey said, flicking out a shining, clanking wristwatch with a practised gesture of display. 'This'll wrap up at six or so . . . about an hour. Where do you live?'

'Pimlico,' I said.

'Perfect. I'll be heading back to Chelsea. I'll give you a lift. We can talk in the car.'

My legs near failed me – I rocked to one side, and leaned against the sink. 'That's great. That's fantastic. Thank you.'

'Have a sit in reception, you look like you're on your last legs,' De Chauncey said. 'I'll find you when I'm done here.'

As the nausea subsided, the sickness returned – the anger and the hatred. I sat in reception with a glass of water like an invalid or a child, tolerated and indulged, told to wait until the grown-ups were finished. The sparks of relief lit by De Chancey's goodwill were extinguished by a tide of corrosive sludge, all my contempt and resentment. I resented that I was reliant on his generosity, that I had to crawl to him for favours, and his civility, his kindness, made it all the worse. They might make you feel at home for a few seconds here and there, but you're never at home. This was their world, your flat was still the possession of an anonymous oligarch or investment fund, and there was De Chauncey oiling the wheels of the system, and making his own fortune as he did so. And Quin, too, via whatever ghastly AI switchboard he had built for them, the slumlord Siri.

And he had been quite right. I might be feathering the nest of some retired *Mail on Sunday* reader I had never met, watching my own future drain away just as it drew closer, but I did almost prefer that to being the serf of an offshore entity, reduced to pleading with an algorithm. Better a sucker paying for someone else's Saga holidays than cattle on a spreadsheet. But I still despised my peonage and everything about it. There were people and institutions who regarded ownership as a burden, that was the horror at the core of it, the gulf of understanding I could not cross – and we call these people landlords. It was a chore, to them, to have the unbeatable investment asset of a London flat sullied by the vile needs of tenants. Not so much of a chore, of course, that they were ever prepared to give up the burden of ownership – just enough to ensure that every human dignity could be considered moot. For me, ownership was an unimaginable privilege, a source of security and comfort so distant that it might be Xanadu. An escape from the exhaustions and humiliation of renting. And why is rent such a treadmill of shame? Because of landlords who regard the responsibilities of ownership as a treadmill. Who resent that the provision of a home interferes with their enrichment.

I sat and seethed and was helpless. Purging myself in the toilets had left me scraped out and shaky, every minute feeling like my last minute of strength. I stared at my phone, letting the glowing screen dissipate the anger – not so that it truly diminished of course, but connecting it to the sea of everyone else's concerns, their dramas and causes, made it seem small and petty and common, turned some of it into sadness and self-loathing. I mentally composed tweets or Facebook status updates that might actually communicate a little of the inner ocean, and

I mentally discarded them. To be overly serious would be to make myself a burden to others, and to ironise and jape was no hope at all, just dishonesty. Best not.

Pierce had left a three-word voicemail: 'I'll text you.' But no text had followed. Instead there was a message from a stranger on Tamesis: 'We good to go?'

The sender's name was Olipi, and it wasn't hard to decode: a stealth account for Oliver Pierce, and a possible literary play on words to boot. A way of using the app without the wider public knowing. I checked back and found that Olipi had followed me during the splurge of activity caused by Quin's post about me. But I had followed back, and I had no memory of doing that. When? Had I known I was following Pierce? I had not gone through all my new followers, following back – on the contrary, I had ignored and avoided that great wedge of notifications. Going through them all was simply too much bother. I looked at the account: it was low-key, anonymous content, but it had checked in at Winterzone the previous night and its connections looked about right, minor London authors, *Vice* writers, people in publishing. Francis Quin.

Anyway. It was done. *We good to go?* No, not me, not in this rain, in this condition. No way was I staying up late for a point-less escapade. But I didn't want to reply, not yet. If I replied to Pierce right now saying that I didn't want to spend a third night wandering with him, I was laying myself open to cajoling and persuasion. I was weak, and might yield to his bullying charm. If I waited until I was lodged tight in my flat, away from Pierce and Quin, near the fridge, I could rely on the Need to save me, to give me the strength to ignore Pierce and stay home.

There were no communications from the office – no missed calls or voicemails, no emails asking where I had gone or demanding I return. And office hours were over. Either I had escaped without consequences, or I had sharpened the blade that was poised over my neck, ready for tomorrow morning.

Another message from Pierce: 'I'm waiting.'

Yeah, me too.

Suits and skirts streamed out of the function room. Some cast me glances, and I felt judged and wanting. The nausea had long subsided, replaced by a deep weariness.

Another message from Pierce: 'Where are you?'

I hadn't replied to any of these messages and I didn't reply to this one.

The exodus slackened. A few stragglers hung on in the lobby, chatting or waiting for rides. Chairs clattered in the function room and staff shuttled in and out, removing trays of glasses and boxes of bottles. The PRs called to each other in happy, end-of-day voices, quite unlike their cultivated manner earlier.

Pierce, again, via Tamesis: 'Never mind. Waiting.' Was that anger? Melancholy? Genuine unconcern? Never mind what? I pictured him at home, staring at the map on his wall, phone hot in his hand, waiting to get word from me. It was a pathetic thought – whatever the reality of the situation, he clearly did not feel himself to be in the driving seat any more. My invocation of Quin had been magic. Never mind that Quin had no useful proof concerning Pierce's fraud, Pierce clearly didn't know that. Or Quin was lying, and did have something; something else, perhaps, some other form of leverage. It was possible. Quin was a man who knew things. And behind Quin was a clean, cold room where banks of servers hummed, panning for secrets in the silt of data that settled under the stream of our lives.

De Chauncey appeared, carrying four YOLO Shoreditch-branded gift bags, two in each hand. 'I thought you might want one of these,' he said, holding out a bag. 'There's some bumf about the project in there. And a pen, and a temporary tattoo, I think, which is fun.'

I mumbled my appreciation.

'How are you feeling?'

'Fine, thank you,' I said. 'Much better. I don't know what came over me.'

'Ready to go?'

'Sure.'

'We'll use one of the office cars. They're parked just around the corner.'

I knew the cars he meant – they had been ubiquitous for a decade, zippy little Minis painted in psychedelic Wolfe / De Chauncey colours, forever parked on pavements and blocking pedestrian crossings. A couple of them, from the Pimlico branch, were left on my little street every night. They always had a visual joke – a driver's door that looked like an X-ray of the driver from the chest down, a transfer in the passenger window so it looked as if they had Will and Kate in the back. I regularly had to fight the urge to run my key along the jaunty paintwork of those Minis.

Outside, De Chauncey opened a large branded umbrella. As it unfurled I was momentarily blinded by a flash of light. I looked up to see what might have been the cause, but saw nothing – nothing apart from the plume, towering over the Shoreditch rooftops, made distinct from the low rainclouds behind by its flickering internal illumination, the upcast light of the fires beneath. No way was it as far as Barking – it could only be a couple of streets distant. The nausea coiled within again as I smelled the smoke, the shattered molecules and chains of poison on the fly.

Thunder grumbled. That's what I had seen – lightning, not the first signs of a fit or a stroke.

'Christ, this weather,' De Chauncey said.

'I'm surprised this rain doesn't put out the fire,' I said.

'What fire?'

'Out in Barking,' I said. 'The big fire there?'

'Oh, that,' De Chauncey said. The frown that had creased his placid face disappeared. 'I thought they put that out already.'

I froze, stomach churning. 'I heard it was still alight.'

'Well, it can't be serious, or it would be in the news.'

'I guess so.'

We started walking. I switched my phone to record and flashed it at De Chauncey. 'Do you mind . . .?'

'Not at all,' he said. 'You'll have to stop me if I go on.'

'Go on all you want,' I said. 'You were telling me about the software that Bunk wrote for you. The robo-landlord.'

'Oh, yeah,' De Chauncey said. 'Yeah, we've been working on it for years, it's beautiful.'

'But I don't understand it,' I said. 'People hate dealing with lettings agents and corporate landlords, sure, but why would they prefer a machine? Isn't that worse?'

De Chauncey chuckled, then looked sideways at me, eyes narrow, appraising. 'It's a little sensitive. F.A.Q.'s a mate of yours, isn't he? I saw on Tamesis.'

'Yeah,' I said.

'Off the record, then,' De Chauncey said, a Bulgari sparkle in his eye. 'The tenants don't know they're dealing with a machine. As far as they're concerned, their landlord is a small-time buy-to-let guy, that's who they're emailing. The algorithm writes its responses like a person – like some random slob who owns a couple of flats on the side to top up his pension. It says "yeah" and "cheers" and so on. It even puts in typos. If it replies at all. That's the beauty of it. It doesn't always reply, less than half the time, and it never replies immediately. Just like a real small-timer.

It's fantastic. It soaks up all the tenant's frustrations, and only occasionally logs jobs for attention, depending on the level of tenant anger, potential risk to the fabric of the property, cost versus yield, and legal liability. Amazing what it can do, what it can decide. They think they're dealing with Dave Stockton, but in fact they're emailing HAL 9000. HAL, only lazy.'

I watched wind-snatched raindrops fall on my phone screen, splashing rainbows in its light. 'Dave Stockton,' I said, mouth dry.

'Yeah, we give them all generic names, Frank Smith, Susan Roberts, Ahmed Khan, Dave Stockton. It's all the same program. "Dave" was one of the first.'

'So—' I began, and I had to stop to try to work some moisture back into my dry mouth. 'So Dave Stockton is an algorithm? A computer?'

'Like a voice assist thing on your phone, but over email. Bunk built it, we just advised on how it should behave and what we wanted from it. But what's clever is that Cortana and Alexa and Google Assist and all those have to be very sophisticated because people expect them to be helpful and useful and fast. No one expects that of Dave, the buy-to-let landlord. They expect him to be a bit shit.'

'Isn't it dishonest?'

De Chauncey shrugged, tipping a spray of water off his umbrella. My phone was still recording. I stared at the jerking line, watching it keep rhythm with the drumming of the raindrops against the material above me and the swish of passing cars. That was what I clung to, hoping that it still contained a link to a form of reality. Not my wet feet or the obvious, morbid biology of my coldness, tiredness and sickness. The phone.

'You say dishonest, I say disruptive,' he said. 'It gives people what they want. Tenants are a group with very low expectations.

As they should be. The software manages that, as well; it records the number and tone of complaints, balances that against the cost of setting things right, and when a threshold is reached, it triggers eviction. We've automated the hardest job a landlord has to do. Such a difficult decision, and we've taken it entirely out of human hands. The emotional labour, and its drag on investment value, is eliminated. You can imagine the peace of mind that creates, knowing that you won't have to deal with a situation of that sort. Beautiful.'

'For the owners,' I said. The journalist's temporary access to the higher lifestyles might look, at times, like corruption – at times, it is corruption. But it also has a strange camouflaging effect. The gilded ones who dwell in the Zebedee hotel, who don't have to give their names to the clipboards, can mistake you for a more elevated element, simply because you are in their space – an owner among owners. They would never guess your actual salary, your actual living arrangement. They would be appalled.

I didn't want to do the interview any more. Damn Eddie and Polly. I had the Pierce story, almost, I could make something out of that. But what would be the point? Another month's salary into the bank, to be electronically deducted hours later to whatever Cayman Islands vault lay behind the artfully demotic syntax of 'Dave Stockton'. The sickness wasn't just in me, it was all around, in my bank account, at work, in the shaking walls of my flat. It had spread out into the world. Like the Need, in fact – it had the same cold implacability to it. Shutting down the options. One deathly Need had revealed another: the need to work at all costs and make rent, the impossibility of stopping or pausing.

On instinct, I glanced up at the plume. I hoped it was serious, that it was spreading, that it took the whole city away. We had been walking at speed through the maze between Great Eastern

Street and Old Street. It was a place I knew intimately, but it was as if the storm and the winter darkness had washed the familiarity from it, made it featureless and dead. I had to take time to fix myself in space, but somehow the plume was exactly where I looked, just over the next line of dark Victorian attic windows. It churned and toiled and looked back at me. Smoke without fire.

All week I had seen it as the result of something that had happened. A tragedy, far but near, that had a beginning and continued and would end.

Now I saw that it was the sign of something yet to happen. It was not moving towards me. I was moving towards it.

'Here we are,' De Chauncey said. We were outside the flagship branch of Wolfe / De Chauncey, a warm slab of light held behind sheet glass. The office was closed, the spots over the desks were dimmed, but the LED-rimmed properties in the window shone like an inaccessible constellation containing habitable worlds. The glass-fronted fridge, a doll's-house version of the store that contained it, still displayed its soldier ranks of San Pellegrino and Cobra. Its blue glow revealed the Street Art wall and the quieted mixing decks where DJs strutted during the day, laying ambient beats over property transactions.

'Home sweet home,' I said. I didn't want to do the interview, but I did still want the lift. I could just grit my teeth and let him talk.

'Cars are parked round the side,' De Chauncey said. Next to the office was a narrow alley, lit only by what reached it from the main road.

As I turned into the alley, the side wall of the office was caught by the sweeping headlights of a passing car. My foot caught on a cobble and I stumbled – my phone slipped from my hand and clattered onto the ground.

A giant cockatoo was waiting in the alley. It stood two storeys tall, feet apart, the yellow feathers on the back of its head raised in a fan. It scowled down at me.

I fell into a crouch, wanting to retrieve my phone from wherever it had fallen, but also to tear myself away from this vast apparition, daring to be certain that it would be gone by the time I looked up. My phone had not broken or landed in a puddle, but the voice recording had stopped. I tried to wipe the dirty water from its screen but succeeded only in redistributing it.

The cockatoo was still there. Its attitude was disapproving, but unchanged. Not a feather had shifted. Another strafe of headlights showed, under its feathers, the texture of the bricks it had been painted onto.

'Do you like our pet?' De Chauncey asked. 'Mascot, really. We sponsor some street artists – they can do amazing things for the image of an area, and values. This was painted by Drabble.'

'Drabble, yeah,' I said. 'I know him.' There was a giant possum, its back swarming with young, near the magazine's building.

'Hold these,' De Chauncey said, handing me the gift bags he had been carrying. Once unencumbered, he took out his car keys and point-clicked. Lights flashed further back in the gloom and an alarm hiccupped. We walked towards the lights.

'Hey,' a voice said behind us.

We turned. A bulky figure was standing at the mouth of the alley, silhouetted against the lights of the street.

'You all right, mate?' De Chauncey said after a moment.

The newcomer walked towards us, purpose in his step, hands thrust into the front pocket of a black hoodie, hood pulled down over the eyes, shoulders shining with rain.

'Is there a problem?' De Chauncey said. There was an edge of warning in his voice, but I wondered if it was covering something else. With my hands full of gift bags, I felt acutely vulnerable. Although I had no idea what was going to happen, I knew what was going to happen.

'No fucking problem,' the figure said. A hand withdrew from the hoodie, bringing a sharp metal point into the second-hand light of the alley. Another rush of white headlights caught his lower face in profile: unshaven, jowly.

It was Pierce – I had known right away, before he spoke, from his build and his gait and his intentions. When he spoke it removed all doubt, though he had tried to roughen up his voice. Just like his writing, I thought, with the reflex of a laugh – but it was like trying to move a limb that had been amputated. I could not laugh, I could not do anything. I knew what he *wanted* to do, but that was not what paralysed me. I was frozen because I did not know how much he was capable of.

'Pierce,' I said, the word muffled by numb lips. Pierce, it was Pierce. I had to say the name, to say the word, because I had been reminded of something Pierce had said when we first met. He had said that names had power, that they steered their bearers. And he was Pierce – was De Chauncey about to get pierced?

De Chauncey glanced at me, but quickly turned his attention back to the hooded form. 'Yeah, peace, brother. We're all just trying to get home.'

'Home,' Pierce growled. 'What do you fucking know about home? How many people have you made homeless?'

De Chauncey scowled at the accusation, indignant but confused. I saw his eyes flick to one side, to the car, covered in the funky Wolfe / De Chauncey branding. He must have wondered, for a moment, how this stranger knew his business, and with that sideways twitch of the eyes I saw him draw the logical, obvious, entirely wrong conclusion: that he was being targeted because of the car. Guilt by automobile association. But the wrong conclusion was the safe conclusion as far as I was concerned. I was in double danger. It had been a mistake to say Pierce's name, it had just slipped out, and De Chauncey's mishearing had been a lucky escape. I did not want him to know that I knew Pierce, that we were all connected. That would make me an accomplice – it would look as if I had been walking De Chauncey into a trap.

Which was, I realised, pretty much what I had done. *I'm waiting*, Pierce had messaged. *Where are you? Never mind. Waiting.* He had been outside the hotel, watching people leaving, watching me wait for De Chauncey, trying to guess at my movements, thinking them all part of the plan – *my* plan. And how had he known I was here? Via Tamesis, and my RSVP. Quin didn't even have to nudge that connection, it could have happened entirely organically, if 'Olipi' had been snooping on my profile.

Pierce took another step towards us, and another. I had been giddy with fear at the volatility of the situation, its ability to turn into any number of horrifying outcomes. But I felt myself steady a little with a realisation: Pierce didn't know what he wanted to do. He had been so vague in outlining the scenario. He had no template to work from. The situation was blank: it could be inscribed.

'Stop,' I said.

Pierce stopped.

'What do you want?' I said.

'Yeah,' said De Chauncey. 'What do you want? Money? Phone? Watch?'

'Shut up!' Pierce spat. He was looking at De Chauncey, angling the blade at him. 'I don't want your fucking money!' In a couple of quick strides he closed the remaining distance between himself and the estate agent, coming so close they were almost chest to chest. He had the knife out, not held almost hidden as it was before but thrust forward, point only inches from De Chauncey's gut.

'Are you afraid?' Pierce asked. His tone was flat rather than mocking or angry, but that only made it more threatening.

De Chauncey certainly appeared afraid. His chin had withdrawn and he looked like he was holding something in his mouth. He closed his eyes, as if offering a prayer, opened them again, and nodded.

I could defuse this, end it perhaps. I could say, *Stop, stop, this man is a literary novelist, he's not dangerous, he knows Lauren Laverne.* I could pretend it was an art project, a stunt gone wrong. Maybe it was, how would I know? But I said nothing, fearful of incriminating myself.

'You're afraid,' Pierce said gently. 'Good. That's it. That's what I want.'

He took a step back and his manner changed. Whereas before he had been wound tight and tense, now his stance was everyday, almost casual. The knife was pointing at the ground, and he returned it to his pocket, embarrassed by it. I half expected him to extend his hand, to say, *Hi, I'm Oliver Pierce, sorry about that, pleasure to meet you.*

'That's it,' he said again, this time to me. 'That's what I want. That's what they need.'

A police siren whooped – the one-off attention-grabbing whoop, not the continuous call. All three of us in the alley jumped, and I looked towards the road. I was afraid again, afraid that the way out would be blocked by the fluorescent flank of a patrol car and strobing blue lights, afraid that Pierce would be arrested and there would be questions, and answers, there would be the truth. But no car appeared.

Pierce wasn't risking it. He turned and ran, making surprising speed for a sedentary man his age and build.

I was left alone with De Chauncey amid the trickling rain.

'Jesus,' De Chauncey said.

We were quiet a moment, and unmoving.

'I thought he was going to, for a moment,' De Chauncey said. The colour had gone from his face. He shook his head. 'Look, I . . . let's do the talking another time. The questions. Not sure I can focus right now. I'll drive, but . . . Jesus. I can't do it right now.'

'That's fine,' I said. It didn't seem to matter.

ELEVEN

A squawk of siren roused me. My eyes were open at once, my body rigid, and I waited for the next noises: car doors slamming, the chuckle of radios, heavy shoes on the concrete steps down to my flat, gloved knuckles banging on the front door.

De Chauncey had not wanted to contact the police. 'What would they do?' he asked me. 'It was just one of those things.' These words were spoken with no bravado; on the contrary, De Chauncey made no effort to disguise how shaken he was. We spoke little when the drive home began, but around King's Cross the silence had become uncomfortable. A backwash of the fright, I guess, the reabsorbed adrenalin making us voluble.

'I don't want to rake over it all again with the police,' he said, as if it had happened years before, not twenty minutes ago.

'I reckon you're probably right,' I said. Naturally I didn't want to encourage De Chauncey to involve the police.

'The police won't do anything anyway,' De Chauncey said. We had been caught by a succession of red lights, and the car rarely moved faster than its thumping windscreen wipers. He started to count off the reasons for his assertion, raising fingers off the steering wheel one by one, little finger first. 'One, no one hurt. Two, nothing taken. Three, no CCTV.'

'No CCTV?' I said, hoping no secret rejoicing showed through a poker face. 'That's a shame.'

'We keep telling the landlord, but . . .' De Chauncey said. 'He'll be long gone by now, anyway.' Evidently I was not the person that he was trying to convince. 'He saw the car and thought he'd try it on. Just a passing scumbag.'

He drummed his hands against the wheel, keeping time with the labouring wipers. 'What gets me is that it's not even right. I mean, I've been blessed, but I worked my way up from nothing, almost nothing. Next to nothing. I'm an immigrant, my dad came over from Cyprus in the seventies. De Chauncey, that's not even my name, my birth name. I'm Alexander Charalambous. I thought De Chauncey sounded a bit more . . . Well, you know. You have to create an impression, in business. You've got to be, I don't know . . .'

'Plausible,' I said.

'Plausible, yeah. I'm not playing the victim, mind. I fucking hate that, I know life's been good to me – the city, this city, it's been good to me, it opened up to me and embraced me.' As he said this, the lights turned to green, a nod of agreement from the silent giant. 'And I guess it just hasn't for that bloke. On drugs, do you think?'

'Obviously not well,' I said.

'If it hadn't been me, it would have been someone else, maybe someone who didn't deserve it.'

'The mugging?'

De Chauncey flashed a frown at me. 'What? No. Success. Anyway, he sees the car, the suit, he thinks . . . he gets it wrong. It's not the whole story, anyway. Maybe that's how we should do this piece? Get away from all that front, all that performance, all that *Apprentice* bullshit. Because, you know, it worries me. I'm not blind to it. The mood's changing.'

'Yeah, maybe,' I said. And he was right, that was a great angle. All of it. But it didn't really matter.

Perhaps he had gone to the police after all; perhaps that was them outside now. With considerable effort, I turned my head towards the window. The curtains were closed. All was quiet, but there was something, something in the light, a bluish flicker . . .

A long, low groan sounded. At first I thought I might have made the sound, but it had come from the fabric of the house. These Victorian terraces made many mysterious noises, mostly when the central heating switched off and they started to cool down.

I snapped from miserable reverie, mind half in last night, to fully awake. If the central heating was off, I was late – late for the Friday meeting, late for the unmissable, utterly mandatory Friday meeting. I snatched up the bedside clock and stared at its treacherous little face. It was a few minutes after nine o'clock. I was late, and more than a little late, but not unsalvageably. If I left immediately, I could be at work at about ten – and possibly the meeting wouldn't have started yet, and I could squeak in.

Urinating in the bathroom, I saw that a crack had appeared in the white-tiled wall behind the toilet cistern, fresh and sharp-edged, running along the grout lines in between the tiles. When had that happened? The place was coming apart. I made a mental note to email Dave – and remembered, a sickening rising bubble, that there was no Dave, just a few thousand lines of software. Software with the power to evict me. What could I say to log the repair without triggering the termination of my tenancy? What were the words or phrases to include, or avoid? Was this the future, then – trying to second-guess the machines overseeing our fate?

I returned to the bedroom and dressed, the Dave question festering away. But there was no time to really dwell on it. If I left right away, I could make the meeting, maybe only snipping the opening pleasantries. I could at least plead my case. There must be a path to redemption, or Eddie and Polly would not have strung me along so far. But what could I say?

Having spent so long in dread, and with so little achieved, I was oddly calm. No more could be done. There were no escape routes, it was all out of my hands. I wondered how many of the aberrations of the past week – the lingering smoke, the gathering cockatoos – might be manifestations of stress, rather than drink, brought on by my desperate efforts to stave off the inevitable, and my growing knowledge of the futility of those efforts. This morning, the fever had broken. All I had to do was turn up, and let events play out.

I unlocked the front door and pulled on it, expecting it to open, but it did not. It stayed firmly in its frame. I pulled again, with more force, and it did not move – not even the slightest flexing of the wood or shift on the hinges. It was like pulling on a doorknob bolted to a brick wall.

The door was secured by a deadlock and a Yale latch. I checked the deadlock – there have been times I have been so wasted that I forgot to lock it, and then the next morning absent-mindedly locked it while meaning to open it. But it was unlocked, I was sure, and as a test I locked it, watching the bar slide across through the tiny gap between door and jamb, then unlocked it again. And the same with the Yale lock – when I turned the knob, the latch retracted, I could see it.

I braced my right foot against the doorframe, took the little metal handle of the Yale lock in both hands, and pulled as hard as I could. At the very least I should have been able to feel the door bend or strain, but it might as well have been stone.

Fingers aching, I let go, and stood staring at the door, as if it might at any moment reveal its secret, or simply spring open under my gaze.

Time ticked by.

'This is stupid,' I said aloud, and resumed trying to yank the door open, again pulling with my foot braced against the frame, then trying a quick succession of short, sharp pulls, as if that might dislodge whatever force was holding the door in place. All I gained was angry red welts on my fingers. Once again I found myself standing and staring at the white-painted wood, breathless with frustration, aware of a rising billow of impotent rage. I had a vital meeting to get to, and I was being thwarted by my own front door. There was an odour, too, a harsh, burning odour, like hot dust in the air . . .

No. Think. Think about it. People aren't trapped by their own front doors, not usually. Think. Could it simply be my imagination? A manifestation of a subliminal reluctance to leave the house? But the pain in my fingers was real. Think clearly and a solution will arise. You'll see what you're missing.

The door had been sticking. It had been stiff to open, and sometimes I had to slam it to shut it. And now it was stuck. Either door or frame must have warped – and it had been raining non-stop since yesterday morning, maybe that contributed. For the second time I thought about firing off an email to Dave. But there was no Dave. The fury bubbled again. No one would come over, no one would sort it out, I was on my own. But if I broke the door down, if I took an axe to it, they'd take an interest then, wouldn't they? I couldn't, of course. This was still my home, even if it was theirs more than mine. What was the cure for a warped door? Sanding back the edge that was sticking – but the door would have to be open for that. Would WD40 loosen it? Where would I spray it, the hinges, the locks? Did I even have any? Maybe in the cupboard under the sink in the kitchen.

The kitchen. I knew what would help me assess the situation. I needed to get out of the gloomy hallway and into the only room in the flat that got any light. Happily it was also the only room with a fridge.

But it was not light in the kitchen. A fractured darkness had claimed the whole rear of the flat, and everything was terribly wrong. Where there should have been a winter morning, there was eclipse. Not night – I was not so intoxicated that I had woken in darkness and imagined it to be the day. The light was blocked out, present somewhere, but occluded.

I imagined rolling banks of fog, or smoke: the plume had reached me, I was in its eye at last, it had enveloped the house, here to choke me. That was not it, of course that was not it; but what confronted me was almost as impossible and threatening. The lime tree had come for me. Its outspread limbs had always interfered with what light made it down to the kitchen, but now the glass roof of the extension was entirely covered in a thick tangle of branches and leaves. They reached down into the garden as well, filling the small space; two days before, I had been obliged to mount the wall to touch the lowest branch, and today I could simply open the back door and lean out. It was as if the tree had vastly grown in the night, like Jack's beanstalk; that or it had broken its moorings and crept up on the house, leaning down to peer in.

To enter the kitchen would be to move into the tree's clutches, but I somehow found the strength. Wood scraped against glass.

'It's a panic attack,' I said to myself, and I liked how confident I sounded. 'You're having a panic attack. You've been having them every day. There's no smoke in the room, there are no evil birds, the tree isn't coming to get you. You're not well, that's what's happening.' I needed to see how the tree could have come so close, to dismiss the mystery as I had the others, to blink and end the hallucination. If necessary I could climb the garden wall again, anything to make the real snap back into place.

Even if I really had wanted to climb the garden wall again, I could not. It was gone. Not quite all of it – but a car-long bite had been taken out of it, visible through the cold jungle that now infested the back garden. I opened the back door to confirm what I could see, and, letting go of the door, it continued to move, falling further open before banging on its hinges. It had never done that before. Once I stepped out, I felt the slope in the poured concrete surface of the garden. A black fissure arced across the ground in front of me, under the dirty white plastic table, to disappear under the kitchen. Everything on one side of this fault line, my side of the fault line, had developed a distinct and novel camber.

No climbing was needed to look into the neighbour's garden today, but I had to push through the rain-soaked boughs that had descended into my path. Cappuccino-brown water had filled two-thirds of their expensive pit, almost submerging the machinery that had been left at its bottom. It was into this mire that the half-moon section of garden wall had fallen, and so had a portion of the concrete slab I was standing on. Creeping towards the precipice, the swamp-shore, painfully aware of the tilt that was consuming the garden, I could see that the sides of the pit were dissolving away in the rain. The pyramid of retained dirt that had supported the tree had collapsed, exposing a ghastly white fist of roots, and the tree had toppled over, coming to rest against my house and the roof of my kitchen. It was incredible to me that the kitchen roof had not simply caved in under the weight of the tree, and I could only conclude that it must have fallen gradually, silently, and that the house itself must be taking its weight. I started to look for signs of damage on our side of the wall, and at once I saw a thick black crack running vertically from where the kitchen roof met the rear wall, up to the lower sill of the ground-floor window. But it didn't stop there, it reappeared above that window and ran up to the sill of Bella's, above; and it continued again through the uppermost level as well, where it was joined by an ugly twin.

And above it, stretching into the heavy grey sky, was the plume. It had not been above the house the other day. Nor had it twisted and tautened in that same urgent way. Was the house itself on fire? No, but it was being consumed all the same. The tree didn't make that crack, it couldn't have. I thought of what had brought it down, the pool sucking away at the ground underneath me, underneath everything.

I rushed back into the kitchen, pulling the door closed behind me. But rather than shutting, the door banged hard against its frame and rebounded into the garden. This jarring impact reverberated in the structure of the kitchen, settling back to nothing as the door shuddered on its hinges. One that won't open, another that won't close, I thought. After a beat of silence, there was a sharp *plink* noise, like an old lightbulb blowing out, and a crack appeared across one of the glass panels in the roof.

Staring up at the broken glass, I backed out of the kitchen, into the living room. A high, squeaking groan issued from somewhere above me – wood and plaster under terminal strain. There was another angry crack across the living room ceiling, forked like lightning. Traces of pinkish plaster moult furred the cans arrayed on the table and floor. From behind me, out in the bathroom area, came a sharp *pop* and a patter of falling dust.

'OK,' I said. 'Time to go.'

I ran down the hall and resumed my desperate tug-of-war with the handle of the front door, but it was still lodged fast. A long, stuttering creak, the building clearing its throat, rang down the corridor around me. I was dimly aware of sounds from outside.

The door was a waste of time. I had to call for help. I took my phone from my pocket and dialled 999. 'Fire,' I said. The highness and the hoarseness of my voice startled me. As the call went through I hammered against the door with the flat of my hand.

The door hammered back.

'Fire service,' said a voice over the phone.

'Fire service!' said a voice through the door.

'You're . . . already here?' I said into the phone, thumbing an end to the call.

'Are you in there?' the voice shouted through the door. It was an authoritative voice, male, accustomed to shouting, in control. There was a frightening urgency to it, like a shot of strong spirit.

'I'm here,' I shouted, again struck by the comparative weediness of my own voice. 'I can't open the door. It's jammed shut.'

'Don't open the door!' the voice said, shouted, the insistence sending a chilled spike through me. I thought of Pierce and the knife, and the silly fear of it.

'I can't,' I said, at a loss.

'Don't! The whole place is about to come down, your front door might be the only thing keeping it up!'

'What whole place?' I said, but not loud enough to be heard through the door. From behind me, in the vicinity of the bathroom, came a sickening grinding noise, rough surface hard against rough surface.

'We've got to get you out of there!' said the voice.

'I've got to get out of here!' I cried in return. 'I've got a meeting!'

'Can you come to the window?'

Yes, I could. I went through to the bedroom and opened the curtains. A firefighter was standing at my front door, in full fluoro-flashed armour and yellow helmet, and another was standing behind him on the stairs. I was stopped by the stance of this second firefighter – her feet were on different steps, not even adjacent steps. She was poised, ready to spring up and away from the house. I was in danger.

With a ping, one end of the curtain rail fell down, spitting plaster and knocking over some of the cans I had left on the window ledge and the desk. A crack had run through the wall where the rail had been attached, and opening the curtains had dislodged the rail from whatever tenuous grip it retained.

The firefighters saw me, but did not acknowledge me, instead conducting a rapid conversation.

'Prop?'

'No time.'

'Quick then.'

'It's reinforced.' The window panes had a grid of wire fired into them, to try to frustrate the burglars who love basement flats. The second firefighter produced a tool, a crowbar interbred with a hatchet.

'Sir! Sir! Turn away from the window and cover your eyes!'

I didn't have to be warned, I knew what was about to happen, and they didn't wait. I shrank back and pressed my arm across my face. The hatchet crunched through the glass. They didn't pause – more impacts followed, accompanied by the tinkling of shards, an almost restful sound in comparison. There was a particularly loud, splitting crack, and more blows.

'Out! Out now!'

A hole had replaced the lower two panes of my bedroom window, the splintered remains of the glass peeled back like a sweet wrapper. The firefighters thrust heavy-gloved hands through, beckoning harshly. I scrambled onto the sill, trying to sweep away crumbs of glass as I did, and take their hands, thinking they meant to steady and assist me. But as soon as they had contact with me, they pushed aside my hands and hooked theirs under my armpits, not helping me but hauling me out all at once. I felt jagged edges catch my trousers and dull razors drag against the skin of my legs.

'Is it just you?' the male firefighter asked. He didn't ask it, he shouted it in my face. 'Is there anyone else in there?'

'Just me,' I gasped. Shining flowers of pain were blossoming where the broken glass had caught me. 'Upstairs maybe—' Whatever I might have said was lost, as I was gripped again and push-pulled up the steps and onto the pavement. Part of me dimly registered surprise that the pavement was empty – was it just these two firefighters? Where was their vehicle? Was no one else about? But there was no time to reflect, we were between the parked cars and out into the road, and they were shouting 'Head down! Head down!' at me – then more hands had me, and my head was pushed under a flapping blue tape, and there were people and lights all around.

Since no one was holding me down any more, I stood up. I was at the end of the street, in a crowd of uniforms and flashing blue lights. A helicopter staggered in overhead. From further away came shouting and siren whoops, and an amplified voice saying, 'Move back, move back! We need this whole area clear right away.'

'Is it going to go?' someone asked. I thought for a second that they were asking me, but the question was directed at the fire-fighter behind me.

'It's going,' she said, pushing her helmet back to rub her temple with the ball of her thumb. 'It's definitely going.'

What was going? I turned back to look at my house. The street appeared as it always did, with the addition of the heli-copter, which had passed over and then wheeled back to hover nearby. But then, clear even against the noise of the helicopter, came a series of reports, a heavy board being dragged down stone steps, and then an ascending noise, the tearing of a sheet of heavy cloth. The facade of the house next to mine folded inwards as if it were no more than a tea-soaked biscuit; then my house moved, downwards, seemingly in a single piece, exactly how I couldn't say, and the facade buckled and everything was on the move at once, crumpling and twisting and turning from solid to liquid, and an uproar of thick grey dust swallowed that part of the street, obliterating our view like a killer whale snatching a mackerel, and everything was noise, not crashing or banging but a continuous rushing jet-engine roar.

The dust arched and twirled and piled outwards, racing itself, and just before it reached the tape cordon and engulfed us, I had the impression of it rising over the broken heart of the street in a thick, malevolent column.

'It's gone,' I said.

Once again, hands seized me, and I wanted to protest, don't touch me, give me a damned moment. But I wasn't being dragged – the arms that had been thrown around me were not manhand-ling but hugging, and a faint note of Jo Malone found its way past the stench of plaster-powder and ruin.

'You're OK,' Bella said, pressing her head into my shoulder. 'You're OK!'

'I'm fine,' I said.

'Your legs, oh . . .'

My trousers had been badly torn, and were now stained by the blood that dripped persistently from a series of scratches and gouges.

'The glass,' I said. 'It's fine, it's nothing.'

'I told them,' she said, breathless. 'They didn't know if anyone was down there, they thought most people had gone to work, and I said, he's definitely down there, he won't have gone out, you've got to get him out.'

I winced – not at the pain from my legs, which was no more than a distant throb. 'I do go out,' I said. I immediately regretted the annoyance in my voice, but Bella did not appear to have noticed it, the proximity of disaster giving her a glittering, jumpy energy.

'It was so close,' she said. 'We saw the tree had moved, of course, and I saw the crack when I got back from my run, and we could hear noises – I called the fire brigade.'

She embraced me again – not swooning onto me, seeking my support, but holding me as if I were the one who needed propping up. Again, I felt the resentment build. But she had possibly saved my life, and she had been made homeless too.

That last thought swung around and struck me like a long plank in a slapstick routine. I was homeless too. I was homeless.

A siren whooped, and then struck up a full wail. A car alarm had started when the houses had collapsed, and continued, only now audible to me. The dust clouds, which had briefly been thick enough to obscure everything but Bella and the luminous moving swatches of the hazard gear worn by the various emergency services, were thinning, beaten and torn by the blades of the helicopter. The line of the street was made visible again, redacted in the middle. All that stood of my former home was the black iron fence and gate.

A firefighter walked towards us, arms outstretched, as if wanting to join in a group hug, but his intention was to herd. 'OK, folks, we need you to move back in the direction of Belgrave Road, the area's still not safe.' He caught sight of my legs and signalled to the green-clad paramedics nearby. 'This one needs attention.'

My bleeding legs meant that we weren't rushed to the outer cordon, but directed to the tailgate of an ambulance. However tender the shepherding, though, there was steel in the hand that guided my elbow. A line of spectators was gathered behind the police tape on Belgrave Road, and they gawped at us as we approached – Bella in her running gear, me in tattered work clothes, both of us coated in dust. The crowd's not-so-secret enjoyment of the sight of us was entirely legible to me: the second-hand thrill of our victimhood, our status as a promontory of the bizarre into the placid sea of the normal, walking exemplars of the not-everyday. They got to enjoy being present at a proper event, while not being as unfortunately over-present as me and Bella. I recognised a couple of the guys who served in the corner shop where I bought my cans. Did they recognise me?

A silver thermal blanket was put over my shoulders, as if I had just run a marathon, and a light was shone in my eyes. I was asked questions. Bella hung nearby, talking into a rose-metal mobile phone, arms clutched in tightly. I thought about my own phone, and took it out of my pocket. Three missed calls. Text messages, too. From Eddie: *Where are you?* From Kay: *GET HERE NOW.*

One of the paramedics came at me with a pair of shears.

'What are you doing?' I said, shying away.

'We've got to get those off,' he said, gesturing at my trousers. 'To treat your legs.'

'You can't do that,' I said.

'They're ruined. This is easiest.'

'No,' I said, pushing away his hand and standing up. 'I mean – I've got to get to work.'

'Call your office then,' he said, indicating my phone with the point of his shears.

'I have to go, it's important.'

He stared at me with an expression of weary tolerance. 'Mate, a building just fell on you. *Call in*. We've got to get you checked over.'

A sensation surged within me, dark and sweet, rich and freeing. I knew it, I knew it by its chemical scent, a cocktail prepared by my own body that was more potent, more intoxicating, than anything I could drink. I had been microdosing on this amazing brew for years, I realised – every time a deadline was extended or I was let off the hook for something, I got a whiff of it. But this was more than a droplet, it was a bucket of it, a tidal wave that surpassed any alcoholic buzz or orgasm. I had only felt this way once, years earlier, in the Olympic summer. And when I remembered the circumstances, I realised it was all a mirage. It meant nothing. Worse, it was a trap. And the chemical tide rushed back out.

'No,' I said. 'You don't understand.'

The paramedic sighed, and beckoned to a colleague, who busied themselves with my legs, rolling up the trousers and cleaning and dressing my wounds. I sat back down to help them. 'You really should look in a mirror before going in,' the first paramedic said. He had started filling out a form.

I didn't need a mirror. I could see my clothes, and I could see Bella – the dust in her hair, the dirt gathering in black lines on her face. She was off the phone and talking to a police officer, a wide-eyed, serious, short-sentence talk, the frugal conversation of emergency. A third figure approached them, in another shade of hi-vis, red this time, but my view of this newcomer was obstructed by their backs and the ambulance door.

'I can go, then?' I asked the paramedic.

'You really shouldn't, but I can't stop you,' he said, raising his eyebrows and scribbling on the form. It was held to a metal clipboard, and I thought of Polly, laying out the case against me while I was helplessly detained here by *force majeure*. 'You'll need to sign this. It says you've refused treatment.'

'Fine, fine,' I said. 'Give it to me.'

Bella and the police officer had turned in my direction – both were pointed at me. The man in red who had been talking with them walked towards where I sat. It was the postman.

'James Bickerton? Basement flat?' he asked.

I nodded, although it seemed a trifle fraudulent to lay claim to an address that no longer existed.

'There's post for you,' he said. 'I suppose . . .' He glanced towards the corner of my former street. 'I suppose I should just give it to you.'

He handed me a cockatoo.

On the rear step of an ambulance, surrounded by professionals, within shouting distance of my cratered home, I was an object of sympathy. The disaster that had birthed my torn and filthy form was obvious and recent, and I was being taken care of, so I could be safely pitied.

On the Tube, I was feared and hated. A bandaged ghoul, separated from my circumstances, I had become a contagious emissary from an underworld of anarchy and corruption. No one knew what had happened to me, but they knew they didn't want a part of it. People put their bags on their laps and pulled their staring children a little closer as I appeared. Talk died away and eyes followed me. Breaths were held, in case I stank as bad as I looked. I was succeeded by a wake of relief as I did not stop or ask for money. I sat in the last seat of the carriage, causing the man next to me to shift and hitch. Don't worry, mate, you're not going to catch anything.

I let out a curt laugh at this thought, and my neighbour shifted again. He was about my age. So I stared at him a while, watching the side of his eyeballs strain with the effort of not looking back at me, before turning my attention to the cockatoo in my lap.

It was a handsome specimen, legs wide on a branch, yellow plumes radiating proudly, a cheeky glint in its eye. I flipped the postcard over to reread what was written on the back.

Dearest James,

We are in Prague again, and saw these splendid chaps at the Zoo. Do you remember Uncle Charles's cockatoo? Such personality in a bird. I generally think them cruel & stupid creatures but it was neither. It kept us so entertained that time it came to visit. Returning Saturday week, via Bratislava and a night in Vienna. Love from us both.

– Mum (& Dad) xxx

For the tenth or twentieth time, I turned the postcard over and looked at the bird. Uncle Charles had a cockatoo. I had not been lying to my friends. It must have been so unlikely to my child-self that it always had the ingredients of invention. But the foundational lie of my lying life was not a lie, it was the truth.

I was in no way redeemed by this realisation. It had not saved me. It merely showed me that the torrent of lies I had told in my time had eroded through to my core. Everything was a lie. I had forgotten the experience of truth.

The postcard was the only thing I held. My bag had been inside the house, as had almost everything else I owned. (My first thought was not my laptop or family photographs or any of my books, but the fridge and its contents.) Almost everything: I had the contents of my pockets, which included my phone, my wallet and my Oyster card. The bedrock of my ability to function. Wasn't that supposed to be all we needed – the premise of those adverts in which twenty-some-things in plaid shirts travel the world on their credit card and data plan? Adverts for credit cards and data plans, mostly. I didn't have a charger or, in all likelihood, a job, so neither could last.

As I walked up the ramp out of Old Street Station, Tamesis chimed. You should update your address information, it said.

'You have got to be fucking kidding me,' I said to it.

The column of black smoke was above the obelisk tower of the Hawksmoor church on Old Street, very near the office. That was west of the station – there was no pretence that it might be in Barking. It wasn't even trying to deceive. And if the cockatoo was real, what else might be?

I was late, but maybe not too late. Even if the meeting had started on time, they could last a couple of hours, and I doubted it would be finished.

But when I arrived in the office, the meeting had already broken up. Or it hadn't even begun. The atmosphere in the room was all wrong, everything was out of place. My eyes were fixed on the aquarium when I came in, expecting it to be full of people, but only Polly and Freya were in there. Ilse was sitting in her little kingdom, and her posture was unlike anything I had seen from her before: she was sprawled back in her chair, as if very relaxed, but her face was tired and preoccupied. Neither of the Rays were in their own duchy – woman Ray was sitting with Mohit, like they were having a chat, but a bad chat. Eddie was on his own in his stockade, on the phone. Kay was standing at her desk, piling up copies of the magazine. Once she had gathered an armful, she carried them towards the main door, and there she saw me.

'What happened to you?' she asked unkindly, before she took in the state of my clothes and face and legs and asked a completely different question, one filled with concern: 'What happened to you?'

'My house fell down,' I said, and the dreaded feeling flickered upwards, and I could not prevent myself from an expression that was almost a smirk. 'I know that sounds . . . It's true.'

'It just fell down?' she said, eyes opaque, a faint sneer of disbelief on her lips.

'There must have been a cause, but really the only important fact is that it fell down.' Once I had said this, I became worried that perhaps glibness wasn't quite the right tone, not with Kay. 'There was building work going on next door. They must have undermined the foundations. I'm sorry, it's come as a bit of a shock.'

'Huh,' Kay said. I expected more. She stepped past me, to the green wheelie bin against the wall. Into this she dropped the heavy load of magazines she had been carrying. They were recent copies, decorated with sticky bookmarks, each one of which represented one of Kay's contributions.

'What are you doing?' I said. 'Don't you need those?'

'Not any more,' she said, with a stiff smile.

'What's going on?'

'Why don't you ask Eddie that?' Kay said.

Eddie, yes. He had seen me, and his brown eyes, peering over the top of his fortifications, followed me as I crossed the office towards him. My terror of the awaiting possibilities was at last overcome by the need to know.

'Jack. You've come to join us at last.'

'I'm sorry I'm late,' I said, although I didn't put much contrition into my tone. 'My house fell down.'

He looked me over, and I saw him pass from the dust on my jacket to the tears in my trouser legs to the blood-spotted bandages on my legs.

'It's a better excuse than usual, I'll give you that,' he said. 'You missed the meeting. The meeting I expressly said you had to attend.'

'Well, I'm here now,' I said. I no longer saw any harm in being blunt. 'Or am I? I'm out, right? Redundancy? Or dismissal?'

Eddie rolled his eyes, as if bored by these questions, and I felt the heat rise in my chest.

'You need to speak with Polly.' He nodded in the direction of the aquarium. I glanced over, and saw that Freya had hunched over, and Polly was leaning across, towards her, grim and concerned.

'Why can't you just tell me?' I said to Eddie.

'Polly,' he said. 'You need to speak with Polly.' He lifted his phone receiver and began to punch in numbers, signalling an end to the conversation. I was momentarily seized by the urge to put my finger on the receiver switch, ending the call before it was dialled, like they do in TV dramas. But I did not.

Both the women in the aquarium were standing. Polly had come around the conference table and was guiding Freya to the door, a gentle hand on her shoulder. Freya's eyes were red and her posture shrunken. She sniffed and hurried past me once the door was open. All that time, even while still mouthing comforting final words to Freya, Polly's eyes had been fixed on me. She ushered me into the meeting room.

It was stuffy inside, spent emotion, like carbon monoxide, pushing out the breathable air.

'I wish we had more privacy,' Polly said with a weary exhalation.

I avoided the seat Freya had occupied as if it were unlucky. Not that luck could have much influence over my situation any more; clearly decisions had already been made, and the roulette ball was lodged firmly on double zero, even if the wheel had not quite ceased to spin. Perhaps poor taste was what I was anxious to avoid: disrespect to the fallen.

Polly had moved to sit where she sat before, but seeing me dodge Freya's chair she changed to sit opposite, pulling all her papers with her. There were a lot of papers. The clipboard was fully loaded, and she had brought through a couple of the purple folders that her documents went into once they graduated from the clipboard.

The Bick file would be in there, for sure.

'Are you OK?' she asked. 'You're all . . . beat up.'

I sighed. 'My house fell down.'

Her frown deepened. 'What? How did that happen?'

I sighed, again – more a groan than a sigh. This was only the third time I had been asked about the house and I was already finding it a chore to explain. There was that initial hurdle of disbelief to surmount, and then all the repetitive details. I had the drunk's desire to obliterate the past, where these tedious matters of context resided, and the future, where there lay further occasions on which I would have to explain them. I wanted to go to the sofa, to the fridge, and when I remembered that they were both buried beneath pulverised brick, I only wanted them more. I had watched my flat disintegrate around me, and it made this meeting, Eddie's opinion of me, everything else, seem trivial. Especially as the chance to avert catastrophe was long past. I was calm. No, not calm – I roiled inwardly. But I was pointed forward, not locked in my usual grid of anxieties.

'I've already been over that with Eddie,' I said, 'and Kay. Do you mind if we skip it, for now? I want to know what's going on, with Kay, with Freya. With me.'

'Sure,' Polly said, smiling without pleasure. 'Of course. You have a right to know. Short version: *big* changes. Eddie is stepping aside, I'm sad to say, and I will be taking over as editor from Monday.'

She was looking at me, for my reaction. I didn't have one. How could I react? My worst speculations had been exceeded. But at the same time it made little material difference to the expected outcome. I swallowed, and said, 'Go on.'

Polly tilted her head, as if she had expected more, and looked down at her notes. 'As you know, the financial picture isn't good. In fact, it's very bad – existential. Eddie has done everything he can to avoid redundancies. But the urgency has become overwhelming. Ilse is taking voluntary redundancy, which' – Polly let a hiss of air past her teeth – 'is probably more expensive than keeping her on, because she's on an Errol contract. We also have to lose Kay, and one of the Rays.'

'Which Ray?' I asked, lips numb.

'Man Ray. I'll be taking a lower salary than Eddie was. A lot lower, in fact. You wouldn't beli— another Errol contract.' She paused, a strange, intense, faraway look in her eyes. 'And Mohit will move up to be my deputy, but not for a while, six months or more . . . the freeze . . .' She tailed off again. 'If we can keep him. He's not happy. No one is. No one likes doing the back. Sorry, I've lost my thread. I don't know what that leaves.'

'Me,' I said. Get to the point. She wasn't handling this well. What did I care about what Mohit would be doing in six months? I'd be gone.

'Of course.' She opened the clip on the clipboard and pulled loose some papers. 'Listen, your work recently . . .'

I lowered my head. I knew what was coming, I was prepared, but I wasn't proud. 'I know,' I said, voice failing on me, almost a whisper.

'Exceptional. Really. I can't thank you enough. We gave you a tough week, I know, but you've excelled, you really have. It's convinced me that I've made the right decision.'

'Excuse me?' I said.

She was holding a sheaf of A4, fresh from the printer and paperclipped together. 'I read this when you sent it over yesterday. It's phenomenal work, really superb. And you say this is just a start? You've got more?'

My lips felt dry, and I licked them. 'I'm not . . . May I see that?'

Polly pushed the document across the table. The cover was a printout of an email.

Here's the first part of the Oliver Pierce transcript.
– Jack

I had the distinct sense of having stumbled sideways into a different world. Could one of my blackouts have been . . . beneficial? A forgotten patch of preternatural organisation and productivity? There were dreams like that, nasty deadline dreams. You imagine it's all done, all sorted, and you wake, and . . . Better than a sweat-soaked anxiety nightmare, maybe, but still horrible. The nightmare is the waking world, the dream the false respite. Maybe this was the subconscious trying to soothe a deeply troubled mind, but it always felt cruel, like a trick.

There were tricks, too, that unscrupulous writers could play, trying to cheat an extra hour or two out of a strict deadline. You could send an email saying, 'Here it is!', but with no attachment, having *forgotten* to include your copy; or you could attach a file with only a title or a couple of paragraphs on it, *accidentally* sending an unfinished version of the file rather than the (not-yet-existent) complete one. An honest mistake! Sincerest apologies. If you were really lucky, you might not get a reply pointing out your 'error' until hours later, or even the next day – or the subsequent Monday. By which time you might have actually achieved a draft. And I was forced to assume that this might be a case like that – Polly might be showing me a blank document or one filled with dummy copy, or a Q&A pulled off the internet and stripped of formatting to resemble a transcript – remembering my recent indiscretions, that seemed possible, or at least less impossible than having actually done the work.

I flicked to a random page. It was all very neat, not like one of my transcripts at all.

> *I had to 'set the record straight'. As if everything is disordered now, crooked, and when I . . . If I go on the record it'll all be properly arranged and neat and tidy. 'The Record'! As if there's a single, agreed text of the past somewhere, in a big ledger with metal clasps . . . Or in one of Quin's servers, now, I suppose.*

That was it, the interview on Tuesday, word for word. All of it.

My stomach twisted. *All* of it? I flicked back a few pages in the transcript.

BICK: *I don't understand. You sounded very eager to talk*
                   to me when we got in touch, but now it sounds as
                   if there's not much you want to say.

[inaudible]

PIERCE: *The thing about* Night Traffic *is that I made it up.*
                   None of it happened. None of it is true.

I stared at that *[inaudible]*. The entirety of my outing as an alcoholic had been redacted, hidden behind a tiny note that looked as if it concealed no more than a couple of mumbled words. It was brazen, but it was probably what I would have done if I had sat down and transcribed the interview myself. Had I done that? It was all too orderly. To my knowledge, I have never produced a line of writing during a blackout. It was appealing to imagine myself living a whole, productive life during the alcohol-induced voids in my memory, calmly tapping away at my keyboard or running underground boxing clubs or whatever, but it was utter fantasy. Blackouts are not magical. In reality, I came out of them knowing that I was lucky not to have choked on my own tongue or drowned in my vomit.

And I had nothing to transcribe from. The recordings had been lost.

Polly was inclined towards me, head tipped to one side, looking at what I was looking at. Her expression changed from pleasure to confusion as I kept leafing through the pages. I had been quiet too long, and I had furrowed my brow. I un-furrowed it.

'Everything OK?' she asked.

'Yes, yes,' I said. 'I'm glad . . . you got this.'

She had said that I had sent it over yesterday. When, yesterday? I returned my attention to the cover sheet, looking for the time stamp on the email: just before four in the afternoon, around the time I left for De Chauncey's event. Impossible. I had not sent it. Could I have been hacked? I looked at the sender's address: jack.bick@bunkmail.co.uk

Bunkmail. I didn't use a Bunkmail account, although it was possible I had set one up in order to register for one of Bunk's services. The *how* of it didn't matter, though – I already knew the *who*. Quin had taken my DVRs and selectively transcribed their contents. The *why*, that was the part I couldn't get. He wanted all the evidence for himself, that was straightforward enough – but why help me out, at Pierce's expense?

'We'll want to go very big on this, of course,' Polly said. 'How many words do you need to do it properly? Four thousand? Five?'

'Uh,' I said, trying to begin a sentence, but only producing a croak. 'We can talk about that.'

'Sure. And, I have to say, I am very excited about your ideas as well. I didn't want to pry inside your creative process, but once again, great job.'

'My ideas?'

'Your ideas for future interviews.'

For a room-revolving moment I had the ghastly thought that Quin might be able to peer inside my head, and had composed Polly's list by telepathy. But even if he was capable of cracking open my skull, he would find little of use within. Had he simply come up with his own?

'I don't remember sending you any ideas,' I said, wary.

Polly blinked and shook her head. 'No. My apologies.' She opened her clipboard and took out a sheet of yellow notepaper. 'I came over to your desk yesterday to thank you for sending over the Pierce transcript, but you had already gone, I think – anyway, this was on your pad. I took the liberty of having a sneaky peek.'

The notepaper she passed me was covered in my own handwriting – a list of names. Alexander De Chauncey, crossed out; Boris Johnson; Mike Butcher; Hugo Pleasance . . . It was the targets list I had drawn up with Pierce, the people we thought might deserve to be mugged.

'Great stuff,' Polly said. 'We could fill half a year, here and now.'

'This isn't really . . .' I began.

'It's a work in progress, I know,' Polly said. 'I'm sorry, I couldn't resist.'

'They're all white men.'

'I know, but we can pad it out with a bit of diversity as we go along. It's an excellent start. Some really unexpected choices.'

'I hate all these people,' I said.

'And I admire you for getting out of your comfort zone,' Polly said. She smiled at me, with real warmth.

A faint ringing sounded in my ears, the song of my own blood, and the smell of burning filled my sinuses. Behind Polly was a rank of windows, looking out towards Clerkenwell and, beyond, the Telecom Tower. And there was the plume, plump and oily, an umbilicus filling the sky with the poison of the earth.

The window faced west, away from the estuary and London's industrial horizon. On Monday, when the Barking fire was raging, we had been watching from the opposite side of the office. This plume had nothing to do with that fire. I feared it might have nothing to do with any fire.

'So I'm not fired?' I said, returning my attention to the room, a feat demanding considerable effort.

'No! We . . . You've more than shown your value to the magazine. I've always been a big admirer of your work, as you know.'

'Kay has value.'

'Absolutely. I know, I know.' Polly frowned, saddened. 'It's been a hugely difficult decision to make. Almost impossible. But you're producing exactly what we need.'

'I've got to say,' I said, shaking my head, 'that I'm surprised. I know that my attendance isn't great . . .' I glanced at the clipboard.

'Eddie did raise a concern about that, said I should keep an eye on it,' Polly said, patting the clipboard gently, like a faithful hound that had earned its rest. 'But we can work on things like punctuality, and it doesn't seem to make much difference to your ability to generate stories. You're unorthodox. A free spirit. I respect that.'

'I'm not well.' It was as if I said the words to myself, that I was telling myself, in the sight of the plume, the impossible smoke column in the west. I'm not well.

I'm not well.

'I know,' Polly said, face again criss-crossed with concern. 'You didn't want to get the news this way. It's a terrible day. I don't mind telling you that this has been the worst morning of my career, and it's been a rough week for us all. It's awful to have to say goodbye to so many talented colleagues, awful. No one wants this to happen, least of all Eddie.'

I had been staring at Polly's clipboard, hardly listening, just as she did not seem to be listening to me, but now I snapped to attention.

'He quit,' I said.

'He couldn't face making redundancies,' Polly said. 'Of course, no one wants to—'

'Of *course*,' I said, standing with enough force and suddenness to send my chair rocketing back into the glass wall of the aquarium. 'No one *wants* to!'

Polly gaped as I spun around and pulled the meeting room door open. The noise of my chair striking the glass had attracted the notice of the few left in the office, who stared at me, their faces masks, unknowing as to what had happened and what might happen now.

Eddie rose slowly from his chair as I approached him. 'Jack,' he said. 'Take a deep breath, and—'

'Fire me,' I said, slashing the distance between us with a few strides. I was at his desk, inside his fort, I could feel my shoulders shaking, my lungs burning, smell the smoke.

'Sit down and let's talk this out.'

'Fire me,' I repeated, louder, spreading out my arms.

Eddie held up his hands. 'Polly has made her decision, and I am not about to—'

'Coward,' I said.

'Excuse me?' There, there it was, an angry light coming on in the eyes, the brows coming down.

'Coward!' I made sure the whole office heard me. All else was quiet, but I did not take my attention away from Eddie. No one was intervening, no hands dragged me away.

'Look,' Eddie said hotly. 'You had better stop before—'

'Before *what*? Before you fire me?' I demanded. 'Couldn't face it, could you? You had to stay everyone's friend. You didn't want to be the bad guy. You gave all that to Polly, always. How long did you delay? How much time did you waste, and money? All because you couldn't . . . When one of your writers was falling apart in front of you.'

Eddie was still scowling, but a shade of doubt had entered his expression, either doubt or bewilderment. His lips parted, but he didn't say anything.

'You didn't do anything. Why didn't you fire me? You could . . . Should . . . When I needed . . .'

I stopped. I was belatedly aware of my tears, which were hotter than my overheated skin, and gritty from the dirt on my face. All this time I had seen my job as a bastion against the Need, the disease – my last strongpoint against final collapse. Now I saw that the Need needed the job more than I did, it had been driving my increasingly desperate attempts to keep it, filling in the gaps left by drinking with copy-pasted quotes and outright fabrications, making me feel that I had to jump through Pierce and Quin's hoops. All those months of scrambling and stumbling had been on behalf of the Need, or to counter its malign effects, not as a defence against it. The Need and the job worked together, staving off collapse, keeping me going, keeping me drinking, preventing me from admitting to myself that I was not well. I was not averting anything. The only way to survive the disaster was to go through it.

'Forget it,' I said. 'I resign.'

What else could I do? I went to the pub.

No one wants this, of course. No one wants confrontation, no one wants to face the obvious, ghastly truth. It will follow you around, it will put itself in front of you again and again. But if you don't want to confront it, if you don't want to have that discussion, that argument . . . Not wanting can be as powerful as wanting. Great stretches of life can be lived, or half-lived, in the in-between space that is created by not wanting. How long had I been carrying on at the magazine, with Eddie knowing what should be done, and yet not wanting to do it? And me not wanting to face the truth myself? As it happened, I had prevailed, I had secured my place. I had won. The Need had won, I had lost.

No one wants this: it had been the same with Elise. We spent a full half of our relationship in the shadow of the conversation – the conversation that neither of us wanted to have, the conversation that we were jointly prepared to invest vast emotional resources and imagination into not having. The conversation that would contain the forbidden, fatal words, the ones that we thought every day. I did not need to have the conversation to know that they were in Elise's mind as prominently as they were in mine. But we never wanted to form them in the air, in the outer realness. That one word in particular: alcoholic. I didn't want to hear that – it was the Game Over sound, when the loop you're holding touches the bendy wire and completes the circuit and a buzzer buzzes. The wire had grown so twisted, and we hung on to the loop with white knuckles, working through the convolutions. I would watch her, terrified, as we had one of the conversations that was not the conversation, and I would have that word in my mind, burning there so clearly that I fancied it might manifest itself in the space between us, letters dripping oily fire, or appear branded on my forehead like a third eye opening. And I'd see it reflected in her eyes, in the glass of the glasses she wore in the evenings but not at work, and I'd be thinking, She's going to say it, it's coming, I know that she's thinking it and she is definitely going to say it this time, and then this conversation will become *that* conversation. But she didn't. We never had that conversation. Not wanting. We went from preferring to stay together rather than have that conversation, to preferring to split rather than have that conversation. What was it all for, then?

To give an example. We were eating dinner in an Italian restaurant near our flat. There are many other examples that I could cite – perhaps this one comes to mind for the setting. It wasn't a tense discussion in the kitchen, or the bedroom, or the living room, the three places in which these discussions took place nine times out of ten. We had gone to this little neighbourhood restaurant, one of a dying breed, in the middle of the week, for no good reason. We were simply both too demoralised to cook. Talk had turned to the amount I drank, I don't remember exactly why or how, but it often did. No, I do remember why, and I don't know why I am claiming I don't. The time had eased past ten and I had mentioned that I wanted to go to the convenience store before it closed. Elise had asked if that was really necessary – didn't I have a can or two in the fridge? Which was true, but I had squirmed nevertheless, and she had picked up on my squirm, my reluctance.

'Jack, the cans, the drinking in the evening,' she said, voice thin with exhaustion, close to a break. 'I'm worried . . .'

And I kept my face calm, all the while thinking, This is it, this time we are going to have the conversation, and she will say the word, and the buzzer will sound and that will be that.

'I'm worried that it's becoming a problem.'

That was as close as we came. Not even: *It's a problem*. Just, becoming. She said how worried she was, and she considerately emphasised her concern for my health and my work. I was not oblivious to her pain. I wanted to soothe it. That was where we differed: the problem that had to be solved.

She wanted me to drink less, to set myself limits and stick to them, bringing everything back to a healthy level. I wanted to make her concern go away, with as few other changes as possible. I wanted her to stop worrying – it was a problem of perception, her perception. I could do a better job of concealing what I drank, that was one priority. But I also needed to make a show of proving that I didn't have a problem – that I wasn't addicted, to use another word that we never spoke.

Hiding the drinking never worked for long. I sneaked pub visits after work, and I filled innocuous containers with lager. I bought the can-crusher. Being drunk, I was sloppy, I made mistakes and the ruses rarely lasted long. They only served to reinforce the impression that I had . . . that there was a problem.

I would have to undergo some genuine deprivation to remove that impression.

The summer of 2012 rolled around. The problem was still *becoming* a problem – both the problem itself and the problematic impression that there was a problem. Nevertheless, we were often happy. We spent long weekend days in the pub, sitting outdoors, reading newspapers and magazines. I spent a little too long one Sunday and became more or less catatonic. This is impossible for me to describe because I have no memory of it, and Elise's account was hobbled by her anger and her embarrassment. I could not be moved, and I had to be helped home by Elise and one of the regulars, taking an arm each. The next day I had to miss work. (I claimed food poisoning, and my absences were still seldom enough for the excuse to work.) Elise spent Sunday night sitting awake beside my motionless form in bed, afraid that I might stop breathing or swallow my tongue. Satisfied that I would live, she spent Monday night at a friend's house. She called me at about 10 p.m. – I had been drinking for hours already, delighted to be out of work and left on my own, and I was unusually drunk for that time on a weeknight. I slurred and forgot things, and she became very upset, and hung up on me.

On Tuesday morning, I called her. Extraordinary measures were needed.

I said I would stop drinking. And I did.

Two empty pint glasses stood on the table in front of me, grey suds clinging to the interiors. A third was full and fresh, still frosted with condensation. My lips had made a little wound at the edge of the foam, but that was the only sign that it had been touched. Perfection. I was in the brightly lit, tacky pub near the office, the one that my colleagues avoided. Friday night was the only time I had seen it busy, full of deafening men in suits and workers from nearby construction sites, but in office hours it had a sleepy air.

Kay dropped herself into the seat opposite me at about four. I would have asked her how she knew where to find me, but I knew already: she would have asked Tamesis for a pub recommendation, perhaps specifying that she wanted to run into people. The app would have done the rest, given that we were T-plus mutuals. No Quin needed – this was just Tamesis doing what it was supposed to do.

She was carrying an early edition of the *Standard*, and tossed it onto the table, folded to the front page headline: ONE HURT IN PIMLICO STREET COLLAPSE.

'Cover story,' she said. 'Another cover. You're on fire.'

'Being on fire would be the end to a perfect day,' I said.

'Want to compare days?' Kay said, with a warning raise of her eyebrows.

'Not particularly,' I said.

She shrugged. 'To be honest, I don't think I could beat "house fell down", even today. Although this morning I did think I was going to be homeless.'

The London question, of course – how did she make it work? And Kay's answer: she shared with a friend, and went payday to payday. My answer, too, although not the sharing part, and that made for bigger gulfs between paydays. I made a mental note to cancel the standing order to Dave, or whatever lay behind the software construct 'Dave'.

'This morning? But not now?'

'I'm back, baby,' Kay said with an acid smile. 'Reinstated.' She put on a voice – a blustering, gruff 'authority' voice. 'Regrettable error, premature, embarrassing, acted without full consultation, sincere apologies.'

'Polly said that?'

'*The publisher* said that. I was taken upstairs. But Polly did it.'

I bent over my pint, and frowned into it. 'Aren't you going to find it difficult working for Polly after this?'

'Yeah. Awkward.' She widened her eyes. 'But I did see a side of her that I liked. After you left – I won't recap the whole thing, but she had a stand-up row with Eddie. Said that she had been kept waiting for years to be editor, doing his dirty work for him, and he couldn't even step down without making her do all the shit he didn't want to do.'

'Wow,' I said.

'I know. I don't think I've ever seen Polly get angry. She's always so calm. It must have been building up a while. It was good. I think she might be a good boss, actually. She might be straight with people. Unlike Eddie.'

'Eddie's an arsehole,' I said, taking a drink.

'Everyone thinks so,' Kay said. 'I need to raise a glass to that. Let me get a drink.'

While Kay was at the bar, I unfolded the *Standard* to look at the story about my house. The splash picture was an aerial shot of the cratered street. A tattered veil of smoke or dust still clung to the heaped wreckage in the crater, like the caldera of a slumbering volcano. The story itself had a couple of quotes from Bella – edited for length, I imagined. The collapse had been attributed to 'nearby basement excavations, weakened by heavy rain'. The street was still closed, it said, while the fire brigade investigated the safety of the surrounding houses.

I pored over the picture, trying to make out features amid the ruins. What was I looking for? The fridge, perhaps, tumbled like a dice. Not that I could get to it. In the lower left-hand corner of the picture was a shape, a curl of white plastic – the edge, I realised, of a drone, part of the circular guard around one of its rotors. That was how news organisation got pictures like this, now, so much cheaper than a helicopter. Would I be on the evening news? Where would I watch it?

Kay returned, with a pint.

'We haven't had a drink in ages,' I said.

She gave me an appraising look, and said nothing. I wondered if I had said the wrong thing.

'This is nice,' I said, raising my glass. 'I'm pleased you got your job back.'

'Are you OK?' she said, and although she didn't elaborate on what she meant, the look she threw at my beer said enough on its own.

'I'm not well,' I said. 'I'll figure it out.'

'Is that why you've been avoiding me?' she asked 'I used to enjoy hanging out with you, but the last few weeks, it's like you don't want to know.'

I didn't reply. At first. And then I realised that I did have a reply.

'Maybe I didn't want to be asked if I was OK,' I said.

'Well, excuse me.'

'No, no. That not really what I mean. I mean . . . I've been having a rough time. I didn't want anyone else getting drawn into it, getting hurt. I really enjoyed hanging out with you as well. I suppose I wanted to . . . preserve that.'

She sipped her lager. I wondered what kind it was, and felt the usual pang of outraged jealousy that came with watching non-alcoholics drink, that it could be so easy for them, that they would reach a point when they didn't want any more, how could they, how could they.

Kay removed a touch of foam from her top lip with a flash of tongue, and said, 'Bollocks.'

'Bollocks?'

'Bollocks. I think you had it right the first time, more or less, not wanting to be asked if you were OK; you've been following your little trajectory, you know where you're going, and you didn't want the hassle of dealing with other people along the way. Getting asked if you were OK might mean admitting you're not OK. You've been streamlining.'

'Bollocks,' I said.

She shrugged, and made a face. 'What will you do now? Tonight? Go to a Travelodge or a Way Inn? Do you have family you could stay with? A friend you can call?'

Another time, I might have taken this for flirting, but it was most definitely not an invitation, though the underlying concern was real.

'Yes,' I said. 'I do.'

TWELVE

It was the time of the Olympics – wholesome athletics filled the television, and outside the sun shone on a rejoicing city. I was in a secret agony as dark and bleak as an Arctic winter. And so, I suspected, was Elise, still shackled to me, still desperate to help, watching and fearing. Not that I saw, in my mirrored cell, every thought reflected inward.

I had stopped drinking, overnight. We had watched the opening ceremony on television together, windows open to the evening air, too far away to hear any fireworks or flypasts, but we could make out the mingled sounds of our neighbours enjoying themselves. And we had fun too, of a pinched kind, clearing the fridge of cans, avoiding thoughts of the next day and subsequent days, relaxing like the 'old times' that were only a couple of years before. Opening ceremony to closing ceremony, that was the deal – if I could fully abstain for that period, we would reopen talks about moderation and rules and setting limits and so on, all the stuff that had failed in the past.

Not that I could see my way to the closing ceremony. I could hardly stand to speculate as far as the end of the next day, the next morning. The future was inaccessible, and any optimistic speculations had a counterfeit air. But the word addict was still absent from our conversations, and when it crept into my thoughts, it came as a devilish intruder. No, it seemed to me that another force was keeping me drinking, quite apart from either free will or addiction – a spook I had never caught in the light. Twisting away within me was an immense contradiction. I believed that stopping drinking would have very little real effect. After all, I was in great shape: an enviable job, a supportive relationship, good health, the world at my feet. Clearing away the drink, and all the problems it had caused, would do no more than reveal happiness, the happiness that had proved elusive so far.

At the same time, I feared stopping more than I had feared anything before. It should have been possible to infer the truth from this – that I was not opening the curtains to a refulgent dawn of contentment, but something else, something worse – but I did not.

If you want to believe, well, that's very powerful, it's very hard to resist.

Work continued. Most of my colleagues had asked for time off during the Olympics, and Eddie hadn't wanted to decline any of those requests. He had tickets for a couple of events, too. So we had all put in extra effort in the fortnight before the games, and I earned some credit for volunteering to forgo leave. But with much of the work done, the days were quiet, so quiet that management turned the office TVs to the BBC coverage, muted, so we could all 'be part of it'.

I was part of nothing. I loitered on the web and picked fights on Twitter, hoping to be taken out of myself for a moment, and then crashing back into shame and embarrassment. I sweated in my seat and pretended to enjoy the sport, feeling alienated from the athletes and the spectators, respective paragons of physical health and communal joy.

Those were the good times. Worse, far worse, were the evenings, when I prowled in our space, temper unbearably strained. The knowledge that my fury was unreasonable did nothing to quash it. I was afraid, terribly afraid, and there was no way of talking about it because I would not be understood. At work I could just about cope, I could divert myself, and there was time yet before the night. In the evening, at home, I was just shut away, and the night was inevitable.

Elise tried her best, and I was not nearly as grateful or gracious as I should have been. Her encouragement numbed me and her compassion repulsed me. And she was so patient with my temper that it made me angry. She filled the fridge with myriad flavours of fruit juice and bought fizzy water in the shrink-wrapped packs of four swollen two-litre bottles. Alongside this were boxes of fancy tea bags: green tea, mint tea, chamomile tea, fruit infusions. She sincerely believed – or wanted to believe – that in one of those pretty boxes lay the methadone I needed, the acceptable substitute for booze that would tide us over to the other side.

Weeks later, she did not take those boxes with her, and when I cleared the flat I threw them away. Half had not been opened.

The permissible drink that gave me any kind of relief was Gaviscon, which soothed the bouts of heartburn that racked me. It was at its most intense when I lay down at the end of the day, nerves tied like violin strings, in order to sleep. Inside, a scorching, corroding sensation would mount. Though it came from the guts, it always felt as if it were dissolving its way upwards into the heart and lungs, somehow both eating away and clogging up all the vital places of the chest, and I would have to rise and swig Gaviscon from the bottle.

Sleep didn't come easily when the heartburn was raging, but it didn't come easily at all. Heartburn was, in a way, a welcome visitor at night, because for all the pain it entailed, it was a connection to the real and the corporeal. Worse were the dreams.

Dream isn't quite the right word. I was not asleep when they came – later in the night they turned into dreams, but they began as paralysing episodes of fear. I would lie in bed, convinced beyond all argument that death was imminent, that I was riddled with cancer or another (torturing, humiliating) terminal disease and I had already left it just too late for the doctors to do anything about it. Given that my insides were boiling and every sinew was aching from withdrawal, this was one of the more believable treats served up by the gruesome cinema of my imagination. I believed that Elise was the one dying, not me, and we had missed our chance to save her by focusing on me. I placed myself in the brutalised aftermath of economic or ecological collapse, fleeing marauders in a wasteland of burned-out cars hissing with corpse-fed nature. I killed off my family individually or in batches, by bacillus and calamity, and I prodded my reaction for its deficiencies, for evidence that I was less than functionally human and undeserving of aid. Nightly, I built hell for myself.

Very worst of all – in the sense of being least explicable and most persistent – were the fantasies of accusation, trial and imprisonment. I would be accused of a crime – naturally, a heinous crime – that I had not committed, or that I had somehow committed without meaning to, and I would hurtle through the machinery of justice on skids of official outrage, landing in prison without prospect of release, abandoned by all who had previously cared for me. Not just any prison: a Piranesi nightmare wrapped in suicide nets and jaundiced paint, the one-handed creation of an authoritarian mind, only in my mind, all for me.

That was cold turkey. It was a prison without escape. It was a living death. And when I think about stopping, it's those waking dreams of prison that come back to me.

I should have made the connection with the conversation that we never had, with the words I never wanted to hear. There I was, every night, imagining an accusation, a charge, and a life sentence, fearing that above all else and not knowing why. And meanwhile, during the day, fearing the words that would traduce me. *Addict* and *alcoholic* – I would have no defence. That's when the talk of moderation and finding a balance would end, and there are no more loopholes or cheats, and you have to stop. For ever.

Ocado bags were scattered in Pierce's hall. Not the fridge and freezer bags – if there had been any of those, he had put them away – but anything that could be left had been left. Profile antennae still twitching, without purpose, I scanned the bags for insights. He liked Krave, the chocolate-filled cereal, which struck me as childish and odd. But his essays did have a sugar-crazed quality. I thought back to our expedition on Tuesday, the police public relations shed in the forecourt of the Ocado depot, right next to the source of the plume. *Don't knock Ocado*, Pierce had said. They had kept him alive in the days following the *Night Traffic* attack, when he couldn't leave the house. An interesting detail to invent, given that there had been no attack and nothing had been stopping him leaving the house. Who had been watching?

I said something about the bags to Pierce. 'Yeah, I've been meaning to get around to that,' he replied. He was already a couple of steps up the stairs; stung, he returned, picked up two bags in each hand, and sprinted back up. I picked up two bags as well, including the one with the box of Krave.

Pierce's flat had not been tidy when I was here on Tuesday, but it was distinctly messier today. Two plates, bearing the remains of two distinct meals, had been left on the dining table, and a couple of empty beer bottles. Not many by my standards, but they would have been the first things to go if he had made any effort to clear up.

He gave me a beer – a Heineken, in a can – and I told him about my house.

'So you've got nothing? No clothes, nothing?'

I nodded.

'Wait here.' He left the living room.

I hadn't said anything about losing my job – about quitting my job. I had quit, not been fired, I needed to be clear about that even to myself. Especially to myself, before a fiction began to cloud and supplant the truth. Nor did I intend to say anything. He didn't have to know, for now.

When Pierce came back, he was carrying a pair of trousers. 'You can have these, they're a bit tight for me now.' He patted his paunch. 'This is, ah, the director's cut.'

While I changed, Pierce turned his back to me, looking at the map that filled his wall. 'Where was it you said you lived, again? Pimlico?'

'Yeah.'

He smoothed the scraps on that part of the map, and picked through them. 'Technically part of the East End, if you believe soil is destiny – built up from the flood plain using spoil from the excavation of one of the docks.'

'Is that so?' The trousers fitted fine, with a belt. This charity had thrown me. I could not have named the instinct that drove me to Pierce's house, but I was angry and – now that the profile no longer mattered – had some vague idea of settling my account, of telling Pierce exactly what I thought of him. But I did not know precisely what that was, and his unprompted kindness complicated my feelings even further, spilling in more resentment and self-loathing. I wondered where the soil scraped out from under my neighbours' houses had gone now – perhaps back east, infill for one of the vast new developments on the river. Returning. Dust to dust.

'Mistress City,' I said.

'Pardon?' Pierce said.

'Mistress City,' I said. 'It's on your map, on Pimlico. I saw it there the other day.'

Pierce folded back the map's hide of notes and clippings. 'Yes,' he said. 'Mistress City. Nickname, because it was where Members of Parliament kept their mistresses, in little rented flats. It's where politicians get fucked.'

'It's certainly where I get fucked,' I said. 'Got, anyway. Thank you for the trousers.'

'You're welcome,' Pierce murmured, still staring at the map. 'Why do you live there, anyway? Why *did* you?'

'I used to share a flat there with a girlfriend,' I said. 'When that ended, I couldn't leave – it was as if leaving the area for somewhere more affordable was an admission of failure. Of being downwardly mobile, I suppose. And the irony is, I had to move downwards, literally downwards, in order to stay. I used to be on the first floor, and I went down into the basement flat.'

'The basement flat of the same house?'

'Same house, yes.' I swigged the beer. 'Another couple live in the flat upstairs. Lived.'

Pierce turned, smiling over his shoulder at me, amused by the story. I could picture him re-telling it, at my expense, for laughs – another little scrap of detail tucked into his vibrant mental city.

'Are we going to talk about what happened?' I asked. 'Last night.'

'It went well, I thought,' Pierce said. He had returned to poring over the map, making tiny adjustments here and there, as if planning a military operation. His casual manner, the complacent way he referred to what he had done, needled me.

'Are you done now?' I said, not disguising the scorn I felt. 'Do you have what you need?'

'Oh, not even slightly,' Pierce said, very calm. 'It's given me an appetite. Thrilling, wasn't it? I used to feel afraid – this ubiquitous fear that I had stopped noticing, it had become part of me – and I don't any more. It's gone.'

I didn't say anything. I didn't know what he wanted, and I suspected that I didn't want to find out. And the same applied to me. Why was I here? To get to Pierce, somehow. To get to the end of his ploys and plans, to exhaust them. But there was more there, always, and indulging him only expanded his desires.

'I liked the way you set it up,' Pierce continued. 'Using Tamesis.'

'I didn't do that,' I said. 'That was Quin.'

He hesitated. 'Yes. But it was a clever idea.'

'It wasn't my idea. It was all Quin. He did it without saying anything to me.'

The map lost its power over Pierce. He turned, not looking around at me, but down, away, to the floor, into thought, brow creased.

'How did Quin know what you wanted to do?' I asked.

'I may have spoken with him,' Pierce said, with a hint of what might have been regret, or even guilt. 'We've been in touch.'

'Me too,' I said. 'He's been moving us about like pins on your fucking map. And I don't know why.'

Pierce kept his gaze away from the wall. 'It's his map,' he said quietly. 'Gather enough data about a person and you can manipulate them, guide their choices, get them doing what you want, and they might not even know.' He turned towards me, and stared. At first I thought I saw the gleam of tears in his eyes, but if they had been there, they went, he overcame them. 'What if that's also true of a city?'

I swallowed, and felt the tightness in my chest. How much dust and smoke had got into my system today? How much of London, as it remade itself?

'All this time I've been wondering why he would waste his time jerking around a nonentity like me,' Pierce said, and the words might as well have come from me, so closely did they match my thoughts. 'What if it's not me, not you? You know' – again he was at the map, as if compelled, up close, eyes flickering from place to place, hands spread out, caressing – 'my little plan, the map, the psychogeographical index, it wasn't just about getting revenge on the psychogeographers, the other novelists. I mean, who gives a shit, really? They're old, old. It was about . . . ownership. Taking ownership. Retaking it. The city was slipping away from me, from us all, and I wanted it back. And the same had applied to *Night Traffic* – trying to own a single moment. Because if I had that, no one else could have the whole. Part of it would always be mine alone.'

'But it was false.'

He didn't look at me, but he winced. 'Well, if it was true, it wouldn't belong only to me, would it? It would belong to . . .

to the ones who . . .' and he trailed away, absorbed in an internal struggle beyond my sight.

I had about a third of the can left, and I drained it. During the journey over, I had discovered a vodka miniature in my pocket, the last survivor of my stealthy office session yesterday. Only yesterday. It was warm.

'Do you have any mixers?' I asked. 'Coke?'

'Lemon squash?' Pierce said absently.

It would do. I went to the kitchen and found the squash concentrate in a cupboard. Beside it was the whisky we had drunk together earlier in the week – about a quarter left. Whatever Pierce's mental turmoil, he hadn't been binge drinking, and I hated him for that.

I took the miniature from my coat pocket. That pocket also contained the postcard from my mother, the picture of the cockatoo. I took that out as well.

Room temperature vodka and room temperature lemon squash alone would be revolting. Looking in Pierce's fridge, I found a full filter jug of water, and a couple more cans of Heineken. I took out another can, and opened it. I still wasn't sure what I wanted from Pierce, but drinking all of his booze was a good start.

When I turned to leave the kitchen, Pierce was standing in the archway. He leaned against the wall as if relaxed, but his whole manner was devoid of nonchalance.

'Making yourself at home?' he said, coming through and checking over the kitchen as if trying to discern what I had stolen. Arriving at a wooden knife block, he tapped his index finger on the handle of each of the four blades it held. Counting them? Checking I hadn't armed myself? Had he used one of those knives the previous night to threaten De Chauncey? Was I in danger?

'What's this?' he asked. In his hand was the postcard from my parents, which I had left on the counter.

'I got it this morning,' I said. Pierce was already reading the back, so it was superfluous to explain who had sent it. 'By the time it arrived, there was no letterbox for it to go through.'

'Huh,' Pierce said. 'Mugged, twice, and then your house falls down. Authentic experiences seem to follow you around. Some people have all the luck.'

'Mugged three times, now,' I said, fixing Pierce with a stare. Or trying to, because he turned his back on me, and opened a kitchen drawer. For a moment I thought he might be putting the postcard in there, but he had left it on the side, and it wasn't clear what he was doing – taking out a small object, a tiny glitter of chrome, a weapon? But it was small enough to palm without my seeing more. Why was I so nervous around Pierce? His behaviour was off, for sure. Did I have reason to fear him? Or was I sensing my own conflicted motives reflected back at me? Did I mean to hurt Pierce?

'I guess that's right,' Pierce said, returning to the living room. 'Three times. You never did tell me about the second time.'

Nor did I intend to. Not at this moment, in any case. My gaze had rested upon the cockatoo, which tipped its head at me, as if waiting for me to say or do something.

'It's weird, actually, what you say about authenticity following me around,' I began, not really knowing where to begin. 'Because for the past few days, I've had the impression that I've been followed around by . . .' I couldn't finish. It sounded too odd, spoken aloud.

'By what?' Pierce's voice came from the living room.

'I don't know,' I said. 'I think I must have got a lungful of fumes when we went to Barking, and it's been messing with my head.'

'We were equally exposed,' Pierce said. 'What's following you around?'

'Smoke,' I said. And as I spoke, my nostrils filled with the smell of burning, unbelievably strong and real.

I clamped my eyes shut. It's not real, I told myself firmly. It's a panic attack. I'm stressed, I can't cope with my circumstances, and my mind tells me to get out as fast as possible. And it creates a reason to do so. That's what's been happening. There's no smoke, it's an incentive conjured up by the flee reflex in the brain.

The smell was only intensifying. I breathed in hard to try to show myself that the sensations were coming from within, not from the atmosphere. The incinerator stench was overwhelming, and I erupted into a coughing fit.

This was ridiculous. It's not real, none of it is real.

The kitchen smoke alarm burst into noise, a staccato electronic peal. I was standing directly beneath it, and it was loud enough to cause pain, a spike driven into the head.

I opened my eyes. Smoke was pouring under the kitchen arch in a solid grey river, drawn by the open window over the sink.

'Shit,' I said. 'Shit!'

I lunged into the living room. Smoke swirled across the ceiling and hazed the rest of the room. Its source was the wall-map, where a patch of flame, centred on east London, was licking upwards and outwards. Its bright orange tongues snaked with easy grace through the dry kindling of the notes and clippings. With every passing second a score of new leaves curled, smoked and ignited. Many detached from the map, carrying fire down to the lower portions of the wall and the floor.

Pierce stood with his back to me, staring at what he had done. In his hand was a lighter.

'Shit,' I repeated. I twisted on the spot, torn between actions – get Pierce away, or combat the fire? It was immediately, instinctively obvious that he would not help. The blaze covered the entirety of the eastern borough of Newham and most of Barking, and had spread as far north as Walthamstow and Epping; flames were licking soot over the cornice and ceiling, which would soon be burning. Meanwhile the fire spread west, marching through the East End, where Pierce's overgrowth of annotations was thickest. Canary Wharf and the Isle of Dogs were ablaze, and the inferno had reached Pierce's home in Mile End – this was what had his attention, watching the fire creep towards the position of his house, even as his real house was on fire.

On fire, and perhaps only seconds away from being beyond hope of control.

I had seen the red cowling of a fire extinguisher in the kitchen. But when I dashed back there, all I found was a fire blanket, fixed to the wall by the stove – good for stifling pan fires, less useful for the kind of conflagration taking hold in the living room. Nevertheless I took hold of the release tags and pulled with such force that the whole affair, plastic cover and all, came off the wall. As I tried to separate blanket and container, I saw the jug of filter water on the side, left there when I gave up making my little cocktail. I grabbed it and ran, as fast as I dared without spilling the water, back into the living room.

It was bad, really bad. Returning to the living room I took a lungful of the smoke, which was thicker and nastier than it had been just seconds earlier, and hung lower in the room. It was as if I had tried to breathe water, polluted water – my lungs revolted, my eyes flooded with stinging tears, and I doubled over, only preserving the water in the jug by a phenomenal act of will.

Pierce appeared unaffected, and continued to watch the fire. Half the map was alight, all of London east of St Paul's. The fire had caught at the cornice and on spots of the floor. I stamped across the floor, scattering smouldering debris, and aimed high with the water, towards Tottenham, trying to quench the fire at the point that it threatened the ceiling. The jug was exhausted in two large sloshes, the third was a pathetic spray of drops, and while some of the rage was knocked from the fire, it was not exhausted, and its boundaries moved ever outwards.

Increasingly light-headed, I turned to the blanket, first holding it out like a sail to see how wide an area I could smother – not enough. But clutching its upper corners in my fists made me think – it was fireproof, right? I changed my hold, trying to wrap it around my hands as best as I could, and then tried to knock the burning notes from the wall, breaking up the largest patches of the fire and scraping firebreaks, stamping on the flames that fell to the floor. Embers went in my hair and eyes and bit at my cheeks; grey pushed in at the edges of vision. I had to stop, after making what seemed like little difference, to retreat and double over, coughing and retching.

But Pierce had awoken from his trance and had disappeared into the kitchen. He reappeared with a blue plastic mop bucket, much bigger than the jug, even only filled halfway, and directed it at the fiercest points of the fire, across Hackney and Leyton.

Without speaking, we worked together. Pierce hit the greatest concentrations of flame, and I swiped and stamped and snuffed the leftovers and fringes with the blanket. We fought for what felt like an age, though it had been less than ten minutes since he had sparked the lighter, and when we were sure the danger was past and all the windows were open to thin the smoke, we splashed across the sodden floor to the couch, coughing and weeping and spitting.

'Why did you do that?' I said, as soon as it was possible to croak out words. 'You could have killed us.'

'I've been meaning to take that down for ages,' Pierce said, with a nod towards the map. It was a ruin, two-thirds of it gone, only west London hanging on, damp and sagging from its pins. The cork tiles that had supported the map were blackened and scarred, some no more than charcoal, others fallen away to reveal the shocking, floury white of spalled plaster. A ridge of debris lay along the line of the skirting board, in a wide puddle of sooty water, soaking into a rucked, grimed rug. Despite the open windows, the room stank of smoke, and a haze of particulates perverted the light.

'The people downstairs are going to be cross,' I said.

'I never see them,' Pierce said. 'Anyway, they can't be cross. I've had a house fire. A terrifying accident. They'll have to be sympathetic. There are rules.'

Yes, malign sympathy. There it was, the sensation I had felt in the morning, sitting breathing the exhalations of my own destroyed house. The lure of freedom. But thought of it was cut short by another coughing fit.

'What were you saying about being followed?' Pierce asked. 'Something about the fumes getting into your head . . .'

I coughed again, and again, trying to dislodge the sack of charcoal briquettes that was crammed in my throat. I could taste blood, a little, and felt as if I were in the late stages of a chest infection. Light-headed, too. Perhaps I should have taken the paramedic's advice and gone to hospital; perhaps I should go now.

'It's gone now, isn't it?' I said, unsure of how to approach the topic and fearful of the answers. 'The column of smoke we followed on Tuesday. It's gone – you couldn't see it today?'

'Today? It had cleared up the day after,' Pierce said. 'They put the fire out. Or it put itself out. From the look of the place there was nothing left to burn.'

'That's what I thought,' I said. 'The thing is – I can still see it.'

'Still see what?' Pierce asked. 'The smoke column?'

'Yes,' I said. 'I've been able to see it ever since. No matter where I am. At night, even. As if it has been following me around. And getting closer, street by street.'

Pierce didn't say anything. I had his attention, at least, although it was impossible to read his gaze.

'It sounds like an invitation,' he said at last.

Cold though it was, the street air tasted good after the soggy ashtray of Pierce's flat. I breathed it deep, and was rewarded with another coughing fit. At least my head cleared a little, enough to remind myself that I had nowhere to sleep tonight. But Tamesis could take care of that, and it was not yet late. Pierce was insistent.

'I'm surprised you haven't done this already,' he said, once more alive with volatile energy. 'Gone to the end of the rainbow, found the pot of gold.'

'A notoriously futile and misguided activity,' I said.

'You said it's no more than a couple of streets away,' Pierce said. 'You must have been tempted? Don't you want to find out what's there?'

'I haven't wanted to acknowledge it that much,' I said. Pierce's persistent questioning was once again putting me under pressure, and a voice within insisted that I was making a mistake. 'Even talking about it with you gives it more significance than I would like,' I continued. 'I don't expect to find anything, and I don't want it to mean anything. If it isn't fixed in a particular place, it must be centred on me. There's nothing else to find.'

'If there's nothing to find, then there's nothing to worry about, right?'

I didn't reply.

'OK, think about it this way,' Pierce said. 'Has ignoring the smoke column made it go away?'

'No,' I said.

'No. It's been getting bigger and closer, you said. So ignoring it hasn't worked. Instead, let's try tracing it, and maybe that'll be what makes it go away and leave you alone.'

There was logic to that. But I wished I had never mentioned the plume to Pierce, because I saw now that he had co-opted it as the basis of one of his adventures.

'Well?' he asked. 'Which way do we go?'

I kicked the pavement. 'What are we doing here?' I asked, not concealing my annoyance.

Pierce shrugged. '*You* came to *me*.'

True. Why had I done that? If it wasn't to follow a story, what did I want from Pierce?

'I'll tell you what I'm doing here,' Pierce said. 'I am *pursuing a process*. We set out to make something happen – to make an event, a real event, to balance out the incident I invented. A truth for a lie. A true interaction with the city. And we haven't quite got there yet.'

'You didn't get that last night? With De Chauncey?'

He shook his head. 'No. It was great, it felt amazing. But . . . I don't like that Quin set it up. It was staged. Tainted. False.'

'False? And chasing around an illusion, a hallucination, is truth?'

'Don't think of it that way,' Pierce said. 'Think of it as . . .

pure. Untainted by outside interference. It's Quin, see. Quin's the problem. I thought he was trying to help, in his way – that he wanted to help the city, that he was trying to get it back. But he isn't.' He frowned hard, biting into a sour thought.

'I know,' I said. 'Last night I learned that Quin and De Chauncey were working together. Projects with landlords, with the police – he's just another scumbag.'

If this was news to Pierce, he hid his surprise. 'It's more advanced than that, I think. But Tamesis is certainly not what I thought it was. It's not going to free the city. Anyway, this plume of yours is different. Nothing to do with Quin, or his little app. It's from another place, a place inside, telling us which way to go. So, which way is that?'

I pointed. There was no need to hunt around for the plume. It had been there all along, over Pierce's shoulder – over both his shoulders, a curtain of looping, gulping yellow-black tar in the star-pricked sky, jaundiced light flickering where it squatted on the Mile End roofline.

'That way, huh?' Pierce said. His enthusiasm dimmed. 'Across the road, I suppose?'

I nodded.

'OK then,' he said, and he turned to fall into step beside me, and we walked south, towards the plume, towards the cemetery park.

The red lights on the cranes crowded over the City gave the western horizon an industrial, petrochemical look, more refinery than business district. Which suited the half-built financial towers well enough – they dug and clawed and pumped as much as they rose and transcended. They were dirty, extractive objects, pummelling more and more value from the land that rooted them, and purifying it into glass and ineffable space.

The smoke indoors was a product of panic attacks, but I had never decided about the plume. Was it a real phenomenon in the world, or a hallucination that existed only in my head? Neither possibility was very comforting, so I had never sought to reach a decision, keeping it to myself and keeping out of its way. Uncertainty was a more desirable state. No action required, no ugly conclusions.

But now Pierce knew about it, and had pushed me into action. The probabilities were collapsing, and the plume appeared to know it. Our path took us directly south, cutting across Mile End Road, but there were no handy pedestrian lights, and I had to divert my attention from the skyline to the speeding evening traffic. Once we reached the other side, I looked again for the smoke, and could not find it. We walked down the side street that led towards the main entrance of the cemetery park, and I kept my eyes on the southern sky, where the plume had been seen last, waiting for it to reassert itself, perhaps with an apologetic cough.

It did not. It was gone. The night sky was rained out, offensively clear, and I could see all of the twenty or thirty stars that London's glare permits, and a nail-clipping of moon.

At the entrance to the cemetery, with its gloomy lodge and war memorial, I hesitated. The plume was no longer there – it was pointless to go in. And I did not want to go in. There were no lights to guide us inside, it was a nature reserve, not a landscaped park, a place for birds and bats.

I scanned the surrounding rooftops, to see if the plume might have popped up in another direction. 'Are you sure about this?' I asked Pierce.

'Are *you* sure?' Pierce replied. 'You look lost. Are we going the right way?'

My hunt for the plume continued, but its absence was as

stubborn and disturbing as its recurrence had been. Time was slipping by. If I was going to find a place to sleep, I should do it soon. Then I could call my parents, or my sister, and try to make some longer-term arrangements. Make my ruin official. Pierce had evaded me to the last. Polly might still try to get a draft out of me, but even if I wanted to do the work, I doubted I could. I took out my phone to look at the time. Tamesis would know about hotels. Quin: he was the one I wanted to confront, but I could not imagine getting close to him.

A wisp, within. The plume would not simply disappear like that. It had meaning. It had to have meaning. I had shunned it and turned from it, and it had persisted, and that persistence had been a promise, that it would reveal itself. And it had not gone as soon as I told Pierce about it, it had been fuller and stronger and angrier than ever, dominating the sky above him, indisputably centred here, at the cemetery. And it had not vanished when we set out to pursue it, but shortly after, once we were committed.

'Never mind,' Pierce said. 'I see it.'

He was staring past me, into the forested dark of the cemetery. When I turned, I saw he was telling the truth. A pillar of smoke climbed avidly above the trees, twisting and bulging with a fierce hunger, underlit by an infernal orange light. It was not the vast, distant cataclysm I had seen before, but it was, beyond question, real. And I fancied I could hear it: a keening whooping on the icy air.

'You see that?' I asked Pierce.

'Plain as day,' he said. He was transfixed by it, the expression on his face the same as when he had stood and watched his map burning. I was reminded of the ghastly fascination the plume had exerted over me the first time I had seen it.

'That's not possible,' I said.

'It's close,' Pierce said. 'Can't you hear it? It's so close.'

Thick lines of crooked headstones like fans of fungus. Headless infants, handless angels. Tombs tipping into the dirt, or rearing from it. Even winter-bare, the trees and undergrowth hissed at our intrusion – this was not our place.

There were no lights, and although the path we trod was clear and level, I had to scurry to keep up with Pierce, and feared that I might at any moment trip or slip amid the fallen masonry. But the plume lit our path, or rather the fire beneath it did, a beacon in the heart of the park. Our destination was a rushing geyser of fire, cupped in the black, skeletal hand of a car frame.

The burning car was parked in an uneven clearing where paths converged. We slowed, feeling the heat on our faces. As we came into the glade, a tyre blew out and the car's body shuddered, coughing up a rush of sparks. All around the naked branches danced and snatched, catching the light of the somersaulting flames. A wet slap of combusted petrol hit the back of my throat and I gagged, feeling again the damage Pierce's arson had done to my lungs.

Another tyre blew, putting a knot in the plume of smoke. We had entered the clearing, but stayed at its edge, near the line of tombs and trees, circling the car.

'The fire's just started,' Pierce said. 'Only a minute or two ago.'

'Should we call someone?'

Pierce was staring into the fire, but his gaze was askew – he was not looking at the funeral pyre of the car, but through it, to the far side of the clearing. The oily light of the blaze had saturated my eyes and at first I took the activity he was watching to be the dancing ghosts of the flames. But it was not – it was people, moving out before the trees. They had tracked us as we circuited the clearing, and now stood in the mouth of the path we had come by, blocking our return: three young men, looped together by volatile youthful energy, jostling and striding and laughing, and looking at us.

Together, thinking the same, Pierce and I turned our heads the other way, to the next path from the clearing. And there were more, another four clustered around a bench, two men and two women, all young, full of strut and angry cheer. Two of this second group broke away and began to approach us. Quite by chance, we were caught in pincers.

Horrid familiarity crept up inside me.

It was happening again.

I looked at Pierce, hoping to see some of the reassuring confidence I recalled from our earliest acquaintance, the good-for-all-occasions cockiness and charm that made him cheek police officers and lad it up with photographers. His face was hollow with horror, mouth a shapeless scrawl.

'Hey! Hey!' the nearest youth said, jutting his chin at us. He was, like his companions, wearing a chunky puffer jacket, and it was impossible to place his age – mid-twenties, though the margin of error could be a decade wide each way. Everything in his stance and step was a challenge to us. Though they were dressed almost identically, the trio on that side were racially diverse; the advance party was black, the two behind them white and Asian.

Exactly as Pierce had described in *Night Traffic*. A few years older, but as he described.

I looked again at Pierce, not that I needed to gauge his thought, not that I needed confirmation.

'I invented you,' Pierce said in a whisper.

You only see the threshold once you're past it. Too late, always too late, you discover that the temper of the moment has passed, and you're in another place, another city.

'You calling someone, bruv?'

To my amazement, I found that this was addressed to me. I had had the sensation – the reassuring delusion – that somehow this might all be for Pierce, laid on solely for his benefit, and would flow past me. Perhaps this was an after-effect of last night, with De Chauncey, when I had been a bystander in a bubble of safety. But that was fantasy. I was here. I was involved.

My phone was in my hand. 'No, not calling anyone,' I said. I eased my phone into my coat pocket. 'We're just leaving.'

'No, you're not.'

Familiar.

I was aware of the other two, manoeuvring at the left periphery of my sight.

'How 'bout you give me that,' the man said, eyes on my coat pocket.

I breathed in hard, filling my nose and lungs with the rough stink of the burning car. Its warmth was the most comforting thing around.

'No,' I said. Not so familiar.

The young man cocked his head to one side.

'No, no, no, no,' Pierce said, voice quiet and wavering where mine had been firmer than I expected. He took a messy step backwards.

'Ffff . . .' one of the pair in the rearguard said.

Our challenger turned to him.

'We fucking know this prick,' his friend said. 'From before.'

Pierce took another step back, and I sensed movement behind me.

A smile spread across the lead man's face, mockingly slanted to one side.

'You going to write about us?'

Pierce emitted a demi-human groan and spun, clumsily, making to run. The lead youth lunged towards him. As the youth passed me, I moved, taking my hands from my pockets and shoving him in the flank. He sprawled over, off the path, into the graves.

It had all happened in an instinctive moment, feeling like precisely timed force, but the scene it birthed was bumbling farce. Pierce had stumbled, and was bent back, almost seated, in an awkward crab-like pose; his antagonist was also momentarily incapacitated, rolling on his side amid the chaos of stone and bramble around the clearing. Rough hands grabbed one of my sleeves, but ineptly, distracted by the low spectacle. Pierce had scrambled over onto his side, and was reaching into his coat. He gathered himself back to his feet as his opponent did, but now there was a spark in his hand, a flash of fire reflected off polished metal.

'Blade!'

I tore myself free of the youth who had grabbed my coat; he was too preoccupied with the unfolding confrontation to improve his hold, or to try to stop me.

The knife had come from the wood block in Pierce's kitchen. He was holding it close to his hip, pointed out, forward, at the young man in front of him. I could see no reason in the writer's eyes, only frothing animal impulse.

'Pierce, listen to me,' I began, but I had nowhere to go.

'I created you!' Pierce shouted, with enough ragged force that the young man quailed a little; for a moment I imagined he might be asking himself if he really was a figment of Pierce's imagination, but it was a quite natural reaction in the face of an unpredictable, distraught person carrying a knife. Even if he was having doubts about his own existence, I found mine melting away. I knew at once that Pierce had invented nothing: *Night Traffic* was the whole truth.

But Pierce sincerely believed that he had invented it – and if he sincerely believed that the people in front of him were no more than phantasms that he, the author, could summon and dismiss, then we were all in terrible danger, not least the man presently under the point of the knife.

'Pierce, they're real, they're all real,' I said.

It was too late. Pierce moved, the start of a charge, intent on carving an edit into his 'creation'. And I moved, incapable of subtlety, astonished that I could be doing the same act twice in less than a minute, no more than a lump of dumb matter, an obstruction that could be placed in the path of disaster.

We crunched together, a clumsy heavy-coated mismatch of joints and weights, and I felt the knife between us, like a tooth-pick caught in closing jaws; then we hit the ground, Pierce on top of me, and the knife, caught between us, did not turn one way or another but went rigidly *in*.

Pain, at my lowest rib on the left side. A point of light.

Pierce rolled off me, and I put my hand to the hurt, expecting worse pain and torn cloth and slick warmth. No.

The three men had backed away, nonplussed at what had happened. One was hissing, 'Fuck sake! Fuck sake!' to himself.

A white shape swooped over me, slicing through the smoke still erupting from the burning car and sending it coiling and curling. I felt the downbeat of wings against my face.

The shape burst into light. I was dazzled, and night was made day. The long, cold grass around me was made green and lush, and every detail of the scene was made perfect. Was I that badly injured, to have come to the Elysian field? I felt fine, not dead, but how should the dead feel but fine? Standing, I thought I might see that I had left my body behind; but it had stood with me, we were still very much connected. I was alive.

I winced into the light and shielded my eyes. Rotors whined.

'This is the police,' said a voice above, an amplified recording. 'Disperse immediately.'

The drone's lights swept the clearing, ending their dazzling focus on me and letting me get a good look at the machine: four fat rotors clover-leafed around a hub of cameras and lights, the blue badge of the Metropolitan Police transferred on its white and yellow hull.

'Disperse immediately,' the drone repeated, and the youths needed no further invitation – they scattered like birds at a gunshot.

Pierce did not budge. He lay exactly where he had slumped after tumbling off me. His hand was still clasped around the handle of the knife, the blade of which was lost inside his chest. He stared into the open night sky, not looking at the drone or the widening smoke from the wreck of the car, not looking at anything.

'Disperse immediately,' the drone repeated in its curt recorded voice. It spoke only to me, and I listened.

I did not go back the way I had come in. I did not fancy returning by the meandering path we had followed from the main entrance, especially if there was any risk that the youths had paused in their flight upon reaching the street – or worse, were being held there by the police. Besides, the nearest gate lay to the north, at the end of a wide, straight path.

Once I was out of the cemetery, I had a clear view along an alley that followed its wall towards the entrance corner, and no blue lights were congregated there, or hooded figures. The smoke from the car was weakening as the blaze burned itself out, and by the time I reached the main road it could no longer be seen. A fire engine streaked past, sirens shrieking, turning towards the park.

There had been no fraud. *Night Traffic* was the truth, and Pierce's confession was the lie. I had understood as soon as Pierce had recognised our assailants in the cemetery – our would-be assailants. All the inconsistencies in his account had evaporated at once, and all his evasions had been explained. Quin had uncovered no evidence of deception because there was nothing to uncover; Pierce could not commit to giving details of what he had done, because he had not done it.

Why, then, had Pierce been moved to confess to a crime that he had not committed? To a crime that had *not been* committed?

I imagined Pierce in his hermitage, and the bright boys and girls of Bunk arriving, sifting his papers, turning up the notes he had made in the distraught days after the attack. He had not feared discovery of a lie – he had feared facing the truth.

The attack described in *Night Traffic* had been real, and so the intense trauma he described there had also been real. He had told how he turned to writing in order to cope with that trauma. But he had gone further. He had convinced himself that by turning the attack into writing, he had turned it into fiction, that his description was his invention. He wanted it gone from memory, so he smoothed it into the realm of inspiration.

When, though? Did the attack slip from fact to fiction during the writing? Possibly, but I suspected that *Night Traffic* became a fraud in Pierce's mind later than that, once it became a success, and he was called upon to talk about it again and again, and to repeat and relive the events of that night over and over. Writing is abandoning. In making a record of our thoughts and experiences, we give ourselves permission to forget them. We *put down* our words – we leave them. But sometimes they get picked up, and brought back to us. I only knew this sensation in a small way, in my continual efforts to escape what I had written, and its mistakes and borrowings and fabrications. For Pierce the sensation must have been multiplied a thousandfold. At some point, sitting on a BBC sofa, his damaged mind had decided that it had created the pain that he was experiencing. The source of the inner conflict was obvious. There was a fraud in *Night Traffic*, in a way, a more sympathetic one: the book was an account of how writing had helped him heal. But he was not healed, far from it. *There* was the lie, or at least the error. And as he was obliged to endlessly repeat it, it contaminated the entire narrative.

So he retreated from view – and then Quin's unblinking eye was turned on his file cabinets, and the polite burglars started rifling through his office . . . The cognitive dissonance must have been intolerable. Inventing the fraud had safely bottled up the attack in the realm of fiction; but was the fraud real if it existed only in Pierce's head, as a story he told only himself? No – stories can't work like that. It had to be shared, it had to be confessed. And who better to serve as witness to this confession than Quin, pious arbiter of digital truth, the man fanatically sifting London's facts from its myths?

That prig, Quin.

I halted at the portal of Mile End Underground Station. The bright pool of light at the head of the steps, the sober white lettering of the station sign, the nicotiney tiles, the warm waft of the tunnels, a haven of electricity and dust – it was all so reassuring, it was unbearable. My knees buckled and I retched. Staggering, I struck a recycling bin, and I steadied myself against it, belching swampy fumes, trying to regain control. My head throbbed. When did I last drink? In Pierce's apartment

– but the memory was interrupted, kicked, by bursts of image. When Pierce said he could see the plume. When we saw the burning car. When we saw the others in the clearing, surrounding us. When Pierce recognised them. When I saw the knife in Pierce's hand. When I saw the drone. They hit me one by one, each a perfect shard of terror – no, facets of a united terror, catching the light in sequence, like a turning gemstone. Only now could I see the whole thing, and find that I could not take it as a whole. I had been in fear, the whole time, and now I was safe. Because there was another light flaring in my gathering recollection of what had just happened: *why did Pierce have the knife?*

Bent against the bin like a busted umbrella, I drew some censorious glances. But I didn't care. I had been through a terrible experience and I didn't care. I could do what I liked.

And there it was again. The feeling. Venomous freedom.

Behind Victoria Station, where Pimlico meets Belgravia, lies a wearying net of characterless streets, distorted around the rail terminus like spacetime around a black hole. A couple of vestigial city grids collide, contorting in the process, with M.C. Escher effect; despite living nearby for years, I often found myself walking a ninety-degree angle to the one I expected, or even the opposite direction. I was never quite able to build a proper mental map of this urban fault. And by a sick joke of planning, this is one of London's gateways, where tourists and visitors totter off airport trains and coaches. They roam ceaselessly in bewildered herds, suitcase wheels grumbling.

It was the pinnacle of summer. The days were warm and bright, though they grew shorter. Elise and I had been to St James's Park, to meet friends and enjoy the fringes of the Olympic events at Horse Guards Parade. Fuchsia mazes of hoardings and fences, exhortations to excel and amaze. Cheerful volunteers and crowds. Distant loudspeaker announcements. Clusters of vans and trailers bursting with antennas and satellite dishes, lounging in the heat of throbbing generators. Little space could be found on the lawns, but we sat and ate a late picnic lunch from supermarket bags, and Elise held my hand. I crawled with discomfort and fatigue – not at the hand-holding, which was sweet and well-meant, but at the daily growing realisation that I was only delaying a horrible crash, that the end was coming, that these times, however good, could not last, and my withdrawal could not be endured. I had been sober a week.

When the park staled, one of our friends – our friends then, her friends now – suggested going to a pub off Ebury Street to watch the sport. Elise cast me a troubled look. But I had no intention of drinking, I wasn't going to give in there. The pub, under her eye and in view of friends, was probably the safest place I could be, which is precisely why I hated it. I watched them with their pints – not Elise, she had orange juice out of sympathy and solidarity, and the ease with which she made that choice rubbed me wrong. I watched them and I held my soda and lime with white knuckles. Every now and then, when the others were diverted, Elise would smile at me and give my hand a squeeze. I hated that. Not because I hated her. On the contrary, I loved her, which made the threatened avalanche of failure all the worse. Not because she was doing the wrong thing. She was doing everything right, precisely as I would wish. She was thoughtful and gentle and generous of spirit – she gave me no excuse, and I hated that. A misstep, a sliver of spite, that was all I wanted, to give me a reason.

When I could take it no longer, I said I wanted to go home. It was a pleasant evening, still light in the sky. Elise was reluctant to leave but prepared to if that was what I wanted, but I suggested that she stay and enjoy a real drink. We had not been there long, and they were more her friends than mine. I was being a drag. I would appreciate a quiet walk home, to clear my head. I expected her to suspect me, because everything I said felt like a lie, even though it was the truth. But she was ready to trust me. And she was right to. I wasn't going to drink, I just wanted silence and solitude.

I had to traverse the Victoria vortex. Many of the streets there are blind, with no homes or shops, only empty offices or high walls blocking off railway lines. Misjudging my bearings, I made a wrong turn, and found myself having to take a longer route. I was not lost; I gave it little thought.

They might have seen me leave the pub, or they had simply guessed that was my origin, spying a leisure-wearing, unladen young man making his directionless way. My head was down, and I was walking without spirit. Perhaps I looked miserable and vulnerable. Perhaps I looked drunk.

There were three of them. I had been dimly aware of them behind me, laughing and larking, but I had not paid much heed, too tied up in the ligatures of miserable thought, the choice between abstaining and suffering or relapsing and suffering. Then, on a walled-in bridge crossing the railways, they rushed past me, as if in a hurry to be elsewhere, to be off that eyeless street. But they did not rush on, and fell into step around and ahead of me, choking off my pace. One of them asked me the time, which was odd, because even as he asked me he was holding his phone, but perhaps he had no battery, perhaps none of them did. For some acute fears, we are slow to believe they are coming true, because we do not want to believe. I took out my phone and told them the time, but that wasn't what they wanted of course, as I was late to realise. There was that moment of dislocation, of confusion, as the interaction changed shape, the threshold was crossed and I entered the other city. I was being mugged a second time.

This time, however, it was different. The whole business is supposed to be a fairly straightforward emotional transaction: threat, fear, valuables changing hands. We fear violence against us, but we also fear being held in a prolonged state of fear, being terrorised, as Pierce was. That usually makes mugging a brisk business, which suits everyone – it's a reliable formula, until it breaks down.

I was not afraid. I laughed. The hard hand on my shoulder made me grin, and the shine on the blade – what was that, a craft knife? – was comic genius. The timing was absolutely fault-less. Life was shit, why not get mugged? They were knocked off their script for a beat, as they considered the possibilities: crazy? Druggie? Off-duty police officer? Charles Bronson psychopath? But they quickly regained their equilibrium, and felt the urgent need to push me off mine. I was slammed against the brick wall and a fist connected with the arch of my eye, a blow I can still feel at times. A foot hammered me on the side of the knee, and I was struck again on the face, across cheekbone and nose. But I continued to laugh, even as I fumbled the contents of my pockets out onto the paving slabs, because I had that feeling. I was free.

I could drink again. I had my excuse – it was perfect. I was released. Elise, my own conscience, they would all be powerless to stop me. This was what I was waiting for, and every blow, every bruise, every visible injury, only helped.

I was delighted – giddy, and not just from the head trauma. The second mugging, the second attack, was the worst thing and the best thing that could have happened to me. I still remember the spreading red drop of blood in the pint I was served in the pub I managed to reach, as the landlord called an ambulance. As if it were being reunited with my body.

Elise couldn't say no to me, and of course she couldn't stay. She was gone before the leaves went from the trees. I had made my choice and we knew it. It was a relief for us both.

I took the Central Line to Liverpool Street and walked up Bishopsgate. Tamesis knew my destination. I had made sure to tell it. And it obliged, showing its birthplace as a spear of heat, an unbelievable concentration of T-plus potential. I would see someone I knew there.

The pubs were near closing, and multitudes spilled into the streets and alleys, despite the cold, to smoke and vape and whinny at each other. Suits rampaged towards the station, where the trains that would take them back to Chingford and Basildon were unloading excitable young people. In Shoreditch the clientele was beardier, more plaid, but the edge was the same. The night did not have long in it, but neither did winter.

Though it was painted in acid colours, in a fractured dazzle pattern, Bunk's headquarters had a more sober air. It was a converted warehouse, and, despite the hour, light glowed behind its grid of large windows. The glass front door was unlocked, though the lobby space was illuminated only by the blue neon logo behind the unstaffed reception desk. I knew where to go – I had been here before. I walked up an echoing concrete stairwell to the fifth floor, aware of the winking red lights of cameras and other sensors in every corner above me. The only sound, other than my footsteps, was a ubiquitous low-intensity hum. At every floor, I could see people in darkened offices, faces floating in screenlight, intent on their tasks.

Electronic locks held shut all the exits from the stairwell, but on the fifth floor the door was propped open, despite red signs

warning to check in with security and have BunkMate identifi-
cation ready. What kept the door from closing was a stack of
copies of the magazine I worked for. Used to work for. This
topmost floor had fewer desks than the others, and they all
pointed the same way. Half the space was given over to clutches
of mismatched stools, benches and bean bags, surrounding a
low dais on three sides. Behind the dais, filling an immense
expanse of warehouse wall, was a map.

Quin called it the 'God Board'. We had been forbidden to
photograph it when the magazine came to visit – or rather,
it had been temporarily switched over to show an innocuous
Tamesis interface. But tonight the God Board was in God
mode, showing the seething hive of London. Thousands of
symbols and icons crawled and pulsed across its heat-marbled
surface – individual Tamesis users, on their way home, out
for dinner, going to clubs. Buses, taxis, Tube and trains, even
emergency vehicles, all had their own symbols, and information overlays slid and flickered, showing traffic speed, user
density and other metrics I couldn't guess at. Jittering data
scrolled at the edges of the map, arcane readings of Tamesis
performance, presumably critical to its operators: system
latency, request response speed, average social velocity, T-link
completion. Just as with Pierce's wall-map, the bombardment
of information was at first overwhelming, and I had to pause
and take it in. But it was possible to skim meaning off the
surface of this deep, churning well of data. The city was visibly
cooling, the T icons trekking outwards and coming to rest.
London was going to sleep.

What would it be like in here in a few hours, when it began
to wake up? Just imagining it gave me a pop of serotonin.

The room had changed in the months since I was last allowed
in. The God Board had been moved to one side, and a second

screen of equal size now stood beside it. This showed the entire British Isles, and while the London screen fizzed with information, the new map was cool and grey and empty. Waiting. There was only one readout that was not resting at zero: a countdown, ticking towards a couple of weeks in the future.

'He's waiting for you,' a voice said from the ranks of desks. I had registered that I was not alone – about a third of the desks were occupied. But none of the workers sitting there had so much as glanced at me when I entered. They were lost in communion with Tamesis, suckling on map-glow.

The BunkMate who had addressed me was seated at the far end of the room, his voice carrying easily through the Wi-Fi-heavy hush. His desk was at right-angles to the others, facing the doors, facing me, and he sat back, picked out by a shaded task light. I recognised him, or half recognised, the glitching partial memory of the drunk. He had been Quin's chaperone in the pub the other night. And we had met before then, exactly here, the first time I had come here.

Behind him was an etched glass wall, containing a private amphitheatre of light. Quin's office.

Quin's desk was a long, wide strip of a glossy composite material, supported by four wooden trestles. I was reminded of Pierce's story about the sheet of mdf he wrote on; but while that was parsimonious and utilitarian, Quin's set-up had the fingerprints of an architect or a designer on its spotless surface. Money had been spent to make it appear unconsidered and practical. Underneath was a dustless labyrinth of toy-bright cables, canalised in wire trays and banded by fat, colourful zip ties. These fed into the four large screens arranged on the desk – three in a triptych at one end, for private devotions, the last at the other, with a wide gap, giving airspace to facetime. The rest of the office was expensively spartan: unshowy leather seats, a thriving fern, little else. The only decoration was a few old Bunk signs on the wall, salvaged from past offices, showing the leaps the company had made in its graphic design and image management since its days as an early millennium start-up.

At first I thought I was alone, that my quarry was not here after all – which led to the ghastly whisper that he might be nowhere, another apparition of paranoia and software. But, of course not, I had met him before, and there he was, behind the group of three screens, like a birdwatcher in a hide. As I entered, he emerged, sliding along the line of the desk on chair castors engineered to total silence.

'That was more difficult than I expected,' he said. 'But we got there in the end.'

I stared at him, and he smiled back at me, satisfied.

'Pierce is dead,' I said.

He glanced back towards his private fan of screens, as if referring to an open document or a video feed. The smile tilted into a rueful expression.

'Yes, I'm afraid so,' he said. 'Not the worst career move. He'll trend. Terrific numbers. Tragedy and mystery do well together. People like to speculate. He'd have been pleased.'

'The police will investigate,' I said. I was only just starting to think it through for myself, and fear building in my gut. 'They'll link me to him, I'll be blamed. Or those guys in the park, they'll get the blame. They didn't do anything, not really.'

Quin shrugged, he actually shrugged, and I quaked with restraint, halting short of launching myself over the desk at him.

'The knife came from Pierce's pocket, he had brought it with him. His will be the only prints on it. You don't have a record, do you.'

The last line wasn't a question – he knew. So I didn't answer.

'The police will interpret the business as a freak accident, or a suicide. A man overcome by his demons, returning to the scene of a terrible event from his past, searching for meaning – and, I suppose, finding it. It's a good story. The investigators will probably be satisfied with it. The loose ends don't matter, they rarely do. Pierce understood that. He wrote a book about it.'

'Bullshit,' I said with vehemence. 'He's dead. Don't you dare try to make that into some satisfying narrative arc. He's fucking dead. He didn't find meaning, or get overcome by demons, or any of that crap. He was just . . . fucked up, he was a fucked-up person and there was a stupid accident, not even a fight, and . . . he's dead.'

Quin closed his eyes and gave a single nod. 'Yes. An entirely reasonable interpretation of events. But not the one that the reporters and obituarists and biographers will choose. As you know. Why don't you sit down?'

'Fuck you, Quin.'

Another nod. 'Fine. You earned that. Please do sit down, though.'

I did not. But I could not be still. My frame shook with undirected energy and tension. Sweat scored a line down my back and stickied my palms. I clenched and unclenched my fists.

'What do you want to do?' Quin said, looking at my hands as they worked. 'Do you want to hurt me? You don't of course. That would be stupid. Or do you want answers?'

'I can listen standing up.'

Quin pursed his lips. 'Listen, then. As it happens, earlier today we were able to regain the signal of the police drone that, ah, went off-grid earlier this week. The Met will be pleased, it was a very costly prototype. Since then we've been doing some testing of its systems for them. And you should be pleased as well, because it has video footage that clears you, and anyone else, of blame for Pierce's death.'

'You're such a fucking liar,' I said, unable to withhold a laugh at Quin's brazenness. 'Been flying around on its own all week, has it? Recharging itself from lampposts, I suppose? Only just found it? And it just happened to be over me and Pierce, right? You've been using it to spy on me.'

'We've had it running a variety of errands. It did look in on you. But your peregrinations have not been my highest priority. We've got a lot to do, preparing to roll out Tamesis nationally. We're busy.'

An orb of rage spun in my core, throwing off instincts that went nowhere. Quin's casual, condescending dismissal of the possibility that I might attack him only made me want to lash out all the more. But lashing out would be the sum of the act – a sordid little flash of action that would achieve zero, or worse than zero.

Instead, I sat down in one of the leather armchairs facing the desk. This made Quin smile – not a nasty patronising smile, but one of the more human expressions I had seen from him: undisguised relief.

'Answers, then.'

'The truth,' I said.

He grimaced. 'Answers.'

'What did you want from Pierce?'

'The truth.'

I ran my hand over my face, exasperated, abruptly tired. Sensing my annoyance, Quin cut in before I could say anything: 'How about you tell me what Pierce told you. Your understanding of his actions.'

'Fine,' I said. 'Pierce was helping you with Tamesis – you were integrating his research into your model, all that esoteric information he had collected. But you were going through the notes for *Night Traffic* and he became troubled. He thought you had uncovered evidence of fraud.'

I frowned, staring down at my hands, which had long stopped making fists, and were meshing together restlessly. It was hard to stay on top of which version of events was the truth.

'So he confessed to you,' I continued. 'Later you told me that the confession was unprompted. You told me that you hadn't found any evidence of fraud. That's because there wasn't any. He didn't make it up. It happened as described.'

'So it appears,' Quin said with a nod. 'Not what I expected, but a useful result. And it came from your work.'

Scowling past Quin's satisfaction with this 'result' and the blood it had entailed, I pushed on.

'You were angry with him and you wanted him to "set the record straight",' I said. 'That was the expression he used, more than once. I was brought in as a tame journalist who could be manipulated or bullied into writing the story that you both wanted. You would have written it yourself in the end, wouldn't you? That's why you stole the recordings.'

'Stole?' Quin said, wrinkling his nose. 'I wasn't going to write anything. Our communications manager here has a way with words, he used to be a journalist like yourself. You would have been pleased with his copy. On deadline, too. But I explained all this to you, in the pub. That's why you gave us the recordings.'

'I did,' I said. It didn't feel quite right, but the capsizing possibility that that was exactly what happened could not be ignored. Pushing the DVRs across the table, a win-win proposition . . . 'So, that's my understanding of what happened. Except I don't really understand it.'

'What part?'

'Any of it, really. Why were you so furious with Pierce? Or rather, why were you so eager to remedy it this way? If you thought he was a fraud, why have anything to do with him? Why involve me, why go to all this obsessive trouble? You could have just walked away. He didn't matter. Neither did I. But you kept . . . messing with us.'

The light around Quin had dimmed while I had been speaking as his various screens went to sleep. They were the only illumination in the room, apart from the cast-off light coming through the glass wall from the God Board, and the technologist had fallen into shadow. With a tiny twitch of one wrist, he woke a screen, and was back, seemingly more pale and stark than before.

'As I told you, we didn't have proof of Pierce's fraud, and I wanted it,' Quin said. 'We needed proof he had invented *Night Traffic*. Because we couldn't find anything. If it was a fraud, it was perfect. No incriminating detail, no inconsistencies or problems in the chronology. His edit of reality had been exquisite.'

'Because it was all true.'

'So it transpires, but we couldn't tell, and it was infuriating. All we had was his confession, and his apparent sincerity. His emotion.'

A shaving of disgust dropped from the last word. I felt a pang of sympathy for Pierce, to have had this crisis, this fracture, in the presence of the calculating mind of F.A.Q.

'But why did it matter to you?' I insisted.

'When he confessed, when we imagined there was this elaborate fiction in play,' Quin began, 'there were possibilities. We were interested in Pierce for more than one reason. But I had to know.'

'Why me, though?' This was really the question foremost in my mind, not just for Quin. It's a routine question for an addict, for whom self-pity comes naturally; and it's a nasty, sticky question, because all too often there are a number of very convincing answers, and we're inviting them to carousel around in our minds. What we mean is: Why not someone else?

'You were pliant, as you say,' Quin replied, with an apologetic shrug. 'Sorry about that. After you made that dishonest dog's dinner of an interview with me . . . I was annoyed, and I had people go through more of your articles, looking for inaccuracies and plagiarism – we found them, too. We were going to do quite a number on you.'

'Pierce told me,' I said. When he had told me, it had come as the most awful news, an abyss opening up. Days later, I hardly cared.

'You got away with a lot. And it was seeping into reality, doing real harm. Your mistakes had made it through to Wikipedia, for instance. You were corrupting the record.'

'If you think I'm the only one, you're more naive than I imagined.'

'It's been a steep learning curve, for sure,' Quin said. He didn't seem at all annoyed or judgemental about it – a transformation from the infuriated, self-righteous F.A.Q. who had complained to Eddie an Ice Age ago. In fact he smiled, and I didn't like it. 'But learn we have, oh yes.'

He rose from his seat and walked around the desk, passing behind me to the door. At the door, he gestured again for me to follow, and left the office.

'Jonathan, I'm taking her for a little ride, if you don't mind,' Quin said to his assistant as he passed. The statement did not leave scope for objection, but Jonathan gave a formal nod anyway.

Quin entered the seating area at the foot of the God Board and perched on a stool. His phone was in his hand and he was thumbing through menus and options at speed, looking up at the board as he did so. The board moved, tiling through overlays, then tracking in on Shoreditch, our location.

'Here we are,' Quin said. It was a skyscraper, in data terms, dwarfing the rest of the city, a spire of information. 'As you can see, there's a great concentration of active users here – my colleagues.' His employees. He was scrolling through the pile of icons heaped at this address. 'Anyone with a BunkMate ID is tinted purple, but – hello! – there's you in the stack, the regular blue one.'

jack.bick said the icon, and there was my avatar, email address and phone number. Quin selected me. He was not using any Tamesis interfaces that I recognised – I wouldn't have been able to pull up any of this information. A bright yellow line appeared on the map, trailing down towards Liverpool Street, twisting about, then shooting off east, towards Mile End. My movements this evening. A squiggle in the streets above Mile End Road, around Pierce's flat. A loop south of that, through the cemetery park. Another, dimmer line also snaked through the same streets – the walk I had taken with Pierce a couple of nights before.

Quin pinched his screen. We hurtled to a satellite's eye view of the city, a faint veil of information passing behind the geographical overlay. And on top, my life: the yellow line, shuttling between Shoreditch and Pimlico, sweeping out to Barking, dangling down to Elephant and Castle. The line was annotated with pointers and dialogues, and intersections with other lines – my searches, information I had referred to, interactions with other users.

'You've kept Tamesis online a lot lately, which is good,' Quin said. 'But as it happens, the software is pretty good at filling in blanks. Tube trips, for instance. When the Tube gets 4G that'll be less of a problem. Other gaps. There's a pub you like around here, on Whitecross Street.'

My mouth was open. Little could surprise me about Quin's knowledge of my activities, but it was no less startling to see it flashed up on a cinema-sized screen.

'Is there anyone you'd like to look at?' Quin asked. 'Your boss Eddie, for instance? Or . . . You had several recent interactions with another user . . .'

A search box popped up. K-a-y . . .

'Stop,' I said.

'We keep these capabilities strictly private,' Quin said, sensing my discomfort. 'We didn't build this system in order to spy on people. But the algorithm has to know all this stuff to do a good job, even if no one else does. This is just a party trick for investors. I didn't show you when you came to interview me, did I? You got the kiddie tour. But you're family now. Here's your search history.'

Quin indexed through my most recent Tamesis enquiries. It was palpably violating, watching him scroll through my insecurities and typos. And he wasn't idly browsing – he was looking for something.

He found it. Street crime overlays. Colour washed over London. Violent crime rates by ward; icons indicating individual incidents at particular times. We were not in the secret, all-knowing back room of Tamesis any more, this was the data I had seen when I asked about the best place to get mugged.

'When we first contacted Pierce,' Quin said, 'one of the things we were trying to understand was *crime*. Street crime, burglaries. Tamesis already uses all available police and Home Office reporting and statistics to inform users about crime rates, but it's very patchy. There's a psychological dimension that's all-important and governs how users behave. Call it fear, but that's not all that it is. And it shapes user decisions: where they go, when, alone or in company. Where they live. And that feeds back into the city. It affects rents and house prices. A street is ill-used at night, so it makes people nervous, they avoid it and it stays little-used. Crime might even rise as the number of possible witnesses falls. Fear isn't always the result of crime – it can cause crime.

'Pierce offered a fascinating case study. He was independently building his own map of the city, one of reputation and myth, precisely what our data lacked. And he had, in *Night Traffic*, written a masterful account of urban fear, of the rippling consequences of a single violent crime. Then he said he had been lying about everything. Infuriating. But, you know, when life gives you lemons, update your seasonal produce model and short-sell Del Monte. Do you know why I built Tamesis, Jack?'

I shook my head. There were all sorts of plausible, reasonable answers I could have given – or insulting ones – but he was just setting up his own, not asking for mine. Let him get on with it.

'No nefarious agenda – it's what I've always said. To bring people together. To create chance encounters, to synthesise social capital, to make innovation and collaboration happen. Because it works. Bringing you and Pierce together – a real leap forward.'

A zigzag of fingers on the phone screen, and the God Board returned to what it had been when I walked in, the busy real-time overview of the Friday night city.

'What do you see?'

This time he did want an answer to his question.

'London.'

'Sure. But, this is not a pipe. This is data, the readouts. It's a dashboard. What's the real city?'

'Outside,' I said. 'Buildings. People.' I rolled my eyes. 'The friends we made along the way. Love. The adventure in the heart of a child. I don't fucking know. You sound just like Pierce, with his fucking riddles. Just tell me.'

'Pierce did have some compatible lines of thought,' Quin said. He was unperturbed by my reluctance to cooperate. 'But you were right, about buildings and people, not the friends shit. Buildings and people are the hardware, or the hardware and the users if you want to go on believing in free will. Really it's all hardware. There's also software – the information governing the environment, the rules and laws, the socioeconomic structures. And the information is as important as the physical fabric. Maybe more so. You rent, right?'

'Used to.'

'Yes, sorry, forgot. And did you select your flat because it perfectly suits all your needs, or because of the rent?'

'Because of the rent,' I said. If it hadn't been for the rent, I would still be living two floors above, in the flat I had occupied with Elise, occupied subsequently by Bella and Dan. But it was all in the same crater now.

'And you only rent because you can't afford to buy, right? I mean, renting is shit. But that's just the way we've chosen to distribute housing, rather than by lottery, or bureaucrats deciding who lives where, neither of which would necessarily be more fair; instead it's all done by market rationing, there's a number attached to each property that sets who can and cannot live there. That information is more important than the physical matter. And again, there's a psychological dimension. Sentiment. Harder to read, to splash up on a big screen, but it's there. We're going to be able to do it, soon.'

He paused. His eyes glittered with the reflected light of the board. He gestured to it with a sweep of the arm.

'London is a machine, running software. And we can edit that software. We can intervene in the city's thoughts about itself. We know something, Jack: crime's coming back. The boom's over, and a crime wave, it fits the political narrative all round. It's the next big thing. Moped gangs, acid attacks. The *Standard* will love it. Fear. Contagion. Property prices will fall.'

'Might not be a bad thing,' I said, feeling cynical. I couldn't listen to reminiscences about the crime-ridden, emptying city of the 1970s and 1980s without feeling half jealous.

'It isn't!' Quin said, all of a sudden passionate. 'I've seen amazing, innovative business driven to Berlin, promising start-ups smothered in the crib, brilliant men and women driven away! All because the rent is too damn high. You and Pierce had it! You had figured it all out independently, you knew what had to be done! I knew I was right. We had Pierce in mind at first to help us guide the program, but he was too damaged. You're even better.'

'Excuse me?' I said.

'You're not well, I know. I thought you were a liar, a fabulist, a joke. But now I see that you're a trailblazer. You've got what we need: you understand the irrelevance of objective truth. You see that experience is plastic, molten plastic.'

The scent of burning polymers filled my nose and mouth.

'We can steer it, Jack. Tamesis can. If people are afraid, they'll rely on us even more. We can make sure the right people are affected, made more afraid, and that the innocent are spared. We can drive out the profiteers and the arseholes. We can make the city ours again. The way it used to be, before it went mad.'

'You want to use Tamesis to *cause crime*?'

Quin shook his head. 'To cause fear of crime, for the right people, and to guide and spare the others. To properly distribute fear. And to ensure that crime happens in the right places. Bring the rents back down, take the pressure out of property, and get into it ourselves. Urban regeneration has run its course, Jack. Urban degeneration, that's what's next. Controlled. Tailored. And, for the right people, very profitable.'

I looked from the map, to Quin, and back. Madness, yes. But no more mad than the boiling human pyramid before me, streams of data rising from it into the empyrean of Bunk's servers. It was the destination, all right, the conclusion: to recognise that the place before us did not exist, that no place did, that it was a fragmenting artefact of 10 million shifting perceptions. To recognise that, yes, what we wrote together in those trails of data could be edited – and would be, whether we participated or not. Here was the future, rising from every phone and computer and device like so much blinding smoke. I could confront it or ignore it, but it was coming. Or I could join it.

But addicts refuse to face the future. Their whole life is a battle against it, one I had been fighting myself for years. And for good reason. The future contains a simple binary: continue and die, or stop and live. That's the truth, the only truth that matters. You can evade and manage, and scrape another day or week or month, but it will only work for so long – ultimately, there's that choice, the one you've been making every day without knowing. Now I knew, and tomorrow would be different.

ACKNOWLEDGEMENTS

I am particularly grateful to my agent, Antony Topping, and to my friends James Smythe and Sam Byers. Adam Roberts, Lee Rourke and Nikesh Shukla all contributed their wisdom and moral support. Anna Minton and Douglas Spencer provided much invaluable reading and discussion. Many ideas were shaped in conversation with Fatima Fernandes. My parents and my wife, Hazel, have been extraordinarily supportive, both now, and then. Philip Crowther gave vital details on the procedures of the emergency services.

At 4th Estate, my thanks go to Nicholas Pearson for his guidance and patience, and to Katy Archer, Michelle Kane, Matt Clacher, Jordan Mulligan and Morag Lyall.

This book could not have been completed without a generous and timely grant from the Authors' Foundation, administered by the Society of Authors.

The essay mentioned in Chapter 7 is 'Mugging as a Way of Life', by David Freeman, and it appeared in the 23 February 1970 edition of *New York Magazine*.

I hope that Tower Hamlets Cemetery Park can forgive my fictional portrayal of it, and I urge the reader to discover the reality of this unique and beautiful place for themselves. Learn more at www.fothcp.org